No L

Ends

by

Ivor McKenzie

Chapter 1

Denny sat on the ground with his back up against a tree, looking down the valley. He could see for miles and miles, over the forests of Bavaria. This view never disappointed him. It was only about ten minutes from the nearest town of Zwiesel in the car, but Denny thought it was like a million miles away.

The warm sun was just starting to get over the hills from the east, and the sunlight was beginning to gently filter through between the canopy branches, with the early mist beginning to rise from the forest floor. One of his German pointer dogs Arno was lying at his feet. While the other one, Udo was left to protect everyone at the house.

What a magical place this was, and he could hardly believe it was all his. One minute you're just a plain guy from a desolate Scottish island called Durma, and after your mum dies, her multi-billion-pound estate, which he knew nothing about, has been bequeathed to you. He still found it scary, and didn't know the vastness of the Albach Trust and felt he didn't want to know. There were people employed all over Germany to run the Trust, and he was happy to let them continue.

Denny was happy looking after the trees, fauna, and animals, as he never felt he was the owner of the forests, just the custodian.

Someone was shouting, and he turned to see his partner, and soon to be wife Helen, walking along the path. He knew she had been coming as Arno had been up on all fours with his ears pricked up, and a low guttural growl was emanating from him. As soon as he recognised her he looked at Denny with pleading eyes to go and meet her. Denny pointed for him to go, and he took off at speed. Helen was kneeling on the ground waiting for him as he bounded into her arms for a hug, and get his ears scratched.

"I sometimes think that you love that dog more than you love me."

"I love both the dogs more than I love you, Denny Foggerty. I get less hassle from them," she shouted back smiling.

1

It was a while after her and Denny arrived in Bavaria that she had given birth to twins, two beautiful baby boys. Finn and Col. Denny had found a retired midwife living in Zwiesel to help Helen with the home births. He found that watching Helen giving birth was the most unbelievable experience he could ever imagine. They were both wondering what was happening when the midwife asked Denny to push down gently on Helen's belly when Finn was being born. She explained later that it was to stop Col turning. When Col came out Denny had said it looked like he had just 'slid out'. Much to the annoyance of Helen.

Both parents were besotted with the boys, and spent most nights with them in the baby slings walking through the forests with the dogs beside them. Denny would explain all about the trees, plants and animals that lived there to the boys even though they were too young, and mostly out for the count. They loved the boys dearly. Life was idyllic for them, but at some stage that was about to change.

Helen came and sat down beside Denny, and started to unwrap the breakfast. They were just waiting for Willie now. Willie came over from Scotland not long after them. When Denny met Willie, it was a dark period for both of them. They both had been cursed with the medical condition called Intermittent Explosive Disorder. At the drop of a hat their rage would take over them, and all hell would break loose. Being dependent on the whisky didn't help them one bit. Both were now sober, and Denny had made Willie the Forestry Manager, and deep down he was thrilled with his title, but would often moan about it just for the sake of it.

Soon, Arno was standing with his ears pricked up and his growl getting louder by the second. It was then that Willie appeared from the trees with a face like thunder.

"Can you not shut up Arno? Bloody hell dog, you know its me."

"Having a bad day, Willie?"

Willie was soaking from the knees down, so he took off his boots and socks. He hung up the socks on a low branch that was now getting the rays from the sun. Denny could see what was going to happen, but was trying not to laugh. Arno was crawling on his belly around the back of the tree where he could get to

Willie's socks. When he thought no one was looking, he pounced and grabbed one of them, making off with it while tossing it up in the air. When Willie saw him he started shouting, but Arno was just ignoring him. It was then that Denny whistled and motioned for the dog to bring the soggy sock back.

"I swear, that one of these days I'm going to shoot that bloody dog Foggerty."

"If you do Time Bomb, then you do realise I will have to shoot you."

"The thing is Foggerty, I know you are not joking."

Willie McLeod had been nicknamed Time Bomb by the community he had lived in on the East coast of Scotland, and the name was well deserved. At any time, his fuse would be lit, and he would explode. They sat there eating rolls with Butterkase cheese and strong German coffee. Helen and Denny were getting married in four days' time, and Helen told him the small marquee had arrived and they were busy erecting it at the moment. All their friends from Scotland were arriving within a day or so, and it was exciting times. Once it was time to get back working Denny had taken a spare pair of socks from his backpack and given them to Willie.

"How's the best man's speech coming along Willie?"

"What bloody speech? When were you going to tell me that I was your best man Foggerty?"

"Think I just did Willie, and take Arno with you down the valley to bond with him. Remember one whistle to get his attention, two blasts for a recall and three for letting him know that there is danger, okay?" Before you both go, I want to have a serious talk with you after the wedding."

"Before I go with this 'mutt', I'm letting you know that we need help in these forests, it's too much for just the two of us as we are being overrun by rabbits and hares. They are destroying the riverbanks."

Helen kissed Denny, and before she left they both stood laughing at Willie walking down the valley mumbling and moaning about Arno. When he thought he was out of sight of them, he had let the dog come into his side, then scratched his ears. Denny thought about the rabbit problem and made a mental note to speak to Otto after the wedding.

Otto had been the previous estate manager and had shown Denny the forests when he had come over from Scotland, and although retired, he still came over one day a week to give his experience and advice to Denny and Willie. He was the one that had kindly given Denny the two young pups Arno and Udo, sired by Otto's dog Ottar. A dog that Denny had a lot of affection for. When Otto brought him over there was only one boss and the pups knew it. They respected him, and if they stepped out of line then Ottar gave them a nip or two.

Helen got back to the lodge, and she often laughed when Denny had referred to it as a shooting lodge, when in fact it was a magnificent six bedroomed house on stilts with annex attached. Willie and Gertie Webber, the house girl, had become an item and had moved into the annex together which was just as well as Denny and Helen were often woken up with the love making squeals that used to come from their bedroom. Willie was always trying hard to please Gertie.

Udo had been lying on the porch and when he saw Helen, he took off to meet her. Helen again knelt down and let him into her arms, then it was a case of being 'slobbered' over. Denny had trained both dogs to a very high standard and Otto showed him how to get them to attack the genital area of any assailant that approached his family. He would take one of the dogs with him when working and leave one at home to guard everyone.

When she saw the marquee going up she realised she was getting a bit excited, and couldn't wait to see their friends again. One of her bridesmaids Jinty, was her best friend from school and had come over at about the same time. Helen had persuaded Denny to buy her a house in Zwiesel, so that she could be near her. Denny had gone one better, and bought her a bakery business with house above. She was making a real go of the business. The only thing that tended to get Denny annoyed, was that she had appeared with her new boyfriend Scottie. Denny had always regarded him as a lazy 'bastard'. Who would laze around, chain smoking, always saying he was looking for work. Helen had persuaded Denny not to do anything about it for Jinty's sake, but he was convinced that there was some verbal abuse going on.

Helen went to see, and feed the boys. They took a bit of feeding, but she was determined to breast feed for as long as she could. Helen told Gertie that everyone would take a share of looking after the twins, so that she could enjoy the wedding and spend time with Willie. Gertie had told her how excited she was for everybody.

"There will be about twenty people attending Gertie, so we will cater for about twenty-five, and make sure there will be plenty of soft drinks for obvious reasons. Absolutely no alcohol. I'm looking forward to the Scottish country dancing. It's been a long time since I had a good 'fling'."

"Miss Helen, I have never had a Scottish dance, and don't know what to do."

"Just let the men throw you around Gertie. By the end of the night, you will be all aches and pains, but you will feel great."

Gertie walked away scratching her head wondering what Helen had meant. After a few hours Willie arrived back, quickly washed and changed, as he was heading off to the airport to pick up his brother Ian and his partner Neala from the airport. They were coming early from Durma as Neala was going to meet Maria at the Albach town house in Zwiesel tomorrow to discuss the Western Isles, Trust which Denny had organised with Neala before he left for Germany. Willie was a bit excited to see them both, but was putting up a front as if it didn't matter to him. Typical Willie. Denny arrived back and proceeded to feed the dogs, and check them over for any parasites they may have picked up in the forest. They never needed bathing as they were in the streams most days. Denny then sat with Helen on the steps to the house holding the boys.

"Do you ever miss the whisky Denny?"

"The craving never leaves some people Helen, but it's never really bothered me now, and when I look at you and the twins, I thank God for small mercies. I think back to what my mum went through. Like me, it didn't take long for the alcohol to get its teeth into her. I don't like the fact that Mum and Dad are lying buried there on a cold, windswept rock, but there is nothing I can do about it. At least their graves are well looked after. Anyway, let's not get morbid when we are holding these beautiful wee boys. Let's go a walk. Maybe we could plan a trip to Durma after the wedding and take Jinty with us?"

"I would love that, Denny."

As they walked, Helen asked him what his thoughts were as to why they were being overrun with rabbits and hares. He told her the only thing he could think of was that their natural predator, the fox, had diminished. The fox's predators were the lynx and the wolf, but it was only very occasionally that Denny had thought he had caught a glimpse of them as they tended to populate the Eastern region which bordered the Czech Republic. After an hour they wandered back to the house and put the sleeping boys to bed, only for them to be woken up by Willie tooting the horn as he arrived back from the airport.

"Denny, would it be such an inconvenience for you if I took one of the rifles and shot Willie?"

"Carry on darling, as I would just bury him somewhere in the forest."

The boys went back to sleep, and they went down to meet their guests. As they stepped out onto the veranda, Arno and Udo were lying there with their usual growls coming from them until Denny told them to be quiet, but rubbed their ears to let them know they were just doing their jobs. As they walked down the steps Ian and Neala got out of the car and it was hugging all round. Helen asked them to come in and get something to eat, but Neala had said that the food could wait as she couldn't wait to see the boys. Before they went into the dining room, Gertie had walked out, and Willie introduced her to the both of them.

"How is he looking after you Gertie? Mind you if he misbehaves then you have my permission to shoot him," said Ian.

"Why is it that everybody wants to shoot me?" said Willie looking a bit peeved.

Nobody laughed, and Gertie walked away to the kitchen thinking how strange these Scottish people were. Gertie had laid on a lovely spread and they were soon eating and chatting, mostly about the upcoming wedding. When Ian had jokingly asked Denny if he had chosen a best man, Willie had 'piped' up.

"He only asked me this morning if I had prepared a bloody speech Ian. He has taken it for granted that I would be his best man."

Helen leaned across the table and clipped Willie on the back of the head again, telling him not to swear in front of the 'bairns'.

"Well Denny, if he doesn't want to do it then I suggest you get one of the dogs to do it, as it will be the same outcome," said Helen.

Everyone burst into laughter, even Gertie getting the joke. Willie joined in the laughter as well. They all helped to clear up after the meal which rather surprised Gertie. As they sat drinking tea or coffee, Denny had announced that if anybody needed anything from, or to go to, Zwiesel then Willie would be the chauffer for the day.

"Does that mean I'm getting the day off Denny?" said Willie feigning that he was having a heart attack at the shock of it.

Everyone had an early night. Next morning Denny had given the names of the people coming over from Edinburgh, and what time their flight would be, to Willie. His old boss from the police Tommy Shearlaw, who had retired not long ago, and his wife Annie were being accompanied by Shonagh Slater, Denny's previous fellow officer from Edinburgh, along with her new partner Jack who was also in the police force. He had never met Jack or Annie, and it would be a bit strange meeting Shonagh again after their troubled time working together, and their intense love making session one night while out on surveillance.

All the folk who were local were going to stay at the town house. Maria was bringing her mum and dad, Max and Elke, as well as Otto and his wife Lina. Maria's partner wasn't sure he could make it, as he was sitting some Law exams over the weekend. Denny had gone down to ask Frieda if she would like to attend the wedding, and she had said she would love to. Frieda was Gertie's gran, and used to be the housekeeper, and lived about twenty minutes from the estate. He had said he would pick her up on the day, but she said not to bother as she was perfectly capable of walking. Frieda must be nearer ninety than eighty.

Denny asked Ian if he would like to come for a walk in the forest as he would like to run things by him. Just as they were about to set off Denny handed Ian a rifle. Ian asked if it was really necessary to have it. Denny said it was, and Ian just shrugged as they headed along the track. Helen watched them go and couldn't quite understand why Ian would need a gun. Ian couldn't quite take in the beauty of the place, and the sounds of all the birds and animals made him feel quite humble. After half an hour,, Denny

7

suggested they sit for a while and take in his favourite view. After a short while Ian turned to Denny and said,

"What's troubling you Denny? I know you wanted to run things past me, but I can't help thinking that you have too much rubbish running through that delicate brain of yours."

"Ian, can you remember when we were sitting on the quay waiting for Helen and me to board the ferry, I told you that I had a niggle in the back of my brain. Knowing what I had done in the past might come back to haunt me. Well, that niggle is growing and only last week my sixth sense was telling me that something's wrong. I don't know what, but my sixth sense has never let me down as you know. I have a feeling that I left too many loose ends back in Scotland."

"Denny, I trust your sixth sense implicitly, but I don't know all about your past so I can't comment. Except to say you might be overthinking things. Have you ever felt threatened since you have been over here? Is that why we both have rifles?"

"My rage has been virtually non- existent since I came here, and both Willie and I are trying hard to keep it that way. However, I owe it to him and Helen to let them know what is going on. I might have to tell them more about my past than they would want to hear. I have told them I need to speak to them, but it would be after the wedding. To answer your question as to whether I have ever felt threatened then maybe the rifle over your shoulder should be the answer. I have more responsibility over here with Helen and the twins. Also, Willie and Gertie, as well as Otto when he is over. Maybe you're right and I am overthinking things, but I intend to 'beef up' security around here not just relying on the dogs."

They both sat in silence for a while, just listening to the bird calls as the sun started to beat down on them.

"The sun always shines on the righteous Denny. Don't worry, and remember I'm only a plane ride away."

As they headed back Ian kept asking Denny about the estate and what his plans were for it. Denny had told him that he was hoping to make it a nature reserve and there would be no shooting on it, or any trees being felled. He realised that he would have to have a small cull of some animals if their food source became scarce and they were suffering. He told Ian that he hoped to introduce trips to the estate for underprivileged children from the inner cities for them to understand nature first hand, but that was only one project that Maria was working on.

When they got back to the house Helen was sitting feeding Col while Gertie was burping Finn. Both dogs ran out to meet them.

"Would you like a 'cuppa' tea and one of Gertie's scones my handsome lover boy?"

"I would love that Helen," replied Ian quickly. Much to the bewilderment of Gertie when nobody laughed or smiled. She thought it would take a while to get to know these people.

When Helen had finished feeding Col, she handed him to Ian to be burped. The look on his panic strewn face was a picture with him asking what he was supposed to do, while keeping Col at arm's length in front of him. Gertie laughed and explained what he should be doing.

After a few minutes, they all thought it might be a bit of a struggle to get Col back off Ian, as he was just sitting with a big grin on his face. He was loving it.

It was early afternoon when Neala came back, and Ian had asked her if she would like a walk in the forests. She said she would love to. Denny thought that would be a great, but on condition that they took the dogs with them. Denny explained how to control them with whistles, and he told them in no uncertain terms that if the dogs started barking furiously, then there was danger to everyone.

As Ian and Neala walked, he told her everything Denny had said about the estate. She couldn't believe the beauty that was all around her. She thought about back home on Durma, and made up her mind there and then, that when her work on the Western Isles Trust was finished, she would try and persuade Ian to come and live here. It was then that Ian told her about his conversation with Denny earlier.

"Oh, please God no Ian. They have such a lovely life together here. What did you tell him?"

"Simply, that I thought he might be overthinking things. However, you know as well as I do that his sixth sense is never wrong. I did say that if he needed my help then I would be there for him. Remember Neala, we don't know even a small part of what he got up to."

Neala sat down against a tree and Ian joined her. She hesitantly asked him if he would ever consider moving out here. He started to laugh, with her wondering if that meant he would never move.

"Neala, I have only been here less than a day and I have fallen in love with the place. When we get home, we should have a serious talk about it. Only if you feel the same way though. The fishing is getting harder and it's becoming a young man's game. I am under no illusion that we haven't landed in paradise, but it's as near to it that we could ever get. Let's not get ahead of ourselves, as we don't even know if Helen and Denny would welcome us coming over. We'll speak about it in a few days."

They got up and decided to walk further as Denny had said the dogs needed a good walk. As they walked, Arno and Udo both had the end of a stick in their mouths and were fighting over it. There was never going to be a winner, so Ian gave them a couple of whistles and they came running to his side. They stood for one last look as the sun started to go down over the hills in the west. Ian put his arm around Neala, and they started to head back with a look of disappointment on the dog's faces.

When they got back, Neala had asked if she could look after the dogs and Denny said she could this time, but generally he preferred to do it himself as he wanted to be in total control of them. Neala never had a dog or a pet in fact, but she was enjoying the interaction with Udo and Arno and wondered if she could get one if they moved here. First things first though.

Everyone heard the rumble of the large four by four truck coming up the track which was Willie bringing everyone from the airport. It stopped at the side of the house and Shonagh and her partner Jack were first out. Then Tommy and his wife Annie, exited. Introductions were made, as well as hugs, kisses, and handshakes. Shonagh gave Denny a long hug which surprised Helen a bit, but she thought it must be her imagination. Helen's first impressions were that they were a really nice bunch of folk. After the introductions, Annie headed straight for the boys who were in their outdoor cot on the veranda. Helen had wanted a double cot so that the boys could snuggle in together to form a strong bond between them.

"Tommy, come and see these beautiful boys will you. Stop talking for a minute and get yourself over here."

Everyone knew then who wore the trousers in the Shearlaw household. Gertie started to serve tea and cakes on the veranda, and they all sat talking about anything and everything. If one of the boys stirred, then it would have taken an Olympic sprinter to beat Annie to the cot. Much to Helen's amusement. Denny asked everyone if they could help with the preparations tomorrow, so that everybody could have a relaxing time on the day of the wedding. They were all in agreement. Denny asked Jack how he was enjoying the police force, and he said it was early days, but it felt promising.

"One thing though Jack, if they ever ask you to go undercover then tell them to stick it where the sun doesn't shine. What do you think Shonagh?"

"Before I met you Denny Foggerty, I had two fully functioning arms, but one night on a police raid organised by yourself, somebody used me for target practice."

"Were you there Tommy? Why didn't you protect the lassie, Tommy? said Annie.

"I think we should all forget about stories of the Edinburgh police, please," said Tommy listening to Denny laughing.

"There is one thing I must tell you about the wedding folks, and that is you will all be expected to give us a song of your choice at some stage during the day."

Everybody was waiting for Denny to start laughing, but said he was deadly serious. There was silence for a while until Willie started to moan.

"Two days for a best man speech and now less than a day to come up with a song. You're bloody unbelievable Foggerty."

Willie suddenly realised what was about to happen when Helen leaned over and clipped the side of his head, only for Annie to do the same on the other side.

"Not in front of the 'bairns' young lad," said Annie. They all started to laugh.

It seemed as though everybody was having a lie in the next morning, but Denny had things to do so he was up early. The dogs

11

had been a bit neglected over the past few days, so he decided to take them a long walk and because of the niggle in his head he had intensified their training. He would up the attack training when everybody left to go home, in case something went wrong. He couldn't wait until Finn and Col were old enough to go on the walks with him.

When Denny got back with the dogs everyone was tucking in to breakfast. Jinty had arrived to stay over and when she saw him, she took off, ran, jumped up and put her arms around him and gave him a big kiss. Jinty had to jump as she was only about five feet and Denny was at least six feet two.

"Helen, I swear he whispered in my ear just now that he would rather marry me than you," she shouted.

"Have him Jinty, he is all yours," Helen shouted back.

Denny thought it might not be too late to grab the boys, along with dogs, and head for the hills to escape these mad people. He asked Jinty where her partner was, and she replied sheepishly that he was ill and won't be coming which pleased Denny as the guy was a chain smoker, and would have been the only guest smoking, apart from being a not very likeable guy. Jinty, from early days, had refused to let Denny go with her hugs so he took the opportunity to whisper in her ear.

"Jinty, I swear that if Scottie ever abuses you either verbally or physically, I will bury him deep, very deep."

"I realise now that it was a mistake him coming over with me, but I thought it was the right decision at the time. Don't worry I'll get 'shot' of him sometime."

"Hey Jinty Thomas, get your backside over here and give me a hand with these chairs instead of lusting over my husband to be," said Helen with a slight smile.

By mid-morning everybody was helping making all the preparations. Gertie always making sure that there were copious amounts of tea, coffee, and biscuits on the go. It was during one tea break that Ardo and Udo suddenly sat up and in unison, got into the attack position and started growling. Denny couldn't see what was going on as they were just looking down the track. Suddenly two figures came into view and Denny took off, knocking over his chair and ran into the house.

"Willie, get your gun and go to the veranda. You know what to do. Protect the boys with your life pal."

Willie didn't need to be told twice, as he too had knocked his chair over and just about Tommy Shearlaw as well. The police instinct came to the fore and Tommy, Shonagh and Jack all walked forward in front of everyone and stood in a protective line. Nobody said a word, as they were wondering what was going on. Denny had come out of the house with his rifle, while Willie stood on the veranda with his gun at the ready. Denny walked slowly taking cover from the trees that lined the track. His sixth sense wasn't telling him anything, so that was throwing him a bit.

The dogs were slowly creeping forward either side of him. Two young lads with holdalls over their shoulders came into view. Denny timed it so that he just walked out from behind a tree and pointed his gun at them, holding it waist high.

"Going to shoot us pal?" said the taller of the two matching Denny's stare.

"Maybe it's going to be death by dog," said the other one.

To Denny they could only have been about sixteen or seventeen, but he was taking no chances.

"What's your names and what are you doing here?"

"More to the point what's your name, and what are you doing here?"

What a pair of cheeky 'sods' thought Denny.

"My name is Denny, Denny Foggerty and I own this estate, so it's now your turn for names."

The older boy turned to the other one and said," Looks like we've got the right place brother."

"Hi, my name's Levi, and this is my pain in the arse brother Bohdi. You phoned Stevie at the Pillars pub in Dundee and asked him over for your wedding, but he couldn't make it, so he sent us instead. Not that we're second best you understand."

Denny walked forward, lowered the gun, and shook them by the hand.

"Bloody hell, Levi and Bohdi, finally I get to meet you. How is Stevie by the way?"

"Getting married like you pal, so he is busy trying to get things organised, but can I ask you something? Can you get these 'dugs' to stop snarling at us, as they are making us very nervous," said Bodhi.

Denny signalled for the dogs to back down, and asked the lads if they would like to come up and meet the guests. As they walked up the track Denny told them that what had happened in Dundee will remain there. Bohdi kept looking at the dogs, as Arno hadn't taken his eyes off him. He asked Denny what would have happened if the dogs had attacked. Denny smiled, and then casually told him.

"They would rip your genitals off young man."

"Good job I lost my virginity last week then," said Bohdi.

"I told you Mr Denny that he is a pain in the arse. He has not stopped telling everyone he can about losing his 'cherry' to one of the 'lassies' from the Downfield estate. He can be such a 'dickhead' at times."

Chapter 2

Denny introduced the lads to everyone and when he came to the police contingent, he swore he saw the lads flinch. Levi turned and looked in awe of the house, and told Denny he didn't think Stevie had any idea of the magnitude of the estate. Just then Helen walked out of the house with the boys and put them in the cot.

"Bloody hell, she's a bit of all right is she not. Who is she?" asked Levi. Helen had heard him and walked over and clipped him on the head. Levi was taken aback.

"Do you see this six-foot two guy who is totally ripped, well that is my husband to be tomorrow, and the clip on your head was for swearing in front of my 'bairns'."

"Very sorry 'missus soon to be Foggerty' but you're still a bit of 'alright.'" Everybody was smiling, and Helen grabbed a hold of them both and gave them a huge hug and thanked them very much for coming to her wedding. She then took the opportunity to say that she hoped they would be singing a song tomorrow and walked away. Although they were a bit bewildered, they looked at each other and smiled. Gertie shouted that she would be serving tea and scones on the veranda. It was a toss up between Tommy Shearlaw and the two young lads who could eat the most scones. Tommy only stopping when Annie told him he had had enough. Him opening his belt was a clue.

After everyone was sated, Tommy caught Denny's eye and gave him a nod to walk with him. Shonagh saw this, got up, and walked with them. When they were out of earshot Tommy turned to Denny and said, "Are you going to tell me what's going on Denny? I saw the way you reacted when the dogs alerted you to the possibility of danger. It could have been anybody coming up that track, but the way you and Willie were running about with rifles wasn't normal son. If you don't want to speak about it, then fine."

"This may sound a bit strange, but if you can think back to Edinburgh and Dundee and how my sixth sense had virtually saved my life at times. Well, it's trying to tell me there is something wrong. Neither of you know what happened in either city, and a lot of people suffered at my hands, but they deserved it. I wasn't a nice person back then, but I have this gnawing feeling that my past is going to catch up with me and I have all the people around me to think of. I put it to Ian that I fear I left too many loose ends back in Scotland."

Tommy sat down against a tree and Shonagh sat with him in silence. After a few minutes Shonagh got up and hugged Denny. It was then Tommy who said,

"I have witnessed your sixth sense Denny and know how powerful it is and you're right, I don't know what you were up to and to be honest I don't want to know. I hope for once your sixth sense is wrong, but if the worst comes to the worst, then I will help you in any way I can, as I'm sure Shonagh will. I am too old to go chasing after criminals now, but I still have good contacts in the force, so if you need any intel then I am here for you."

"Thank you both very much, but rest assured I will never put your life in any danger. If I have to do anything I will do it myself with my family and friends far away from it. Please remember not to say anything to anyone."

Denny suggested they walk back and not think about it anymore as they didn't want to spoil their trip over for the wedding. When they got back Willie was moaning as usual about having to do all the work when in fact it was practically finished. Helen had asked them where they had been and Shonagh had said they had been reminiscing about the heady days of police work in Edinburgh and Dundee. Helen had said that Denny had never spoken about his time on the force, but maybe he would tell her sometime. There were looks all around, and nobody said a word, but Denny thought it might be sooner, rather than later.

"Any chance we can go for a walk in the forests Mr Denny? We won't go far," asked Levi.

Denny had a long think before saying, "Only if you take the dogs with you. Can either of you whistle?"

"Oh, not the 'dugs' Mr Denny, they put the fear of death into me. The thought of them ripping my balls off has been going through my head since you told me what they are capable of."

16

"No dogs? Then you are going nowhere. What would Stevie say if I phoned him and said that I lost you in the forests, never to be seen again," said Denny.

"Stop being a 'woose' Bohdi, you've never liked dogs since you read Hound of the Baskerville at school. We would love to take the dogs Mr Denny."

Denny explained about the whistles, the most important one being the one for danger and the furious barking of the dogs. They both said they understood, and Denny called the dogs over and told them to 'go' with the lads. They had just started walking when Denny said,

"Remember lads, if there is any real danger, I'm not fussy about you pair getting back, but I am about my dogs."

The look on their faces said it all. Denny walked away smiling but knew he would have to detrain the dogs and start again when everyone was away home. He needed to be the only one in charge of them. Especially if his sixth sense was right. The lads arrived back after an hour looking like they had just won a prize, both with big smiles on their faces. The Albach estate magic had worked again.

Everyone was just sitting around relaxing. Helen had just finished feeding the boys when she walked over to the two young lads and put a baby towel over each of their shoulders. There was a look of 'what's going on here' between them. She then brought Finn and Col over to them and asked them to burp them. When she gave the twins to them, she thought there was real fear on their faces.

"What's happening here Mrs Denny? What are we supposed to do now?"

It was then that the Olympic sprinter Annie rushed over and started to explain what they were supposed to do. It was only after a minute or so that Col burped, bringing some sick up onto the towel. By the look on Bodhi's face, you would have thought the end of the world was near. Levi was a natural, but was glad he was under the watchful eye of Annie. The rest of the guests thought it was amusing, until Helen had said everyone would get their turn, as well as the nappy changing. Helen thought she saw Jack visibly shrink, while trying to hide behind Shonagh.

Helen saw Neala looking wistfully at the babies and went and sat down beside her. They were at the end of the veranda where nobody could overhear them.

"I saw you looking forlornly at my babies Neala. You do realise that I will be checking your luggage before you leave in case you have any thoughts on trying to steal my beautiful boys," Helen said jokingly.

"I'm going to ask you a question Helen, and I want you to answer me truthfully please. I'm nearly forty-two years old now and my biological clock started ticking a few years ago, but do you think I am too old for a having a baby?"

By the look on her face, Helen could see that she was in a bit of a turmoil over this and although Helen would tell her honestly, she knew that Ian's feelings would have to come into it.

"Neala, I really don't think you are too old, seriously. I think you would make a great mother, but most importantly it's Ian you should be sitting down with and talking this through."

"Another thing was how Ian and I have felt about this place since we arrived. I can't help thinking what a beautiful place this would be to live."

"Neala, just wait until the day after the wedding and Denny will make a 'wee' announcement."

It was a little while after that the two lads started to shout for Helen when it was obvious that the boys needing changed with Bodhi holding Col as far away from him as possible. Helen shouted on Shonagh and Annie for help. Annie rushed forward while Shonagh was a bit hesitant, but they both got down to changing them. Shonagh being extra careful not to prick Finn with the safety pin, this being her first time.

Gertie announced that dinner would be in the dining room in about an hour, so if anybody would like to freshen up, then fine. Denny had organised for the young lads to stay in the annex with Willie and Gertie, primarily so that Willie would look after them, but he had thought they were a pair of level-headed boys. The house was quiet for that hour as everyone took the opportunity for a bath or shower. Each room was ensuite and the bathrooms were just as opulent as the bedrooms. So, it was lovely lying back in the bath just savouring the moment. However, Tommy was getting it in the neck from his wife due to the length of time it was taking him to decorate their own bathroom back home. Annie was small, but very feisty and not to be messed with, while Tommy had learned to turn a deaf ear to her protestations.

Jack had been getting amorous, but Shonagh said she didn't want to make love as she was in someone else's house. The real reason being that seeing Denny again made her feel a bit awkward. She had kept on thinking back to their love making in that car during one night of surveillance. She could never forget the intensity of her climaxes, and she hadn't had that same experience since. Each time she made love to Jack her mind often drifted to Denny and his beautifully sculpted body, and how well-endowed he was. Hopefully these thoughts might dwindle and the only person she would think about was Jack.

As they were lying on the bed after showering, Neala had turned to Ian and asked if he ever thought about missing out on being a father. She thought that his body had gone a bit rigid, and then he had turned to her and asked her to spell it out as to what she was meaning. Very slowly, she said that over the last few months she had had the feeling of missing out on having a family and wondered what their life would be like if they had one. She was surprised when he told her he wondered why she had never brought it up before.

"Does that mean what I think it does Ian?"

"No Neala, what it means is that we have such a lot to talk about when we get home, but as we are lying here naked maybe we should keep on practicing," he said with a wicked smile on his face.

Everyone started to drift into the dining room and were walking around looking at the paintings on the walls. Levi and Bohdi had turned out in jeans and checked shirts. When they got to the painting of the white stag, they were taken aback by it and asked Denny what it was. Everyone had moved to the painting, and Denny took the opportunity to make a small speech.

"This is the white stag that roams these forests, or should I say it's descendants do, as that painting was done a long time ago. I thought that the day after the wedding that whoever was up for it might go on a small shoot, as we have a serious rabbit and hare overpopulation. However, it is highly unlikely we would see the stag on the shoot as I have only caught small glimpses of it. If it does appear then on no account does anybody take a shot at it. If that animal dies at the hand of anybody from this estate, then serious bad luck would befall the whole estate, and everyone on it. Is that clear?"

They all nodded their heads.

Gertie had excelled herself for the meal. Starters was a traditional vegetable soup with crusty bread baked by Jinty at her shop. The second course was Bockwurst, a German sausage accompanied by Bavarian Radish Salad. Ice Cream with strawberries and raspberries was the sweet if anybody could manage it. Tommy had tried hard, but was beaten into second place by Levi and Bohdi. Denny didn't know where they put it all as there wasn't a 'pick' on them. When they were all finished, Bohdi turned to Gertie and said, "That was lovely miss Gertie. With your looks and cooking skills I reckon you might want to get rid of Willie, and come and see me in Dundee. What do you think?"

They all just looked at him before he turned to everyone and said, "What?" holding his arms out. Denny laughed which set everyone else off, although with Willie it was a bit of a forced laugh. After they all helped to clear the large dining room table, they started the washing up with only one plate being dropped and smashed. Willie got the blame.

After everything was cleared away, they sat out on the veranda for tea and coffee along with fudge biscuits that Gertie had baked. Her speciality. The sun was just going down and the sky was blood red, beautiful but a bit scary if you had never seen it before. As they sat there in peace and quiet it was Ian that decided he was going to sing a sea shanty for everyone. He started to sing Blow the Man Down which Denny, Helen and Jinty had learned at school and helped with the chorus. Nobody could believe how good his voice was, and Jinty and Helen were singing with a tear in their eye. No matter what, Durma was still in their hearts. Gertie had grabbed the bottom of her dress at the knees and was swirling it from side to side while she danced around everyone, giving all the men a kiss as she passed them. Much to the annoyance of Willie, until she came to him and gave him a long, lingering kiss while sitting on his knee. Willie looked at Levi and Bohdi with an air of 'that's how it's done boys'.

Not to be outdone the two lads stood up and asked everyone if they could clap along to the song they were about to sing. This was a bit surprising, but they all nodded in agreement. They started to sing 'Bonnie Dundee'. The lads sang their hearts out, and everyone was clapping and singing and gave them a resounding cheer when they had finished. Surprisingly it was Shonagh who got up and gave them both a hug. When they were sitting down, she asked them what they were studying at school. Levi had said he was hoping to go to university to study Psychology, and then Bohdi said he was already in his first year at college studying Forestry and Land Management. Everyone was waiting for them to start laughing, but they had been deadly serious. As soon as Bohdie had spoken, Denny had immediately sat up and stored that piece of information in the back of his brain.

"By the way lads, I have been rude as I haven't asked you what your surnames are and I never asked Stevie either," said Denny.

"Levi and Bohdi will do just fine pal, and best if you leave it at Stevie from Lochee," replied Levi.

Tommy started to laugh and told Denny he had a 'right pair there'.

Next day was the wedding so nobody wanted a late night, so they all dwindled away to their rooms. Denny had gone to Helen and suggested he sleep in one of the spare rooms as with all that was going through his head he kept tossing and turning and disturbing her. Helen agreed, as she told him he had been talking and shouting in his sleep. When they were in their room, he kissed the boys and Helen goodnight and told her she still had time to call it all off if she wanted with a smile on his face.

"I want nothing more in my life than to marry you Denny, so that we can have a wonderful life together with the boys."

He started to walk downstairs, and Helen asked him where he was going. He told them that he was going to sleep with the dogs in the room out the back. It didn't surprise her, so she just blew him a kiss and then he was gone. He walked into the room and the dogs came to greet him. He laid the mattress and pillow in between the dogs beds and lay down and fell asleep immediately. During the night he must have been shouting in his sleep as he woke up to find the dogs ready to go into the attack mode. He comforted them, and they all went back to sleep.

This was the day of the wedding and over breakfast Helen asked everyone how they had slept. Annie said that Tommy's snoring had kept her awake and wondered if the animals in the forest had been kept awake as well. Helen had suggested Denny go for a long shower when he went up to the room as she didn't want to marry someone stinking of dogs. He was standing in front of their bed and didn't hear Jinty come in. She ran and jumped on him, and he ended up turning and falling onto his back on the bed. She quickly got onto the bed and straddled him.

"Last chance Foggerty it's me or Helen."

"Before you get amorous Jinty, have a smell at him."

Jinty put her nose to his chest before getting off him and lying on the bed holding her throat, pretending not to be able to breath. Helen told him to get all his clothes off and put them in one of the spare rooms as he wasn't to see her in her wedding dress until she walked down the steps of the veranda. Willie had already put his clothes in the room just so that they could get ready together. Helen had asked Gertie to bring her clothes to the main bedroom so that the three of them would be together before it was time.

Denny and Willie had gone to Munich to get their kilts and all the accessories. They thought it might be difficult, but Otto had pointed them in the right direction. Denny had bought a record player and dozens of records for everybody to dance and sing to. It wasn't going to be a big wedding, but it would be a happy and joyous day.

An hour later Maria and her mum and dad, Max, and Elke, along with Otto and his wife Lina arrived. It was lovely for Helen and Denny that they all wore thistle buttonholes.

"Denny, I hope you don't mind, but I have had to bring Ottar as I couldn't get my usual dog minder to look after him."

"Never apologise for bringing my lovely pal to see me Otto."

Denny went to the back of the four by four and opened the hatch. Ottar walked forward and started to lick his face with Denny scratching his ears. Ottar slowly jumped down and walked towards everybody. Denny thought he was such a proud and magnificent specimen of a dog. Arno and Udo came down to see

22

him, but made sure they walked at his side and always slightly behind him.

Helen came down the steps with the boys cradled in each arm and introduced everyone to each other. She was so glad that she had all these lovely people at her wedding. When Ottar saw Helen, he ran to her, and Helen handed the boys to Elke and Lina and got down on her knees and let him in for a cuddle and ear scratch. As they were standing there Bohdi said, "Oh no, not another bloody dog." Helen had heard him and crooked her finger beckoning him to come to her. He knew what was going to happen, so he walked forward and put his arms around her waiting for the inevitable clip around the ear, which duly arrived. He whispered in her ear that Maria looked 'fit' and asked if she thought she might be up for dancing.

"Hey Maria, this young lad thinks your 'fit' and will you be up for dancing today?" she shouted.

"If it's that young handsome guy that's hanging on to you then I definitely would be."

All Bohdi could do was stand there while everyone was laughing with a face redder than last night's sky. Denny could feel the warmth coming from the group and decided to try and put his niggling doubts out of his head for the duration of the wedding celebrations.

The ceremony wasn't until two o'clock, so there was time to spare while everyone got to know each other. As they all sat on the veranda, Denny and Helen walked a little with the boys strapped to them before Denny turned to her and said," We are two lucky people darling. Do you think we will be having them all back here for our first-year anniversary?"

"Let's all make a pledge before they go back home that we will meet up again in a year. What do you think my beautiful boy?"

Gertie had been out with the tea pot again, and some ginger biscuits. Helen thought she was an absolute gem, but knew that she might want to move on at some stage. Everyone sat on the veranda. Denny thought there had been a lot of sitting around over the last few days, but it was a nice time for everyone to get to know each other.

"Denny, we are going up to the room to get ready now and suggest everyone else does the same, especially the young lads as I don't know how they will be turned out. Remember the minister will be here soon, and please don't jilt me at the altar."

Denny wondered if God had spent too much time creating women. He must have been overthinking, as they are very complicated and talked a lot of 'drivel' at times. It was then that the three dogs stood up, Ottar very gingerly, with the usual guttural growl coming from them. Denny looked down the track to see the minister Bruno Fischer coming up with his notes in his hand. Denny quietened the dogs and went to meet him. He was a tall, ruddy faced chap with a very gentle smile. He had been up at the house a few weeks ago and had loved meeting everyone, especially the boys, and had said a few words over them as they lay in their cot. Helen had loved that.

Denny made all the introductions, and then Annie went and made him a coffee along with fudge biscuits which he polished off in no time. Denny turned to the guests and suggested that everyone go and get changed and could they please look after the boys.

Denny and Willie were first out. Both of them wore McLeod tartan kilts because Willie asked Denny to wear it as there was no Foggerty tartan. Denny was proud to do it. As everybody emerged, all the men wore kilts except Tommy who wore a pair of tartan trews. The ladies had dresses of all kinds and colour. Everyone from Scotland wore a heather buttonhole. They were only waiting for Levi and Bohdi and old Frieda.

It was then that the two lads walked up the side steps onto the veranda and stood at the top of the steps. They were absolutely resplendent standing there. Both had on a white Jacobite shirt, while Bohdi wore a kilt of the Pringle tartan and Levi had one of the McKenzie tartan. It was then that all guests looked down at their footwear only to see both were wearing a pair of old baseball boots. No socks. Denny and Willie started to laugh setting everyone else off. Even the minister couldn't help himself. As they started to walk forward Denny heard himself saying," God bless the pair of you."

Otto said that the dogs were up on their feet and Denny looked down the track only to see Frieda walking up. Without being prompted the two lads took off down the track to help her. As they started to take an arm each she started to protest and hit them with her walking stick. No matter what the lads tried to do, they were in danger of being swatted. Eventually she arrived, and everybody got into their seats with Neala and Lina holding the boys.

Max had volunteered to play the music, so he stood over at the record player ready for Helen and her bridesmaids Jinty and Gertie to appear. There were dozens of albums to cover every taste. Helen and Denny had spent weeks thinking about what songs or tunes they wanted for today and hoped everyone would enjoy their choices.

Denny had no doubt that Helen would be late just for the sake of it, and she didn't disappoint. The minister was obviously used to it as he stood there with a smile on his face. After another ten minutes the French doors started to open. Jinty and Gertie walked through and stood to the side. They were dressed in beautiful green dresses, and each carried a posy of wildflowers which had come from the forest. Neither wore any shoes.

"What's happening here Denny, I didn't know Gertie had been asked to be a bridesmaid," Willie whispered in Denny's ear.

"Sometimes I wonder what planet you're on Willie."

A few minutes passed then Helen walked out and stood in between them, they all moved nearer to the top of the stairs. She wore a slightly different green dress. As well as her posy, Jinty had made her a head garland of the same flowers. No shoes. Everyone thought she looked stunning. Denny and Helen could have had the biggest wedding with no expense spared, anywhere in the world, but they wanted it here with their friends and their boys. Willie started to fidget, and Denny had asked him what was going on.

"They are three beautiful 'lassies' Denny. How lucky are we?"

It was then that the music started, and the skirl of the pipes introduced Highland Cathedral as the girls started to walk forward. All the ladies were soon in tears, and Denny thought he saw Ian wipe a tear away. He noticed that when the lads saw the girls in their bare feet, they nonchalantly slid their baseball boots off and kicked them under their chairs.

"Don't you start 'greetin' Foggerty as you will set me off and that could be the end of my image. A pretty rubbish image mind you."

As Helen walked towards Denny, she never took her eyes off him. Never wavered one bit. When she got to him, she gave him a loving kiss. It was then that the minister took over and started the ceremony. Denny held her hand and thought she was shaking a bit, so he just gently squeezed it. Mr Fischer started talking about marriage, and how it was so special for both Denny and Helen. How they had brought two lovely boys into this world and how the name of Foggerty would carry on through the generations. They both made their vows which was them saying how much they loved each other. The mister said how lovely it was that all their friends had come for their special day and having good friends was a rarity, and hoped that they might all come back for the weddings of Cal and Finn. There were a few looks of 'not sure about that'. Then Mr Fischer did a strange thing. He put his hands on their foreheads and held them there for about a minute with his eyes closed.

He then asked the best man for the rings. Willie started to panic and looked at Denny with his arms out.

"You never gave me any rings Foggerty. What's happening here?"

"The rings are in your sporran Willie. I put them in when you were showering earlier."

Willie took them out and handed them to Mr Fischer. Both rings were crafted to look like two branches intertwined with each other with reference to the forests their lives were encapsulated in. They put the rings on each other's finger and the minister said, "I now pronounce you man and wife and you may kiss the bride Denny. As he did so everybody started to clap and cheer which got the dogs standing up wondering what the hell was going on. It was all hugs and congratulations from there on. Helen walked over and took her boys in her arms and cried tears of joy. She didn't get to keep them for long as Annie was hovering around.

Denny hugged Jinty and Gertie and thanked them for being there for Helen. Jinty doing her usual hanging around his neck forever. It was then that he walked over to Willie and shook his hand.

"Willie, I don't how to say this. I don't have any family so I would be so proud if I can call you my brother. What do you say?"

"Foggerty, you're hell bent on getting me crying today. Aren't you? I might not show it all the time, but I've always considered you as my other brother, although I'll always be the good looking one."

They smiled and hugged, but had to stop before it became a bit of a wrestling match with Helen giving them a stern look. It was time for the meal and the men walked to the side of the lodge and carried back a large round table to the centre of the marquee ready for the meal to be served. Gertie had been working miracles all week preparing the wedding fayre and now it was everybody's turn to help out. Place mats and cutlery as well as glasses were set out around the table, before all the ladies went down to the annex kitchen and brought the food to the table.

Everyone sat down to Leberkase which was a rich meatloaf accompanied with veal strips. There was also Kasespatzle, soft gooey little noodle dumplings in cheese topped with crunchy caramelised onions. Lastly was Kaiserschmarran for a sweet. A dish of caramelised pancakes with berries. When everyone was seated they gave Gertie a round of applause for all her efforts. With the round table, nobody was left out of the conversation. Helen held Denny's hand and they both looked around the table smiling. It seemed that Tommy meant business as he had loosened his trews at the start ready for any competition which the two lads would bring.

There were smiles, laughter and genuine joy around the table. Everyone had thoroughly enjoyed the food. Even Tommy had to admit defeat to Levi and Bohdi giving them a slight nod at the end. Ian had then stood up and announced that they were going to do the speeches now. A time that Willie hoped would never come. Ian didn't sit down. He just looked at Helen and said, "Helen, I hope you don't mind, but Denny asked me a while back on the phone that as your own Dad wasn't going to be here, then could I give the father of the bride speech. I have known you for what seems a long time and I am proud to be standing here giving this speech. You are such a lovely 'lassie', and I had no doubts that Denny would come back to you. When Denny was away cavorting around Scotland and over here, Neala and I got to know you very well and if truth be told if I ever had a daughter then I would want her to be like you."

Helen ran round the table and gave Ian a huge hug with tears streaming down her face. Willie whispered to Denny that he thought this was supposed to be a happy occasion. Denny just shook his head. Willie never ceased to amaze him. When Ian was finished they all clapped, and Neala sat there with a single tear coming down her cheek. So proud of Ian. It was now time for Denny to give his speech.

"Ladies and gentlemen. On behalf of my amazing wife and doting mother to Fin and Cal, we would like to thank you for being here with us today. All we ever wanted was a small and intimate wedding with those we love with us. I can't say that the last couple of years have been very easy, especially for me, but we have come through it stronger people. I once told Helen that if I couldn't kick the whisky then she was to shoot me while I stood on the edge of the cliff on Durma. That's how bad I was, but she stuck with me. She is an amazing 'lassie' folks and I thank God she is now my wife. Sorry mister Fischer, but I do believe there is some sort of God up there. I hope you all enjoy yourself today and please raise your glasses to Helen. Thank you."

Everyone clapped and some of the ladies had a 'wee' tear in their eye as Denny sat down and gave Helen a big kiss.

Ian stood up and said it was now the turn of his brother, the best man, to make his speech.

"Well folks, can I just say that Foggerty here gave me only a few days' notice that I was to be his best man and make a speech. So, I have been 'bricking' it ever since. I tried writing something down, but after several attempts I gave it up as a bad job. I then thought I would just 'wing' it. I can see Foggerty sitting there with his hand over his eyes wondering what I'm going to say next. However, what I will say will be from the heart. Just before these three beautiful girls came out Denny asked me if he could be my other brother as he had no family. I thought it was a ploy to get me 'greetin' and he almost succeeded. It was the nicest thing that anyone has ever said to me. I am a little bit lost for words now. What can you say about the three stunning 'lassies' sitting next to me. Firstly though, I would like to say that if Helen did try and shoot Denny on the cliff on Durma, then she would have taken two or three tries seeing as she is a woman. That was supposed to be a joke folks seeing as none of you are laughing. I like to think of them as my sisters but that would be a bit weird as I am sleeping every night with Gertie. Sorry minister. It might seem a bit strange, but I love them with all my heart. So quickly raise you glasses to the 'lassies' as I feel I really am about to shed some tears."

They all gave Willie a thunderous round of applause and believe it or not Willie actually bowed. Denny leaned across and hugged him. After the speeches it was just a case of sitting around and chatting, and Helen felt they were all beginning to bond with each other. Ian eventually asked for all the men to help lift the table out of the way and the ladies just left the dishes as they didn't want to get any stains on their dresses. Seats were put around the outside of the marquee leaving a large square of grass for a dance floor.

It was now time for the bridal waltz and Ian had announced that Helen and Denny would like everyone to follow them once the music started. The bride and groom stood ready at the top end of the grass square and Max started the song. The beautiful song 'The Wonder of You' by Elvis played, and everyone wondered if the animal residents of the forest had ever heard Elvis before. Levi had beaten Bodhi to dance with Maria, so Bodhi had walked over to Jinty, held his hand out, and asked her very eloquently for this dance. She smiled and threw her arms around him. Even the minister had got Frieda up after a bit of persuasion.

The dancing went on for hours. The music was sometimes slow dances with even some German waltzes thrown in. After a while the three girls had brought out jugs of fresh orange so that they could all quench their thirsts.

"Ladies and gentlemen or should I just say friends. Gertie has never experienced Scottish Country Dancing, so I think it's time we showed her."

"Mr Ian, I only said to Helen that I had never experienced it, so you don't have to do it for me."

"If anybody doesn't know how to do it then follow Willie, as he once got a certificate for it for dancing in front of Queen Elizabeth when she visited the Highlands."

"I think I'll stick to Denny being my brother," said Willie who was slightly embarrassed.

The Eightsome Reel was first and after a bit of getting everyone in their places the music started. Jack had gotten Annie up, but think she would have preferred to stay sitting. Elke was happy holding the boys. After about five minutes the dancing was wild. All the ladies were being thrown about, and the men were fairly swirling their kilts around.

"Mrs Helen, do you see what I am seeing? All the men seem to have forgotten their underwear as they are showing us far too much," shouted Gertie.

Helen just gave her the thumbs up and laughed. Everyone from Bavaria adapted very quickly to the dances and were a bit disappointed when each dance finished. There was Strip the Willow, Eightsome Reel and Dashing White Sergeant along with a host of others. Max thought it prudent to space out the dances so that they could all get their breath back. No one wanted them to end, so Max just carried on.

At the end of one dance Otto gave Denny a quick whistle, and pointed to the dogs who had been sleeping on the veranda, but were now up on all fours and ready. He told Helen he would be back just now as he had to see what the dogs were up to. As he walked past Willie he whispered that there might be a problem. Willie followed Denny and as they both looked down the track they saw a guy who was looking very unstable on his feet. They immediately recognised Scottie, Jinty's boyfriend who seemed drunk, very drunk. Denny walked faster as he wanted Scottie as far away from the celebrations as possible. When Denny intercepted him, Scottie tried to barge past, but Denny wasn't going to let that happen.

"Scottie, your drunk, so why don't you just go home. Jinty doesn't want to see you like that. She will be home tomorrow. You'll just upset everyone at the wedding."

The smell of alcohol and cigarette smoke coming from him was making both Willie and Denny feel nauseous. The smell from Scottie was absolutely rank.

"Just because you own all this Foggerty, you think you can boss everyone around. Well, you're not going to do it to me. She is my girlfriend and I'm going up there to see her and you and your sidekick aren't going to stop me. Bring it on you broken down alcoholic."

Willie had never seen Denny move as fast. Denny grabbed him by the throat and started to squeeze. He wasn't letting go and Willie thought this was going to be a problem as Scottie was beginning to go blue in the face. Eventually, Willie had to grab Denny's arm and with all his strength managed to free Scottie's throat. Scottie fell to the ground, but Willie could see that Denny's rage was about to kick off. He grabbed him around the chest and told him to breathe deeply. After a few minutes Denny responded and calmed down.

"Here is what's going to happen you smelly bastard. Jinty will be here for another couple of days and when she gets home you had better be gone. You will never contact her again. If you do, then she will phone me and I will come and get you, stake you out in the forest and let the wolves eat you while you are still alive. I believe they start with the genitals. Do you understand you 'prick'."

Scottie could only nod his head. As he got up Denny smashed his nose with a punch. Scottie wandered away with blood spurting out his broken nose. As they walked back Willie said, "Denny, it looked like you were going to throttle him just now. What's going on with you. Is it to do with your talk to Helen and me after the wedding? And why did you break his nose?"

"Yes, it is about my talk to you Willie and why did I break his nose? Simply, because I could brother. So, let's see who is fast enough to get the next dance with Helen."

They both took off, but it was a no contest as Denny's big stride was eating up the ground leaving Willie in his wake. When they got back there was still a lot of dancing going on. As they sat watching everybody enjoying their self, Jinty had sat down beside Denny.

"I was at the toilet and saw you out the window Denny. Was that Scottie? What happened?"

Denny told her and she started to cry, saying she was so sorry, but Denny reminded her that he doesn't like tears. So, he suggested they give it a 'birl' around the dancefloor.

The day was getting on so Denny suggested that it might be time for everyone to do their party piece and sing a song or two. He had purchased a small amp with microphones along with lots of albums, where the lyrics were missing so that anyone could sing the missing words to the song. It was a mad rush to get the tunes that they wanted, but everybody seemed happy with their choice.

Surprisingly, it was the minister who was up first. Nobody was going to get in his way. Max started the music and Bruno gave everyone a very energetic version of' You're the Devil in Disguise' by Elvis. His hips were gyrating, and he was jumping about like a man possessed. When he finished he gave a theatrical bow as everyone gave him rapturous applause. Everybody, bar a few, who point blank refused to sing got their turn. Some coming back for two or three songs. It was nearing the end when Ian asked Willie and Denny to come and stand beside him for his song. As they stood either side of him he took the mic, no music, and belted out 'What shall we do with a Drunken Sailor'. Everyone just stood, not saying a word, while looking at Denny and Willie. Denny looked at Willie and they started laughing and joined in with Ian, much to the relief of the guests.

The time had come to finish up the wedding although nobody wanted that to happen. Denny then announced that the Bavarian folk would like to sing a song which is dear to their hearts. As they all walked forward it seemed that everyone knew what the song would be. Deutschland, Deutschland. Everyone else stood in respect. They sang it with love in their hearts and tears in their eyes. Even Frieda sat and waved her stick in the air. There was a lot of hugging after the song finished. Denny then asked the Scots to see what they could do. They got up and walked forward to the mic. Levi and Bohdi started to argue over who should have the mic and the feud was settled with a clip over their heads by Helen.

Denny passed the mic to Ian who shared it with Tommy. Levi and Bohdi stood waiting with a hand on their hearts. Flower of Scotland started, and they gave it their all. The ladies were unashamedly crying, and Tommy was singing emotionally. Shonagh linked arms with Jack and Annie. Helen put her arms around Neala, Jinty and Gertie who insisted she wanted to try and sing this song. When they finished they got into a huddle with all the other guests and hugged and hugged. They then retired to the veranda for tea and biscuits. Frieda said she would have to get home, so the minister offered to take her. He seemed a bit disappointed about the biscuits, but Helen had picked up on it, so she made up two bags. One for him and the other for Frieda. Denny and her thanked them both very much for helping to make their wedding so special. Denny handed him a thick envelope for officiating on the day.

"Mr Foggerty, this is far too much for my services today."

"Well, Bruno it was really for your Elvis impersonation, not just marrying us," said Denny laughing.

"I know neither of you are religious, but I hope my God looks after you, especially the boys."

Bruno and Frieda walked off down the track.

While taking tea, Elke had asked if they could come over from the town house tomorrow morning for the men to go out shooting and the ladies to indulge themselves in tea and gossip. There was the nodding of heads all around. It had been a big day, so everyone started to drift home to the town house or to their beds. Jinty had said she was taking the boys into her room overnight. Helen had expressed milk, so Jinty was all sorted.

Denny and Helen went to their room, and they were no sooner in when she quickly took off her dress, slowly took off her underwear teasing Denny, lay on her back on the bed and said," C'mon big boy, let me see if you still have it. I could do with multiple orgasms tonight my lovely husband." Denny was erect right away and they were soon making love with an intensity that they hadn't experienced since the boys came along. Helen had been very vocal, but neither could care less if any of the guests heard them. Eventually they lay back exhausted.

"Denny, please promise me that we will continue to make love for as long as it's physically possible."

"Helen, I've told you before that I will never stop loving you and when I am ninety I will be making love to you albeit, with not the same intensity and you might need to give me a hand to get me on top of you."

They both laughed and held each other until they fell asleep.

Chapter 3

It was the noises coming from the animals in the forests that woke Denny. He lay back and tried to identify all the calls and whistles. God he loved this place. Helen was lying peacefully and looking very content. There was time for a shower before he changed and took the dogs for a walk. He only took Ottar a short way before sending him back. He felt exhilarated and started to run with the dogs, but he knew he was kidding himself on as Udo and Arno were just toddling alongside him, probably asking themselves if this was the best he could do. When he got back Helen had just got into the shower and Denny felt he needed to shower again, after sweating profusely on his run as it had been hot in the forest.

He went into the shower and backed her up against the tiles, lifted her up, slowly entered her and started to make love to her with the same intensity as last night. Helen thought the wall might cave in until the bedroom door opened and Jinty shouted "Are you two still at it. Keep it down for God's sake or you'll wake the bairns."

Helen, Jinty and Gertie started on the breakfasts, and it wasn't long before Denny heard the roar of Max's Opel off road truck bringing everyone from the town house coming up the track. Denny had offered to buy Max a newer, quieter model, but he had refused point blank as Denny had given him more than enough. As they all gathered in the dining room Denny thought they all looked bright and breezy. Even although they would be going home in a few hours.

Just before the breakfast was served Denny stood up.

"I hope to make this my last speech for a 'wee' while, trust me. What I am about to say may come as a surprise to you. It is really for my friends from Scotland. Helen and I were wondering if any of you would like to come and live on the estate. Not necessarily work, but definitely to live. I don't know if you noticed, but at the bottom of the estate where the track ends there is scrubland either side. Well, if anybody would like to come and live here, then I would build them a house not dissimilar to this, but smaller. One which they would then own. The house can be completed in six months.

I realise for the four of you living in Edinburgh it would be a massive wrench leaving such a beautiful city, but the offer is there. Ian and Neala, we can have a talk before you go."

"Have you forgotten somebody Mr Denny? What about me and Bohdi? Can I say though, you had better put us down for one each as I can't stand much more of his snoring."

By the looks they gave each other Denny thought a fight might ensue.

"Sorry lads, but you are going home to complete your education, but there are always holidays for you to pop over, and I will make sure I send money to Stevie for your flights."

The lads didn't look too happy, but Denny knew they would get over the disappointment. Tommy said that he thought that he and Annie would struggle to leave Edinburgh, but would be more than happy to come over for a holiday. Shonagh agreed with Tommy as did Jack, but the thought of coming over whenever they could was very appealing.

After the breakfast was over Denny suggested that the men go and change for their little shooting expedition into the forest. Otto wanted to bring Ottar and Denny agreed. Max said he would stay behind as he needed to check out something on the car. As they were standing waiting for the lads to appear Willie then shouted, "For the love of God you pair, just have a look at yourselves. No chance of doing any stalking today then."

The lads stood there with camouflage tops that Denny had found for them and bright blue swim shorts. So bright that they could have been seen from the moon. Everybody just shook their heads and laughed. Denny had suggested to Otto that four guns would be enough, and he had agreed. One each for Denny, Otto, Ian, and Willie. Jack was quite happy with that, but the look on the lad's faces was one of sheer disbelief.

Denny saw this and quickly told them not to worry as they would get their turn like everybody else. He did advise everyone that it would be Otto in charge, and as there were guns and ammunition involved whatever he said was gospel.

They set off and walked at a steady pace. When Denny was alongside Otto he asked him about the scarcity of the foxes.

"There are a couple of reasons that come to mind Denny. One, that they have contracted a 'pox' of some sort and would pass it down to their offspring. Rabbits can also get it and if the fox eats them then it will contract it and die. Secondly, have you ever thought that they may be getting trapped. Fox's pelts can still command a fair price in Munich to be used in ladies' coats."

"I think if it was a 'pox' Otto then I would see evidence of carcasses lying around but I don't see any. I never thought about the trapping side, so I will try and speak to anybody who can tell me."

The day was beautiful, so they weren't in any hurry to get to get to the East valley. After a while Otto suggested they walk in silence for a few minutes. They came to a stream and over on the far banking dozens of rabbits were enjoying the sunshine on their backs. Denny never liked killing animals, but when it came to humans he had no bother with it, if they deserved it.

Everyone took their turn to shoot. Ian, Tommy, and Willie were top notch at it, but Jack's technique left a bit to be desired. When it came to the young lads they literally never missed putting each bullet through the middle of the rabbit's head. It made Denny think back to his early years. Levi got a telling off from Otto for firing once from the hip, but still putting it dead centre of the rabbit's brain. Otto telling him he watched too many cowboy films.

Otto suggested they move further up the valley, and while they walked Tommy asked the lads where they got their prowess with a rifle.

"Well Mr Tommy, when you've lived on some of the council estates that we have, you learn to shoot after you have learned to walk. .22 pellet guns were often passed down from brother to brother, even sister to sister. How many times did you go into a council estate, and you had to dodge the .22 pellets fired at you? Bet you got hit a few times Mr Tommy."

Tommy could only smile as Levi was spot on with that. Denny had told everyone that he wouldn't get the dogs to pick up due to the possibility of the rabbits having a pox. They would leave the carcasses for the scavenging crows.

"By the look of the dogs Mr Denny, they are desperate to go and retrieve judging by the 'slavers' hanging from their mouths. Either that or they've got rabies. What do you think Mr Denny?"

"Bohdi, I think if I accidentally discharged this rifle, and the bullet went dead centre into your forehead, then I don't think anyone here would bother too much, although the crows wouldn't get much of a feed off you."

Everyone either shook their heads or shrugged their shoulders.

"Thanks a bunch, you guys," said Bohdi.

The mist had descended on them a little bit, so Otto warned everyone to keep clear of the banking at the stream as it got steeper as they climbed. They pretty much walked in silence until Ottar suddenly stood stock still and growled. Otto put his arm out and quietly said that nobody was to move. Both Arno and Udo started to growl standing either side of Ottar, which unnerved Bohdi. There was nothing to see until the mist parted and there standing in a clearing no more than fifty yards away was a magnificent white stag just looking down on them. It must have been about eight feet high with twelve-point antlers. As the sun broke through the mist the beast truly gleamed. A real Royal Stag.

Slowly, Denny walked forward with Otto telling him not too, far. He stood and looked the stag straight in the eyes and it then raised its head and snorted. It seemed like a stand off, until Denny realised that this was not his domain, so he slowly walked backwards, never taking his eyes off this awesome beast. When Denny stood with the rest of them, the stag started to throw his head in the air and stomp the ground. Everyone knew, including the dogs, who was the master here. It slowly and proudly, with his head held high, turned, and started to walk away only once stopping to look back. It then wandered off into the mist.

Nobody uttered a word and Denny bent over with his head in his hands covering his face. When he looked at Otto they both smiled knowing they might never experience anything like that again. They all looked around at each other with smiles starting to appear on their faces. Denny looked at Bohdi who had obviously been scared and for all his talk about dogs, was standing with his hand on Ottar's neck.

"Well folks, I don't think we will ever beat that, so maybe it's time to wander back. Lads, could you do me a favour and trot back with Udo and Arno as they need to stretch their legs". The lads took off and gave the impression that they were in charge of the dogs, but everyone knew it was the other way round.

When they got back to the house they all sat having sandwiches and cakes, while Denny and Otto regaled them with the story of the white stag. Those who hadn't been there were in awe of their experience.

"Miss Maria, I wasn't scared, and I just stood there protecting the dogs, honest," said Bohdi.

"Young man, what is it like to be so handsome and so brave?" asked Maria.

"It just comes natural to me Miss Maria," replied Bohdi. No one could stop laughing with Bohdi wondering what was going on until Levi gave him a proper punch on his upper arm and told him to keep quiet. The time had come for everyone to start packing to go home. Maria and her family along with Otto and Lina said their goodbyes with the expected tears and long hugs. Finn and Col got their fair share of kisses and cuddles. Everyone waved until they were down the track and out of sight.

Next was Tommy and Annie as well as Shonagh and Jack. Ian and Neala were on a later flight as were the lads. Willie loaded their luggage into the four by four and waited while everyone said goodbye. As Annie held the boys she couldn't hold back the flood of tears, with Tommy just shaking his head at her. When Shonagh gave Denny a hug she whispered in his ear to contact her if he needed any help. As they took off down the road Helen broke down and started to cry.

"Don't worry Mrs Helen, you've still got Levi and me," said Bohdi.

"I think that might be why I'm crying son," replied Helen.

Later that afternoon Denny sat down with Ian and Neala and asked them their thoughts on what he had said earlier. Denny thought it prudent to include Willie in the conversation. As they sat outside, the sun was low in the sky and casting some weird and wonderful shadows throughout the forests. Ian didn't say anything as he sat holding Neala's hand before looking into her eyes and saying.

"I think I can say for the both of us that we would love to come and live here Denny. It's been three and a half magical days, and we have talked about how the fishing is a young man's game and the catches are getting smaller and smaller. Can I say though that we have put some money away and would like to contribute as much as we can to having a house built for us. However, it might be best if it's three bedrooms at least."

"Why would you need three bedrooms Neala?" said Willie.

"Willie isn't it obvious? We are going to try and make you an uncle. We were going to talk about it when we got home, but we have both made up our minds and now is the time to share our thoughts with the people we love."

Willie just sat there trying to take everything in before asking Denny that if Ian comes to work here will he still be the Forest Manager? Denny nodded and the biggest smile came over his face. Willie got up and walked over to Neala and Ian and gave them a huge hug. Denny told Ian that he wouldn't be contributing anything to the house, and he could have it built in about six months.

Denny shouted for everyone else to come over and hear the news. When they heard, Helen Jinty and Gertie started to hug Ian and Neala with the usual tears. Denny said he was going to check on his boys as he couldn't stand any more tears. They all sat in silence until Levi tried hard to get Denny to change his mind about him and Bohdi coming to live there.

"Education is so important son, but I'm going to make you a promise. While you are at college and university, Helen and I will sponsor you to help with your studies. All monies will go through Stevie and if you ask for any and he says no then that's it. However, if things don't work out for you, then you will be more than welcome to come and work for me and before you ask I will build a house for you, but hopefully that is years down the line."

"That's very kind Mr Denny, but can I ask you a very important question? What's the chance of me bringing that 'lassie' I lost my virginity to from the estate with me?"

"Willie, Ian, can you get a key for the gun cabinet so we can get a gun with the highest calibre and shoot him, putting us all out of our misery?"

The look on Bohdi's face said he really thought Denny meant it. Jinty came over and sat on his knee and put her arms around him and told them to stop teasing the poor boy.

"Who's teasing, Jinty? Oh, and by the way it will be me that is taking you home tomorrow, for obvious reasons. Okay?"

"Fine Denny, but if he is still there then I will deal with the situation. I know you would knock his head off just for the sake of it. Wouldn't you?"

Denny just shrugged his shoulders and smiled.

It was time for Ian, Neala, and the lads to go so, Willie got all their luggage into the four by four. Suddenly, the lads ran into the annex and returned with a small bag each, which they gave to Denny and Helen. When they opened them, there were presents from Stevie. Purple and white heather plants.

"He said it's so that you never forget Scotland, Mr and Mrs Denny. Nearly four days we've been 'lugging' these things around."

"Thank him very much lads and I will thank him personally if I ever see him."

Before they left there were the promises of keeping in touch, whether it was to be by phone or letters. As they all hugged, Denny had to tell Bohdi to let Jinty go so that she could come up for air. Just before they got in the car the three dogs came running down the steps. Everyone paid them attention before Bohdi knelt down and put his arms around Ottar, scratched his ears and then did the same to Arno and Udo.

"Not so scared of 'dugs' now son, said Denny."

"I've just got the knack Mr Denny. Oh, and before I go, can I say something Mrs Helen? Look after my 'bairns' will you?"

As the four by four was nearing the end of the track Helen went and put her arm around Denny's waist and said, "I'm going to miss everybody Denny, but especially the lads and that enigma called Bohdi." A single tear rolled down her cheek.

"I don't think it will be that long before I see them again."

Denny went to look after Col and Fin while Helen helped Gertie and Jinty to get the house back to some semblance of order. Laundry was going to be the name of the game for the next few days. Helen came out onto the veranda, and started to change the boys. She could see that Denny was looking troubled so she suggested he take the dogs for a walk, but leave Ottar here, as Otto might turn up at any time to pick him up. Denny sat on the steps with Ottar. Just speaking to him while his arm was around his neck. He knew the dog was getting old and frail and might not have long to be running around these forests. The most important thing Denny thought was that Ottar has had such a great life, and there would be no regrets when he went.

He took Arno and Udo and walked towards the South valley to see what Willie had been moaning about a few days ago. When he got to the bottom of the valley he got a bit of a surprise to see the state of the place. Tracks were being overrun with weeds, some trees had fallen down the banking, ending up in the stream with the potential of catching debris and blocking the flow of the water. Denny realised that Willie was right, and they needed help but who? With all the nonsense going through his head he had to get someone he could trust.

The sky was starting to cast over, so he decided to walk the dogs back as he had to take Jinty home. When they arrived back Otto was just about to leave with Ottar, but the dog still wanted to come up to Denny for an ear scratch and a growl at the other dogs when they got too close. Denny asked Otto if he would be over next week, and he had given Denny the thumbs up.

It was time to take Jinty home, so he put all her bags into the other jeep and after the usual goodbyes they started toward Zwiesel with Jinty shouting out the window.

"If he isn't back in a few hours then I think he will just be staying with me Mrs Foggerty. What do you think?"

"Fine by me you 'hussy' Jinty Thomas."

Willie was back and Denny told him that he was in charge and to carry his rifle with him wherever he went. As they neared Jinty's house and bakery, Denny knew something wasn't right, but didn't say anything as he knew it was going to be hard for Jinty going back to an empty house. Her bakery was in a busy area of the town, so business was brisk. After parking up, he got her luggage out the back and they wandered around the side of the building, but he could see the apprehension on her face as they climbed the stairs. They were only halfway up before Denny could smell the 'reek' of stale cigarette smoke emanating from under the door.

"Give me your keys Jinty and let me go in first. I can see your going to argue, but please don't. Give me your bloody keys."

Denny went through the door first and as he walked into the lounge he couldn't believe the mess he was seeing. Small bowls used as ashtrays, all full to overflowing. Food cartons with half eaten food were lying over the floor as well as empty beer bottles. The wet patches on the floor were anybody's guess. Jinty was in tears. He walked over and put his arms around her. He said to her if she wanted to come back to the estate then fine as he would get a company in to clean the house from top to bottom.

"No, you're fine Denny. This is my house and I'll just put on a pair of gloves and get on with it."

She suddenly took off down the outside stairs with Denny following her wondering what was going on. She went in the back door to the bakery, and opened a small cupboard. Denny could see immediately that there was a safe in there, but the door was open and whatever was in it was gone.

"What is missing Jinty?"

"About five hundred Deutschmarks and both our passports, but most importantly a necklace that belonged to my grandmother. I'm going to clean this place out, phone the lady who helps me in the shop and we will be open tomorrow. Nothing is going to drive me away from here."

It was then that Denny told her to find a pair of gloves big enough for him, and they were soon cleaning the place, with the opening of the windows the first job. As Denny was cleaning, it was all he could do to keep his rage in check, but he knew that if Scottie was still around he would find him soon enough and deal with him. Maybe the wolves would get a good feed soon.

"I'm going to leave you soon Jinty. Have you any other money? I will make up your loss and don't say a word please. I feel I may explode at any time, and as you have been a witness to it before you know it's not nice to see. I need you to promise that you will phone me or Helen every second day. When I get back I will immediately phone an emergency locksmith and he will be here within the hour to change all the locks"

"Don't worry about money Denny, I have a bit stashed away, so I'll be fine. Go home and kiss the 'bairns' for me and I will 'pop up' in a couple of days to see everyone. Just give me a reassuring hug before you go."

As Denny drove home his driving was a bit erratic, as his mind kept drifting to what he was going to do to Scottie. Whatever it was he would make it very unpleasant for him and if his rage took over then he would make no promises. When he got home he had the unenviable task of telling everyone what had went down.

"Only two days ago we had a lovely wedding and now this scum bag does that. Best that I never see him Denny or the 'Timebomb' will explode, and his head will explode with me," said Willie.

Helen had suggested that everyone calm down and it would all work out. They all looked incredulously at her, and she realised that she had spoken out of turn, looked at them, then said, "Okay, then let's rip his fucking 'balls' off if we catch him. Agreed?" They all stood and looked at each other not saying a word until Gertie suggested they go in for something to eat. The wedding had been such a wonderful day, so Denny wasn't sure when he was going to bring up the subject of his sixth sense giving him cause for concern. However, it had to be done and the more he was putting it off the more his brain would be in turmoil.

Denny had told Willie that he agreed with him regarding help in the South valley and he would be helping him until he could find some guys to help them out. It was work as normal the next day, but Denny was going away early, as he needed to go and see Felix about the tightening of security around the estate. Felix had been a bit of a hero during the war and had given Denny some words of wisdom when he had been over before. He knew he would have to search for him as Felix liked the Jägermeister, so it would be a case of trawling the bars looking for him.

That afternoon Denny had tried all the bars he knew in Zwiesel and was running out of hope of finding him, until he saw a sign up a small side street advertising Jägermeister, so he thought it might be worth a try. As he entered it was busy for an afternoon and as he stood looking around he couldn't see Felix anywhere.

"Looking for me Denny?"

He was slightly startled, and when he turned round here was Felix sitting behind the door with his usual glass in his hand. Denny walked over and shook his hand.

"As it happens Felix I am. I'm looking for some advice from you. I am needing to increase the security up at and around the big house in the estate and also the town house here in Zwiesel. Do you happen to know anybody that can help?"

"I know the exact people you are after and I will have to explain about them, but if I'm going to be talking a lot then I will need a Jägermeister and a large one at that please."

Denny walked to the bar with a smile on his face. He ordered a large Jägermeister and a coffee for himself. When he paid for them he asked the barman if he could pay for another two large drinks for Felix when he wanted them. As Denny sat down Felix had commented on his coffee.

"I believe you had a bit of a problem with the alcohol son. Max was telling me all about it, but more importantly what a good job you are doing with the estate."

Denny told him the reason he wanted to increase security. Felix was a bit taken aback by his reasons.

"You're going to all that trouble because you have a feeling that there may be danger around the corner?"

Denny then explained about his sixth sense and how it had never let him down and he knew something was going to happen. When, he didn't know. Felix sat there not speaking, just sipping his drink.

"Well son, I'm going to recommend somebody to you. They are a couple of brothers who were in and out of jail for a while for burglary. This might seem strange, but if anyone can tell you how to stop intruders getting near your house then it will be this pair. They are going through a bit of a lean spell as their reputation has gone before them and they are not getting a lot of work, but I will vouch for them."

Denny sat with Felix for a while before saying he had to go and see the guys regarding the security. After shaking his hand, Denny had said that he had the feeling he would be speaking to him about other things.

Denny followed Felix's instructions and eventually came to a seedy little back street where he saw a dirty looking sign hanging on the wall which read, HOFFMAN BROS. As Denny walked through the door two men stood behind a counter. By the look on their faces, they must have thought the imposing figure of Denny was from the West German Secret police.

"Relax lads, I trust you can speak a bit of English? I need some help."

As soon as Denny mentioned Felix's name the brothers seemed to relax. Denny told them all about the job required and what could they do for him. Their eyes lit up at the possibility of working for the Albach Trust and when Denny told them there was to be no expense spared, their eyes were practically bulging. One of the brothers told Denny that there was new technology on video security systems out, developed by a lady called Marie van Brittan Brown, who comes from America.

"How about you come out to the estate tomorrow at four o'clock so that we can go over things? Oh, and one last thing lads. I know you have done your time for what you did, and if truth be told, if they had caught me for what I've done, then they would have thrown the key to the cell away. So, if you mess me around I will have no problem in making you disappear. Okay?"

All the brothers could do was nod.

When he got back to the house it was just a case of walking Arno as he had been standing guard while Willie had taken Udo down the valley with him to work. As they sat around having supper Denny told them about the brothers coming tomorrow.

"Are you sure you can trust them?" said Helen.

"I trust Felix, but the Hoffman brothers are under no illusion as to what will happen to them if they cross me."

"It seems to me that you're a bit of a bad 'bugger' Foggerty," said Willie as they all burst into laughter.

It was then that Helen had said to Denny, was he not going overboard with this security problem. Denny thought that this might have to be the time to tell everyone what was going on.

"Right, the lot of you please listen. I've dreaded this day that I would have to tell you all about my past. If you don't want to hear it then please go and do something else. I'm going to be brutally honest with you. During my previous time over here, I badly hurt a few people for poaching on my land. It wasn't very pleasant for them, but they had the option to walk away from it, but they were too arrogant to do that. You know that I met Willie up in Helmsford, and together we dished out a lot of violence to people who we thought deserved it. When I was in the police in Edinburgh and Dundee I did the unspeakable deed of killing two people, maybe more, I don't know. I then took the law into my own hands when I returned to Durma and took great satisfaction in disposing of four drug runners. They were using the island to transport their filthy poison to the mainland. Helen, the boss of that operation was Scoug. I shot him stone dead.

My sixth sense has been telling me that something is about to happen, but I don't know what or when. My theory is that I left too many loose ends back home and now they have come back to haunt me. I'm not sorry for what I have done, but I am sorry for getting you involved in it. If any of you want to leave the estate then I fully understand. It's my fight."

Helen's face was as white as a sheet as she got up, walked over to the boys and picked them up. Denny and Willie didn't say a word and Gertie was just dumbstruck. Helen walked back with the boys and gave Finn to Denny.

"Please, promise me one thing Foggerty, that you will protect our boys no matter what."

"I'm going nowhere brother, and I too will try my best to keep everyone safe. Especially the boys, as I am their adopted uncle for God's sake."

Denny could only smile at him.

"Mr Denny, wherever Mrs Helen and the boys go I'll will be with them and if anyone tries to hurt them then I will shoot them. Is that okay Mr Denny?"

Denny reassured her that it would be fine and hopefully it wouldn't come to that, but once and for all it has to be Helen and Denny, no Mr or Mrs.

"Rest assured I will protect everyone with my life. Tomorrow, I would like us to start talking about the security of the house when the brothers are over, and Willie, I'll leave it to you to teach Gertie how to use a rifle and God help you pal. First thing to explain is that please, please put the safety on when we are around. Being the best shot I would do it myself but I'm too busy."

47

"Yeh, right Foggerty you couldn't hit a cow's arse with a banjo."

"Oh, I forgot to say that I'm phoning Otto to ask him if I could borrow Ottar for a while."

Tomorrow came soon enough, and they were all up and going about their jobs. Udo was left with Helen and to be honest he never minded as he loved all the attention he got from her. He always sat below the boy's cot and Helen wondered what would happen to someone if they approached the boys when they shouldn't have.

Denny and Willie took off down the South valley and worked like Trojans until just after lunch, when they headed back to wait for the Hoffmans to arrive.

They arrived bang on time in a clapped-out old jeep. Denny introduced them to everyone, although the Hoffmans seemed a bit wary. Gerti produced her magic and served tea and coffee along with cheese scones. Denny was keen to get on with it, so as soon as the brothers were finished he showed them around the house and immediate grounds. The brothers seemed to know what they were doing and on occasion they would have a little argument with each other. After an hour the older brother asked Denny if he would like to write down everything that would be needed.

When Denny had finished the list he was quite impressed by their thoroughness.

"You will have all you need within a week at the latest, and I have added a few items to your list for myself. Six of the best two-way radios and binoculars that money can buy. On looking at your list I see you have asked for several animal camera traps. Why? It's not animals about which I am worried."

"It's amazing what images you find on these things. Place them on trees at head height and make sure you check them every day or night. Before we go, can I ask you something? Are you preparing for a war Mr Foggerty? It certainly looks like it and can I just say that my brother and I would be only too happy to help you. Lots of times we staked out a place for a few days at a time with the owners walking only a few feet past us without realising."

"I appreciate your offer Gunther, but I don't want to put you and your brother Karl in any danger. Just in case though, can either of you shoot?" I take it that's a yes by the way you're laughing. I would also like to say if, and it will be a big if, you are going to work with the trust which may be all over Germany, then you need to get a new shop as that seedy little shop isn't the best image for you. I will sort it out just as soon as I can sort my own 'shit' out."

"Does that mean we have to get rid of the guns in the back shop?"

Denny never said anything, but made a mental note to check the guns out.

When the Hoffmans were leaving Otto drew up, opened the back door of the vehicle and out strode Ottar. Denny was glad to see his magnificent pal again even if it was only a couple of days since he was here last. Denny took Otto aside and told him why he wanted Ottar here.

"I need him here all the time to watch over everyone. I know he is getting on a bit Otto, and I only want him as a deterrent and wouldn't put him in harm's way. I can't remember if I told you that my sixth sense is scrambling my brain at the moment, and I need Udo and Arno out with Willie and me when we are working in the forest. I have a feeling of impending danger Otto."

"Don't worry son, as much as Ottar is getting on he still needs a purpose in his life and I'm sure he will love being with Helen and you, and if he ever has to protect any of you then God help the person who will be getting his genitals ripped off."

Just as Helen came out of the door, Denny had said that her pal was here to see her. When she saw Ottar she ran down the stairs and knelt down and waited on the 'big man' coming in for his hug. Denny told her that Ottar would be looking after the house while he and Willie were out working with the other two dogs, putting a big smile on her face. However, Denny thought the smile was a bit forced as she still wasn't sure what was happening.

While lying in bed Denny asked Helen if Jinty had phoned. She said she hadn't, but that was just Jinty's way. Denny told her he wasn't happy with that and wanted her to phone Jinty tomorrow first thing. Helen thought that he was beginning to freak her out with all the turmoil in his head.

After seeing to the boys in the morning, the next thing Helen did was to phone Jinty. There was no answer so she thought the shop must be busy, so she tried in about an hour, but still no reply. She was still trying at two o'clock, and at that stage she knew something wasn't right, so as soon as Denny came back she would tell him. He and Willie were late coming back and as soon as she told him he jumped into the jeep and headed off to see Jinty. As he drew up he knew something wasn't right, but he was getting totally 'pissed' off always knowing that things weren't right. As he was climbing the outside stairs he shouted that it was him so that she wouldn't get a fright. No answer. He got to the door and knocked while looking through the letter box. He got no answer and couldn't see anything from the letter box. It was the smell of stale smoke and body odour that made his mind up to put the door in. Slowly he walked into the lounge only to see Jinty curled up on the sofa with a blanket around her. Her eye was swollen and her lip split. Denny knew he had to stay calm, so he walked over and sat beside her and put his arm around her shoulders. She started to sob and kept on saying how sorry she was.

"You don't have to say sorry to me Jinty, but in your own time please tell me what happened and please don't leave anything out."

"Scottie crept up the stairs behind me. I was so tired that I never heard him, he then shoved me in the door and locked it behind him. He then forced me down onto the sofa and tried to stick his hand up my skirt, but I managed to push him away and that was when he punched me in the eye. I was so scared Denny that he was going to rape me. His eyes were glazed, and I swear he was on drugs of some sort. The smell that was coming off him was awful and I was trying hard not to vomit when he was near to me. He came at me with his fists clenched and asked me where I kept my savings. I had to tell him. I'm so sorry. After I gave the money to him he punched me on the mouth and eye then told me not to tell you or Helen. He did mention one thing and that was nobody would ever find him or the squat he was in."

50

She started crying again and Denny told her to pack a few things as she was coming back with him. He asked her if the lady who worked for her could look after the business and Jinty had said it would be no bother, as she would just get her sister in to help her and she would phone her from the estate. Denny noticed that Scottie had pulled the phone line out as they went out the door.

As they sat in the car, Denny told Jinty to find some good music on the radio, but no music from girl bands as he couldn't handle that. On the way back Denny felt he was going to pull the steering wheel off if he didn't calm down. When they arrived back Jinty got out, but she nearly fainted, and Denny had to act fast to catch her and carry her into the house. Helen started shouting about what had just happened and she was getting hysterical before Denny told her to get a grip and see to Jinty. With everything going on Willie and Gertie came flying up the stairs and as soon as Gertie saw Jinty's face she started to cry.

"Stop crying for God's sake woman, and get the medical kit out," said Willie.

"Willie, let's leave Helen and Gertie to tend to Jinty as I need to talk to you outside."

He told Willie everything that had happened and what Jinty had said. He had to be careful that he didn't tip him over the edge as his Explosive Disorder would take over.

"I can see the rage rising in you Willie, but we have to talk about this and work out how we are going to find him and especially what we are going to do with him."

"I should have left you that day to rip his fucking throat out brother. There are no promises from me when we catch him Denny although we have to be careful about the authorities. No point in both of us being 'banged up' for the rest of our lives."

"We have to find out where the squats are around here, and if that means greasing a few palms then fine. I'm going to phone the Hoffmans to get Jinty's flat secured, and I can ask them if they can give us any information on squats, but that could simply mean 'dossing' down in somebody's house. Do you think we were bad 'buggers' in an earlier life pal."

"Nah, just this life pal. Trouble seems to follow us, but I am so looking forward to catching that bastard Scottie. We can't change who we are so why try."

Denny went inside and into their room only to find Jinty coming out the shower with just a small towel drying her hair.

She grabbed a towel and put it around her, but Denny had told her she was too slow with the towel. Helen had come in and told him to get out, but Denny asked Jinty if she had a photo of Scottie. She said she did unfortunately, and it was in her purse. Denny took it out and told her she wouldn't get it back. He also told her that Scottie wouldn't be troubling her again.

He phoned the Hoffmans and told them to meet him at Jinty's address in half an hour. When he got into Zwiesel, the brothers were already there. Denny liked that about them.

He told them what had happened, and he could see genuine anger on their faces. The brothers immediately went to work securing the front door, with all the windows next. They suggested they put a high gate halfway up the stairs so that once you were through it, would spring shut blocking the stairs from anyone behind. They worked on the doors and windows to the bakery shop as well before saying to Denny that was as much as they could do. The gate on the stairs would have to wait until it was made tomorrow morning.

"That's fine, and now I would like to speak to you about something. You said to me how you considered yourselves the best at surveillance, so how about we put that to the test? Here is a photo of the bastard that assaulted my friend. Please make a few copies and if you can do your magic by carrying out surveillance on the property day and night, taking it in turns. If this guy shows up then I need you to follow him and find out where he lives or generally ask around. If you see him then do not make an approach. Phone me immediately. Come and pick up one of the jeeps we have at the estate tomorrow first thing just in case somebody is transporting him around."

"Don't worry Mr Foggerty we have our own jeep here."

"No disrespect Gunter, but what you have is a heap of 'shit' and sounds like a traction engine. What you need is stealth. I hope you consider yourselves working for me now and I will pay you a good wage plus bonuses."

52

He knew that this was probably the kindest thing anybody had ever done for them in a long time. Karl was about to shed a tear before he said, "Don't shed one fucking tear Karl as I've had enough of that crap to last me a lifetime."

Denny left them to it.

When he arrived back Jinty was sitting outside with Helen, just watching the boys sleeping. He walked forward and gave Jinty a hug and announced that she had quite a nice body on her. Jinty just laughed, but Helen threw one of the boy's burping blankets at him. He just smiled.

"Here is what is going to happen girls. Willie and I will deal with Scottie, and you will never hear from him again. So please forget about all this as much as it pains you."

It was an early night for everyone. Willie had made sure the dogs had been walked and Denny had checked and double checked the doors and windows of the house. When he had been in bed for about half an hour he got up and did the same again with Helen wondering what the hell was going on. It was about one in the morning when the thunder and lightning started accompanied by torrential rain. Helen had cuddled into Denny. You would have thought she was used to it coming from a windswept rock called Durma. She asked Denny if the dogs would be okay, and he told her they would be fine with Ottar lying in between them. He laughed and said it was Willie he was worried about. Denny was up early and as he sat under the roof of the veranda with the dogs, Willie came out with a coffee for him. The rain was still coming down in sheets and he told Willie he had heard a few cracks during the night which meant that a few trees were down, or some large branches had been hit.

"After I have had my drink I'm taking the dogs for a walk whether they want to go or not. Please be here for the Hoffmans and give them the blue jeep and I will have Maria send us another one as quickly as possible."

Denny wasn't shy at spending, and money never bothered him. He had set up personal accounts worth hundreds of thousands of deutschmarks for everyone on the estate. Especially Finn and Col. Also, hundreds of thousands of pounds in accounts in Edinburgh. One day soon he would tell Willie and Gertie about their accounts. He thought they might get a 'wee' surprise when he did. Denny and Helen worked off a very large expense account. For every deutschmark he spent the trust was making millions more. He just wished he could have shared some of it with his mum and dad.

Denny took off with the dogs and after a short while he sent Ottar back to save his legs. He thought that Ottar wasn't too happy, but off he trotted back to the house. As he walked he could see a bit of destruction caused by last night's violent storm. After an hour he decided to return home having seen as much as he needed to. As he was nearing the house he thought that the thunder was starting again, but then realised it was just the Hoffman's jeep trying to get up the track. When it arrived, Denny asked them in, and Gertie did her usual and immediately got the kettle going. As they sat drinking tea Jinty walked out, and Denny introduced the brothers to her.

"Jinty, these two guys have put as much security on your house as possible and when or if you go back then they will have twenty-four-hour surveillance on your home. Get to know their faces just in case you think there is somebody lurking outside."

It was then that Karl got up, excused himself and went outside and was prowling along the veranda. Just walking back and forward.

"You will have to excuse Karl everyone, as he saw a lot of violence directed towards our mother by our father when we were young."

"Tell him I'm fine Gunter, and not to worry. Oh, and by the way Daniel Rey Foggerty, I will definitely be going home as there will be nobody there standing watching me coming out of the shower like last night."

Gunter was wondering what he was getting into, and Willie and Gertie just looked at each other. As the brothers prepared to leave, Denny handed them the keys to the jeep and as they wandered around the side of the house it was Karl who spoke.

"Mr Foggerty, this jeep is nearly new we can't accept something as good as this."

"Take it, it's yours, and I will tell you where to fill up with diesel and for any repairs you should need. Oh, one last thing. Do you both have passports?"

They both nodded and said that when they went to jail they had to surrender them, but when they came out they had managed to get new ones which had surprised them both. Karl was disappointed he wasn't driving the new jeep and had to settle for the 'traction engine'.

When they were gone, Willie sidled up to Denny and quietly asked him what the hell was going on regarding passports for the brothers.

"Just covering all bases Willie."

Denny had already told Gunther that he wanted a daily update with regard to the surveillance of the bakery and house although he didn't think Scottie would be that stupid, but because there was the possibility of drugs involved then anything was possible.

Two days later all the security equipment arrived at the estate and Denny wasted no time in phoning the brothers. They came out the next morning and got right to work. Denny was impressed with their work ethic as they never wanted to stop for a break, but it was Gertie who insisted. It only took them a day to have the house secure. Karl then asked Denny and Willie to follow him into the woods to show them how to set up the animal camera traps.

Karl suggested that they put them up on the trees which had some foliage and have them cover the areas where the house was the most approachable from. Six traps covered quite an area so Denny, who had been a bit sceptical about them at first, ended up being quite impressed, but the proof was still to come.

Chapter 4

Over the next few days Willie and Denny had to work harder than ever to make up for lost time. There was still no evidence of fox carcasses, so it was more than likely that someone was poaching them, but he wondered how the hell he was going to find out who? They were both trying out their two-way radios and it was Willie who would send spooky noises to Denny or try and do animal sounds. Denny just laughed, as some of animal noises didn't pertain to Germany never mind Bavaria. They were making inroads into clearing the tracks at the South valley, so Denny was a little more relaxed. Unlike Willie, who had been taking Gertie out for shooting practice at nights. He always came back so flustered and one night when they came back Gertie was so happy with a big smile on her face.

"Mr Denny, I managed to hit a tree with the bullet."

"Yeh, but not the right bloody tree Gertie. There are millions of trees in the forests so I'm in fear of my life every time I go out with you. Denny, I've told her if anybody comes at her then she should just turn the rifle around and hit him with the bloody thing."

Willie had realised what he had just said, but when he had looked over to where the boys should be he saw that they weren't there, until Helen clipped him on the back of the head. He was startled until he looked around and saw that she had moved the boys to the far end of the veranda.

"Not fair Helen, that was just sneaky."

The girls had to be shown how to work the radios, and Denny found it amusing that they would call each other from the next room, when shouting through the wall would be easier. He never wanted this for everyone, but knew it had to be done. One day while Willie and him were sitting having a break, Denny had said to him that his sixth sense was playing up again and to be prepared for anything.

"Denny this 'voodoo' has been going around inside your head for a little while, but nothing seems to be happening. Are you sure something is going to happen?"

"Willie, every night I lie awake wondering who might be coming after me, and for the love of me, I can't think of anybody. It's driving me crazy. I haven't had a decent night's sleep in weeks, but I do know one thing brother, and that is they are coming."

When they got back to the house that day Jinty was packing.

"I need to go folks. My business needs me, and I won't let an 'arsehole' like Scottie drive me out. The security you have put on my building will deter anyone, never mind him."

As much as they weren't happy with this, they all fully understood and felt she would be safe especially with the brothers on surveillance. Denny would drive her home and said that a phone call every night was a prerequisite of her going home. She had agreed and said her goodbyes to everyone, especially the boys.

He drove into the small road next to the bakery making sure there was nobody around. As Jinty gave him a hug and went through the gate on the stairs with it snapping closed behind her. Denny suddenly turned and grabbed the person next to him by the throat.

"For fuck's sake Karl, where did you spring from?"

"If I told you Denny then I wouldn't be doing my job."

Jinty was laughing as she went through the door and blew them a kiss. Denny's heart was thumping, and he grabbed Karl and hugged him until his heart rate started to slow.

"Well, there is one thing Karl, this proves I made the right decision to hire you and your brother, but please don't creep up on me again if you value your life."

Karl didn't know how to take that, so he just smiled as Denny walked away and got into the jeep. He thought however that Denny Foggerty was one powerful guy. When Denny got home he told everyone what had happened, and Willie thought it was hilarious that Denny was trying to kill off the employees. He told him he was too wound up and said that he and Gertie would take the boys for a long walk before bedtime for him to relax.

After supper, Willie and Gertie put the boys in the slings and along with Arno and Udo, they started to walk through the forest. Helen didn't waste any time as she grabbed Denny's hand and led him upstairs.

"Let's not rush as they will be away for an hour anyway Denny, but you have been neglecting me 'big boy,' so I want to be thoroughly satisfied by the time they get back so get your mind in gear."

Helen then started to do her usual and very slowly take her clothes off. When she had removed her bra she started a slow massage on her breasts and nipples just to tease him. It certainly was working as Denny stripped as quick as he could and stood there with his big erection. Slowly, she started to take her panties off and she went onto the bed, turned over onto her hands and knees, and waited for Denny to enter her.

She started to squeal as Denny was thrusting into her and after a few minutes she had shouted for him to stop.

"Denny, what are you playing at? You're hurting me. It's as if your enjoying doing that to me. You once told me you would never have sex with me only love making, but I don't know what the hell that was just now. I'm sore."

They both lay beside each other and when he tried to hold her hand she pushed it away

"I'm so sorry Helen, there is far too much rubbish going through my head just now and it's making me angry and if I took it out on you then please accept my apologies. I never meant to hurt you."

She was too sore to enjoy intercourse, so she just started to masturbate Denny, but after a while he knew he wasn't going to climax, so he just slid off the bed and started to get dressed. After half an hour they could see Willie and Gertie in the distance holding hands as they walked back with Fin and Col. When they walked up the steps Willie said, "Well that was lovely folks. Gertie is becoming a right good storyteller, albeit in German. By the look on your faces, you didn't have such a good time. Either of you want to speak about it?"

Neither of them took up his offer so Helen thanked them for looking after the boys and took them up to their beds. Willie gave a nod to Gertie, and they wandered down to the annex, so that they could leave them alone.

The wind howled all night and usually Helen would cuddle into Denny, but not tonight. She lay as far away from him as possible. He watched every hour on the clock pass until five am when he got up and showered before walking the dogs. Ottar was in the mood to walk further so Denny just let him tag along. He knew he had to make up with Helen and would try and speak to her tonight, but he knew it wouldn't be easy. After a while of walking, he saw Arno and Udo fighting over something. At first he thought it was a stick, but when he recalled them, he found it to be a leather strap. It had holes in it like a belt and he couldn't work out what it was. Then it suddenly struck him. It was a strap to hold down the front of an animal trap. It was relatively new, so Otto had been right. The foxes were being trapped.

Everyone was eating outside when he got back, so he went and picked up his sons and bounced them on his knees. Helen still wasn't giving him a second glance and he didn't blame her. He told Willie about the strap and about Otto being spot on.

As they both walked to the forest, Denny said to Willie that he and Gertie should have taken a two-way radio with them when walking the boys last night. Willie started to rage at him asking why he didn't take a radio with him when he took Jinty home.

"You've got double standards here Foggerty. You expect us to know what is going on in your thick skull, yet you don't even know yourself for fuck's sake. If anything happens then we will be ready for it, trust me."

"Will we brother?"

The next few days were just normal with Denny putting up some animal camera traps where he thought foxes might want to have their lairs, but he knew it might be a long shot. Eventually, Helen had come around and things were back to normal except in their bed as she said she was just getting over what had happened that night. It was one night that as they were getting ready for bed she walked over to him, with Denny expecting a warm embrace, but she just kicked him in the genitals. Denny just hit the floor and lay there.

"What was that for?"

"Now you know how I felt that night don't you?"

Denny put his hand up as if asking Helen for a lift up and when she grabbed his hand he pulled her down on top of him. He kissed her tenderly and Helen responded and suggested they get into bed.

"I don't know what you're expecting Helen, as after that kick I won't be able to get hard for about a week. Trust me."

"You've got two days Foggerty or else."

That night Helen did cuddle into him, and they both knew it would be fine.

Two nights later, Willie had come running to the house quite excited with a couple of the camera traps in his hands. He quickly showed the first pictures to Denny, and they showed grainy images of quite a stocky guy with some dead foxes hanging over his shoulders. Unfortunately, they couldn't get a clear image of his face.

"Now Denny, when I show you the next camera please control your temper. Okay?"

Denny just nodded his head. Willie showed him the next pictures.

"Oh my God Willie, I would recognise that face anywhere. It's that bastard Scottie. I don't know who the other guy is, but I definitely recognise the drug riddled apology for a human being that is Scottie. Why the hell would they be walking in the woods, especially at night and so close to the house? Let's sit down and try and work this out Willie, as this is not good."

As they sat throwing suggestions at each other as to why Scottie had been there, they realised they had no bloody idea.

"Let's forget about the guy with the foxes just now and concentrate on the other two. Firstly, I don't know about you, but we need more cameras and saturate the immediate forest approaching the house. My gut instinct is telling me that Scottie is not the cause of my sixth sense playing up, but you can never be sure. I'm going to phone the Hoffmans right now and see if there is any update on their surveillance and we need one of them out to help put up some more traps as we might not be doing it properly. The main thing is why would Scottie be anywhere near here knowing full well that if we caught him we would rip his head off his shoulders?"

Gunter arrived early next morning, with Helen insisting on giving everyone a good breakfast before they set off into the forest. As they walked along Denny was quizzing Gunter about anything strange happening around the bakery. He told him that both he and Karl had noticed a beat-up old VW campervan that had been sitting across the road from the bakery a few times. It was strange as it didn't have any number plates and they were running the risk of being stopped by the police. He said it gave him the impression that it belonged to the hippie commune that were squatting in a large house on land at the outskirts of Zwiesel. Denny asked him to right down the directions when they got back to the house.

Gunter told them to move some of the cameras and put some a bit higher or lower. He advised them to get as many as they could without alerting any intruder to their presence. Basically, have a barrier in the trees covering all approaches to the house.

After Gunter had gone it was back to work as normal and Denny knew he had to get more help and quick. The way things were with his head he didn't know who to trust. When they had finished for the day he asked Willie if he could look after the two dogs and give Ottar a short walk when they got back, as he wanted to walk with Helen and the boys through the forest before supper.

"Don't be too early getting back Foggerty, as I feel that Gertie is in for a bit of loving tonight."

Denny just shook his head as normal.

As they were working next morning Denny turned to Willie and said that they needed a plan on how to find and deal with Scottie. Willie then said he agreed with Denny's first idea of staking him out in the North valley, where there was more chance of wolves getting to him, but they had to find him first.

"Are we just going to take his life Willie? What does that make us my brother? Evil I think."

"How many people have you despatched from this earth without the blink of an eye? How about you and I go and suss out the address that Gunter gave us, but we need one of the brothers here to look after the place."

It happened about an hour later as they were clearing trees from one of the streams. Shots rang out from the North. It didn't seem real to start with, as they both just looked at each other. Denny then kicked into self-preservation mode.

"Willie, get over the stream and head up to the North valley, but come in from the West. I am taking the dogs, and I am going

61

to meet this danger head on, so please be up there to have my back. Don't get into danger, please."

Willie was mumbling something about never getting a chance to shoot somebody when he ran through the stream. Denny took off at a fast, but sensible pace. He knew that you should never be totally out of breath when you meet your opponent. He didn't know how Willie was getting on, but having to run uphill was a struggle, however the dogs were literally taking it in their stride. They knew something was up and Denny had to keep giving them instructions to come to heel as they were getting too far in front at times. Suddenly another couple of shots rang out and he 'hit the deck' with the dogs dropping down beside him. He never felt any crack or snapping sound, so if they were shooting at him then they must have been awful shots.

He slowly got up, and was trying hard to see if he could identify where the shots were coming from. At this point his heart was pounding and he decided to get off the animal track and advance through the trees. He took off running, but found the going tough as the tree branches were continually whipping and scratching his face. It was always in his mind to watch that he didn't turn or break his ankle as that would be catastrophic. As he ran he marvelled at the dogs' agility weaving in and out of the branches. There was no chance of seeing where Willie was, and they had decided not to use the two-way radios just in case the people in the forest heard them.

The sky was getting grey, and he wondered if the thunder and lightning might start. Just something else to dampen his mood even further. Another shot rang out, and he knew he was getting close. There had to be at least two off them as he identified two separate rifles. Now was the time to take it slower and he made sure the dogs knew not to get in front of him. After another fifteen minutes he could see what was happening. Two guys with rifles had been shooting rabbits and hares. One of the guys was bundling up the animals and tying them to a branch at each end ready for carrying them to wherever they came from. The other guy who was much smaller was leaning back against a tree holding his rifle, but Denny could only see the side of him as the tree was blocking his vision.

"I can see what you are doing, but why are you doing it on my land? Please don't go for your rifle, or I will have to put a bullet in your head. Hence the red dot that is attached to your forehead."

"Well, then my brother Tomaz would have to put a bullet in you."

Denny had seen the brother slowly turning the gun to point at him, but he wasn't worried.

"Maybe you should tell your brother to very slowly look down, don't move his gun, whereby he will see my two dogs with their teeth bared, ready to rip his throat out and his genitals off."

Arno and Udo had silently crept around the tree and were just waiting for Denny's command.

"Then, it will be left up to me to decide whether to waste a bullet by putting him out of his misery. Although it would be interesting to see 'death by dogs,'" said Willie who had walked from behind a tree to the left of Tomaz.

Nobody said a word for a few minutes and the dogs never took their eyes of the target.

"It seems we have an impasse Mr Foggerty." said the older brother.

"There is no fucking impasse here pal. We have the upper hand, and we won't hesitate to shoot you where you stand and leave your bodies for the wolves. How do you know my name? You are on my land killing animals. Why? For your sake I had better believe what you tell me or a nod to the dogs and you will have lost your brother. Okay?"

"Okay, my name is Yuri, and this is my brother Tomaz. Please don't ask him anything as he won't reply as several years ago he was in a terrible accident and has never spoken since. He can hear very well, but it's just his speech that's a problem. To answer your question about why we are poaching on your land is basically that we need to eat. Simple as that. We live with our old and infirm father in our farm which is just over that hill, but I'm sure it is in Slovakia. I make no apologies for wanting to eat and look after my brother and father. I know you own these forests, and I thought that as you are over-run with these animals then you weren't going to miss them."

"Willie, put your gun down it will be all right, but keep it near to you. I have never known what it's like to be hungry, so maybe we can sit down and talk about this situation."

"Mr Foggerty, can I ask you to stand the dogs down as Tomaz could collapse at any time. Please."

Denny gave a command for the dogs to stand down, but he was positive there was a look of sheer disappointment on Arno's face. Tomaz slid down the tree and Yuri walked over and took his gun off him and laid it next to his. When they were all sitting, Denny gave Tomaz a drink of water from his flask.

"I assume you don't have any jobs" asked Willie.

"Around here there is nothing, and our farm isn't workable as we lost all the livestock to wolves a long time ago. The bogs are encroaching towards our farm, and it is impossible to plant any crops. It's a dire situation and we often find our dad in tears when we come back from job hunting or just looking for a food source as we have nothing for him, hence we poach your rabbits."

Denny asked about Yuri's history and not to leave anything out. Yuri was thirty-three years old and had been serving in the Czech Special Services, but an altercation with his commanding officer one night had made him flee the army and technically he was on the run, but he had enlisted under a different address so he doubted they would come looking for him. He said that Tomaz was only twenty-five and his life changing accident was at an early age when he had tried to chase a wolf which had a lamb in its mouth. Filled with rage he ran after it, but ran into a particularly bad bog and got stuck. It appears he was crying for help for hours while slowly being sucked under the bog. He was lucky that our father came back, and it was fortunate that our old tractor started, and he managed to pull him out after several attempts.

While Yuri was talking, Tomaz sat with his hands cupped over his ears. Although Denny had known them only a brief time he felt sorry for them, especially Tomaz.

"Don't jump or shy away, just keep still Tomaz."

He watched Denny giving the dogs hand instructions, and they slowly walked over to Tomaz and lay by his side. It only took a minute for him to lay his hands on their necks and slowly stroke them.

"Mr Foggerty, would your dogs really have attacked Tomaz on your command?"

Willie started laughing and said," attacked? I think a better way to explain it would be 'ripped to bits' pal."

Denny was at a loss as to what to do, but after a few minutes of deliberation he spoke to Yuri.

"I'm going to make you a proposition Yuri. If you don't like it then please stay away from my land, and if I catch you poaching again I will shoot the both of you. How would you and Tomaz like to work for me? It will be hard work and Willie would be in charge of you. I will give you a good wage, so that you don't have to go hungry again. The work is basically looking after the forests and the animals in them. I will give you both new rifles and expect you to have them with you each day. There will be no indiscriminate firing of them, especially if you see the white stag or I definitely will shoot you both. From what you have been telling me your farm is a little bit away, so I will provide you with powerful ATVs to get you over the hill and back. You don't have to give me your answer right now, but the offer is only open for twenty-four hours."

"No need for another day Mr Foggerty, I know I speak on behalf of Tomaz when I say we accept your offer, and we will walk from the farm each day until the vehicles come and we thank you from the bottom of our hearts. As will my father."

"Please be at the big house by eight tomorrow morning and we will take it from there. If you cross me or let me down then I will consider shooting you."

"Don't worry Mr Foggerty we won't, and may I ask if you are in the habit of shooting people?"

"Yes I am, and my name is Denny not Mr Foggerty. Please take the rabbits you have shot away with you, and we will see you tomorrow at eight. Don't be late, okay?"

As the brothers tied up all the rabbits, Yuri had turned to Tomaz and said, "that is one very troubled man brother." Tomaz stood looking down the track for a while before turning and nodding his head, but Yuri could see there was a small niggle of doubt in Tomaz's head.

Nothing was said on the walk home, but Willie could see Denny's brain churning.

"What's bothering you pal? You haven't said a word in twenty minutes, what's eating you?"

"Willie, I don't know if I have made a mistake by bringing two strangers into our lives on the estate. I have everyone's interest to think about."

"Please, put your rifle down. Just humour me."

As Denny bent over to lay the rifle down, Willie kicked him up the arse. Denny fell forward against a tree before he made a grab for his rifle with such an evil look on his face, but Willie was standing with his gun pointed at Denny's head before he could grab it.

"What the fuck was that about?"

"Because I'm sick fed up with your moaning Denny. You really need to start enjoying your life pal or you will drag everyone else down with you."

They both walked on in silence until they got home.

That night Denny had sat troubled on the veranda. He had told both Helen and Gertie about Yuri and Tomaz arriving tomorrow, and both were fine with it. However, he reckoned he could have told Gertie that the moon was made of cheese, and she would have believed him. Helen had sat down beside Denny and linked her arm through his. She could feel how tense he was, so she told him the boys were asleep and they should go upstairs and try for a night of loving. Denny looked at her and smiled.

That night Denny had Helen in every love making position he could think of. He had promised her a night of passion and he was going to make that happen. Helen wondered where he had experienced some of these love positions as some of them were new to her. She realised they were apart for years, so it must have been with other women, so she fully understood, but when it came down to it he was hers and she would make sure nobody would take him away from her. That night she thought her body was going to explode with the amount of orgasms she was having, but she wasn't complaining. They fell asleep in each other's arms and when they woke in the morning the bed was soaking with sweat from their lovemaking exertions.

As they were having breakfast, Helen had turned to Denny and said," Hey lover boy would you have any objections to me going for a run in the forests, as I need to get fitter if I have to keep up with you in the bedroom stakes?"

She didn't see Willie behind her, and he said, "Well loverboy is there any sign of your two pals from Slovakia? Oh, and Helen if you had entered in a lottery I feel you would have got second prize with Foggerty here. Me being the first prize of course."

She ran and jumped on him knocking him over and straddling him. Shades of Jinty he thought. It was then that the brothers walked around the building and the look on their faces was one of bewilderment.

"Come on up lads. I knew you were coming because if you look behind you'll see why, but don't be frightened. The dog in the middle is the father of the other two, but still more protective than the others. As the brothers slowly turned round there stood the three dogs in a line with their teeth bared. Please come up and have something to eat with us, but only after I have told the dogs to ease off."

Denny sent the dogs into the forest and the brothers came and sat down.

"This is my wife. The one who was straddling my brother, and this is Gertie his partner. My two boys are lying over there in their cot. They are the most precious things in our lives, and we would all, and I mean all, would give our lives for them. I'll show you what I mean but don't scared. Understand Tomaz?"

Denny stood, gave three whistles and within a minute the three dogs appeared and then Denny shouted an instruction. They bolted up the steps knocking over anything in their way to lie beside the boys cot with again their teeth bared. Yuri had thought that Udo might knock his head off as he jumped over the sofa that he was sitting on. The dogs were just staring, taking everything and everybody in with their top lips still up. Denny could see that Tomaz was a bit scared, so he called the dogs off and sent Arno and Udo off to play. He instructed Ottar to go and sit beside Tomaz. Yuri understood what he was doing.

"That was very impressive Denny."

Denny explained to them about what their work would be, and they wouldn't always be working together. Also, they would have to have at least one of the dogs with them at all times so Tomaz would have to get used to them very quickly. After he told them about the security measures he had put in place, he had tried to explain his sixth sense.

"I noticed all the animal cameras and the security systems you have when we came in. What is it you are afraid of Denny?"

"I don't know Yuri, that's the problem, but let me tell you something. I am not afraid of anything or anyone I can see, but if anybody threatens my extended family then I will shoot them stone dead. What about you and Tomaz?

Denny looked at them and they gave a slight nod of the head. It was then that Willie in his usual tactless way said," We may have a problem Denny if Tomaz has to use the two-way radio. Maybe if I 'boot' him in the 'balls' he might come out of it. What do you think?"

Denny was about to say something, but Yuri put his hand up stopping him.

"Willie, please never say that you might hurt my brother. I know it is only a temporary affliction that he has, but rest assured he can look after himself. I'll ask you this question and after you have answered it please stay perfectly still. How quickly could you raise your rifle, cock it and fire at Tomaz?"

Willie had started to say three seconds before a knife embedded itself in the wooden pillar next to his ear. Helen gave out a squeal which had alerted Ottar.

"You would now be dead with a knife in your throat my friend."

"Everybody calm down please, you've made your point Yuri, and that was also impressive Tomaz. I never even saw that coming and by the look on Willie's face he didn't either. Tomaz, please remove your knife and then we can all eat."

When Tomaz took the knife out of the post he lifted up his shirt revealing a large belt with about six other knives and put the knife back in. Both Denny and Willie were suitably impressed. Gertie came out with croissants, meat and cheese along with the usual strong coffee and they were soon enjoying their meal. None more so than the two brothers who Denny thought might enjoy it more than rabbit.

As they sat eating they heard a jeep coming up the track. The dogs were in the attack position on the driveway and Willie and Denny had their guns ready. Denny noticed Tomaz had a knife secreted in his hand. How he had done it so quickly baffled Denny. Denny put his hand on Tomaz's arm and told everyone to take it easy.

Jinty stepped out of the jeep and shouted.

"Hey Foggerty, tell your smelly 'dugs' to stand down before I give them a right telling off."

Jinty walked up the steps and gave everyone a hug before jumping on Denny and wrapping her legs around his waist and giving him a full-on kiss. Much to the amusement of the brothers.

"Who are these two good looking lads Helen? Where did you manage to 'rake' them up from?"

Denny butted in and introduced Jinty to Yuri and Tomaz. She gave them both a hug with Denny noticing that she had held on to Yuri for a little bit longer, but he thought she might as Yuri was a good-looking guy.

"Are you here for another free meal Jinty Thomas," said Helen.

"Well, it's not to see you lot, but most importantly just to hold my two 'bairns'. Are they over there in the cot?"

She walked back with the boys in each arm and started to give them to the brothers. Tomaz was fine, but Yuri was hesitant.

"Stop being a big 'fanny' Yuri and take the 'bairn'. You're about as bad as the last two brothers who were here, although I must admit I do miss them."

Denny looked at Helen and they both realised they hadn't given their wedding guests a lot of thought over the last few weeks. Denny suggested they give them all a phone tonight.

It was time for the brothers to go, so Jinty took the boys off them and put them back in their cot. Willie and Denny shook hands with them and Helen and Jinty giving them a hug with Jinty looking into Yuri's eyes when she had finished. Denny had spoken quietly to Yuri just before they left.

"You may have to walk in tomorrow, but your ATVs should be here for you going home. Maybe, one day soon we can come and visit your farm and meet your father?"

As they were about to leave Helen had motioned for Tomaz to kneel down on the ground with her. He was reluctant at first but eventually he did. It was then that the three dogs came bounding in for their hugs and ear scratching. Yuri just stood back and watched Tomaz being licked by the dogs and copying Helen when she scratched their ears.

"Thank you Denny. Both Tomaz and I appreciate the warm welcome you, your family and friends have given us. C'mon Tomaz, we need to get home to check on our father."

Tomaz seemed to be enjoying himself, but got up and waved his goodbyes.

"Well, everyone, what did you think of them? Do you think they can be trusted? If you have any doubts about either of them then please say now."

Nobody said a word, so Denny was quite happy.

"Don't plan on any of your legendary love making sessions tonight Willie as we have a squat to look for."

Willie seemed a little bit disappointed, but the thought of them running into Scottie made him feel a bit better. He suggested that they go out and do some work as it was a continual struggle to keep the forests clear. After quite a gruelling day clearing large branches from the streams, they had returned home tired and hungry, but they both knew they had a job to do tonight, and it had to be done right. After dinner they jumped into one of the four by fours that they didn't use very often, as Denny had said that there was a slight chance that Scottie might recognise one of the other vehicles. Helen and Gertie knew better than to ask where they were going.

"Where is it that we are actually going Denny and what's the plan if we see that scum Scottie?"

Denny handed him a piece of paper with a street name on it and directions how to get to it. He told him to look out for a beat-up old VW campervan, which Karl Hoffman had seen a couple of times. The rain started and it was coming down in 'sheets' which reminded him of his time on Durma. Unfortunately, the rain was making visibility difficult.

They parked on the street just along from a big, dilapidated house. The front door had rotted away a long time ago and there wasn't much glass left in the windows. Karl couldn't be sure that this was where he would be. Just an educated guess from him. Willie sat there looking bored before asking Denny," Well partner have you come up with a plan yet or do we just wing it as usual?

I'm getting rather pissed off just sitting here getting colder by the minute."

"Willie, shut the fuck up for a minute. I'm thinking. Remember this has to be done so that it looks like Scottie has had an accident and nothing, and I mean nothing, can be traced back to us. It might sound strange, but I want the police all over this. First thing tomorrow I want us to check all the camera traps and see how many images of Scottie are on them. The more the merrier. Right, stay here and get in the driving seat I am going in for a look."

Denny took a hooded raincoat from the back seat and got out.

He walked over to the building pretending he was staggering through drink or drugs. After all, did enough of this while undercover in the police force in Edinburgh. Just as he started to go through the door entrance, two young lads came out and barged into Denny. He quickly uttered a slurred apology in German which seemed to placate the guys and they walked off. Willie was ready to intervene if they had started on Denny, but then again there was only two of them so he might have just sat back and watched the 'fireworks' from his brother. Just then Willie looked in the mirror and saw a police patrol car coming along the street. He slid right down to make sure he wasn't seen. The car stopped outside the building, but nobody got out. He wasn't worried for Denny as he could look after himself. The car moved off and it was only a few minutes after that an old VW campervan came along and parked outside the door. The rain was getting heavier, and he was struggling to see who came out of the van. He could see it was two people but couldn't say for certain if it was Scottie or not.

Denny came from around the side of the house and headed towards the four by four. He got in and threw his wet waterproof into the back seat.

"Well?"

"You wouldn't believe the state of that place Willie. It's like a rabbit warren and by God we have enough of them where we are. I tried to look into every room, but some were locked if there was a door at all, but all I was met with was a torrent of abuse if they were indulging in intercourse or if they were trying to shoot up. The smell was awful Willie and a few times I wanted to throw up, but I devised a plan as I was holding back the vomit. I reckon Scottie is going to be a sailor, but this has to be done to perfection. Are you in?"

"Don't be bloody stupid Denny, of course I am, but I need you to tell me all about it tomorrow so that I can get my head around it. I take it you noticed the campervan sitting there?"

"Yeh I did, and I thought I caught site of Scottie through one of the side windows. Now I need to go home and see the boys and Helen."

As they stepped out of the car Wille turned to Denny and said, "You do realise brother that when we get Scottie we will be committing murder?"

"I've done it before to some bad and evil people Willie and I honestly believe I am stopping him before he hurts Jinty or worse."

Willie just shrugged his shoulders and went to see Gertie and find out if she was up for a bit of loving.

Next day Yuri and Tomaz arrived early, and Denny thought they might be hoping for a bit of breakfast which Gertie duly obliged. Denny said that Willie, Tomaz and Udo would team up and for Willie to try and learn a way to communicate with the younger brother.

"Remember Tomaz, you must learn to work with Udo and learn to trust him. If you can whistle then one to get his attention, two to recall him and three that he is in danger. I take it you can whistle?"

Tomaz nodded his head. And smiled. It seemed he had a purpose in his life now and Denny knew he would be fine. Before they left, Gertie came out with four bags which was their lunches and gave them a bag each and an even bigger smile came over Tomaz's face. Denny told Helen they would phone their friends tonight and to use the radios when they needed to.

Denny headed into the North valley while Willie headed South. The weather wasn't looking promising, but that was just what working in the forests was all about. If it got too bad they would finish up and start again tomorrow. After about four hours work with a small break half- way, Willie told Tomaz they would take their lunch now. While sitting eating, Willie tried to engage him in a way where he could understand what his response was.

72

It was going to be difficult. As they sat, Willie told Tomaz as much as he thought appropriate about the forest and how to look after the dogs. While Willie was eating he reckoned that Tomaz had finished his double quick and was eyeing up his bratwurst sausage. He handed it to him and Tomaz just nodded his head, giving Willie the thumbs up. He thought he would have to tell Gertie to make bigger portions for Tomaz in the future.

Up in the North valley, Denny and Yuri were really starting to bond with Denny being impressed with his work. It was during lunch that Yuri had brought up the subject of the missing foxes. He told Denny he was certain who was trapping them and where he lived, but assured him he was a pure bastard, and was sure he used to come up to the farm to steal anything he could. His name was Albescu.

The rain was getting heavier, and Willie answered his radio which was Denny telling him the work was over and to meet up at the track to the house. Willie told Tomaz that they were finishing up for the day. All of a sudden two extremely loud whistles punctuated the air. Willie got such a fright he had to hold onto a tree. It had been Tomaz recalling Udo and as they both stood there he put his thumbs up to Willie.

"That's the only bloody thing I have heard come out of your mouth Tomaz and it nearly gave me heart failure."

Tomaz just laughed.

They met at the start of the track to the house which was a bit misty, and Denny said he would speak to everyone before they all retired for the day. They were near the house when a shot rang out knocking a branch off one of the trees high above their heads. They simultaneously 'hit the dirt' with everyone scrambling to get their rifles from the scabbards. There was a bit of a panic, until they heard somebody shout.

"I can't see who you are, but I am protecting the boys, and I will fire again if I can find out where to aim the rifle at."

It was Yuri who started laughing first, who then set off Denny and Tomaz. Willie lay there with his face angrier than Denny had seen for a long time.

"This is all your fault Foggerty, insisting that she learns how to fire a gun. Gertie put the bloody gun down it's us."

"Who is us?"

By this time the other were lying there laughing uncontrollably.

"It's Denny and Willie, Gertie, so please put the gun down.

"Willie, we might have to get Tomaz to show her how to throw a knife. What do you think?"

"I might have to go back on the whisky at this rate Foggerty. Helen, please take that bloody rifle off Gertie before she does some real damage."

Helen had been with the boys upstairs, but she had ran out and took the rifle off Gertie, put the safety catch on and shouted that the 'coast was clear,' whereby they all got up and walked to the house with Yuri still laughing.

"Go and make some tea and bring some biscuits for the boys Gertie please, as I have to finish changing the boys."

"And go and get your eyes tested," shouted Willie after her.

As they sat drinking their tea Denny had asked Helen and Gertie to leave them alone so that they could talk. As soon as they were out of earshot, Denny started to explain to the brothers about the problem they were having with Scottie.

"It is our intention that we snatch him and bring him back here for him to have an accident, but you and Tomaz have to stay out of it. For the next week when you come in with the ATVs, please stop just inside the forest and look towards the house. If there is police car or a mortuary van outside then just wander into the forest until I give you the all clear on the radio. Understood?"

They both nodded.

"Can I ask what he did to the girl Jinty, Denny."

After Denny explained, Yuri's demeanour changed before he said," I think we should help you Denny, it is not a problem to us."

Denny looked over to Tomaz who was drawing his finger across his throat.

"No, definitely not. He is a bad person Yuri and when bad people threaten my family I have no problem dispatching them to Hell, and please not a single word to the girls."

It was then that a low loader truck started to come up the driveway, but Denny was expecting it. On the back were two brand new ATVs. Once they were unloaded, Denny suggested that Yuri and Tomaz get used to them and showed them where to fill up with petrol. They were very quick learners and just before they left Denny took them into the secure room at the back of the house. It had one door in from the house itself and no windows. Denny handed them two brand new rifles and scabbards and told them to keep their old ones handy. He then asked them to choose some workwear, ammunition and boots and if they needed replaced at any time, then they were just to say. Denny then handed them a week's wage each just to keep them going and despite them protesting, Denny said he wanted to do it.

After they had left, Denny turned to Willie and asked him to get out of his bed half an hour earlier tomorrow morning so that they could go over the plan to eliminate that scumbag Scottie. All Willie was bothered about was that Gertie might be in the mood for some loving in the morning. Denny had walked away shaking his head as usual.

The rain battered of the roof all night, and he wondered if they would get any work done as the rainstorms could go on for days. In one way it might help his plan for Scottie. They would collect the memory cards from the animal cameras and see how many of them showed Scottie. Denny lay awake most of the night. He was wondering if his demons would ever leave him. Probably not, as his sixth sense was still telling him of impending danger at some point. He was up early as there was no point in lying there just waiting to see if the rain would stop.

He was sitting on the veranda with a strong coffee when Willie appeared.

"What God-awful time is this Denny. I could have been still lying in the arms of my beloved."

"Ah, shut the fuck up McLeod, you couldn't even spell the word beloved."

"Bit tetchy this morning are we not brother."

"Right, here is my plan. In a few days we take the old truck to the squat, and we wait until we think the time is right for us to go in. There will no doubt be people still going about as some of these lazy bastards will sleep most of the time unless they are knocked out with drugs. When we go in we will have our hoodies on covering as much of our faces as possible. We will pretend that we are drunk or under the influence of some 'shit' and be holding on to each other. We will pretend that we are that far gone we can't even speak. Then we will start the search from top to the bottom. It is best that we stick together in case we come across Scottie. If that happens we need to put him out with one punch and carry him out pretending that we are all out of it. I will put a cover in the boot, and we will drive straight back here and dispatch the rat.

"You make it sound so easy brother. What if it there are complications?"

"We wing it Willie, but remember we only have one chance at this."

"I take it you have thought about giving him a good beating and not killing him then?"

"And have Jinty looking over her shoulders for the rest of her life. No chance and remember the Hoffman Brothers can't be staking out the building for the rest of their days. Having second thoughts?"

"Not me my friend. I'm just going to say the big boy made me do it."

Willie started to laugh, and they could both hear the roar of the ATVs coming through the forest. The dogs were crouched waiting for a command, and it was Willie this time who told them to lie down. Yuri and Tomaz walked up the steps and took their waterproofs off. As soon as they had sat down, Helen had come out with the boys and handed them to Willie and Denny. They always had a verbal competition going as to who could get one of the boys to either say Willie or Daddy. If the boys passed wind then they would argue that he had spoken either name.

Helen had said the breakfast would be a few minutes and she told Denny that Gertie had something to ask him. Willie just shook his head wondering what she was going to ask. They had only started eating when they heard a car coming up the track. Denny leaned out over the handrail, saw it was Jinty and calmed the dogs down. As she got out of her car Denny shouted," Here for another free meal Thomas or are you here to see anybody in particular?"

"Don't know what you are on about my big Scottish lover."

Tomaz had looked at Yuri who just smiled and shook his head. Jinty came up the steps with bags of fresh bread, rolls and cakes. Enough to feed an army. Helen took them off her and then proceeded to give two of the biggest bags to Yuri and Tomaz insisting they had more than enough with the other two bags. It was then that Gertie came out.

"Mr Denny, I think that Gertie has a good idea. I think it best if you get me one of these handguns instead of the rifle as I find it a bit heavy. Also, one of these holster things to put it in so that I can look after the boys with two free hands. What do you think?"

Yuri almost spluttered out some of his breakfast while holding back a laugh. Willie sat with his head in his hands.

"Nice that you are thinking like that Gertie, and I will certainly look into it."

Helen was at the back of Gertie shaking her head and mouthing no. The rain started heavier now, and they all sat on the veranda enjoying each other's company and taking turns with Finn and Col. Tomaz was really getting into it, but Yuri was still a bit reserved. Denny noticed that Jinty was taking every opportunity to sit nearer to Yuri when anybody moved. He couldn't blame her after what she had been through, but he was going to have a quiet word with her about rushing into another relationship. Denny had said he was going to look at the camera traps, but Yuri had said he would go as he felt he had to justify his wages. Denny said that didn't have to be the case, but Yuri said that was just who he was.

Before Yuri went out into the forest, Denny told him to bring back any memory card that had images on them other than animals. He was about to go before Denny told him forcibly to take his gun and Ottar with him. It wouldn't be too far for Ottar although the dog didn't look too enamoured going out in that rain, but Denny knew he had to keep his legs going.

When Yuri came back Denny asked him and Willie inside so that they could look at the cards on the special viewer. What they saw was rather disturbing for them as Scottie and his 'pal' were on them, all on different dates.

"Denny, we still haven't worked out why Scottie and his anonymous pal are hanging around in the forests, have we?"

Yuri asked them to tell him all the dates he was seen on and what positions the cameras were in at the time. Denny had them all written down and showed Yuri the copies of the memory cards. He asked them to give him a while to digest the information. It was a bit of a hang on for Willie and Denny as they paced about the dining room waiting for Yuri to tell them his thoughts. Yuri then came through and asked them to sit down.

"The answer is simple my friends. These two people are on recognisance of your property. Probably checking for entrances and exits through the trees. Nobody just wanders aimlessly through these forests without a purpose. You did say that the one you know is full of drugs, well I expect the other guy has persuaded him to come to the estate to show him the lay out of the forests. Most likely for payment. Has the one you know been up here, and been walking in the forests?"

"Yes he has Yuri. How sure are you? I can't believe I have been so fucking stupid."

"It was my job in the army Denny, so yes I am one hundred per cent sure."

It was then that Denny picked up one of the chairs and smashed it on the floor, shouting and swearing like a man possessed. Willie gave Yuri a nod and they both dived on Denny and pinned him to the ground. This wasn't Denny in full flow, but it took the two of them an age to calm him down. It was like pinning an out-of-control wild animal down. Eventually, as they lay there exhausted, the door opened and Helen popped her head around and said, "I heard a noise, what is happening?"

"Fucking get out Helen and leave us alone."

Helen knew to make herself scarce. When she was gone, Willie sat up and put his head in his hands. Yuri still lay there and looked over at Willie, but he gave a slight shake of the head as if to say please leave it alone. When Denny got up he said that the four of them, which included Tomaz, had to sit down to work out a plan and hopefully they would get more information out of Scottie, even if it meant torturing the bastard. Willie and Yuri just looked at each other.

When Denny walked out he went over to the handrail and just stared out into the incessant rain. Helen came over and put his hand around his waist.

"I'm sorry Helen, you shouldn't have to be involved in that. I need to have a break from the estate. I need to get away. How about we book flights and get over to Edinburgh and then back to Durma for a few days but not until the end of the week. I've got some unfinished business."

As the weather was to be like this all week, Denny suggested to the brothers that they go home and spend time with their father. They weren't too happy, but Denny explained that nobody working for him lost any money when he planned his workdays like this.

Yuri and Tomaz headed off with Jinty's baking in a waterproof bag which Helen had supplied. Denny asked Jinty for a quiet word and he took her into the kitchen.

"Jinty, don't think I haven't noticed the way you are looking at Yuri and I can't blame you as he is a good-looking guy. However, can I please ask you not to rush into anything. You still have the remnants of bruising on your face, so until Scottie is out of the equation then please tread carefully will you?"

"Denny, I don't know if we will ever see that bastard again and I will promise that I will take it easy with the next person. Unless you're going to leave Helen for me?"

A big smile came over her face until he picked her up and she started screaming. He walked out onto the veranda with her over his shoulder and told her to say cheerio to the 'bairns' and head home. When she said cheerio to everyone she walked down to her car, but not before blowing several kisses to Denny.

"Get lost Thomas. Your nothing but a trollop. I don't know why I have you as my best friend," shouted Helen.

When Helen was out of earshot and Gertie was in the annex, Denny turned to Willie and said," Within the next two days pal we are going to exterminate that cockroach Scottie, but not before we try and get some answers. My plan has slightly changed as I think we need the help of Yuri. Agreed?"

"That's fine by me my brother. If you are justifying to me that we commit murder, then let's go for it."

For the next few days, the rain was coming down 'heavens hard' and although Yuri and Tomaz arrived every morning there was not a lot that anybody could do. Tomaz had helped by taking the dogs out a walk, but it was mostly everyone just doing any maintenance on the buildings and outhouses as well as cleaning the guns. Tomaz seemed a 'dab hand' at checking over all the ATVs and Denny had also let him loose on the four by fours.

When he asked Yuri why he was good at it he said the vehicles on their farm had to be continually repaired and parts made, as there was no money to buy new.

Denny had walked with Willie on the second day towards the first stream which was just past the track. It was in full flow, and he knew it would be perfect.

"Willie, this is where it is going to happen to the scum Scottie. He is going sailing tomorrow night."

Willie just nodded, but wondered how Denny could be as cold and calculated as he was. After all they were going to take a guys life. An arseholes life, but still a human being's life. He was feeling a bit nauseous, but he knew that would pass. When they got back Denny had a word with Yuri and asked if he was still up for helping them tomorrow night. Yuri nodded his head. He told Tomaz and Yuri if it was still as wet tomorrow then not to come over, but he asked Yuri to be over by midnight and to bring a top that would cover his face.

CHAPTER 5

In the evening Denny was prowling about like a caged tiger. All he could think about was what would happen to Yuri and Willie if it all went wrong, but he couldn't understand why he wasn't thinking about himself, as he had the twins and Helen to think about. He wondered if he was in one of his self-destruct modes he experienced every so often. Every scenario was going through his head, and it was giving him a raging headache. Everyone knew to stay away from him when he was like that.

Denny tossed and turned in his bed, with Helen ending up sleeping in one of the spare bedrooms and she was beginning to worry about him as his mood swings were terrible at the moment and he would 'fly off the handle' at the smallest thing. She knew he had went through a lot in his life, but she thought he might get over his problems through time. However, that seemed a long way away just now.

When she looked out she saw Denny starting to go on a run with Arno and Udo. He had told her that you should never run a dog at speed, but he was pounding his legs into the dirt with the dogs blissfully unaware that they shouldn't be chasing like that. Eventually she lost him in the mist and rain and went to see the boys. When she brought them downstairs, Willie was sitting outside with a cup in his hand looking very thoughtful.

"Willie, do you know what is going on with Denny just now. I know he has this sixth - sense 'mumbo jumbo' going on in his head just now, but it seems to be consuming him. What's happening?"

"Helen, please never, ever underestimate his 'mumbo jumbo' as you call it. He has probably kept himself alive because of it. Hopefully, after this week things will calm down."

"Why this week Willie? What's going to happen?"

"Nothing Helen, so just drop it please as you are beginning to sound like a nagging wife. A 'fit' wife according to Levi mind you."

Willie was laughing as Helen walked away with a smile on her face, but she still wasn't happy with what he had just said. A while later he heard one of the dogs coming through the mist. It was Udo with Arno coming just behind him. He had often wondered if dogs ever thought about who was going to be the first back or was it just instinct. Denny was coming in a poor third and he ran straight up the stairs, stripped off and put a towel around him.

"Enjoy your run and coming in a lousy third behind the dogs brother? Or are you going to give me a lame excuse."

"This coming from someone who couldn't run a message. Oh, and by the way it will just be you and Yuri working together with Tomaz watching the house while we are away in Edinburgh and then Durma. You okay with that?"

"I'll just have to be wont I, but it would have been nice with a little bit more notice."

Just then Gertie came out with the breakfast and was a little bit put out seeing Denny with only a towel round his waist. Helen then walked out after her and told her not to get flustered as there was not much to see under the towel. Willie started to laugh, and he thought he saw a slight smile on Denny's face.

The day dragged, with no let up from the rain until about nine in the evening when Yuri and Tomaz walked out of the mist, facing three savage looking dogs.

"I wasn't expecting you until about midnight and it's obvious the dogs can't tell the time."

They all watched from the veranda as Tomaz made some signs to Yuri.

"He is asking if he could call the dogs off Denny as it would be good practice."

"Tell him to go ahead and see what happens Yuri."

Tomaz gave out two very loud whistles. The dogs then very slowly walked towards him showing more teeth than before. Another two whistles wasn't stopping the dogs and by this time Tomaz had put his hand over his genitals expecting the worst, and walked behind Yuri. Denny then gave the command to stand down and the dogs all walked in unison to greet the pair. Much to Tomaz's relief.

"Why did the whistles not work this time he is asking me Denny?"

"Simple Tomaz, you are approaching my family in near darkness, and I never gave the command to the dogs to say it is okay. After a while they will begin to trust you and only, as I have said before, that you trust them. If you had been a stranger and they had sensed danger then they would have been fighting over your scrotum by now pal. You okay with that?"

Tomaz had nodded his head and Yuri said he thought it was a good idea to bring him along to protect everyone while they were in Zwiesel. Denny had said that was good thinking, but he was raging inside, why he hadn't thought to do that himself.

"Gertie, can I ask you a big favour please. We have been unable to get in to the village to get provisions and Tomaz is getting so fed up of rabbit stew, so I was wondering if you could make him a light snack or something please."

Gertie said something in German and then took off to the kitchen.

Half an hour later she emerged with a plates of meat, cheeses and fruit that would have 'choked a horse'.

"C'mon Gertie, look at the size of that plateful. You feed him better than me for God's sake."

"That is because I like him better than you Willie."

She immediately turned and looked at Helen for approval. Helen gave her the thumbs up. All stage managed of course. There was a bit of tension in the air for the next couple of hours while Helen kept on looking over at Denny wondering what was going on, and where they were going. Denny never looked her way as the least she knew the better.

At about eleven thirty Denny had said it was time for a little drive in the car. The girls were away to bed and Denny had told Tomaz he was in charge of looking after his family. If anybody approaches this house and you don't know them then you can either shoot them or leave the dogs to rip them to bits. He stood there looking at Tomaz who gave him a reassuring nod and a look that Denny was happy with.

Denny insisted on driving as he still hadn't heard from Maria if the two brothers were on the insurance and didn't want any problems if they were stopped by the police. Nobody spoke on the journey and with the rain coming down hard Denny was hoping that there wouldn't be many people about. He thought the

83

rainwater might deter the smelly hippies from coming out. When they arrived at the rundown house, they sat there for about ten minutes before Denny turned to Willie and Yuri and asked if they were sure about what they were doing. The silence told Denny they were up for it.

Willie and Denny got out and put their hooded tops on before Denny put his head in the car.

"Stay in the driver's seat, and if it all goes belly up then get the hell out of here."

Denny and Willie put their arms around each other's shoulders, started to sway about and staggered towards the door. Yuri had then slid down in the seat and waited.

As they walked through the door Denny whispered to Willie that he had a niggle in his head that they should start at the top. Some people were still walking around, but not many. They started to climb the central staircase still holding on to each other.

"Hate to tell you this brother, but I seriously need to vomit with the smell in here."

"Swallow it if it comes up. Don't you fucking dare throw up pal."

When they eventually got up they started methodically opening doors and looking in. Denny was the one putting his head in so that Willie wouldn't throw up. If any door was locked then Denny had his jemmy with him which easily opened it. It was the last room on the top floor when they hit the jackpot. As Denny looked in he saw Scottie lying on a stinking makeshift bed. He motioned to Willie and they both went into the room with Willie holding his nose and trying hard not do a 'five finger spew.'

Slowly and quietly, they walked to Scottie's bed before Denny lunged forward and smashed him on his chin. Willie had never seen such a powerful punch in all his days of fighting. Scottie went out like a light, but Willie suspected he was probably half-way there already with the drugs he was taking. Willie had to pull a scarf he had brought, tight over his face as the smell that was coming from him was overpowering, but they got him up and started to carry him as if he was drunk. They got to the top of the stairs ready to go down when a voice said," Where do you think you are going with him?"

Stepping on to the top landing was a guy dressed in a multi-coloured caftan, sporting a greasy ponytail. His eyes were glazed, and he was slightly unsteady on his feet.

"I am the master of this commune, and he is one of my followers so please take him back to his room. Then leave my house."

Willie left Denny to hold Scottie up, then ran forward and smashed the heel of his hand into the hippie's chest sending him flying upwards and heading down the stairs. He hit every step on the way down until there was a thud when he hit the floor at the bottom. They then dragged Scottie unceremoniously down the stairs lifting him over the guy who was blocking their way. Before they got to the door, Denny looked back and saw a pool of blood coming from the hippie's head. He knew he would be smoking his 'shit' in Hell tonight.

They dragged Scottie out the door and headed for the car. Yuri had been keeping a look out and jumped out of the car and opened the boot. Denny then lifted Scottie into the boot and quickly tied his hands and feet loosely and stuck a rag into his mouth. He never thought he would have had to do this again after Dundee. They sat in the car for a minute to gather their senses before Denny drove off.

"Yuri, put the windows down in the back and if we are stopped can you act drunk?"

They were nearly at the turn off for the estate when a police car came right up the back of them with lights flashing.

"Should have kept your mouth shut brother. Now what?"

"Both of you let me do the talking. There is no way they could know what we have done. Keep calm."

When Denny had pulled over he saw a single policeman exit the car and move towards them. He came up to the window and said that did they know that they had went through the traffic lights when they were turning to red.

"I'll put my hands up officer. I didn't see that as the rain was blurring my vision. I'm probably in too much of a hurry to get this guy in the back home as his wife is going to 'kill' him."

Yuri was rolling about in the back singing some song in a dialect Denny didn't know.

Then the office asked Denny for identification. When he started to read it he suddenly stopped and said," I see you are from the Albach Estate sir? I have always wanted to see the forests as I am a keen ornithologist, and I could imagine there is a massive variety of birds in them."

"I own the estate as well as the whole Albach Trust officer, so at some point why don't you phone the estate, say in a few weeks, and we can organise for you to go 'twitching' in the forests."

The officer had just been given the chance of a lifetime, so he thanked Denny and told him to drive carefully before taking a step back and giving him a salute.

"Well, I never thought I would see the day that the German police are saluting you now. What is the bloody world coming to Foggerty?"

They were a little apprehensive when coming up the track, until they saw Tomaz leaning against one of the posts with his rifle aimed at their vehicle. "I hope his trigger finger doesn't twitch," said Yuri. When they got to the house, Denny quietly asked him through the window if there had been any problems to which he answered no by shaking his head.

"Stay here Tomaz as we will only be another half an hour. Okay?"

Tomaz gave them the 'thumbs up' and they headed along the track to the forests. Denny glanced over at Willie and saw that he was actually sleeping. He couldn't believe him. Forty-five minutes ago, he had just thrown a guy down the stairs killing him, and now he was sleeping. Unbelievable.

When they couldn't go any further they stopped, and Willie came too. They hauled Scottie out of the boot and dragged him down the banking and put him up against a tree, but not before putting his head in the fast-flowing stream to try and get him awake.

"Right, you pair, there has to be as few marks on his body as possible, so I will be asking him the questions."

"Yeh, yeh Foggerty, you always want the fun," said Willie.

Eventually Scottie was lucid, so Denny wasted no time in questioning him.

"Okay you scumbag, your answers will depend on whether you leave this forest alive or not. Why have you and your pal been scouting out these forests, and who is he?

Scottie never said anything, so Denny smacked him in the mouth.

"As if they aren't going to notice that one," said Willie.

The look that Denny gave him made him keep any more comments to himself. Denny threw questions at Scottie, but was getting nowhere until Yuri took a knife out, knelt before him and started opening his trousers. Scottie was beginning to panic, and Yuri had asked Denny if he could cut his 'balls' off. It was then that Scottie started to talk, but at times he was just laughing.

"You think you are a big man Foggerty, but you have messed with the wrong people this time. You fucked up back on Durma, and now they are coming for you. You're going to be dead meat at some stage."

"Who is coming for me and when?"

"I can't tell you that, as I was approached by a guy who wanted information on the estate, but why he came to me I have no idea, but they will get you, you bastard. You don't know who you are messing with. Now untie me and piss off and let me go then maybe I'll go and pay that bitch Jinty a visit to show her what she has been missing."

Denny was nearly knocked over by Willie grabbing Scottie by the back of the neck and shouting at Yuri to cut the ties on his feet and hands quickly.

"You're going nowhere you fucker, apart from meeting your smelly hippie master in Hell."

Willie dragged him to the water's edge with Yuri's help, before putting his head under the water. Scottie was thrashing about, but Willie held his hand on the back of his neck until there were no more bubbles coming up. An evil smile came over Denny's face.

The three of them stood and watched Scottie's body float down the stream as if it was just a matter of fact.

"Yuri, when we get back to the house you and Tomaz head back home and don't appear until mid-day and remember if you see any police or official cars then just stay in the woods. If the girls ask, we went hunting for Scottie last night, but couldn't find him. Are we all okay with that?"

They both agreed on that and got into the four by four and headed back to the house. When they were nearing it they saw Tomaz in a kneeling position ready with his gun. The dogs were growling at the side of the house, but Willie went and told them to be quiet. When Yuri left with Tomaz, Denny had said to Willie he would take the dogs out early and find where the body had floated to, come back and phone the police.

The rain was still coming down heavily when Denny got out of the bed at first light, trying not to waken Helen. He wandered down to the dogs room on the side of the house and let them out. The rain was starting to ease off which wasn't what Denny wanted as he thought the police, when they arrived, would spend as little time as possible investigating if they were getting soaked.

He got about twenty minutes from the track with the dogs, before they started barking furiously down by the edge of the stream. Scottie's body was lying face down with his arms outstretched. Job done he thought. He started to walk back with the dogs following and when he went into the house he immediately phoned the police station and said there had been an accident and fatality on the estate. Denny thought it a good idea to keep mentioning the word accident to get it ingrained into everybody's head. They said they would send officers as soon as possible.

Helen had heard him on the phone and came running downstairs and asked what had happened. Just then Willie came up from the annex and he asked both of them to come into the dining room as he needed to speak to them.

"Helen, I was out walking the dogs and I found Scottie's body floating in the stream. It looks to me like he must have slipped, hit his head, and fallen into the stream which is pretty swollen with all the rain we have been having."

Helen's face paled and she had to sit down.

"What was he doing up here Denny?"

"Denny, show her the photos from the cameras will you," said Willie.

He walked over to the dresser, opened a drawer and took the photos out asking her to have a look at them. Her hands were shaking before she spoke.

"What the hell was he doing all the times he was here Denny, and who is the person he is with?"

Willie interrupted and said it was a mystery which they couldn't fathom out, but maybe the police could.

"Helen. Denny and I along with Yuri went out looking for him in Zwiesel last night as we still felt he was a danger to Jinty. We left Tomaz to look after you all. There was no sign of him, and we got back about midnight, but it is obvious that he was up to no good, so good riddance to him."

Helen had said she was going to start the breakfast and if it was okay she would explain to Gertie and phone Jinty.

"That's fine Helen, but Jinty isn't to come over until the police are away. We don't want her getting upset if she sees the body. Play everything low key please."

As Denny walked outside he just gave Willie a slight nod.

It was half an hour before the police arrived and Denny was so glad to see it was the 'ornithologist' they had encountered last night. He was with a young officer, and they had been followed up the track by a grey mortuary van with what looked like two even younger guys in it. Denny walked down the steps and greeted them.

Denny pleaded ignorance to what the procedure would be. He knew it would be no different from Scotland. He asked all the officers up onto the veranda out of the drizzle that was still coming down.

"What is it that you want us to do officer. You're the experts here. If we can give you a hand to get the body up the banking then fine. Do you have waterproofs and boots with you?"

They all looked around sheepishly at each other before the guy in charge admitted that no, they were ill equipped today.

"Why don't you all come into the store room and get kitted out and Willie and I can take you to where the body is but for security purposes I insist on taking one of the dogs with us, but please don't try and interact with any of the dogs."

After Denny had got them all suited and booted they got into the two four by fours and headed along the track. When they got as far as they could Denny asked them to get out and they would have to walk the rest of the way. They got to where the body was, and he could see that a couple of the young lads didn't feel they were up for the job.

"How about my Forestry Manager and I go down and drag the body up the banking, but only if that won't destroy any evidence. What do you think sir? We can all then carry it to the four by fours. Can any of you drive a four by four?"

Officer 'twitcher' really didn't have a clue and Denny was leading him all the way which was fine.

"That would be best I think. Do you know the deceased Mr Foggerty?"

"We all do sir, and we are all a bit cut up about this, but probably best if I explain it all back at the house."

One of the young lads drove one of the vehicles back with Willie and another officer and Arno sitting on the cage at the back, while Denny drove the others back with the body lying on the cage at the back. Denny didn't think that the girls should see Scottie like that, so he radioed to Willie to get Helen and Gertie out of the way before they brought the body in.

It was just a case of putting the body on a stretcher and covering it with a blanket before it was put in the back of the van. Once that was done the two mortuary attendants drove away to what Denny supposed would be the morgue. He suggested that they all go in and get a hot drink and some biscuits. Denny had found out that the officer in charge's name was Meyer and he was all for the drinks and biscuits. Denny thought this was going to be easy to persuade him that what had happened was an accident.

As they all sat in the dining room he could see the two officers looking at all the paintings on the wall and the opulence of the place. Gertie had brought through a large pot of coffee with homemade biscuits of all varieties. Willie had brought the photos of the camera images and handed them to Officer Meyer who, give him his due, took his time studying them.

"Mr Foggerty, what is your opinion as to why this person was over here."

"Well, to be honest we all think he lost his way in life and when he inflicted violence on my wife's best friend we had heard he had fallen in to the drug scene and I think the reason he was over here was to cause the estate trouble. I was sure I had heard somebody outside, as did the dogs a few times, but by the time I got out whoever it was had gone. I think he was under the influence and while walking in the forest he has slipped and hit his head and drowned. I can only think that it could be death by misadventure. What do you think Officer Meyer.

"I concur Mr Foggerty. I think it's been a tragic accident and that's what my report will say as I am sure the toxicology report will tell us that there is drugs in his system."

Before Officer Meyer left, Denny asked him if it was appropriate to give him a couple of bags of Gertie's biscuits unless it broke any protocol.

"Don't worry Mr Foggerty, I will gladly receive the biscuits and pass them around the station tomorrow."

"Before you go Officer Meyer, can I thank you for the way you have handled this incident and the Albach Trust will be conveying this to your senior officers. Oh, and please remember to contact us here to organise a few days out bird watching."

Denny had never seen as big a smile on anybody's face than was on Officer Meyers. As he waved the officers away, Willie came out and jumped on Denny's back and wasn't letting go, until Denny swatted him away like a fly.

"I am positive we are fine brother. We have only one person to sort out now and that is the guy who is poaching the foxes."

"Bloody hell Foggerty, we should put a sign up at the bottom of the track saying 'Murder for Hire,' but I must say you manipulated him brilliantly."

They both turned as they heard Jinty's jeep coming up the track and Willie had said he wasn't going to speak to her about Scottie and it would be up to Denny.

As she got out of the car Denny could see she had been crying.

"Right Jinty Thomas, don't you fucking dare shed any tears at my home over a scumbag like Scottie. Got it?"

She ran forward and hugged Denny and wouldn't let go until Helen walked out and came down the steps and put her arm around her.

"Jinty, it will be a 'wee' while till Yuri arrives." said Denny.

91

"You are so bloody cold and insensitive, husband. Why don't you 'bugger off' as I'm sure you must have something else to do."

Denny had suggested to Willie that they get Gertie to make up lunch for the four of them as he was sure the brothers would appreciate it when they arrived. Denny and Willie took the dogs along the track to the forest, and it wasn't long before they saw the brothers standing beside their ATVs.

"Did it go all right Denny?" said Yuri.

"We're sound Yuri, but we will meet back here at five o'clock and go over it again and again till we are word perfect. That okay for everyone?"

Heads were nodded. Denny had said that he and Tomaz would take Arno, head down to the South and see the others later. When they started walking Tomaz was making an awfully good job of looking after the lunches. Denny couldn't help but smile.

"Remember Tomaz, Arno is a bit different to Udo. More ferocious and I wouldn't want to have my 'balls' ripped off by him. He is like a devil dog when I tell him to be."

Denny was trying not to let Tomaz see him smiling and noticed him moving to the other side away from Arno. He suggested they have something to eat before starting to work which seemed to please Tomaz. After eating, Denny sat back against a tree. God he was tired, and his head was hurting so much from the nonsense going through it. He just nodded off. He fell into deep sleep and a nightmare was consuming him. All the shadows in the forest were coming for him. All different shapes and sizes. They were dark and scary. There were faces in each one and they were contorted in pain. Were these the faces of the people he had killed before?

Eventually, Denny was awoken by Tomaz trying to hold him down which was a bit of a token gesture. Denny shoved him aside, grabbed his gun and was staggering about in some sort of trance ready to shoot anything that he thought might be a threat. He was shouting something about him being ready for anybody that comes for him. Arno was on high alert with teeth bared, but was confused as nobody was giving him a command to attack.

Denny came out of his dream like state to see Tomaz sitting on the ground with one hand covering his eyes and the other

92

covering his genitals. When fully in the land of the living, Denny said, "Tomaz, your fine. I'm sorry you had to see that and maybe if I tell you all about myself it will explain everything."

For about an hour Denny told him everything about his life and when he looked over Tomaz was looking really scared.

"Remember my good friend. One day I will sail into Hell, and then that will be one beautiful battle with all the people I have killed, trust me. C'mon let's get some work done."

Tomaz was glad for his world to be back to normal, as he started clearing branches from the banking. Willie started to do his usual pathetic animal impersonations on the radio and Denny had motioned to Tomaz to do two clicks on it so that Willie would put it to his ear. Denny then told him quietly to give a blast of three whistles into it.

"You little bastard Tomaz. I know that was you. I'm bloody deaf in one ear now you little prick. Wait till I get a hold of you."

Tomaz was on his knees laughing which was strange for Denny, as no sound was coming out of him. Arno was running around wondering who he had to come back to. Denny laughed with him, and they both carried on working.

They all met up at five o'clock and started walking back to the house with Willie giving Tomaz 'daggers'. Tomaz made sure he kept on the other side of Denny. As far away from Willie as possible. Denny said he would speak to everyone in the morning so that Yuri and Tomaz could get back to their father.

When they got back Jinty was still there sitting with Helen and the boys on the veranda. Yuri walked forward to her with Denny wondering what he was going to say.

"I'm sorry to hear about your friend Jinty, even though hadn't been very nice to you. A terrible accident."

Jinty got up and gave him a big hug. She saw Tomaz waiting there as if he was waiting to say something but couldn't, so she gave him just as big a hug. Helen smiled at Denny and then he knew the girls would accept Scottie's death as an accident. Jinty had asked to speak to Denny in private whereby she had asked him to come to the mortuary with him to identify the body. Normally Denny wouldn't have wasted a second of his time on an 'arsehole', but seeing it was Jinty he told her he would do it and organise a cremation for him as Jinty had told him she had no idea where he belonged and had just appeared on Durma one day. He made a mental note to Officer Meyer tomorrow. He was going to ask for a cremation as quickly as possible, as he thought Scottie had some religious views on that. Denny wanted the body burnt as quickly as possible, so that any evidence would burn with him.

Yuri had declined Helen's invite for tea as he said he had to get back for his father. Much to Jinty's disappointment.

"Yuri, why don't Willie and I come over first thing and meet your father. I will get the Hoffman brothers over to protect the estate. What do you say?"

"My father would consider that an honour Denny, and we will look forward to seeing you."

It was decided by Helen that Jinty would stay the night and it was a rather sombre time, although she said she felt more shock than anything. Ottar still needed walking so Denny had suggested to Jinty that she might like to come a short walk with him. She had agreed and they took Ottar and started walking along the track.

"Denny, I really don't understand why he was prowling around in these forests. Helen said he had been across countless time with another guy. I take it you have no idea who he is?"

"Not a clue Jinty, but I intend to find out and ask him why and if I don't get a good answer then God help him. You're a really good friend to us Jinty, and I hope you can find a bit of happiness as you deserve it, but please don't put all your eggs in one basket with Yuri."

"I won't Denny, but at least I feel safer now that Scottie is no longer with us. Maybe I'll get to know Yuri better and things might develop, but who knows."

She linked her arm through Denny's, and they walked for a bit towards the North valley.

"We could always keep walking and we would end up at Yuri's farm. Who do you say?"

Jinty started to playfully hit him before Denny picked her up and put her over his shoulder.

"Bloody hell Foggerty not again and I thought you were supposed to protect me you smelly 'dug'."

Ottar gave her one quick glance and went on sniffing at everything and anything. Denny had decided that they better get back as he wasn't sure about the weather.

They walked towards the house and Jinty shouted to Helen who was sitting with the boys," He only managed to ravish me three times Helen, what do you think?"

"I think he must be losing it, or it might be he just doesn't really fancy you anymore and is just using you for his animalistic sex. What do you think you hussy?" They both started laughing and Denny escaped by saying he was going to put Ottar in the kennel room.

When he was in the kennel the dogs were all over him, so he sat on one of their beds and started to think about what Scottie had said. It could only be associates of the people he had killed on the fishing boat which was dropping the drugs off. Apart from Scoug, they were just random people. He wondered if it could be connected to the incident with Scoug in the pub in Sea Haven, but Scoug's crew then were just a few misguided guys who wanted to make money at other people's expense. He sat with his head in his hands and really didn't have a clue who was coming after him, but he was going to prepare for it.

That night Willie and Denny were doing their best to see who could get one of the boys to walk, until Helen had put a stop to their childish game as she referred to it. After the last dog walk, Denny said he was going to bed as he was going to be up early before he went to meet the brother's father with Willie. He must have been tossing and turning all night, as when he woke up Helen had vacated herself to another bedroom again.

When he sat outside having a quick something to eat he heard a motor and when he looked down the track he could see the Hoffmans coming up. He invited them in for something to eat and drink.

"Right lads, you know the score. Willie and I will be away for a few hours so please protect the property and the people in it with your lives. Do you need any rifles? or do you have your own guns?.

Gunther had asked Denny to follow him to the boot of the car and when he opened it Denny said" Bloody hell Gunther, you've

95

come prepared for a war. All you need now is some bloody hand grenades."

Karl had said he could go back to the shop and get some. Denny had said their rifles would be enough. That's all he needed, grenades on the estate.

"Please accept my apologies, but I meant to phone you last night to say that you no longer have to put surveillance on Jinty's property. Her ex-boyfriend won't trouble her anymore, but I am still going to pay you each month as I want surveillance done on this property and the forests. I'll speak to you soon about what I am looking for. When all this is over you can move into your new premises. It is being fitted out to a high standard and the contractors will contact you for your input. Its Savigny Platz no 13." There was a look of pure surprise on their faces.

"Denny you have done so much for us and now this. How can we repay you?"

"Just keeping my family safe is enough."

Willie came out and suggested they head off. Denny said he was taking Ottar in the cage on the back of his ATV as he wanted the other two dogs left here. He shouted to Helen that she was in charge of the dogs, and she knew the 'drill'. As they headed off, the Hoffmans took up their positions on the veranda and Denny thought they had been a good 'find'. They travelled up the track towards where the brothers lived. Ottar was leaning forward with his chin on Denny's left shoulder. Denny knew where he was going as he just followed the tyre tracks from Yuri and Tomaz's ATVs from their daily journey to the estate.

Denny got to the brow of the hill first before Willie pulled up next to him. They both looked down on the land and farm house.

"What a fucking 'shithole' Denny. I don't know what is keeping the buildings standing?"

There was old machinery lying around just being devoured by rust. They both knew what Yuri was on about when he had said the bogs were encroaching on the house and farm buildings.

"It makes me feel how lucky we are. I'll see what I can do for them, but it is still early days, so I'm not going to rush into anything."

They took off down the hill to the farm house. Tomaz came out to greet them and there was genuine pleasure on his face. He ushered them in. Sitting beside the log fire was his dad Artem. He looked a shrivelled old man, but with a lovely beaming smile, trying to get as near to the fire as he could. Yuri came through and introduced them to him. Denny was surprised how strong a handshake he had. When Ottar walked over to him the look he had on his face was of pure joy. Ottar lay down at his feet.

Yuri had made some strong coffee and they just sat around the fire talking. Artem's English was good as he said he had been a communications officer during the war and had taught Tomaz and Yuri. His wife had died when giving birth to Tomaz, so he had brought the boys up on his own. They sat for a good hour before Yuri had said they had better head over to the estate to do some work.

"Are you able to get out and about Artem?" asked Willie.

"Only around the buildings to keep my legs going and get fresh air."

"Well, remember to keep your rifle with you in case you get a visit from the wolves."

"I don't have a rifle Willie, but I do have a big stick."

Denny and Willie looked at each other before Willie went over to where his was propped up, came back and gave it to him.

"I can't accept this Willie. It's such a generous gift."

"Keep it Artem, and your boys will bring an adequate supply of ammunition for the rifle, but remember, no firing if you see the white stag."

Before they left Artem asked them if he could say something to Denny and Willie before they left. Yuri tried to stop him, but he was insistent.

"Lads, can I tell you that I don't know how long I have to live as God has decided that I am to have the cancer. I have been blessed to have had two beautiful sons, but when I go please look after them. Will you?"

Tomaz started to shed tears before Denny shouted at him to remember that he didn't do tears. Tomaz quickly wiped his eyes with his sleeve. Artem smiled.

"Artem, I promise I will take them into our family when you go. Hopefully not too soon."

A big smile came over him and he gave Willie and Denny a curt bow.

They headed back over the hill to the estate with Willie trying hard to race Denny to be first there. When they got back Willie was only in third place as Yuri had taken him on the last bend much to Willie's surprise. Tomaz was quite far behind as if he didn't know you could press the accelerator down any further. Denny could see the Hoffmans standing guard on the steps to the house. Both looking around the estate as if on high alert.

All the girls came out, including Jinty who seemed to be a permanent fixture on the estate.

"Hey Jinty, isn't it about time you were back feeding the hordes of Zwiesel with your bread and cakes. Just let me know if you want a house built on the estate and it will happen, just as long as you're not pestering me all the time."

Jinty ran and jumped from the top of the steps and threw her arms and legs around Denny. He caught her, but started to topple backwards before falling on his back with Jinty still straddling him.

"You promise Foggerty?"

"Yes, I promise you. You 'nutter' Jinty Thomas. As long as you promise to stop throwing your legs around me."

"Can't promise that, but let's be fair Foggerty, you know you love it."

Everyone just stood watching the side show play out before Gertie appeared with the breakfast and everyone got stuck in.

When the Hoffmans were leaving Denny asked them if business had picked up and they said that thanks to word getting around that they had done work for the Albach Estate, more and more people were coming to them. Denny had went into the house and came back with an envelope and handed it to Gunther.

"No, no, please Denny we were only too pleased to help. Any time."

"Take the bloody money or he will be moaning about it all day."

Willie saw Helen rise and walk slowly towards him.

"Oh no, I didn't swear did I?"

Willie just accepted he had and took the clip on the head from Helen with Tomaz finding it funny.

Willie looked at him and said," Wait till your back talking and then you're in trouble, trust me."

Everyone started laughing.

Jinty said she was heading home, and the men started to get ready to go to work, but not before she gave them all, including Willie, a big hug with Yuri getting a lingering smile after his. When the girls were out of hearing range, Denny had told the men to meet up at four thirty where the track meets the forest for a chat after the revelations from Scottie.

The mist seemed to be coming out of the forest to meet them and if you had been a stranger then it would be a bit frightening, but to the guys it was just another day. Denny was with Tomaz again, and during the day he felt he was understanding what he was trying to say even though it was Tomaz's own crude sign language. After lunch Denny did his usual and sat with his back to a tree and started to think about what Scottie had said.

He knew it couldn't be anybody associated with Scoug, so he had to find out who the other people were, but how did anybody know it was him that had shot them. He decided that he needed help, so he was going to phone Shonagh, either tonight or early tomorrow morning. The meeting at four thirty with everyone was going to define what was going to happen over the next few months.

At about three in the afternoon, he told Tomaz to stop as he was going to show him how to control Arno. Tomaz looked very hesitant, verging on frightened, but Denny reassured him he would be fine. With Tomaz not speaking it was going to be difficult just using hand signals so he asked him if he could make any guttural sounds at all. When Tomaz gave out what sounded like a growl, Arno got down in the crouch position, bared his teeth and was ready to pounce on him. Tomaz ran behind Denny, before Denny started laughing and told the dog to ease off.

"I'll have to do a bit of thinking on that one Tomaz. What do you think?"

Tomaz stood there furiously nodding his head.

When they met at the track Denny asked them to listen to what he was going to say, and if they had any reservations they should speak up now and don't hold back.

"You all know what Scottie had said on the night he went 'sailing'. Well, I'm telling you this now. They will be coming after me and if anyone doesn't want to be in this fight then I fully understand. I am taking the family and Jinty back to Durma next week to give them a break and to see if there is any answers there. I am asking the Hoffmans over to protect the house and the three of you will work together. Willie, you'll be in charge and if you need to shoot anybody then you have my blessing."

A smile came over Willie's face.

They all agreed that they were up for this fight. However, Yuri had said they needed a strategy. He and Tomaz couldn't be way over the hill if something kicks off here on the estate. He also stated that they needed back up plans if things go 'belly' up.

"No disrespect Denny, but we need to put this down in black and white in the form of a map of the estate. All possible entrances and exits should be covered. If you bring in Gunther and Karl then we still only have six people, and we don't know how many of them there will be. We need to have areas marked out as to who will be covering them. I'm sorry Denny, but we are nowhere near ready yet."

"You're right Yuri, I have been blinded by that scumbags rantings and there is far more planning to be done. How about the three of you sit down with the Hoffmans, after I have asked them if they are in or not and we can take it from there."

They headed back to the house and the brothers said their goodbyes, but not before Yuri telling Denny he would start putting some ideas down on paper when he got home and when he was satisfied with them he would bring them over. Before they left, Helen and Gertie came down and put two large bags of baking in the baskets of their ATVs.

"From your secret admirer Yuri and I bet you can't guess who that is?"

She rolled her eyes and laughed, then asked Denny to come into the dining room as she wanted to speak to him. When they were out of earshot of everybody she asked," Denny I know you, Willie and the brothers have been having what seems like secret meetings lately, so I want to know what the hell is going on and how much danger are we all in."

"All I can tell you Helen is it seems the threat is real, and if it happens then prepare for you and Gertie to take the boys and go to the town house. No bloody arguments. Okay? I promise you this, love of my life, that I won't let anybody hurt you or the boys.

Quietly speak to Gertie so that she knows what she has to do when or if the time comes."

She knew her husband, so she just looked at him and nodded. Denny had said to her that he needed to speak to Shonagh back in Edinburgh in private on police business and she must not try and listen in. She said she understood. Denny firstly phoned the Hoffman brothers and asked them to come over at seven thirty in the morning. Next was to be Shonagh.

When she answered the phone her first words were," What is wrong Denny?"

"Shonagh, I have had some credible information from a source who I can't tell you about, that apparently certain people know what happened on Durma or at least they think they do. They are sending people to eliminate me Shonagh. I am not scared of them, and I will have made security provisions within a few days. I will give them the war they want Shonagh. You know me. Here is where you come in. You and Tommy know it was me, I know that, but who else could know? Can you try and find out the identity of the guy who was lying on the rocks and who the trawler was registered to. I think it was called Endless Summer. I know it can't be anybody from John Scougal's family as there is only his mother. The guy who got blown up with the boat couldn't be identified, but I was wondering if you identified the guy with the hole in his chest. It has to come from somebody either in the police or Durma. I can't see any connection to the Thomson family. What do you think?"

"Denny, please give me time to think and tomorrow I'll have to pull in a few favours and try to get copies of files, but it won't be easy pal."

"Please don't get caught Shonagh as that is the last thing I want, but can I just say that I have a feeling that this will be all played out on your home turf, well in Scotland anyway.Helen and I, along with the kids and Jinty are coming over to Edinburgh and then on to Durma next week, so it would be nice to meet up, but remember Shonagh, no lifting your top up for me as I am a respectable married man now."

Before she could reply she heard Denny laughing and him putting the phone down. She started to smile as she knew he would never let her forget that. As she sat with a tea she feared that this was not going to end well for somebody, so she was going to do everything she could to help him.

Before he went to bed he took his rifle and both dogs, leaving Ottar at home and walked into the woods. He needed to think, and he needed the solitude for that to happen. He did his usual and sat with his back to a tree. He thought how magical these forests were even at night. The dogs were just lying down beside him as if they were looking at the black shapes of the trees and shadows in front of them. Apart from the owl calls throughout the forests nothing stirred. Denny felt at peace, but he knew that wouldn't last.

"Well, my friends, war is about to descend on us all, so I hope you are all up for it and let's see if I have trained you well enough. Remember no quarter given."

The dogs were looking at him as if they knew what he was saying before they put their heads down on their front paws, waiting on Denny announcing that they were going home.

Denny sat on the veranda with the Hoffman brothers early the next morning and told them what was happening. He had asked them if they were in or out, but there was to be no half measures. They were to stay in the house while he was away, and Willie would be in charge. They had looked at each and both had said they were one hundred percent in, and they would have no compunction in killing anyone they thought was evil, or was threatening the estate or the people in it. That was music to Denny's ears, and he told them that Willie would call a meeting with everyone to discuss a strategy for when the time comes.

"Can we bring our own arms Denny?"

"You can bring hand grenades if you want lads," said Denny jokingly.

Denny saw them glancing at each other before he said, "Don't tell me you have brought the grenades in your car for 'fuck's sake. Have you?"

Denny walked away not waiting for the answer.

The next two days were as normal as possible, but Denny really didn't want to leave the estate with everything that that was going on. Helen had asked Jinty a few days ago if she would like to go to Scotland for a few days and she could hardly contain her excitement, saying she would get cover for the bakery.

102

Maria from the Trust had made all the arrangements which were really just first-class tickets for the three adults from Munich to Edinburgh. She had left the return flights as open tickets, as Denny didn't want to commit as to when they would be returning.

The morning of the journey came, and it started with Willie complaining about how much luggage they were taking for only a few days. The 'kitchen sink' had been mentioned a few times. The journey into the airport was a nightmare as the boys wouldn't settle and they had cried most of the way. The rain was battering off the windows which wasn't putting anyone in a good mood, but Denny thought it would acclimatise them for Durma no doubt.

Hanging around the airport terminal hadn't been that much better. Denny couldn't settle as he was on edge, continually looking around to see if he recognised any faces in the crowd. He didn't envy these people who had to constantly fly for their work. They were all grateful that as soon as the flight had started the boys had fallen asleep, as had Denny.

Denny's nightmares gave him no respite during his sleep on the flight. Several times Helen had to reach over the aisle and gave him a push to try and waken him up. The lady next to him was getting a bit frightened, and when the plane was coming into land Denny apologised most profusely to her. She had leaned across and whispered in his ear," Try and get some help son. You need it."

While they were waiting for their luggage Denny had phoned Robert Trapp at the hotel to confirm that everything was still okay, but he knew Maria would leave nothing to chance.

When they arrived at the hotel Robert came out to meet them. He shook hands with Denny and gave Helen a hug as well as Jinty after he had been introduced to her. He was especially pleased to see the boys, and told Helen he had organised his niece to stay over to look after them while they had their meal.

"The meal is for seven people tonight and I hope you all like haggis."

"Who are the seven?" said Denny.

"Maria has organised for Tommy, Annie, Shonagh as well as Jack to dine with you tonight. She thought that might come as a pleasant surprise to you all."

They all just stood there smiling.

"Why we don't we show Jinty the sights Helen, as she didn't have much time in Edinburgh before she came across to Zwiesel to stay, but let's go and freshen up before Jinty starts to smell."

Jinty did her usual and jumped on Denny before running her tongue up his face. Denny pushed her off shaking his head.

"Does she do that often Denny?"

"Every possible chance she gets Robert, believe me."

After showering, they took the boys in a double push chair Robert had acquired and walked along to the lovely Princes' Street Gardens. They sat having a picnic that Robert had prepared for them and although it was a bit cold they savoured every minute, just people watching and admiring the beautiful buildings in front of them.

While Denny sat there he hoped above all else that he would not have to bring his war to this beautiful city. He knew now that it was going to be a war with many casualties, but there was only going to be one winner and he wasn't going to be second best. Every day he felt stronger, and he was beginning to feel sorry for the people who were coming up against him. He turned away and an evil smile came over him.

In the evening Tommy and Annie arrived first. Annie couldn't wait to see the boys, taking Helen's arm and virtually dragging her up to their room to see them. Helen felt sorry for the babysitter Morag, as Annie was giving her the Third Degree on her experience in looking after babies, until Morag said she was the manageress at a nursery here in Edinburgh.

"Well, if you need help at any time I will be just down the stairs and the name is Annie. Okay?"

Helen was trying not to laugh while standing at the back of Annie. Morag thanked Annie and looked at Helen with a wry smile on her face. By the time Helen and Annie had gone down stairs Shonagh had arrived. They all sat having a soft drink with Jinty telling Shonagh of her interest in one of the estate workers called Yuri as her boyfriend Scottie had met a terrible accident on the estate. When Shonagh looked at Denny and Helen they both just rolled their eyes, but she knew by the look on Denny's face that there was to more to it than meets the eye. Shonagh had said that Jack wouldn't be coming due to work commitments, but he sends his regards. Robert had excelled himself with the meal even making sure Tommy was given seconds much to Annie's disgust. Denny could see that Helen seemed far more relaxed and he hoped to be the same when they landed on Durma.

The evening seemed to come to an end far too soon, with Annie and Shonagh creeping up to the room to see the boys before they left.

"Denny, can I have a word with you while the ladies are doing their usual bloody hugs and tears."

"Sure Tommy, let's get out of earshot of the ladies."

"I was wondering if there have been any developments on the security front for you and the family?"

"Unfortunately, Tommy, I have found out that the threat is real, and it stems from what happened on Durma. It seems as if I have pissed some people off big style. I have been making plans back home to make the estate as secure as possible, but you know the size of it and it's not easy. I'm hoping to get some answers when I'm over on Durma."

"Denny, you know that what you did on Durma wasn't right, but totally understandable. The people you shot were evil people, but evil people have brothers and sisters, and revenge is all too easy for them. Have you asked Shonagh to give you any information she can?"

"Tommy, I know what I did wasn't rational, but you know I'm not a rational person. If someone needs to go to Hell and I can do it, then I will. By the law of averages, it has to catch up with me some day, but I hope it's when I'm a wizened old man. Let me ask you something Tommy. Do you think there is any chance that people have found out about me from someone in the police force? I have went over it time and time again and the only people who know for definite are you and Shonagh and I would trust you with my life."

"It seems to me that someone on Durma knew that you and John Scougal had a grievance between you, and they have put two and two together. It's a small island Denny, and John's body was recovered from the sea. His mother was notified and advised he had got himself mixed up in a drug feud, as that was the official statement that I personally put out. If there are any answers then I'm sure you will find them on Durma."

Lately, Denny had been casting his mind back to that fateful night and a thought kept appearing in his head, but he really hoped he was wrong.

Before she left for the night, Shonagh had discretely taken out an envelope from her handbag and gave it to Denny.

"These are copies of the transcripts from the investigation into the Durma incident. As you will see there is not a lot to go on as we identified three bodies including John Scougal, but to be honest they only appeared on our systems with minor convictions. The boat belonged to an old fisherman from up north, but he died a few years ago and his widow had said someone came to her door and offered her good money for it. He had paid cash, and she was glad of the money. The boat had never been called Endless Summer and had never been registered in any port, so that was a bit of a dead loss. If you want my opinion then I think, and I hope not, someone you know has been feeding information to the parties that are after you."

Denny had thanked her and gave her another hug.

Denny's sleep that night had been fitful and in the morning got such a fright to find Jinty lying in bed beside Helen and him. She had said she had been cold, but he suspected she was really apprehensive about arriving back on Durma without Scottie.

"Helen, I don't know how you ever get any sleep as I was being prodded in the back by something hard all night."

"Well, Jinty that something hard was going to be put to good use if you hadn't turned up in our bed."

"Okay, okay I get your drift. I'm away for a shower in my own room. Enjoy yourself without me."

"Trust me, I will."

Helen had been thoroughly satisfied with their love making, but she felt Denny's mind was somewhere else. She didn't want to ask him about it, so she just told him how lovely their love making had been.

After breakfast they started to load their gear into a small mini-bus that Robert had sourced for them to take them to the ferry as they thought the train and bus might be too much for the boys. Denny had brought down a small envelope with him and handed it to Robert. When he opened it he started to protest at the size of the cheque, stating that Denny had given him enough the last time. Denny just shook his hand and told him that they hoped to be back at some point and that hopefully they would bring their friends with them.

"Denny, I get the sense you have a lot troubling you just now. Are you in trouble?"

"No Robert. Other people are going to be in trouble. Trust me."

Nothing else was said and five minutes later they were heading off to catch the ferry to Sea Haven and then on to Kismay. The journey was long with several stops to get the boys out of their car seats. Denny couldn't believe the time he had done it in the train and a beat up old bus. As they sat in the small building that served as a waiting terminal Denny looked out on to the Durma Sound and thought the wind was starting to get up. He could see the waves starting to roll and he thought this might not be a fun sailing.

He told Helen that she might want to have some towels and clothes handy for the twins. She said that they would be fine, but that was Helen. Being a woman, she always knew best, or she thought she did.

When they finally boarded the twins came alive and they were becoming a handful, so they were taking it in turns to push them around in the prams. Back and forward, back and forward. Denny never knew if it was best to sit at the stern or at the bow so he decided on the bow so that they could at least see Durma getting nearer.

They were about half an hour from Sea Haven when the wind really started to whip up and the rain started. Welcome to Durma he thought. He wondered if his mum and dad had the same weather when they first came here. He turned to see Jinty leaning over the hand rail depositing her breakfast into the sea. At least this was the first time she had shut up since they had left Edinburgh. He was slightly concerned for her as the boat was starting to roll a bit and the wind was getting stronger, so he went out, steadied himself and put his arm around her waist.

"Don't think about 'copping a feel' Foggerty while I am in this vulnerable position or else."

"You're quite safe Jinty as I would struggle to find anything worth feeling. Remember I've seen you coming out of the shower."

Jinty tried to laugh, but it made her wretch even more. Helen shouted from the window wondering if she was okay and Denny just gave her a nod of the head. Eventually Jinty was finished feeding the fishes and they both went back inside. There was an announcement that they would be disembarking in fifteen minutes, so they sat waiting and thanking God that they had made it. Jinty started to dry wretch after seeing one of the crewmen walking around, while eating a large cream cake that must have been fresh about a week ago, with the cream turning a light shade of brown now.

"Right, everybody let's go as I'm sure that is Ian's four by four waiting for us. Jinty I would suggest you go and rinse your mouth. Here is a mint. Yuri would think you're a right 'scrubber' with breath like that."

"Fuck off Foggerty or I will try my hardest to push you over the side."

There was sheer joy on Ian's face when they walked up to him. He suggested that they keep the greetings until they were at the house as the weather was getting worse. After a while Ian said, "I can see by your glum faces that you aren't that happy to be back on Durma."

"It's just that it was a particularly bad crossing Ian. Of course, we are really looking forward to seeing you and Neala. It will be strange, but nice to see what the Western Isles Trust has started, "said Helen.

They past a newish building and Ian pointed out it was the new school for Sea Haven. Everyone was impressed with its size and design.

"Neala had made sure that Miss Glover and Miss Bryant had a big say in how it would look when finished."

"I see they haven't done anything about this road Ian. If you hit anymore bumps then we might have to stop for Jinty."

"Don't listen to him Ian. Wait till I tell you about him trying for a 'feel' on the boat."

108

"Did you really Denny?"

Denny just smiled and shrugged his shoulders before Helen told them to change the subject as she was sitting in the back. Eventually, they got to the brow of the hill and Ian stopped. They looked down on Kismay and couldn't believe the difference since they were last here. A new school was almost built, and new cladding was being put on all the cottages. There was a start on the widening of the harbour mouth. The three of them thought that they had never seen Kismay looking so fresh.

"I see Scroggie's bar has resisted the temptation to move into the twenty first century Ian."

"Not for the want of trying on Neala's part Denny. Many a night she would go down to the bar and try and persuade them to let her put some investment into the place. However, to no avail."

As they drove towards the house Denny was having mixed feelings about being back on the island. He wanted to visit his mum and dad's graves and see the progress that Neala was making through the Trust. It was great seeing Ian as it would Neala, but he felt there wouldn't be many other people he would go out of his way to visit. What he wanted to do was find some answers.

Chapter 6

Neala was waiting for them at the house and there was the usual excitement from everybody. Neala greeted everyone, but Helen could see she was more interested in the twins. Denny noticed that they had decorated the house to a high standard. Denny thought he might have some regrets about the house, but he knew he had moved on and was happy that Ian and Neala were enjoying it.

"You up for a walk along the cliffs Denny now that the rain has stopped? It'll let the women catch up."

"Sounds good to me Ian."

As they headed South along the path Denny had said," Have you ever thought much about Isla. I must admit she has come into my thoughts a few times, but that's not surprising with all the rubbish that is floating around in there just now."

"Only occasionally Denny. I have a good life with Neala and if we manage to start a family then it would be complete. I'm glad
that Hamish is languishing in Hell as we speak. Dare I ask you what is happening on the estate after you told me about your sixth-sense."

"I will tell you if you promise that you won't come over to try and help me. I don't know if I should tell you this, but Scottie beat up Jinty quite badly. He also stole from her. This was after she kicked him out or should I say I helped her get rid of him. He was heavily involved in drugs and was living in a squat in Zwiesel."

"I feel terrible Denny. I'm struggling as what to say. How has she coped with it?."

"I think she hides a lot, but she seems keen on one of the guys I have employed to work the estate. His name is Yuri. Him and his brother Tomaz are two nice guys and with what I think may be coming, I know I can rely on them."

"Is Scottie still in the town?"

"Scottie had an accident on the estate Ian. He went sailing one night."

Ian stood trying to work it out for a few minutes before it suddenly twigged.

"Oh, for 'fuck's' sake, please tell me you didn't drown him did you?"

"Not me Ian, Willie did."

Ian's face immediately lost all its blood, and he stood there not moving a muscle before he asked why. Denny told him about Scottie giving information to the people who were after him. He took the photos which the animal cameras had taken out of his pocket and showed them to Ian. He had to sit while looking at the photos.

"So, it's real then Denny, but did Willie have to drown him?"

"While we were speaking to him he confessed to helping some guy to give him the lowdown on the estate. Probably for drug money. He had then threatened to pay Jinty another visit to teach her a lesson, so it was a toss-up as to who did the deed. Willie got there first. I'm sorry to be the one that had to tell you Ian, but as far as I am concerned it's just another evil bastard sent to Hell. Before this is all over there will be quite a contingent sitting down there around the meal table waiting to see if I arrive.

"What do think pal? Oh, and as far as the girls know, Scottie had an accident."

Ian just sat there before eventually saying," what a bloody mess this is getting Denny. Are you prepared for what might happen? This is going to get ugly, very ugly."

"That's why I don't want you anywhere near it. I've got four guys, apart from Willie, who are unfortunately expendable. Is it enough? I don't know, but it's all I've got at the moment."

Denny had said that he hoped to find some answers while he was here on Durma and asked if he had recognised the guy in the photo. Ian had said no, but there were a lot of strangers on the island working on the schools and harbour. Only one person has asked about you and Helen and that was Mike Stewart, just asking how you were getting on.

"How much did you tell him Ian?"

"Nothing much Denny, I just met him down at Jeannie's store and I was telling him what a great time we had at your wedding."

"Did you tell him where you were at the wedding?"

111

"I may have done. I really can't remember, but I do remember telling him what a good job you were doing through the Albach Trust. Oh no, surely you can't suspect Mike is involved in any of this."

"At this stage I don't know who I suspect Ian, but what I do know is that somebody here on this island has the answers I need, and I will find that person."

Walking back, Denny had asked him if Neala and him had any more thoughts on coming to Bavaria. Ian had said that there was quite a few things to consider. The house, boat, doctors position and Neala's involvement with the Western Isles Trust, but she was hopeful that she had someone lined up. When they arrived and went into the house there was a nice spread on the table, and they all got in about it.

"What were you two talking about on your walk then?" asked Jinty.

"The price of fish Jinty. "said Ian.

God bless her thought Denny, as she just sat there nodding her head, before saying that the cost of fish in Zwiesel was high. Both Denny and Ian had to turn their heads away so that she didn't see them smiling. After their meal, Helen put the twins to bed, and they all sat for the next few hours just catching up.

"Willie sends his regards, and he was asking if there was any chance he could be an uncle before he was an old man?" said Denny.

"Believe me it's not for the want of trying, is it Ian? "replied Neala laughing.

Denny never thought he had seen Ian blush before, but there was a first time for everything.

"Why have the pair of you not asked me about Scottie for God's sake."

Helen could see that there was a hint of a tear in her eye.

"Jinty, I have just been told by Denny while out walking and I am so sorry. This is the first Neala has heard of it."

"Well, I'm not after what he did to me. It's my grans necklace that I am sad about."

It was then that Denny had went into his pocket and brought out the necklace and handed it to her. She was stunned and just sat there looking at it before the tears started.

"Oh, give it a rest with the tears Thomas. I can't handle them."

It was then she ran around the table and jumped onto Denny's lap knocking the chair and the pair of them onto the floor. She did her usual and straddled him before asking where he had got it from. She was giving him kisses all over his cheeks. He told her he had Karl Hoffman trawl all the pawn shops in the town looking for it. The description she had given him had helped.

"Thank you so much Denny, I really appreciate that. Helen, I think for the first time in my life I may be getting him excited as I feel something hard down there."

"Jinty, have a look down and I think you might find it's his belt buckle."

"Ah bugger."

Next day the sun had shown on Durma, and everyone seemed happy as they sat having breakfast. Finn had been up a couple of times during the night which was understandable considering the traveling they had done. Over breakfast they decided what they were going to do and who they were going to see. They had all wanted to go and see the new school being built and of course Miss Glover and Miss Bryant. Ian had said he would take Denny down to see the workings of the new harbour. Jinty had said she would pop in and see some of her old customers. They all wanted to do as much as they could as they would only be there another two days.

As they walked down to the school Ian had discreetly asked Denny for one of the photos and quickly pocketed it. When they were passing Scroggies' bar, Ian had excused himself and made the excuse he needed to see someone in there and said he would catch them up. Denny had looked at Ian to see if he wanted him to come with him, but a slight shake of the head had indicated no.

They thought that they might arrive at the school at a bad time, but the look on the teacher's faces was one of surprise and sheer delight. They told their classes to read some pages in the story book. Treasure Island. Miss Glover and Miss Bryant immediately took to the twins and as Denny suspected they were gushing all over them. Miss Glover couldn't hold back, and she just let the tears flow which set off all the rest. After a while Miss Glover asked if they would all like to meet one of her classes. Helen had said why not, and they all walked along the corridor and into the class. They sat at the front and the pupils were then encouraged to fire questions at them.

Some were directed at Helen and Jinty about their time as the Kismay Queen and her Lady in Waiting. Neala was asked if she was the one in charge of building the new school. Suddenly, one little imp of a boy stood up at the back and asked if he could ask Denny a question.

"Is it true Mr. Denny that not so long ago you were ill because you took too much whisky, but you're better now and you have become the richest man in the world?"

Denny smiled.

"Well, I won't lie to you son, I took too much whisky and at times it didn't make me a very nice person. As to being the richest man in the world I couldn't really tell you, but I am very, very rich, and I am trying to put all my money into doing good around the world."

"How much pocket money do you get."

"Maybe my wife can answer that."

"It depends whether he does his chores or not."

"There is always a catch to getting your pocket money Mrs Denny isn't there."

The class started to laugh.

"Please, Mr Denny can I ask you one more question. When I am old enough can I come and work for you?"

"Of course, you can. What is your name?"

"Tam sir, Tam Bogle and I'm a really hard worker."

"Well, Tam if you stick in at school and when it's time to leave, Miss Glover will contact me, and we will get you over for a job. How does that sound?"

Tam started to punch the air, and everyone started cheering. With one glance, Miss Glover regained some semblance of order and suggested they went to see the new school. They were all impressed with the design. Instead of just two classes there were several which meant that all the student were in their own age groups. One room was going to be a music room, and another was to make a new library. They were all very impressed.

Before they left Miss Glover made sure they would bring the twins back before they went back home. Denny was last out the door.

"Oh, by the way Denny did your friend catch up with you. He came in one day and said you and him had lost contact and do I know where you live now."

Denny just froze. He regained his focus before taking a photo out of his jacket and showed it to her.

"Is this the man Miss Glover?"

"That's him Denny. I could only tell him what I knew and that you now lived in Germany. I trust that was okay?"

"That's fine Miss Glover I'll catch up with him at some point, but may I ask if you have seen him speaking to anyone else?"

"Probably the only other person was Mike Stewart son."

As he caught up with everyone his head was pounding. There might be a reasonable explanation for it, but Denny was beginning to think otherwise. He needed space to think so he had suggested to everyone that he head off to the graveyard and for Helen to come over in a while with the twins as he wanted them there for his mum and dad.

Denny sat down between his mum and dad's graves and put his head in his hands. He couldn't believe this was happening. No, not Mike Stewart for the love of God. Helen and Jinty had been knocking on some doors to speak to friends and they were given a warm reception from everybody. Neala had gone to meet Ian as the girls arrived at the graveyard. Jinty had said she would give them privacy, but Helen had told her to stay where she was.

As Denny sat in between the graves, he asked Helen to hand him the two boys and as he held them both he was telling them all about their grandparents. Denny started to tell his mum and dad about his idyllic life in Bavaria, and all the people who knew and missed his mum.

Eventually, Helen took the boys from him and said they would give him a few minutes and for him to catch them up.

As they walked back towards the house Jinty had said they should pop in and see Jean Scougal in the shop. Helen quickly looked at Denny and could see on his face he didn't really want to go in. The only thing that changed his mind was the chance to ask Jean if anyone was asking about him. As they walked in Jean was shocked, but so happy to see them. She was sitting behind her make-shift counter and the girls went round and handed the twins to her. She started to cry, and it wasn't the tears that affected

Denny this time, it was the fact she didn't know he had killed her only son.

The rain started to batter off the windows and Jean had told them to come through the back and she would make them all a cup of tea. While sitting Denny, had asked her if she had been approached by the Trust to have the shop and house renovated.

"Neala has told me to expect the head of one of the building companies to visit me, so that I can tell them what I need to happen."

"Jean, have you ever thought about moving away from Durma. I know it hasn't very good memories for you now. The reason I am saying that is I have a good bakery business where we all live, and I was hoping to expand. There is a shop next door with a house above which is the same as mine and I would need someone on who I could rely on. The house is big enough where you could do your dressmaking as well if you wanted. What do you think?"

"This has come as a bit of a shock Jinty. Are you in agreement Helen and Denny?"

It had come as a shock to Denny, but Helen and Jinty weren't shy at spending Denny's money.

"C'mon, Foggerty you've got plenty of money. What do you think of my plan?"

Denny was lost for words.

"I think it would be a great idea Jinty, and if Jean wants to come over she can be there as soon as the house above the shop is ready."

"Is Germany not a long way away though?"

"Just a hop, skip and a jump Jean. If you decide yes, then contact us and I will come over and accompany you over to Bavaria."

"Well, that has given me a lot to ponder over, but are you sure I won't be a burden to you all?"

The three of them told her that she was more than welcome and to just let Neala know what she decides.

"Before you leave, can I ask you something Helen and Denny, although I really don't have a right to ask this. If and at the moment it's a big if, I come over, there then I know the twins don't have grandparent, so if I could be their surrogate grandparent then that would please me more than anything?"

Helen walked forward and said, "That would be such a wonderful thing Jean, of course you can."

They said their goodbyes and started to try and get back to the house before they were soaked. It wasn't long before Denny turned and ran back to the shop. As he walked through the door, Jean asked him if he had forgotten something.

"No, don't worry, I was wondering if this man had been asking after me?"

He took the photo out and showed her it. She sat there contemplating before saying," You know I do remember him son, as he wasn't a very nice man. He asked me a few months ago if I knew where you lived now and did you come back and visit the island. I told him that you lived abroad, but where, I said I didn't know, as I didn't. However, I did see him walking down the road with Mike. Is everything okay son?"

"It's all good Jean, thank you."

He walked forward and gave her a hug and a kiss on the cheek. When Denny walked through the door everyone was getting their coats off and Helen had said she was going up to put the boys down for a nap. Denny said he would help and try for a twenty minute nap himself. When Helen laid the boys down they were out like a light, so Denny lay down on the bed intending for a quick nap. He was no sooner on the bed when Helen joined him. She quickly unbuckled his belt, put her hand into his jeans and exposed his penis. She lifted her skirt and slowly took her panties down before straddling him and put his now erect penis inside her.

"I can't promise that I'll be quiet when I climax Denny so you will just have to accept it. Jinty isn't the only young hussy who enjoys straddling you."

It was like Helen meant business. She was grinding her body into his and at one stage she was up on the balls of her feet bouncing up and down on his penis, until she started to climax. She let out one almighty scream. Denny thought that the men in Scroggies would have heard her. Denny climaxed soon after and they lay back on the bed holding hands. As they lay there Helen had asked him why he was acting a bit strange around people.

Always the last to say goodbye and then going back to speak to them and what was Ian and him talking about when out walking along the cliffs.

"I am here to enjoy myself Helen, but for the sake of my family I am here for answers. Our problems back home are not going away."

"Have you found any Denny?"

"It looks like it and really not the answers I wanted to find, but I promise no matter what I find out it won't spoil our trip here."

"Did you enjoy our lovemaking Denny?"

"It was lovely darling, but I was just wondering who would be best at straddling me. You or Jinty, seeing as she has had enough practice at it."

He just managed to get in the bathroom before a hairbrush had clattered of the door.

"You can't hide in there forever Foggerty. Remember you have to sleep sometime, unless you can sleep with your eyes open."

When they got down stairs Neala was busy making dinner and Jinty wasn't very happy looking.

"Here was me thinking I might get a 'kip' for a wee while until the animal like screams from a couple of baboons came through the wall."

"You know what Jinty Thomas, Denny admitted I straddle him better than you."

"You'll regret saying that Foggerty. Just you wait."

Ian defused the situation by asking Denny if he wanted to walk to the harbour to see what progress had been made seeing as the rain had stopped. Denny was glad to escape. They sat on the seat just outside Scroggies and looked over the building work that was going on. Both Ian and Denny knew it was supposed to be progress, but neither were sure that they thought about it that way. Denny's mind wandered back to wee Archie and thought what a waste of a life, all because of drugs and greed.

Ian didn't say a word, but just handed Denny the photo he had given him earlier.

"You don't have to tell me Ian. It looks like Mike Stewart has been feeding people information on me."

"Yip, it looks like it pal. I would never have dreamed it would be him. He was seen a few times in Scroggies having a drink with the guy in the picture. Telling people, he was his cousin. He had sounded out some of the fishermen and they knew where you had gone through Scottie, before he arrived at the estate with Jinty. I feel for you son. Nobody should be going through this."

"Ian, I don't want you worrying about me. I will try and make sure Willie will come through this unscathed, but I did give him the option of leaving before anything started."

"What did he say?"

"He said I should stop being an 'eejit' Ian. He would be at my side no matter what happens."

"Typical Willie. What are we going to do about Mike Stewart, Denny?"

"There is no 'we' in this equation Ian. I will sort it before I leave and don't worry, there won't be another death on the island at my hands. I need to extract as much information from him as possible and I got an envelope full of information from Shonagh."

"Do you think we should pop in for a whisky before we go home Denny."

Denny started to laugh which lightened the mood a bit. As they walked home Ian suggested that they all went for a walk tomorrow and take something to eat with them. They could sit and reminisce about the good old days before Daniel Rey Foggerty imploded on this piece of rock. Denny smiled. He had just laughed and smiled within a few minutes. Maybe there was hope for him yet.

When they got back to the house, Ian had asked everyone if they were up for what he had said to Denny. They all seemed keen. Denny had phoned Willie that night and he had been quite dramatic by telling Denny it was 'all quiet on the Western Front.' He had sensed that all the men were getting a bit nervous with him not being there. He had asked about his brother and Neala and Denny said he would put them on before he ended the call.

As they sat round the fire after dinner Ian had said," Denny, I don't know if it's the right time, but remember you offered for us to come and stay with you on the estate? Well, if the offer is still there then we would love to come over."

119

"Ian, Neala we would love to have you come and stay. When I get back I will send you plans and designs of houses that can be built and you can both sit down and design your own house. It will only take six months to complete the house. Any size you want. Please put the problems I am having behind you and look forward to coming over."

"What problems are they Foggerty?"

"None of your business Jinty Thomas."

Jinty stuck her tongue out at him.

It had been a stormy night, with the wind howling off the sea and the waves in the distance could be heard crashing off the cliffs. Yet when they got up there wasn't any wind and the sun was trying it's hardest to see if it could get through the clouds, but it was struggling. There was a bit of a sombre mood around the kitchen table as they knew that this would be the last time they would all be together for a while. It didn't seem to affect Denny's appetite as the morning rolls were being scoffed as if they were to be his last.

"These rolls are much better than yours Thomas. You might want to go down and ask the 'lassie' that makes them how to do it."

"Piss off Foggerty. You know it was me that taught her everything she knows, before I left so get lost."

"Right, Denny get off Jinty's case. Deep down she will still be feeling a bit sad about Scottie," said Helen.

"She will be feeling sad cause she is missing her handsome Czech stud going by the name of Yuri. What do you say Jinty?" said Denny.

"That doesn't concern you Foggerty," she retorted.

Then a big smile came over her face and she blew him a kiss. Ian had suggested that they wind up the 'circus' and they start getting ready for their walk before the weather changed. As they left, Denny had Finn in one baby carrier and Ian had Col in the other. Neala had never seen Ian look as happy. Jinty had linked her arms through Helen and Neala's, but Denny told them to be careful as the path wasn't that wide and if anyone went over then they would be fish food.

The morning was glorious for Durma. It wasn't long before Helen had said to Denny did he remember this cove. Denny smiled and said how could he forget.

"What's so special about this cove you pair?"

"Nothing to do with you big ears Thomas," said Helen.

"Oh, don't tell me. This is the place you did the deed. Wasn't it?"

Helen and Denny just shrugged their shoulders with Jinty laughing her head off. They had walked South in keeping away from the cove where Isla was found, although Denny had thought the girls hadn't realised. The boys had been good, and they seemed to be taking everything in. After a couple of hours walking Jinty started to complain that her legs were hurting and could they have a rest.

Denny looked over to see a clump of trees he recognised and suggested they sit over there for a while in case the weather changed. When they sat down Neala had handed the food bag to Ian and 'demanded' that she was looking after Col. Helen and Jinty got the food and drinks out, and they all sat quite happy eating and looking out to the blustery waves. A sure sign that the wind would get up at some point.

"Hey, Helen is there any more places along the coast that you and Foggerty did the business?"

"I think I will tell her Denny. Probably on the ground right where you are sitting Jinty."

Jinty jumped up as if she had been bitten on her arse by something and said," Ah yuck. Could you not have told me before I sat down for God's sake. That's awful."

"Trust me Jinty, Denny was such an energetic lover that day."

"Please, don't tell me any more before I feel sick."

Neala sat there wondering if moving to Bavaria was such a good idea.

The waves were getting higher, and both Ian and Denny had said they would all be better right under the cover of the trees. Denny had said to Jinty she should have stayed where she was, but said she would rather sit on a rock. The rain came down heaven's hard and it was only Jinty that was starting to get wet. She quickly moved and lay in Denny's lap and put her arms around his chest. Everyone kept talking and it was only ten minutes later that they saw she had fallen asleep. Such a diminutive figure lying on top of Denny.

The squall didn't take long to pass over and it was then that Neala suggested they head home as the rain was becoming more frequent. As soon as Denny moved, Jinty woke up.

"I wasn't sleeping," she immediately said.

"Well, you must snore when your awake then, and you were dribbling over my top. Not sure Yuri will find that very attractive."

Denny laughed, but Jinty wasn't looking too happy.

They were lucky in as much as the rain was only slight now and again and they got home relatively unscathed.

"Helen can you and Neala look after the boys as I have someone I want to call in on as we will be away early tomorrow, but Neala, Helen will give you our flight tickets so can you please phone and book us on a flight for mid-afternoon and give Willie a call please to let him know when our flight will arrive in Munich. Also, can you phone that number and see if the same Edinburgh taxi company can pick us up from the ferry.

As he started to walk out the door Ian caught his eye, and he knew he was going to see Mike Stewart.

He had rehearsed what he was going to say and had promised himself, time and time again, that he would keep his rage in check. He knocked on the door and Mike Stewart opened it.

"Oh, it's you Denny please come in. It's nice to see you."

"Not sure you will be happy to see me after what I've I have got to say to you."

Denny knew from the look on his face that he had him like a rat in a trap.

"Right, here is how it's going down. I am here for answers and if you refuse to give me them then your life will end right here and now. I know you have been giving information to a guy with regards to my whereabouts. You have also been asking people from all over Durma if they could supply you with that information. I can see by your face that I am right. What I want to know is who he is and why he wanted that said information. Just as importantly I need to know why you did it."

"I'm not going to lie to you Denny. I really don't know the guy's name. He approached me and asked if I could give him any information on the night the incident happened here on Durma. He asked if I knew who had wiped out the fishing boat."

"And who did you say Mike?"

The words couldn't come out of Mike's mouth. It was like he had frozen.

"Spit out Mike. Who did you say it was?"

"I said you were heavily involved in it Denny. Let's be fair, you know you were. So, what was I to say?"

"You could have said fuck all Mike. You had no definitive proof it was me and as an ex-policeman you should know you can't make someone guilty on a hunch. Did he say who wanted the information, as it's obvious he was just a 'goffer', so I need to find out who he is."

"The guy did let slip after a few pints that the man he was working for was high up in the British Government, but attached to the Scottish office. However, he was speaking through drink, and I didn't press it."

"Okay, my last question is why the fuck did you sell me out?"

"Simple, Denny. I did it for money. I had promised my daughter that I would help my granddaughter through University, and as you know my police pension wouldn't even look at it."

"You sold me out for money you rodent? You put my family and extended family in danger?"

"Well, here is what is going to happen. After I have dispatched these people to the earth, I will come back, and if you are still here then your death will be long and slow. Or you can go to Tanna Head and see if you can try and fly from it. Your decision Judas."

Denny opened the door and then threw the photo of the guy at Mike. He turned and gave him an evil smile which started Mike crying.

As he walked through the door Ian asked if everything was okay.

"Job done Ian, and no I didn't before you ask. Please don't go near Tanna Head for a few days."

The last night was a very quiet affair with a lovely meal and talk of when Ian and Neala hope to arrive on the estate.

"What I am about to say to you goes no further. I am expecting a baby, but as you know when that happens to a women of my age, then there can be lots of complications. So, I would appreciate that you don't make a fuss over me and please don't tell Willie, or he will be on the phone every day."

They all wanted to give Neala a hug, but understood her emotions at this time.

It was an early night for everybody, as they had to leave early to catch the first ferry. Before they set off everyone said their goodbyes with Neala getting more hugs whether she wanted them or not. As they passed Mike Stewart's house, Denny and Ian just looked at each other, but nothing was said. They stopped at the school to say cheerio to Miss Glover and Miss Bryant.

"Miss Glover, please forgive me if I'm wrong, but it can't be long until you retire, so here is a proposition for you. Why don't you think about coming over and living with us in Bavaria? It's my intention through the Trust to have underprivileged children from all over Germany to come to the estate for adventure weekends. Also, to learn about the varied nature we have in the forests, and I propose to build some small buildings to use as classrooms. We would love to have you over to oversee it.

"Denny, you would do that for me? I'm in a bit of shock to be honest, but at the moment that feels like a beautiful idea. Let me think about it and I will contact Ian to get your phone number. Does that mean I will get to see the boys often?"

"Of course, it does and don't worry about living accommodation as Denny is building houses on our land for friends and family, except for Jinty Thomas here as you know how disruptive she can be."

Jinty was about to argue, but one look from Miss Glover defused the situation before it started. Things never changed.

"What about you Miss Bryant? I realise it's a while before you retire, but why wait? If my idea to have the children on the estate works then we can expand the adventure. Running the Western Isles Trust can easily be passed over to other people. Maybe some of the ex-pupils from Kismay?"

"Denny, I'm like Miss Glover here. I am struggling to speak, but please give me time to think about it and I can guarantee that I will get no sleep tonight for thinking about it."

They headed to the ferry after the boys had been smothered with hugs and kisses. Denny wondered when he would get his hugs. Maybe not.

At the ferry they said goodbye to Ian and started to walk on the boat before Denny said," Remember Ian, no matter how bad things get, then don't you dare come over. I will look after your 'wee' brother, promise. They shook hands and the Bavaria contingent boarded the boat on their journey home. The only eventful thing was Helen and Jinty sitting with their arms around each other at the stern watching Durma disappear. Denny stood looking out the window of the passenger waiting area wondering if he would ever see Durma again. His thoughts drifted to see what he could do to get his mum and dad's bodies exhumed and brought to Bavaria. Was that really fair though. Was it all about him.

True to their word the taxi was waiting for them, and they were soon on their way to Edinburgh and then the airport. Eventually, they were at the car parking at the airport terminal with the rain belting down. As Helen and Jinty made a run for it to the terminal entrance with the twins, Denny asked the taxi driver how his business was doing. He had said he was just keeping his head above water. Denny then pulled out an envelope from his inside pocket.

"There will be other people coming from and going to Durma, so I hope I can rely on you to give them the same service as you have given us. This is for you and remember you never picked us up and you never dropped us off here. Okay?"

As Denny walked away the driver opened the envelope and shouted," Hey mister, this is far too much, I could buy another cab with this."

"You keep it pal and remember, not a word."

The way Denny smiled the driver knew there was something evil about this guy, but with that amount of money tucked in his pocket he would drive the Devil around if he was asked. Maybe he just had.

Everyone was glad to be back in Munich with Willie driving them back to Zwiesel. Denny was sitting in the front and when he looked over he tried to work out what was wrong with him.

"What's the matter Willie? Your face is telling me you are worried about something. What is it?"

"Since you have been away I could see a lot of tension on the guy's faces. Probably just wondering when or if trouble is going to happen."

"There is no longer an 'if' in this equation Willie. It is going to happen as people have spent a lot of time and effort trying to find me and they have, according to the information I have procured. I will speak to everyone tomorrow before breakfast."

As they drove up to the house and parked, the dogs came out to meet him. Udo and Arno started to run to him, until Ottar give out two sharp barks and the dogs knew they would have to wait their turn as Ottar walked into Denny's arms as he knelt down. Denny felt it was good to be back, but he knew the hard work was about to start. Dangerous work.

Gertie had made a beautiful meal and they all sat outside eating. Denny had thanked the Hoffman brothers for helping to look after the estate with the usual wad of cash given to Gunther. They had protested as usual, but Denny had ignored it. He had asked them to be over by eight o'clock sharp tomorrow, but to enjoy the evening meal with everyone.

"How was that God forsaken 'shithole' of a rock called Durma, Denny?"

"Still as resplendent as ever brother and your loving brother and future sister in law send their regards."

"Future sister in law? Does that mean I am going to make another blooming speech Denny?"

"Seems like it Willie, but if you want some good news then here it is. They are coming to stay with us. As soon as we can get a house built for them in the fields at the bottom of the track. That is something I have to speak to you about. Whether you and Gertie want a house of your own down there as well."

"Not sure about that pal as the annex here has been our little love shack for a while now. Although you are all a bit close right enough when Gertie shouts out her 'Banshee' like squeals while we are making love."

Everyone just sat their laughing while Willie was looking perplexed as to why they found it amusing.

"Let's just leave that for another day brother." said Denny smiling.

Denny took the dogs out for their last walk, but sent Ottar home after a while which the dog seemed happy about. He went to his favourite spot to sit and watch the beautiful sunset. As the dogs sat with him he said, "Well boys it's definite. Evil is coming to us, and it won't be nice, but I have said this before. I will do everything humanly possible to protect everyone on this estate."

Denny looked at the vastness of the forests and wondered how in hell they were going to protect this mass of land. He knew that the meeting tomorrow would be a make or break time as to whether protecting this area was feasible or not. He also had to go and see Felix to ask for his help. When Denny got back they were still sitting out, so he sat with them playing with the boys before making an announcement.

"Just to let you know folks, that I won't ever be going back to Durma. Although there are some good memories, there are far too many bad ones and I'd rather they stay there. Mum and dad's graves are there, but they are elsewhere, and I know Ian has asked someone to look after the graves for me. If there is anything to do with the Western Isles Trust then Maria can deal with it. Maybe it's time for her to take a trip over herself."

They just looked at each other and let Denny make up his own mind.

As the light came through the window the next morning, Denny decided to get up as he hadn't got very much sleep at all. He showered and took the dogs for a walk. When he got back, Gertie was up, and she came out and asked how many would there be for breakfast. He told her six guys, and he wouldn't have minded if the men were served first, as there was to be a meeting as soon as they had eaten.

Yuri and Tomaz arrived early and there seemed a genuine look of relief on their faces seeing Denny standing there. Tomaz looked as if he couldn't wait for breakfast to be served. The Hoffmans arrived soon after and they all got stuck into breakfast. Denny wanted this meeting to be out of earshot of the girls, so he had wandered in and told them to stay away from the veranda until he told them it was okay to come out.

127

As the meeting started, it was Yuri who had said that he had drawn out a map of the forests and had marked on it the most likely directions that any perpetrators would come from, but he said it might not be possible, but they needed to know when they will be coming. Denny said he would contact Felix and he would able to keep an eye on the village accommodation and would be able to tell us if any strangers appear.

Denny asked if anyone could photocopy Yuri's map with a copy for everyone. Gunther said he would do that, but first he wanted to mark on the map where they should put bright spot lights up, so that the forest would light up like it was on fire. He said he could get the lights and they can be switched on by one remote control. A small trench had to be dug to take the cable to the main light and then connect it to the other lights with a simple thin cable through the branches. All lights to be sensor activated.

"Can I say something though Denny? Your arsenal of weapons is woefully short for what we are expecting. We have to have rifles with infrared scopes, and we have to carry hand guns. Also, knives. Whatever we all prefer."

Thanks Gunther and Yuri, you are filling me with a lot of confidence. Can you get us the guns Gunther?"

It was then that Jinty came onto the veranda asking if anyone wanted tea. Basically, to give the eye to Yuri.

"Jinty, get the fuck off this veranda, before I throw you off. I told you not to come out until I said it was okay to do so."

Jinty was about to argue.

"This is my house Jinty Thomas, so my rules. Now, get to fuck."

Jinty could see the evil look on Denny's face, so she ran inside.

"Anybody got anything else to add. Willie?"

"What have you planned about getting the girls and the twins away when it starts to kick off?"

"I am going to get them away as early as possible once I hear from Felix. Hopefully a day or two before, but remember I don't know when they will be coming. Then I will put them into the town house, but I haven't thought about how we will protect them there."

It was then that Gunther said to Denny that he had an idea, but he might not like it.

"After our release, we had to attend a rehabilitation course for newly released prisoners, otherwise we could be hauled back inside. A lot of these guys still have no jobs and are really struggling both financially and mentally. How about we ask half a dozen if they would be prepared to patrol the area around the town house when needed. We can't arm them obviously, but some of these guys are tough and not to be messed with. Remember though, they will be driven by money.

"Sounds like a plan Gunther, choose who you want, and we will have a meeting with them as soon as possible. Get back to me please. Right, that's us guys, we need to get to work. We know what is about to happen will be dangerous and possibly life threatening and as I have said before I won't hold it against anyone if they want to back out at this stage."

Nobody said a word.

"Right Thomas, if you want to flirt with Yuri then you have five minutes before we have to leave to do some work."

"Piss off Foggerty," came the reply from Jinty inside the house.

Helen came out before Denny left and asked if he could meet her at the start of the North trail, and she would bring his lunch along, as she wanted to speak to him. Everyone else would take theirs with them. Helen and Jinty started the laundry, and it wasn't long before lots of nappies were on the lines and blowing in the wind. It was obvious that this was going to be a day of loads of cups of tea and biscuits. While they sat watching the boys crawling around the veranda Helen had said to Jinty," How serious are you about Yuri, Jinty? Or is it you being caught on the rebound, after all its only been a few weeks since Scottie's accident. Tell me what you think Jinty."

"It feels like it might lead to something. You must admit he is quite a handsome guy, but he might snore in his sleep or have terrible wind problems, or he might be a really nice guy and awesome lover."

"Well, that just about covers the important points Jinty."

"Willie snores sometime girls, but he has no wind problems," said Gertie.

The girls started to laugh.

129

Chapter 7

Just before lunch Helen had said to the girls that she was away to take Denny's lunch to him. She said she would take Ottar with her, and she would have her radio with her, so she would be fine.

As they say, you never hear the bullet that is destined for you.

Denny had just said to Yuri he would have to head off to see Helen when he heard the shot and got on his radio.

"Was that you Willie? What the hell is happening down there?"

"I wasn't us Denny, but it came from down here somewhere. Wait a minute, I can see a white vehicle of sorts. I'm going after it and sending Tomaz back up to meet you."

Willie ran into the forest as fast as he could, while Tomaz sped off to where he would meet up with the other guys. Yuri and Denny were racing as fast as they could and eventually they could see Tomaz coming towards them. As they turned on to the home trail they heard a further two shots and hoped Willie was okay.

As they ran past a clump of trees they saw what they were dreading. Helen was lying in a heap at the foot of a tree. Ottar was standing there on three legs with his teeth bared, ready to protect Helen. Denny told the other two to stay back while he walked slowly toward Ottar with his hand out, telling him to take it easy and what a good dog he was. Eventually, Ottar lay down beside Helen.

"Oh God no, please no," roared Denny.

Helen lay there with the top of her jersey covered in blood and Ottar with blood dripping down his front right leg. Just then Tomaz appeared and ran forward to where Helen lay. He immediately took out a thin knife. Denny tried to stop him, but Yuri held him back. Tomaz delicately cut Helens jersey away around where the bullet had went through and gesticulated that he wanted something to put on the wound to stem the flow. Denny had a clean hankie and handed it to Tomaz who gently put it on the wound and put pressure on it. After a few minutes Tomaz removed the dressing and asked one of them for water. Yuri handed him his flask and Tomaz soaked the hankie, wiping the blood away. The bleeding had stopped. They could see that the bullet had ploughed a furrow across the top of Helen's right breast ending up in the tree she was lying up against.

Tomaz pointed to Helen and gave Denny the thumbs up indicating that she would be okay, before Denny picked her up and started to carry her back to the house, while asking Yuri to contact Gertie or Jinty on the radio to phone the local hospital and get a doctor up to the estate as well as the police as quickly as possible. Willie was sprinting to catch them up and when he saw Helen he completely lost it. Shouting, swearing and telling everyone what he would do to the person who had done this to Helen. Denny had told him to calm down.

Once they got to the house, Jinty and Gertie had prepared a bed in one of the downstairs' bedroom. They had the first aid kit and hot water and towels ready, and they cut Helen's jersey and bra off. Tomaz covering his eyes as he didn't want to see Helen's naked breast. He turned and grabbed Denny's arm and pointed towards Ottar and then pointed to himself. Although Ottar must have been in pain he was still standing looking at Helen. Tomaz indicated that he would need tweezers and bandages from the kit and Denny nodded. Tomaz took Ottar out of the bedroom and sat with him on the veranda just getting his trust before he could do anything.

Gertie asked everyone except Denny to leave the room to give Helen peace and quiet. It was then they heard a vehicle coming up the drive. Willie started to get his gun ready, but Denny could see it was the doctor, so he put a hand on Willie's arm. Following close behind was a police car and when it drew nearer Denny could see it was Officer Meyer. The doctor walked into the house and straight into the bedroom. Officer Meyer had been told it was the wife of the estate owner who had been shot, so he knew immediately to come to Denny. While everyone was seated Jinty came out with sweet tea and biscuits for everyone. Denny just gave her a smile.

When he looked over, Tomaz caught his eye as if to get permission to start patching Ottar up.

"Do you need a hand Tomaz? I could come and hold Ottar for you if you like?"

Tomaz was furiously shaking his head and pointing to himself. Denny watched him start taking out the splinters from Ottar's leg. The splinters that emanated from the tree bark when the bullet hit the tree. Denny marvelled at how gentle he was with the dog. He washed the wounds and bandaged them up. Two months ago, Tomaz would have run a mile from any dog.

The doctor asked Denny to come in to the bedroom.

"Mr Foggerty, your wife was a very lucky young lady. She has a deep laceration at the top of her right breast. I have stitched it and unfortunately there will be a scar, but it's something she will just have to put up with. However, please think what would have happened if she had taken another step and where the bullet would have ended up."

Helen was quite lucid when he bent over to give her a kiss.

"I'm sorry Denny, should I have had my rifle with me?"

"Don't worry, darling. Carrying a rifle wouldn't have stopped this. Try and get some sleep and I'll come in after and see how you are."

Denny thanked the doctor and asked if his practice could send his invoice to the trust in the town house.

"Of course, Mr Foggerty and remember she has to have rest and I will be back in a few weeks to take the stitches out. Goodbye."

Denny suggested that Yuri and Tomaz go home, but he would need to speak to everyone tomorrow morning.

"Do you think this is the start?" asked Yuri.

Denny just shook his head. He knew this was completely different. Before Tomaz left, Denny walked over to him and gave him a hug and thanked him with all his heart for looking after Helen and Ottar. Tomaz just gave him a smile and his usual thumbs up. Denny gave him the thumbs up back.

He sat down with Office Meyer and gave a statement, as did Willie, but Denny noticed that Willie had left a few details out and wondered why?

"Rest assured Mr Foggerty, we will do our best to apprehend these people and I will keep you updated."

He gave his usual salute and left.

Denny then went into the house and phoned Ian. He was out on the boat, but Neala was devastated by the news. She asked about the wound and told him not to worry as she had been very lucky. She asked if this had anything to do with what he had been talking to Ian about.

"No, I'm sure it hasn't Neala as my sixth-sense hasn't been telling me anything different, other than what has been going on lately. There is something in my head that I just can't fathom out, but it will come to me."

"Denny, do you think we should cancel our plans to come over. We would only be another couple for you to worry about?"

"Don't cancel anything please Neala. I swear on that beautiful wee scar on my wife's breast that it will be all sorted out before you even step on a plane. If Ian wants to phone tonight then great. Look after yourself please."

"And you Denny, and tell Helen we are thinking of her."

Denny then phoned Otto who wanted to come over straight away, but Denny had said no. Maybe in a few days and could he let everyone else know.

"Otto, can I tell you about Ottar. Even though he was bleeding, in pain and standing on three legs he was still prepared to protect Helen. At first I couldn't get near him as he was fixated on protecting her. He is fine now as one of the guys fixed him up with so much care and attention."

There was silence on the phone.

"Sorry, Denny I was a bit emotional there. He is such a lovely dog and wish I could have him forever, but we know that's not going to happen. If you want I could come over and pick him up?"

"I don't think he would thank you for that Otto considering all the attention he will be getting from everyone. Especially Helen."

Otto had told Denny he would thank the guy personally for fixing Ottar up.

Gertie was personally taking care of Helen, while Jinty had the boys. Willie had been a bit more shocked than he let on, so he had locked himself away in the annex. Denny needed time to think, so he shouted to Willie at the annex door that he was going to walk the dogs and that he was in charge of the house. All he got from Willie was a 'grunt', but that was normal at times from him.

Denny walked and jogged until he came to his favourite spot and sat down with the dogs who were just aimlessly wandering about sniffing for any smells they could find. He didn't want to put his head back just in case he fell asleep. The rain started to come down heavily and the dogs got under the tree with him, although he thought he might end up getting pushed out from under it. After a while he put his head in his hands and said to himself, 'I don't expect to cruise through this darkness Foggerty, but for all our sakes I promise, as I've promised before, that I will not leave any loose ends this time. If it means sacrificing myself, then I am prepared to do it.'

Denny was tired and he needed sleep. He really hoped that he would get some tonight, but he couldn't guarantee that. When he got home he went to see Helen who, was remarkably sitting up having a laugh with the girls.

"I thought you were supposed to be resting Helen?"

"I'm fine Denny, the girls have been cheering me up. Are you going to explain to me why you think this has happened. Do you think it was poachers Denny?"

"Not today Helen. We're both tired and I need to get my head around this. I have the answer tucked somewhere in my head, but I just can't get to grips with it. Maybe in a few days we will talk about it. Neala and Ian are asking after you and expect a visit from the town house within the next few days. When Willie comes in please try and placate him as he is feeling really bad about what has happened to you, as we all are."

"Denny, Jinty tells me that it was Tomaz who attended to me in the forest. Is that right?"

"Yes it was Helen. He was so gentle and knew exactly what he was doing, but was really embarrassed when your jersey was being cut away. He even hid his eyes."

"Oh, bless him Denny and I believe that Ottar got hurt and Tomaz attended to him as well."

Denny told her how Ottar stood protecting her even although he was injured and in pain. Helen shouted on him before Denny tried to tell her not to. Ottar came limping from outside into the bedroom. Even although she was in pain she grabbed him around the neck and hugged him.

"Thank you so much Ottar. You really are my beautiful boy."

Denny knew that was it, as Ottar started to make himself comfy next to her bed and Denny didn't fancy asking him to move. It was then that Gertie ushered Denny out as Helen needed sleep.

He sat outside with the boys and Jinty came out and joined him.

"I'm not sorry at shouting at you Jinty, but what happened to Helen could have happened to you for not doing as you were told."

"What, would somebody shoot me?"

"No, not somebody Jinty, me."

They both laughed, but she then got up, walked over, sat on Denny's knee, put her arms around his neck and cried her eyes out. Delayed shock thought Denny. It was then the phone rang, and it was Ian.

"What the bloody hell happened Denny? We are both in shock. You told Neala you didn't think it had anything to do with what is going to happen."

"No, I don't think so Ian, and I am beginning to think that she was in the wrong place at the time. I think it was me the shot was meant for, but I will work it out in the next few days. Please don't worry about coming over pal, as I told Neala I am going to sort this out and we will all be fine. You can wait until the house is built or come and stay with us. Although I think the former might be the correct decision with Neala being pregnant."

"You could be right Denny, but I wish I could be of more help."

"Ian, I don't want any more people out here. I have based all my plans on the amount of people I have here. Take care, and I will phone you in a couple of days or Helen will. Cheery."

Daylight was leaving the estate, and a full moon was staring down on him. This was when all the crazies were supposed to come out. Maybe one crazy with a rifle had come out a bit early. He wandered in and took the phone of the hook and went into Helen's room. She looked pale and tired, so he just gave her a kiss and told her to get rest and he would see her in the morning. Ottar wasn't for shifting so he left him happily beside her.

"Don't worry Mr Denny, I will sleep in this room tonight and Willie had said he will try and entice Ottar out for a last 'pee.'"

135

Denny could remember getting to his room, but that was all. The usual nightmares came and went, but when he woke he felt unusually fresh. He showered and went downstairs to see Helen. It was early and she was sitting up and chatting with both girls and feeding her boys.

"Don't say a word Denny, it's what I want and must do. I'm feeling sore, but overall better. Please come and have breakfast with me."

They had just finished eating when they heard the roar of the ATVs coming along the track.

"Are you up for seeing Yuri and Tomaz, Helen? I'm sure they will want to see you."

"Yeh, not a problem just show them in."

The two came in and stood either side of her bed with Tomaz slightly hesitant at first. Come here, she told him, then held him tight and kissed him on the cheek. He was a bit embarrassed with a red face and then tried to mimic how he had cut away her jersey and stopped the blood flow. To show her how he had been embarrassed he covered his eyes with his hand. She laughed and shouted for Jinty to come through as there was someone here to see her. It was a bit of a surprise for her to see Yuri standing there as she hadn't heard the ATVs coming. She walked around the bed and gave Yuri a long hug. He wasn't for letting her go. They laughed when they saw Tomaz hiding his eyes with his hand.

"Helen, half of Bavaria will be over to see you. I can see the Hoffman's jeep coming up the track. Do you want to see them?"

"Of course."

"Bloody diva." murmured Denny.

He called a meeting with all the men and again told the women to stay inside.

"Right, listen up guys. Don't anybody think that was the start of what is to come. It won't start with a single gunshot through the trees. Willie, you omitted to tell the police officer something. Can you please tell us what it is."

"Simple pal. After the initial shot you heard two other shots, and they were fired by me. My sight was blurred by the trees, but I managed to get off two shots into a vehicle speeding down one of the tracks. It looked like some sort of pickup and was either cream or dirty white. The bullet holes give us something to go on

136

to catch the bastards that did this, and then it will be 'curtains' for them as I don't think the police are capable of catching them."

"Sorry to disappoint you Willie, but we are doing this by the book. We are going to find them, but then hand them over to Office Meyer. We can't have the estate under the spotlight with what is coming up."

"Are you joking Foggerty? Your wife is lying through there having nearly been killed and you want to hand them over to the police? What are you about thinking pal?"

"Trust me Willie. I have something to show you all."

Denny walked inside and came back with a bag and then produced the jersey that Helen had been wearing. He then asked everyone if they recognised it. They all knew in an instance what he was getting at. It was his jersey. He had worn it many times while out working.

"Helen must have picked it up and put it on before coming to meet me. They weren't out for Helen, they were out for me. I told some of you that something in my head was bothering me about all this and I'm finally figuring it out. A good few years ago, on my first visit here, I encountered some poachers for want of a better word. I asked them to leave, but they refused, and it ended up badly for them. Their mode of transport that day was an off white pick-up. Willie, could the passenger you briefly saw have been a girl?

"Every possibility Denny."

"Okay, everybody just be on high alert and let's all get back to work, but remember if any of the girls ask then we just say it could have been a lone poacher."

As Tomaz got up, he pointed to the bedroom where Ottar was lying and asked in his own way if he could change his bandages. Denny had given him the nod to go ahead, but told him not to change the dressing on Helen's breast. Everyone started laughing as Tomaz went in to the bedroom with his hand over his eyes.

Before they went to work Willie said," Denny, can you imagine what would have happened if Helen had been carrying one of the boys?"

"It's went through my mind a hundred times. Don't worry Willie, they are not going to get away with it. I promise."

137

The day was uneventful which everybody was thankful for, and when they got back to the house Helen was up and about.

"Hey Jinty, I think you need to go back to that bakery business you have in a few days. We love you and we have appreciated your help, especially with the boys. Maybe Yuri would like to come down one night to see the house and bakery. What do you think?" said Denny.

"I would love that, what do you think Yuri?"

Yuri just smiled and nodded.

"Bloody hell, you're a man of few words aren't you?"

An even bigger smile came over his face.

That night, Denny had told everyone that he was off down the town to see Felix. After parking the jeep, he must have looked in six bars before eventually tracking him down. As he wandered in he heard Felix shout to the barman for a coffee for Denny and a large Jägermeister for him. Denny knew it would be him paying, so he went to the bar, paid, and left enough for Felix to have a few drinks when he left. The usual agreement.

"Felix, I am sure you will have heard what happened to Helen, so I am wondering if you can help me. I'm looking for a white or off white pick-up truck driven by a guy with possibly a women passenger. The passenger side will have two bullet holes in it. I'm sorry I can't give you more information."

Felix just tapped the side of his nose with his finger and winked.

"I am sorry to hear about your wife Denny and I wish her a speedy recovery. Rest assured you will have your answer within a couple of weeks at the latest. Unfortunately, I am going away for a few days, or I would be contacting you sooner. Denny and Felix sat talking for a while, before Felix had said Denny should be back home with his wife. Just as he was about to get up, Denny slipped an envelope under the table with Felix pocketing it swiftly.

"You might need to grease some palms pal."

"You think?"

After a few days Helen was getting back to normal, so Jinty had decided to go home.

"Thank you so much Jinty for all your help. We don't know what we would have done without you and Gertie. Please pop up soon. Oh, by the way what do you really think of Yuri or is this just you on the rebound?"

"I'm still a bit confused about him Helen. Some days I get a bit excited thinking about him and others I am thinking I might be rushing into things. Although to be honest I would like to see him naked before I make any judgement."

Jinty then gave a dirty laugh.

Helen gave her a kiss on the cheek and whispered in her ear that she was just a 'hussy'.

One lunchtime, Denny and Yuri were sitting eating and Denny said he would like run things past him. He told Yuri all his plans to keep everyone on the estate safe once the turmoil kicked off and wondered what he thought. Yuri sat pondering for a while.

"Your plan is sound, and I am sure we will all come through this unscathed. However, remember what you have been continually telling us, and that is you will not leave any loose ends this time. Well, don't you think they will just send more and more people after us if they fear we have dispatched the first lot on their way? Also, what do we do with the bodies? I know Karl wants a run through with your plan and that is a good idea. I would also like your thoughts on how many men do you think they will send?"

"I'm glad you have asked these questions Yuri. Firstly, I think the people that will come will just be hired thugs looking for a quick pay day. I don't think there will be a lot of planning and I don't think they will send more than five or six men as they will be expendable. To send anymore could attract interest from the authorities. The bodies? Well, if your dad is still able and your excavator is still working, then could you ask him if he could dig a hole big enough to accommodate the dead bodies. Preferably in a bog just far enough away from your house, but without compromising himself or the excavator. Once Gunther and Karl have put the lights up I think we should do a run through of the plan, but not just once. Let's do it time and time again. To go back to your question on loose ends then I have a plan to take the fight to them Yuri. I am going back to Scotland to finish it. Do you fancy coming with me?"

When they all got back to the house after work Helen was sitting feeding the boys. Denny hadn't realised how big they were getting and promised himself to spend more time with them.

The Czech boys headed off and Denny had asked Willie to come for a walk with the dogs through the forest as he needed to speak. They weren't far from the house before Denny told him his plan for when the time comes. This made Willie feel important, as if Denny was asking for his approval. Willie never came up with anything more than Yuri had, so as far as Denny was concerned he would run it past Tomaz and the Hoffmans and stick to it. No matter what.

After their evening meal the phone had rung, and Gertie had answered it and shouted to Denny it was for him. When Denny had answered it he found it was Ian.

"Hi Denny, we were just wondering how Helen was. We have been thinking about her. On a more sobering piece of news, I thought I would let you know that Mike Stewart is dead. He was seen just walking off the edge of Tanna Head yesterday. One of the guys picking up his lobster pots had seen him just walk forward and fall. The fisherman had said there was nobody with him."

"Helen is on the mend Ian, but she will take a bit of time to recover. What I have discovered is that she was wearing my jersey. She just picked it up on the way out to meet me. That shot was meant for me Ian and I think I now know who it was, but I intend to go down the route of turning them into the police, but as I have told Willie they won't get away with it. Good news for me with regard to Mike Stewart though."

"Bloody hell Denny. When we were over, Neala and I had taken the boys in their slings for a walk. It could have been either of them. It doesn't bear thinking about."

"Do you think I am doing the right thing by turning him or them into the police Ian?"

"I'm not sure pal. Morally yes. Personally, I would put a lump of lead in between his eyes."

"That's the problem I am going to have with Willie though. He would just shoot him and to hell with the consequences, so I have to be careful with him Ian. Anyway, I will get Helen to phone Neala tomorrow night."

When Yuri arrived with Tomaz in the morning he told Denny that they had come across several dead foxes on their way home the previous night. They hadn't been stripped of their pelts, but just dumped.

"What do you think happened there Yuri?"

"It seems to me that he either dropped them as he couldn't carry them, or he just didn't notice that they had fallen."

"I think it might be the time to have a word with this guy Albescu. If I come over in the next few days can you show me where he lives? Or possibly where he drinks? Anyway, how is your father?"

"He woke us at four thirty this morning with the bloody excavator going. This was him starting to dig the hole as you requested. I told him he didn't have to do it right away, but he is not well at the moment, and he just possibly wants to get it done This will be him now until the hole is deep enough. Only then will we get some sleep in the mornings. Mind you there is a storm brewing over the mountains at the back of the farm and it looks bad, so I think the hole will be filled with water sooner rather than later."

Yuri had no sooner spoken when Denny felt the first few spots of rain.

"Let's not head out to the forest just yet, as I really don't want to be sitting under a tree for half the day. I think some strong coffee might be in order."

As they sat outside the rain was getting worse. Tomaz motioned if it was okay to go and see Ottar. Denny just nodded. He was no sooner inside when he came running out again with his hands over his eyes again.

Helen came out laughing and told them that Tomaz had caught her with just her bra and pants on.

"Lucky him," said Willie.

"Give it a rest McLeod," said Denny.

Willie then grabbed Tomaz and took his hand away from his eyes. He jokingly started to rub his knuckles over his head and pull his ears and nose. He turned round laughing and looked at Yuri and Denny who weren't even smiling.

"He's got a knife aimed at my heart hasn't he?"

"Pretty much," said Denny.

141

Willie looked down to see Tomaz smiling, with a large thin knife aimed at his heart.

"How the hell does he do that?"

The rain was getting heavier so Denny told the brothers that they could go home anytime they wanted. Denny thought Yuri might try and hang around to see if Jinty would appear.

"Yuri, why don't you take one of the jeeps and go down and see Jinty for an hour or two? I need to show Tomaz how to step up Ottar's recovery."

"Are you sure that would be okay?"

Denny nodded and said he would see him sometime. Yuri headed off and Denny said to Tomaz that he was going to tell him what to do with Ottar.

"Right, call him now."

Tomaz gave out a very sharp whistle, whereby Willie nearly jumped out of his seat.

"Bloody hell Foggerty, can you not explain to him to keep the volume down with his whistles. I'm away to clean the guns and then see if Gertie might like a bit of loving from Willie the Love Master."

This time Denny didn't even shake his head. Instead, he put his arm around Tomaz and took him to see Ottar. Denny showed him how to stretch Ottar's legs and gently massage him along his back.

"Ottar has been lying about getting pampered for too long, so I'm putting you in charge of getting him fitter with stretching and gentle exercise. When you and Ottar are ready I will tell and show you how to get him to attack the genitals of a perpetrator. Ottar knows what to do, but he needs certain commands, but we will need to show him hand gestures obviously. So, if you want to stay over sometime and look after him, then fine by me. What do you think?"

Denny thought his head might drop off with the nodding he was doing. Just then Helen came out and asked if her little hero was still here. She walked over, put her arms around him and kissed him on the cheek, then told Denny she was going to phone Neala.

"You get more kisses from her than I do Tomaz so cherish them."

Tomaz got on with looking after Ottar, albeit with one very red face. He started to take off Ottar's dressing and gave Denny the thumbs up. For never really having known the dog, Denny thought that Tomaz was showing a lot of trust in him. Tomaz stretched out Ottar's legs and then took him for a short walk into the wood. Denny had shouted and told him off for not carrying his rifle, Tomaz ran back and collected it along with his radio, looking very sheepishly.

About an hour later Yuri had arrived back in the jeep and Denny had asked him if everything was okay down at the bakery. Denny got his answer when Yuri opened the back of the jeep, and it was stacked full of breads and pastries. Denny told him to take as much as they both could carry on the back of their ATVs. He had supplied them with waterproof sheets to cover the goods on the back.

For the next few days, the rain teamed down and work in the forest was nigh on impossible. Denny would have been as well telling everybody not to turn up, but he wanted them to be on as high alert as possible. He told Yuri he could use the jeep to go and see Jinty, but only after the work time was over. Denny phoned the Hoffmans and asked where the security lights were and Karl had told him they were coming over that morning, but they had to be careful using electricity in this weather. When they arrived, Denny had insisted that the lights were to go up, rain or no rain, ready to be connected when the weather lifted.

Karl and Gunther had worked tirelessly putting the lights up and were continually getting soaked until the lights were up. Denny told them to come into the house and remove their waterproofs. As if on que, Gertie had produced a large pot of steaming hot coffee and plum jam sandwiches.

"I will tell you something Gertie, when you get fed up of the Love Master, then I think I will look into having you as my second wife, what do you think?" said Denny.

"Please Mr Denny, your making me blush. I don't think Mrs Helen would like that."

"It wouldn't bother me Gertie," said Helen as she walked out the door. "It will make a change from him pounding incessantly into me Gertie."

"Please, the both of you stop, as I really am getting embarrassed now, and Willie is sitting over there."

"Don't listen to them Gertie, the Love Master is only getting going and he has a few quirky moves still to come from Willie's book of Masterful Love Making."

"Is that quirky or perverted Willie," said Denny.

Denny knew he had to get them focused, so when they were finished eating he said, "Okay, please listen everyone. We have to get ourselves prepared for the onslaught, however large or small it's going to be. What we are going to do is that every morning we are going to have a trial run of our plan to repel the bastards that are coming for me. It doesn't matter the weather. I want you to get angry, very angry when we are going through these trial runs. More angry than you ever thought you were capable of. It will keep you alive. The way my sixth-sense is telling me is that I believe it won't be long, but what I do know is it will give me a heads up. Also, there is a man in the village that should be able to tell us when these scum arrive and when they propose to come for me. His name is Felix. However, I must firstly find the person that shot my wife and hand them over to the police in Zwiesel. Felix is going to give me his name sooner rather than later. Anybody got anything to add?"

"Yes Denny, Karl and I have a few bits and pieces in the boot of the car that you asked for plus a few extras."

When Karl had opened the lid of the boot Denny was a bit shocked and what went through his mind was that if he needed to kit out an army, then he knew who to come to. He shouted to Helen and Gertie to go inside and then for Tomaz, Yuri and Willie to join him.

"Everyone take a rifle and infrared scope each, as well a handgun of your choice. I'm not sure about what knives we should have, but our little expert here will let us know what we need."

Tomaz was in his element showing everyone what they could do with each knife. Unfortunately, Willie was the person that Tomaz was demonstrating on, and everyone was smiling at Willie's grimaces.

"If everyone is happy with their choices then I suggest that you and Tomaz carry them with you at all times Yuri, as well as the knives which I can justify you having them while working in the forests. However, both you and Karl, Gunther will have to leave your guns here as I can't have you driving about with them in the car. Willie, can you take the handguns along with the spare knives and we will put them in a metal container and put them in a hiding place that has easy access. The spare rifles and radios can go in the gun cabinet in the gun room. We can't justify too many guns around here."

He knew he had to lighten the mood, so he shouted on Helen and Gertie to come out.

"Girls, sorry to spring this on you, but we are going to have a party tomorrow for everybody. Yuri, how long do you think it would take you to bring your father over if you used the jeep? I'm not sure which roads you would use though. Assuming he is capable, and he would like to come. Helen, you can contact Jinty, and I'm sorry I have never asked you Karl and Gunther, if you had partners. If so, please ask them if they would like to come."

Helen just looked at Denny, shook her head, but gave him a lovely smile. She knew why he wanted to give the party. He needed everyone's spirits raised.

"Let's be over here for two o'clock and we will start our trial runs the day after. Karl, please get the electricity to these lights pronto, as I want to see them working. Remember, it's your strategy we are enacting so please get it right. I will pay you cash for what you brought over in boot."

"Denny, give me three hours tomorrow and they will be ready."

Yuri said he would ask his dad and if he used the jeep it would take him just under an hour to get here.

"Take the jeep Yuri, and if your dad is not able to go back then he can stay here with Tomaz.

"Are you inferring I might be staying elsewhere Denny," he said while smiling.

Karl was true to his word and after Gunther and him were finished they headed home saying they would be back for the get together.

They had all arrived before two o'clock and it was introductions all round. Yuri had introduced his dad Artem to the family and there was a bright smile on his face when the girls had given him a hug. The Hoffmans had introduced their partners as Ada and Gisela. Before they all went into the dining room, Denny had introduced them all to the three dogs. The dogs just stood there looking, until Tomaz called for Ottar to come to his side. He then pointed to him before pointing to himself, as if Ottar was his. His dad looked at Tomaz and smiled with tears in his eyes.

"Remember Artem, no bloody tears from the men in this house. Helen and Jinty have the rights to them."

Artem laughed and wiped his eyes with his hankie. Denny knew he wasn't long for this earth and seeing Tomaz happy made him emotional. Introductions over, they all paraded into the dining room. Denny saw the look on the Hoffman partners and Artem's faces at the opulence.

"Ladies, Artem, although we have all this around us we are just simple people so don't think anything else. Let's go and eat. Tomaz get that bloody dog out of the dining room, you know he's not allowed."

Tomaz looked crestfallen and put his hand on Ottar's neck and made a hand gesture to him which Denny had never seen before. Ada and Gisela were lovely looking girls, and their English was pretty decent, so conversation amongst everyone was good. He wondered how they had hooked up with the Hoffmans. Tomaz made up for his lack of conversation with his hand gestures and laughed in his own way. More a smile than a laugh.

The food was exceptional as always, and Denny thought that after everything was settled they should do this again. Assuming they would be alive.

The get together went on until five o'clock. Ada and Gisela spent a lot of time with the boys and even Artem was telling them a Czech fairytale, which to Denny sounded a bit 'dark'. The two girls offered to help Helen and Gertie with the dishes, but they said it was fine. Denny and Willie got to know the brothers better, and it appeared they had led a very chequered life. Denny didn't want to enquire too much, but was glad he had them as friends instead of enemies. After another hour the Hoffmans were away. Artem and his boys were sitting under the roof of the veranda with the rain 'belting' down, so happy and content. Denny approached them and sat down.

146

"How about tonight, that you and Tomaz stay with us Artem and Yuri can head down the road with Jinty. If nothing else it will get her from under my feet. You will then get to experience Gertie's fabulous breakfast."

Both Artem and Tomaz started to protest that they didn't have any clothes to sleep in before Denny said, "Lads, where I came from it was often minus two degrees with a windchill factor of minus five and there was no clothes worn in bed. In Scotland it is sacrilege to wear anything in your bed except for a bare naked lady, so you are not going to go to bed with any clothes. You're going 'butt naked'. Sound okay?"

Artem couldn't stop laughing, and Denny wasn't sure that Tomaz really knew what was going on. Just then Jinty walked out, and Denny said that she was taking Yuri home tonight. Denny told her he was fed up of seeing her here. She put on an angry face and ran, did her usual, and with her legs splayed landing on Denny's lap knocking him over in the seat. As she straddled him she said, "Listen Foggerty, before I let you up, just admit that you will miss me." Artem couldn't believe what was happening. He looked over at Yuri who just shrugged his shoulders. Then at Tomaz, who was imitating a yawn.

"Yuri, please come and catch your 'wee Scottish lassie' will you?"

Yuri walked over as Denny lifted her by the waist and literally threw her into his arms. Artem was shocked at the strength of Denny, but a smile came over his face seeing his son with a lovely girl in his arms.

Willie had slept through all of this while lying on one of the outside sofas.

Helen came out with the coffee and sat down beside Artem, at one stage it looked like she was force feeding him Gertie's biscuits.

"Right, Tomaz let's go and get some waterproofs and we will walk the dogs, but not Ottar as that will be your job when we get back. Remember any wet dog has to be dried with a towel, especially their legs."

When they were walking through the forest, Tomaz was trying out his newly made up hand signals on Arno and Udo who were basically just ignoring him. Denny was trying hard not to laugh.

"Tomaz, I want to ask you a few things. Please answer me truthfully. Do you know why you can't talk or was it being stuck in the bog that did it?

Tomaz turned his head and Denny was sure he was going to say something, instead he just shrugged his shoulders. It was then that Denny knew that the little 'bugger' could speak anytime he wanted to, but chose to be in his own wee world.

"The last, but most important answer now Tomaz. When we have to fight these people that are coming for me, can you kill any of them?"

Tomaz thought for a minute before drawing his finger over his throat and smiling. Denny thought that would do for him.

They soon turned and headed home, but before they took the dogs in Denny said," Tomaz, what is it that you whisper in Ottar's ear when you are supposedly teaching him hand gestures?"

Tomaz quickly turned to Denny with a surprise look on his face.

"Don't worry wee man. Your secret is safe with me, but if you ever have to shout to save somebody's life then you will bloody well do it."

Another smile crossed Tomaz's face. They dried the dogs and then Tomaz wandered off to get Ottar. When Denny walked in to the house Artem had said did they mind if he went up to his bedroom, and he might just end up going to bed as he was very tired. Both Helen and Denny had said that was fine and Helen would take him up. When she came down she asked Denny if he knew if there was anything wrong with Artem?

"Come and sit with me Helen. I don't want you getting upset, but Artem is dying of cancer and may not have a long time left. When that happens I don't know what will happen to Tomaz if Jinty and Yuri become an item. I have no doubt that Yuri will look after him, but if they happen to start living together, then they will want their own space and privacy. The way they look at each other I can see that happening at some stage."

"What's going to happen to Tomaz though Denny? Will he come and live with us?"

"No Helen. It will all work itself out, trust me."

Denny phoned Gunther and asked him if he could set up the meeting with the ex-cons for tomorrow night. Gunther said he could and wondered if Denny would be okay with holding it in one of the back rooms of the local bars. Denny didn't have a problem with that and to make it for seven o'clock. He knew things were falling into place and just needed Felix to come through.

Next day all the men were assembled ready to go for a trial run. Yuri had arrived back with a smile on his face and Tomaz giving him the thumbs up. The rain lay heavily on the forest which tended to keep the light out.

"Okay, everyone remember that this is Karl's plan and if we have to tweak it to make it better then we will do it when we come back, not during the exercise. Over to you Karl."

Karl had spoken to Denny previously about his plan and Denny had agreed with it although he was keen to see it in action.

"Both Denny and I agree that it's most likely that they will come from the south west and it will be at night and through the trees, but they will use the tracks that are already there. Even given the fact that they have been given a heads up by that bastard Scottie giving them a tour round the forest. The bank of trees running parallel with the main track is virtually impenetrable, so the chance of anybody coming through that way is nil, but I suggest that we leave Ottar sheltering under one of the trees ready to pounce if somebody does come through. Each dog to be trained to rip any of the perpetrator's balls off. Willie, can you be waiting at the far end of the bank of trees where you can cover some of the animal trails. If by chance anything goes bad then high tail it back to the house and take up a defensive position with one other person still to be decided on."

"Does it mean I can put a bullet in their brain then Denny?"

"Of course, now no more interruptions unless it's important. Got that Willie?"

Karl then gave everyone a new radio and put them all on the same wavelength. He then showed them all where they would be positioned, all hidden by bushes, but protected by a tree in front of them. He told them they were to open fire when the lights went on, not before.

"I have the remote switch ready to light up the forest, as I will be well in front of you all and I will wait until they have all walked past me. Please, though I am relying on you to do the shooting, as I don't want to be firing back at you. Denny, please keep the dogs well protected until we have everyone accounted for, but if anyone does a runner then unleash them. Okay, we go back to the house and then go full throttle this time where I will disappear, and I will call you all on the radio to get you all into your positions, fast. I want you to fire one shot only into the distance as soon as the lights go on."

"What about you," said Yuri.

"Yeh, what happens if they find you and shoot you Karl," said Willie.

"Then I would be dead Willie," he said laughing.

Willie didn't quite get the irony.

"Don't worry about me, you and the guys that are coming won't even know where I am never mind hit me."

They were all waiting nervously when the call came through. They ran as fast as they could with Denny positioning Ottar under a tree with plenty of foliage and within only a few minutes they were all waiting for the lights going on. Even though it was daylight the forest was as bright as a sunny, summer's day when they did go on. They could see for miles through the trees. The commencement of shots started and finished just as quickly. The silence was eerie. Denny looked at the dogs and found them salivating, wondering what they had to retrieve. Their radios crackled.

"Okay, I am switching the lights off so can you please move forward to where the stream is. I want to show you the effect of the lights."

They all moved forward and then stood facing where the lights were positioned. Nothing happened, until Karl pressed the remote again. The lights were blinding everyone. Even the dogs were running around yelping."

"Switch the bloody lights off Karl for God's sake," shouted Willie.

Everyone stood trying to get their eyes adjusted after the lights went out. Denny went on the radio and asked Karl if that was it for the day, but there no response. He tried again, but still nothing.

"Okay, everyone let's head home," said Denny.

Willie had just started to ask where they thought Karl was when a hand went on to his shoulder and Karl said he was here. Willie just about passed out with fright.

"Don't you ever fucking do that again Karl. I was ready to shoot you."

As they all walked back, Karl had said they needed to shave at least a minute off their time otherwise somebody might die. Denny said that was a sobering thought.

When they got back the Hoffmans left, but not before Denny telling Karl what a great job he did this morning and saying to Gunther he would meet him at the shop just before seven o'clock.

"Right, everyone let's get some work done while the rain stays off. Artem, please look after Ottar for Tomaz and make sure the girls pamper you."

"Okay, Denny I will try my best to let the girls look after me."

Denny walked away from Artem who had another big smile on his face.

"Remember Tomaz, that as soon as you finish work you have to tend to Ottar."

Denny put his ear down to his mouth wondering if he would say anything, but all Tomaz did was slowly shake his head and grinned. Not a smile this time, just a grin.

After tea, Yuri used the jeep to take Tomaz and his dad home, but Denny had said he wanted to speak to him first thing tomorrow.

Denny was early outside their shop. As he sat waiting he wondered how he had got himself, and others into this mess. Had he just been pure evil when dealing with the scum he had encountered in his life. However, could he not have just turned a blind eye to what was happening around him. He wondered if other people thought the same way as him. Probably. He promised himself it would soon be over. Just then Gunther came out of the shop and got in the car.

"Just tell me where to go pal. Is there likely to be a problem with any of the guys tonight? I can't say I am in the mood to get 'crap' from anybody."

151

"Don't worry I can vouch for them all, although one young guy can be a bit of a hothead, but that might not be a bad thing considering what we are asking them to do."

Ten minutes later they were walking into the bar, with the barman just nodding to Gunther. When they walked into the back room, six men sat around a table eyeing up Denny. Gunther greeted them and introduced Denny. They just nodded at him.

"Thanks for coming lads. Hopefully you can understand English, if not Gunther will translate. I don't know if Gunther has explained what the job entails, but if not, then here goes. Within the next month or so, some bastards from where I used to live are going to try and take me out. Maybe even my family and friends. I'm not going to let that happen. When they do come, then I am taking my family and a few friends to the Albach Town house where they will be protected inside. However, I need the six of you surrounding the building making yourselves as highly visible as possible. Unfortunately, you cannot have any firearms or knives. You will only be a visual deterrent. If you feel someone is a danger then deal with them. I will square anything away with my good friend, Officer Meyer. Any questions on the job itself."

One lad enquired as to the length of time the job will last?

"As from tonight all of you, if you accept my offer, will be on my payroll until it's over. I expect the incident, for want of a better word will only last a night and a day. However, I expect you to be on standby at a moment's notice. On the night in question, you will hear shots coming from my estate, but ignore it. We will be killing the scum that have come for me. The excuse will be that fireworks are being let off for my boys' birthday party."

"How much force can we use? Remember we are not long out of jail."

"As much as you need to, considering they attacked you and the Trust has the finest lawyers in the whole of Europe who will prove it was justification on your part. I will pay you a week's money tonight and Gunther will pay you at the end of each week until the job is done. Also, if you do a good job, then I will try and get you a job within the Trust, assuming you want it. It might not be great, but at least it's work, and you will be receiving a good income. Please leave your phone numbers with Gunther and he will contact you daily. Remember though, as soon as Gunther contacts you saying it is happening then you move and move fast."

Denny went in to his inside pocket and took out several wads of cash and handed one to everybody. When they saw how much Denny had given them they just looked at each other.

"Mr Foggerty, I thought you said you would give us a week's money? This is more than I used to earn in six month."

"If my family are safe after all this, then I will give you a bonus that will make your eyes water. I'm leaving now, but I will put some deutschmarks behind the bar for a drink. Stay safe."

"Are you not staying for a drink Mr Foggerty?"

"Best not," said Denny as he walked out the room laughing and went into the bar and handed the barman a wad of cash for him as well as the drink money for the men.

"Remember, none of us were here."

He was leaving nothing to chance.

The barman put a crooked forefinger to his brow, then Denny and Gunther left the bar. As he drove back, Denny again thought how easy it was to do things when you had a lot of money. The next step in his plan was to speak to Yuri tomorrow morning. His head started to hurt. His temples were throbbing. Why did his life have to be like this? He just wanted to be with Helen and his boys. How hard could that be. He knew that when he got home he had to phone Shonagh.

"Hi Denny, nice to hear from you, but I fear this is not going to be good news, is it?"

"I suppose you could call it both good and bad news Shonagh, but before I start can I ask how you and Jack are and how both your jobs are?"

"We are both fine Denny, although I'm still getting a small bit of nerve pain in the arm near to the shoulder. I have it under control with medication, but I have been told that it may get worse. The job is okay, but I miss being out on investigations and the odd raid. Jack is studying hard for his sergeant's exam with ambitions to go into the CID. Other than that, we just get on with it. There is one thing I must say to you and get it off my chest. That is, I can't get our love making that night out of my head. I know it sounds silly, as Jack and I have a good relationship, but he hasn't given me the fulfilment you gave me that night. I keep hoping that it will come, but no. Sorry Denny, I just had to say it and maybe now I can move on, but I'm not holding my breath. Anyway, what were you phoning me about?

"That was a bit of a revelation Shonagh. I also have thought back to that night, but I remember you telling me that we had to keep our relationship professional, and it couldn't happen again. You were right to think like that as I was a drunkard, and ready to press the self- destruct button. I hope we have a good friendship, and it will carry on through the years. However, I am going to make you a once in a lifetime offer. In Munich there is a world renowned Neurosurgeon based about an hour away from us. How about you fly over, and I will get him to examine you to see if there is anything he can do. If he can't then you will just have to carry on with medication. What have you got to lose?"

"Denny, you surprise me every time I speak to you, and I will give your offer some serious thought. Okay, your turn now."

"You know we were on Durma for a short visit, and it was lovely I suppose for Helen and Jinty, but my head was full to bursting about who was coming after me. In the end I found out who was giving my enemies all the information about me. I don't know if you want hear this but here goes. Mike Stewart."

There was silence on the phone as Denny waited for a reaction, but eventually he had to say.

"Are you still there Shonagh? For fuck sake say something will you."

"So sorry Denny, I can hardly speak as I am too shocked. He was such a nice man when I met him. Are you definitely sure? I'm not disbelieving you, but bloody hell he was an ex-policeman. An Islander. Shocked doesn't come close to how I am feeling. How did you find out it was him?"

"I had photos of a guy that was prowling around our estate for a while, and when I showed people on the island if they knew him they had said he was often seen with Mike Stewart."

"You do know that he had an accident when he fell off a cliff. Oh, please tell me it was an accident Denny and not you?"

"Shonagh, I will tell you the truth. I sat in his cottage listening to his pathetic excuses about how he wanted to help his granddaughter through university, but he was struggling on his police pension. He also said that he didn't think he did anything wrong by giving information to the guy, seeing as he thought I was heavily involved in the incident. So, he took the thirty pieces of silver. However, I did give him two options Shonagh. The first was that after I had despatched the scum that are after me to the earth, then I would come back and end his life in a horrible fashion. Or he might like to think about trying to fly off Tanna Head. I knew he had taken the second option when Ian had phoned me. I make no apologies for my actions Shonagh, as that 'rodent' has helped to put my family in grave danger."

"Oh, what a screw up this is Denny. I feel for you and the family. If there is anything I can do then I will."

"There is one thing, but I think it could be a long shot. Mike Stewart did say that the guy had let slip that he worked indirectly for someone who was high up in the British Government, but was connected to the Scottish office. I realise though it could be anybody."

"Denny, the best person for this is Tommy with his connections. He can ask if any of his previous colleagues have presently anybody on their radar, but be warned Denny, going up against a Government official is playing a very dangerous game. The police would always be on his side. I will speak to Tommy."

"Don't worry Shonagh, I am going to end this once and for all. I don't want you to get involved, but during the course of your job if you hear of anything that might be related to me, not specifically by name, but by nature then please let me know. Oh, and I have thought about your problem with you and Jack. You haven't asked him to put his hand up your shirt."

"Foggerty you bastard, you're never going to let that go are you? Denny? Denny?"

She was then speaking to herself. It had been lovely speaking to him though. She then smiled.

Everyone was inside and Denny sat alone on the veranda contemplating what was going to happen in the next few days or weeks. It was making him so tired, but he knew he had to be on top of his game if everyone was to survive. He woke up about one o'clock having fallen asleep in the chair. He still had his rifle tucked under his arm. He looked out into the forest and wondered if he had put a curse on this place. His demons were still with him. He gave his usual evil smile and raised his rifle to the forest. There was nobody there. He headed off to bed to get some sleep for what is was worth.

The men arrived early, and Gertie had everything ready for their breakfast. Denny said to Yuri that as soon as he was finished then he needed to speak to him.

"Yuri, I am having a problem with where you and Tomaz are living while this episode is going on. I'm hoping that I can give us as much notice as possible as to when this might kick off, but I can't say for definite. The problem is that you and Tomaz are at least thirty minutes away, but I really need you nearer. As you know we have a shooting lodge just five minutes away in the North East forest. When I arrived here I had some workmen over to renovate it. I personally think it would be okay to live in for a while. Also, there is ample room for the three of you. I'll give you the keys and make a slight detour tonight on your way home and see what you think. Obviously, you can head home after this is over if you all wish. Let me know tomorrow morning, but to be honest I can't really take no for an answer. Right, we need to have another run through as I see everyone is waiting."

Day after day they went through the drill, until Karl had said they were as ready as they could be. The Czech brothers and their dad had moved into the lodge, and they all seemed happy with the arrangement especially Artem, as he would often wander down to see the boys along with Helen and Gertie for a bit of a 'blether'. Naturally, with a few coffees and cakes thrown in. Denny had asked him if Yuri had told him about what was going to happen, and he said he had and if there was anything he could do then he was up for it. Denny knew that when it was time he would ask him to stay behind with his rifle just in case anyone approached from the main track up to the house.

It was now just a case of waiting, but there was a nervousness about the place.

Before he left to work Denny had spoken to the Hoffmans and asked if they could start coming over each day from now on, as he was getting more and more agitated and when the time was near then they would stay in the house. They were fine with that and said they would get their cousin to cover the shop.

156

All Denny had to do now was speak to the girls, and he would include Jinty as well. He would do that tonight. His head was playing up and his sixth sense was beginning to play havoc with his senses. Now all he was waiting for was a phone call from Felix. He had never felt as nervous as this in all his life. Maybe all his misdemeanours in Durma, Dundee and Edinburgh had been masked by the whisky.

He radioed Helen from the forest and asked her to ask Jinty to come up at about seven o'clock tonight and to make sure the boys were fed and in their cot.

Denny's head wasn't in the work, so he radioed Willie and told him to come back as that was it finished for the day. When they all arrived back, Denny had sat them down and asked them to please listen carefully.

"Well, it's been a long time coming, but if my sixth sense is playing ball with me then within the next few days we will be under attack. It all depends on when Felix will call me, and then it's game on. There will be no more work from now on and as hard as it may be, I want you to sleep with your radios switched on just waiting on Karl's call. When I deem it to be the right time, then the girls and the twins will be driven to the Albach Town house and protected there.

Everybody, including Karl and Gunther will stay here in the house. Make sure your guns and knives are spotless and your ammo stocked up. Because of the weather if you want to wear waterproofs then get them from the tack room. Personally, I find them restrictive, so I will be wearing just a warm jersey. Wear what you are okay with. We will speak every morning to see if anyone has any more ideas, but we will not deviate from the plan. Additional ideas will be looked at though."

Willie, Denny and Yuri walked into the forest to see if their vantage points were still clear, leaving Tomaz to stay behind to look after everyone with his arm around Ottar's neck. After about forty minutes they were walking back and as they neared the house Denny thought that something wasn't quite right with Tomaz and Ottar. The dog was standing with his eyes transfixed on the three of them with Tomaz whispering in his ear.

"What's going on with that little 'bugger' Denny. He's pretending to speak to Ottar isn't he? I'm not sure that I am liking this Denny," said Willie.

Denny thought he knew what was happening, but wasn't sure and he was just going to let it play out. As they were getting nearer Tomaz was at it again. Willie was walking slightly slower.

"I'm not sure we should be going any further folks," said Willie with genuine apprehension in his voice.

"Get bloody on with it McLeod. Stop being a 'fanny' as Jinty would say."

They were only twenty yards from the steps when Ottar crouched down and went into attack mode ready for a signal. Willie and Yuri had panic written all over their faces. Tomaz just sat there smiling, and then bursting into his own fits of laughter.

"Foggerty, tell that wee bastard to get that fucking dog under control."

Tomaz just laughed all the harder as he whispered into Ottar's ear.

"Right, that's it Foggerty. Just tell me who I've to shoot first as I'm getting sick of this. Speak to me Foggerty, which one?"

"Calm down Willie. Okay, fun and games over Tomaz, give him the command to stand down please. Now."

Tomaz cupped his hand to Ottar's ear giving the impression that he was giving him instructions, but Denny noticed his other hand was squeezing on the other side of his neck. Ottar then walked down the steps and Denny knelt to let him come into his arms.

"Put the gun away Willie, as I'm beginning to think Jinty might be right and that your just a 'fanny'. A disgrace to the Scottish race my brother."

Denny then sent Ottar over to Willie who reluctantly gave him a rub of his ears.

"Tomaz, no more of your little jokes okay?"

Denny walked away smiling and was glad of the little distraction that Tomaz had given them.

"Yuri, I need to speak to your dad later. How about you come down for something to eat and no need for you to go down to see Jinty as she is coming up," Denny said with a wee smirk on his face.

Yuri smiled and said he would be down at seven o'clock if that was okay?

Denny went for a shower, and he was glad to just stand there and let the hot water wash over him. He was praying for the day when this would be all over, but he knew it wouldn't be anytime soon. One part would end and another start. So be it. He was just about to take three days of growth from his chin when he decided to leave it. Why? He didn't know, but at some point it would come to him.

Before they ate Denny had asked the girls for privacy to speak to Artem and his boys. The girls left them to it.

"Artem, I'm going to ask you a big favour and if you say you are not up for it them no problem. These people will be here soon and what I need is someone positioned here with a rifle to cover anyone of us having to retreat. Although that will be highly unlikely. Trust me."

"It is an honour that you have asked me. Please let me tell you though, I may have been in communications during the war, but I was still a crack shot. I know all of the men here and if I don't recognise somebody then I will put a bullet between their eyes. Does that sound good to you Denny?"

"Sounds fine to me Artem thank you. If you can give me a bit of time to speak to the girls then we can all eat."

Denny walked into the kitchen.

"Hey, Thomas have you traded your jeep in for a time travel machine? Every time you know Yuri is here then you are here within the blink of an eye. Right, everybody stop what you are doing and listen very carefully. Do not interrupt me. Got it? I am certain that these people who are coming for me will be here within the next few days. Not weeks. Days. Jinty I have no right to ask you this as it's not your fight, but can you stay here until I ask you to take the girls and the twins to the Albach Town house. You don't come back until I tell you to. Maria has made provisions for you all to be protected inside the house. Also, there will be some unarmed men patrolling outside so don't be concerned as they are friends of Gunther."

"Why do you say it's not my fight Denny? You have all told me time and time again that I am family, so yes I will go home

159

and get clothes for the next few weeks and if you want to give me a gun then fine."

"Thanks for that Jinty. Please make sure you have plenty of knickers to change into seeing as you will be thinking of Yuri a lot I would also appreciate that you don't jump and start straddling me for a while and no gun. Okay."

Denny should have kept his mouth shut as she just ran a vaulted onto his lap. Fortunately, not knocking him over this time. As she sat on his lap she said," I promise Foggerty, but when this is all over I can't promise anything." She gave him a kiss while stroking his stubble leaving Denny just shaking his head. Followed by Helen shaking hers.

Denny went and phoned the Hoffmans and told them to get their cousin organised and be over tomorrow morning with enough clothes for several days. As everyone sat eating, Jinty headed off to her house. Then the phone rang, and Helen came out.

"Denny, it's Felix for you."

He said he would take it in the dining room.

"Evening Felix, how are you?"

"I'm fine Denny. I have the information you asked for. I hope you are ready up there, because five men booked in to one of the hotels last night. They have left their booking open and are expecting a delivery tomorrow, but they told the owner they wanted complete privacy when it arrives. They have rented a dark blue four by four from the airport. How about you come down in a bit of a disguise and we will have a look at who you will be up against?"

"Sounds like a plan Felix. I will meet you in the town square and if it's not too far we can walk to the hotel. See you in about twenty minutes."

Denny ran in to the tack room and found an old torn jersey and waterproof coat. Otto had left several hats when he departed, so Denny found the scruffiest and then headed up to the veranda. He looked like a tramp. Both Willie and Yuri looked at him and he gave both a slight nod. He told everyone that he would be back in an hour and to stay put.

He took one of the jeeps and headed down the road. Felix was standing waiting, so Denny parked up and went to meet him. As they were walking to the hotel Felix had said to follow his lead.

"As you go through the door, only have your eyes on the bar and the barman. If these people are in the bar then they will be eating or drinking so hopefully they will be concentrating on what they are doing and not us. I will sit with my back to them so that you can look over my shoulder and you can size them up, but you can't stare. You okay with that? Oh, and I hope you don't smell as bad as you look, or we won't be served a drink."

As they went through the door of the hotel the owner was working behind the bar and gave the slightest of nods to his left pointing out five guys sitting in the corner. Felix ordered two large Jägermeister and shook his head slightly as Denny started to protest. Felix gave one to him and nodded that they should sit over by the window so that they could watch the table in the corner. The hotel owner's wife started to bring out the men's meals and they were soon eating and drinking. It was obvious that they had been drinking before their meal, as they started to get louder throughout their meal. Felix gave Denny a look and started trivial talk so that Denny could look over his shoulder and suss out the guys. After a while Denny had seen enough, although there was one man sitting with his back to him all the time. Denny had noticed that Felix switched glasses and was now sipping on the one that he had handed to Denny.

Just as they stood up the guy who had been shielded from Denny turned and shouted for more lager. Denny got such a shock as it was the same guy who had been prowling around the estate and asking questions on Durma. Denny went to the bar and paid with a large amount of money and Felix said to the owner he would be waiting on his phone call night or day. The barman just raised his eyebrows in acknowledgement, before Felix and Denny left the hotel.

As they walked to the car Felix asked Denny what he thought.

"They are just amateurs Felix. As I expected they are unfit and just over for some quick money."

"It doesn't matter if you are an amateur or not Denny, you can be dangerous with a gun in your hand. I will phone you as soon as I hear anything. Oh, and one more thing son. How many telephone poles are there between the house and the main substation?"

"Only one Felix why?"

"Then I suggest you put razor wire as far up it as you can in case they want to cut the wires."

They said goodbye with Denny shaking his hand and telling him how much he appreciated his help.

"Oh, by the way son I have found out who shot at your wife, but I will leave that until all this is over."

When Denny arrived back Jinty was back, so he went to see the girls to ask if they were all ready to move to the town house. Helen had said they were fine, but Denny had noticed a slight tremble in her voice. The men were all sitting outside and told them he would speak to them in a minute. He got on the phone and asked the Hoffmans if they could stop what they are doing and come up and stay at the house. He asked if they could bring fifty meters of razor wire with them.

It wasn't a problem and true to form they arrived twenty minutes later.

He had asked the girls to stay inside while he spoke to the men.

"Okay, folks. I went down to the town after Felix had phoned me. The guys that after me are here. Last chance to leave the estate. No? Okay, there are five of them, including the guy that was prowling around here with Scottie. It was pretty apparent that they are not trained killers, just amateurs who will do anything for money. They didn't look fit and one of them even had a massive beer belly and didn't look capable of walking or running anywhere. However, as Felix pointed out, anyone is dangerous with a gun in their hand. They are expecting a delivery to their hotel tomorrow which I suspect will be their guns and ammunition. I can't tell you if it's happening tomorrow or the night after, but I will know the minute they leave their hotel to come here.

"Karl, I need that razor wire on the telephone pole down the track so that they cannot cut any communications as we have to phone the police immediately after we have finished with them. Karl, you suggested we use fireworks after to make it look like we had a party for the boys. Do you still have them in your car?

162

Gunther, there is a slight change of plan. After you have phoned the men to tell them to get into position from tomorrow morning early, I need one guy at the substation to make sure nobody is going to launch an attack on it. Leave him one of the old jeeps for him to sit in just in case the weather is bad. Tomorrow will be a long day, but I suggest we work round about the house here. Always in pairs and with our hand guns strapped to our waist along with our rifles over our shoulders. Any questions?"

"Yeh, I have my brother. What are we doing with the bodies?"

"Artem kindly dug a big hole for us on his farm a while ago, so they will go in there and left to rot. Remember, from now on you sleep with your clothes on and your radio switched to the right frequency."

"I'm not sure how Gertie will react to the Love Master being fully clothed in our bed of passion Denny."

Everyone laughed, except Willie, but it was a very nervous laugh thought Denny. As if on que, Gertie opened the door slightly and shouted was it okay to bring out the coffee and cakes, slightly frightened that she would get a bollocking from Denny. He shouted that it was fine, and the girls brought out what appeared to Denny was a banquet.

"Bloody hell girls, what have you prepared for us, the Last Supper? Remember, we are only going to despatch some evil bastards to the Under World."

An angry cheer went up, and the dogs were up, startled and wondering what was going on.

Denny then knew they would be okay.

Helen and Gertie had made up the rooms to accommodate everyone with Jinty in beside Helen, as Denny had decided he was going to sleep with the dogs. Although sleep would be hard to come by. It was to be an uneventful night and Denny had thought about Karl lying in his hiding place although he had taken out a couple of blankets with him. He walked in to the house at about seven o'clock and Denny was waiting for him.

"Hard night Karl? I take it there was nothing happening in the forest?"

"Only some wolf calls that made me a bit nervous to be honest."

"Go in and get a few hours' sleep and I will put two of us along the line of the lights for two hours at a time." Everyone was sitting on the veranda by eight o'clock getting their breakfast when the phone rang. It was Felix.

"Morning Denny, I trust you all had a peaceful night. However, you won't tonight. A van drew up and a large heavy holdall was handed over to one of the men. From what I can surmise it looked about the length for rifles. It has to be tonight as they cannot have these guns lying about their rooms. Get yourselves ready, and I will phone you as soon as they leave the hotel. That should give you about thirty minutes. Good luck my friend."

Denny shouted on the girls to get ready to move to the town house. "No panic, but don't 'piss about'." He went in and grabbed his boys and brought them out with everyone giving the girls a hand with their luggage. When the four by four was packed and the boys inside, Helen came up and put her arms around Denny and gave him a big kiss.

"No heroics my husband. Just do what you have to do, and we will come back."

The vehicle took off down the road and Denny went in and phoned Maria telling her to expect them and were there men outside keeping an eye on the building?

"Okay, we are ready here, and yes there are several unsavoury looking men walking about outside. I'm so glad they are on our side."

Denny thanked her and then ended the call.

"Okay, everyone please listen. We have to take turns at watching the forest from where Karl put the lights up. Two of us at a time for two hours. Everyone else can either sleep or get on with something they want to do. According to Felix, and my throbbing head from my sixth sense it will be tonight so get angry. Tomaz, it's me and you on first watch and before you ask, yes you can bring Ottar as I will be taking Arno and Udo."

As they walked out, Denny looked at Tomaz and he could see that he was as nervous as hell.

"Don't worry wee man, you will be fine tonight. I will make sure of that. It's not a nice thing I have landed you with, but try and relax a bit and make sure your shots count though."

164

Tomaz smiled at him, and wondered why this man was so cold and calculated, when he was about to kill people. The more he had been around him, the bigger the mystery Denny had become. After two hours, Willie and Gunther came and relieved them, and so it went on throughout the day and into the early hours of the evening. At nearly midnight Karl said he was going to his hiding place in the forest and not to try and contact him, but to wait for his signal.

At about two o'clock in the morning Denny told everyone to get on the veranda and be ready as he knew it wasn't going to be long. Artem was already sitting with a blanket around his shoulders and his rifle aiming down the track.

The silence was so intense. Denny sat just watching the forest with the dogs either side of him and Ottar lying next to Willie. Yuri, Gunther and Tomaz were just sitting staring into space, not really knowing what the night would bring. Denny sent the dogs out to relieve themselves, but it was as quick as they could cock their legs before they ran back. He was sure that they knew something was up, and when he ran his hand over their backs he felt tension in their bodies. Ottar just lay there with his eyes fixed in front of him. It was then that their radios crackled, and the single word 'move' was said.

"Let's go lads. Please be safe, but kill the fuckers."

They ran and within minutes they were in their positions and had their rifles ready. Willie had put Ottar under a tree and whispered for him to stay. Denny put Arno and Udo behind him giving them maximum safety. They waited and waited. What was a few minutes seemed like an hour.

Suddenly, the lights went on and there in front of them were the five men trying to shield their eyes while trying to point their rifles. Yuri took out the guy in his line of site and then it was Tomaz who shot the next guy, but only 'winged' him. A shout came over the radio that they had a runner to the North, whereby Tomaz ran behind Yuri's position and took off after the guy. Gunther was giving him cover fire. Denny killed the next one stone dead with a bullet between the eyes.

"Another runner is heading back the way they came."

Denny then grabbed the dogs, pointed to where the guy was running and gave them the instruction to kill. The dogs took off, and unbelievably they both leapt the stream from the top of the banking at the near side to the far side. They were gone and Denny hoped they would be safe.

"A runner to the South. Up to you Willie."

"Willie, it's Denny. Try and 'wing' him if you can."

A shot went out and then Willie came over the radio saying he had shot him, but the guy was trying to scramble away, and he was now going after him with Ottar.

It was then that everyone heard the most blood curdling screams coming from the forest where the dogs were.

Willie came over the radio saying that he and Ottar had the guy trapped as he was trying to hide under the banking which had fallen away.

"It's Denny here. Is everyone safe?"

They all said they were except Tomaz who was missing.

"Yuri, where the fuck is Tomaz?"

"He ran North to get the guy he shot. I'm going after him."

"Gunther, you stay here in case Willie needs help, as I'm going after the dogs if it's okay Karl?"

"You're fine Denny, it's all clear."

Denny ran through the stream and sprinted as fast as he could in the direction where the dogs had gone. He was being directed to where they were in the trees by their loud growling. When he got there both dogs were still in the attack mode, but he stood them down as the guy was obviously dead. Disembowelled, with his throat ripped out.

Denny stood looking at the guy for a minute, before his evil smile came over his face.

He spoke into the radio and asked for help to help bring the body back to where they were. Karl had said it would be him and Denny had directed him to where he was waiting.

"Bloody hell Denny, that's horrific. I feel like vomiting."

"Don't you dare Karl."

The dogs were wandering about with their muzzles covered in blood just sniffing around, before Arno walked over and cocked his leg on the body. Denny knew he shouldn't, but he couldn't stifle a laugh. Karl realised then that Denny was even more evil than he had thought. Denny had said that they should try and carry the guy, as he didn't want any drag marks as

166

evidence. Karl was trying hard not to look at the guys injuries. When they got back to where everyone was, he told Gunther and Karl to hurry and bring the ATVs from the house and attach a trailer to the most powerful one. Somebody had to bring Artem with them.

It was then that he saw Yuri and Tomaz walking down the North trail.

"Well, what happened to you Tomaz?"

Tomaz made gestures of him shooting and then throwing something.

"What he is trying to tell you Denny is that he shot the guy, who then ran into the forest, before Tomaz trailed him and put a knife in his back. The guy is lying beside the stream behind a tree so we can pick him up when we go to our farm."

"Maybe, he should just tell me himself."

Yuri just looked at Denny and then Tomaz wondering what was going on.

"Hello, is there anybody there. It's Willie, remember me? I need a bit of help down here."

Denny had told him on the radio that Tomaz and him would be there in five minutes. So, they took off running with Tomaz trying hard to keep up with Denny, which was a bit of a mismatch. When they got to Willie, he and Ottar were standing guard next to an overhang on the banking.

"He's under there Denny. I haven't sent Ottar in as I don't know how much 'intact' you want him. Think we should shoot him and leave him for the wolves?"

Denny jumped down on to the banking before he said, "right you scum, I can't get in to your little bolt hole that you have squirreled into, so let me tell you how it's going to happen. You are coming out whether you will be in one piece or several. I am going to tell my little friend here to instruct his dog to grab you and pull you out, and just to let you know that your red headed friend no longer has any genitals or throat. It's up to you."

Denny and Willie stood there looking at Tomaz and Ottar and wondering who was salivating the most.

"Okay, my little friend, instruct your dog please."

Tomaz whispered something in Ottar's ear, and then gave him a couple of gestures. Ottar jumped down onto the banking and landed on all fours facing into the guy. He then let out the most ferocious snarl, with his teeth showing, that both Willie and Denny had ever seen or heard from him. His growl would have frightened anyone. Willie had actually jumped back in fright, although he would deny it later.

"Okay, okay I'm coming out, but get that bloody dog away."

As the guy came out Willie was about to start punching the guy, but Denny stopped him.

"What's going on Foggerty? We can't let him live, never mind go free."

"Tie his hands Tomaz, and I want him taken back to the log store and tied up with absolutely no chance of escape. Guard him well. When I come back, we will tend to his injuries. We will be back within a couple of hours and please, take all the dogs back. You're in charge, but I want Arno and Udo's faces to be washed in the stream. All the blood to be gone."

A large smile came over Tomaz's face.

"You don't have to come over Willie if you don't want to as we have plenty of bodies. No pun intended."

"I'll just wander back and make myself a sandwich I think."

"For fuck sake McLeod, we've just killed four people, taken another one prisoner and all you can think about is your bloody belly."

"Just a bit peckish big man."

Denny walked up to where the bodies were, then stopped and turned to watch Willie strolling along holding his rifle over his shoulder singing a song he couldn't quite make out.

"Okay, let's get three of the bodies in to the trailer and put the last one over the basket on my ATV. Artem get on the back with Yuri. They didn't waste any time heading over the hill to the farm.

When they got off their machines they quickly dragged the bodies to the large hole that Artem had dug out. Denny picked them up one at a time and unceremoniously threw then into the hole.

"Go to Hell you bastards. Right, Artem fill the hole in please."

Artem started the digger and began to back fill the hole. He wasn't wasting any time and after half an hour he was flattening the soil on top of where the hole had been.

"Artem, please position the digger on top of the hole and set fire to it. We don't want anybody trying to see what might be underneath it or trying to steal it."

Artem had such blind faith in Denny, that he walked to the old barn and came back with a full can of kerosene and a box of matches. He took the can and doused the machine before setting fire to it. Everyone stood as far back as possible before the diesel tank went up with a woosh.

"Yuri, did you all bring all your personal possessions with you to the shooting lodge?"

"Just a few bits and pieces are left Denny. Why?"

"You and your dad go and get them as quickly as possible."

Ten minutes later they appeared with two small hessian bags. Denny went into the barn and brought out another can of kerosene. He started to douse the house and sheds with it.

"Denny, what the fuck are you doing?" shouted Yuri.

He gave Yuri a quick glance before looking straight into Artem's eyes. Artem gave his son and then Denny a slight nod of the head before saying to go ahead. It didn't take long for all the buildings to catch fire. Artem stood just looking at the home he had moved into with his wife so many years ago, and the house he had brought up his sons in. A tear appeared in his eye, but Denny gave him a stern look and he quickly wiped it away with his sleeve.

"Artem, you and your boys are coming to live on the estate. Is that okay with you? What about you Yuri?"

They both nodded and smiled.

They started back and the rain came pouring down making the trail a bit slippery to navigate On arriving back, Karl was lighting fireworks, but dousing them in a bucket of water soon after. That reminded Denny that he had forgot to phone the police. He took off inside the house and dialled the police station. Fortunately, it was his pal Officer Meyer who answered the phone.

"Officer Meyer, I owe you a big apology. Last night we had a small celebration for my boys and there were fireworks involved and it did go on for a while. So again, I'm sorry."

"Don't worry Mr Foggerty. We have had a few phone calls about it so we have to investigate, however it will just be a matter of course. I will send one of my junior officers up in say about an hour if that suits?"

"That will be fine, but if you are going to be up here bird watching I would prefer if you called me Denny."

"Of course, Denny I will look forward to being on your estate and we get to know each other better."

Denny shook his head and wondered at the things he had to do just so that he could kill people.

He then told everyone to go into the forest where they were positioned and make sure they picked up all the empty shell casings as a police officer would be here within the hour.

"Tomaz, your with me so let's go and see this guy in the log store."

Tomaz had certainly tied him up alright. Not even Houdini could have escaped with the amount of rope that he had tied around him.

"Keep him gagged Tomaz and kept out of sight as there is a police officer arriving soon. The less people that are around the better. We will have a word with this scumbag after the police have left."

Ten minutes later a police car was coming up the track and the rain was coming down heavier than ever. This is perfect thought Denny. He went out to greet the officer who looked like he was just in his early twenties.

"Come up to the veranda officer and you can ask me what is it you want to know. I can offer you tea and a cake if that sounds appealing to you."

"That would be lovely Mr. Foggerty. Officer Meyer said you would be very hospitable."

Willie then walked out and started to complain to Denny that he never got much sleep due to the bloody fireworks being set off half the night. The officer sat down with the three dogs just staring at him, unnerving him a bit. Then Denny came back with the tea and a large piece of Gertie's sponge cake, which never looked like it 'touched the sides'.

"Mr. Foggerty, do you use the dogs for hunting in the forests?"

"No, we don't do any hunting here, it's all about conservation. Sometimes we have to cull certain species when food becomes a bit scarce for the animals which is unfortunate, but that's just the law of the land. Sorry, I didn't get your name officer?"

"It's Hans Schmidt Mr. Foggerty."

"Please to meet you Hans. Just call me Denny."

"There was something I was going to ask you Denny, and that is my hobby is botany and I know you said that Officer Meyer could come onto your land to enjoy his bird watching. So, I was wondering if you would show me the same courtesy and let me study my pastime in your forests."

Denny wondered what he had started, before he thought having an ornithologist and a botanist might be great for his plans for under privileged children visiting.

"Absolutely Hans, but only under the supervision of our Forest Manager William McLeod who you just met. There is high security on this estate, and I can show you an example."

Denny whistled on the dogs who all jumped up and stood in front of the officer ready for attack. Hans just about 'passed' the cake he had just eaten into his pants. Denny quickly stood the dogs down.

"Sorry about that Hans, but these dogs would be here for your protection as you never know who would be here in the forest."

"Thank God these dogs would be here looking after me. Okay, Denny I must go, and my report will state that you were just letting off fireworks. Good day to you."

"Maybe you and Officer Meyer could come over together?"

"That would be great."

When the car was down the track, Willie came back out and said, "Foggerty, that just about made me 'puke up' you sucking up to the officer like that. You're not going to let them on the estate are you?"

"I have a wee plan William."

"You can cut the 'crap' calling me William. Gertie shouts out Willie when she gets climaxes from the Love Master, so that will do for me."

"Willie, I wish you had been on the other side of the lights earlier, and I would have told everyone to make you the bloody target."

"I don't believe a word you are saying brother. Oh, and next time I have to shoot somebody for you, and you shout, 'wing him,' then try telling me where you would like him 'winged about."

Denny couldn't take much more of his incessant nonsense, so he walked inside to phone Helen at the Town house.

Chapter 8

It was Maria who answered the phone and immediately asked Denny if everything was okay?

"I am almost certain it is Maria, but I need them to stay with you for another couple of days just to be on the safe side if that is okay?"

"That will be fine, and I will put Helen on the line as she is standing here eagerly waiting to speak to you."

"Denny, Denny I take it you are all okay? I have been worried sick."

"Helen, we are all fine, although I don't think it was a very pleasant experience for any of us. However, I need you to stay there for another couple of days. Then you can all come home, and we can get back to something that resembles normality."

"I'm so glad that will be the end of it."

Denny knew it was far from over, but he couldn't tell Helen that, well not yet anyway. He wasn't looking forward to when that time came.

He told everybody to go home, as Tomaz and him would finish up as they had to have a word with the guy tied up in the log store. When they entered the log store the look on the guy's face was one of a terror-stricken animal. From the smell coming from him it was obvious that he had wet himself. Denny knew he had to put his plan in to action and hope it would work. Suddenly, he remembered Felix, and ran in to the house to phone him, but not before telling Tomaz to guard the guy. The phone was eventually answered.

"Good morning Felix. Without your help I probably wouldn't be standing here phoning you."

"I take it that everything went well and none of your men were injured?"

"Not quite a turkey shoot Felix, but not far away, and it will be impossible for anybody to find the bodies. Can you please give me the name of the guy that shot at Helen. I intend to go down the route of turning him over to the police. Do you think I am doing the right thing Felix."

"It doesn't really matter what I think Denny, it's how you feel, but be warned, his father is a wealthy businessman who has been known to line a few pockets to get his son out of trouble. The son is just a spoilt brat, who has been in and out of university courses all his life. He is always surrounded by a few pals, especially a girl with long hair, who all hang on to his every word. Maybe, you should have a backup plan in case it all goes wrong."

Felix gave Denny the name of the guy, where he lived and said he would find out where he and his pals drank and would get back to him.

"Thanks Felix, I will make a note to myself to put some money behind the bars of the establishments you drink in."

"Remember Denny, since meeting you I only drink large Jägermeister now."

Before he hung up Denny could hear him laughing.

He shouted on Willie to come out so he could go over his plan for the guy in the log store. Willie sauntered out as if tomorrow would do.

"Willie, I am going to run a plan by you, and I really need you on my side with this. Firstly, I am going to get Tomaz to clean up and stitch his wound which looks like your bullet went cleanly through his shoulder. I can see you looking at me, but please trust me. I then want him taken to his hotel, let him do a quick change and you and Tomaz take him to the airport, and put him on the first available flight to where he came from. I'm hoping it was Edinburgh, but his ticket will let you know. Tell the hotel owner to get rid of all the other guy's belongings and I will come down and pay him handsomely for his work. You got that? I will let you know what the next part is when you get back."

Willie just nodded and went to get a jeep ready.

When Denny went back in to the store Tomaz was waving a large knife in front of the guys face.

"Put the knife away will you. Okay, you cretin I need to know who sent you over?"

"I can't, I can't as the bastard who employed us would have no problem hurting my family. Just do what you want with me as I can't help you."

Denny could see that he wasn't going to be of any use.

"Here is what is going to happen you 'worm' and that is my friend here is going to stitch you up. Then you will be taken to the airport and put on the first available flight to Edinburgh. It was Edinburgh wasn't it?"

The guy just nodded, and at that Denny knew where his flight would be going to.

"Please tell your so called boss not to fuck with me again. Got it?"

Another nod, and then he told Tomaz to clean up the wound and not to be gentle about it. When the guy was cleaned up, Denny told Willie to take Tomaz with him and go to the hotel first, before heading to the airport with Tomaz sitting in the back with him.

"If he asks to make a phone call then pretend your indifferent to his request and let him do it. He will probably be wanting someone to pick him up at the airport. I won't know who, but I need to know what the registration number of the car that does pick him up is, and from there we can find out who owns the car. Phone me immediately you know what flight he will be on and when it will arrive in Edinburgh."

"Okay boss, I can see you're a scheming big bugger. There will be no problem from my end."

Denny watched Willie grab the guy by his injured shoulder and he started to scream, before throwing him in the back seat where Tomaz was waiting with his knife in his hand, ready to slightly press it against the guy's ribs while keeping it out of sight. At the hotel, they escorted him up the stairs to his room where the owner let them in. He knew not to ask any questions. The guy quickly changed and only took his passport and a small amount of cash with him. Willie had said that Denny would be down to see the owner, and he would be admirably rewarded if he could just get rid of the belongings of the other four men.

"That won't be a problem, as we have a large incinerator out the back. Please tell Mr. Foggerty that no names have been written in our hotel register and there will be no trace of any of these people ever staying here."

Willie thanked him and they started off for the airport.

"Remember, if you try to escape either from the car or at the airport then my little man here will put a blade in to your heart.

The only thing I can tell you is that it will be a quick death. Understand?"

The man just nodded and sat back in the seat.

The airport was busy, so Willie explained to Tomaz that it makes it easier for somebody to slip away from his captors. Tomaz acknowledged that he understood. It was just after they had booked the guy on his flight that Willie had made a phone call to Denny telling him the flight details and when it would arrive in Edinburgh.

Denny immediately phoned the Pillars Bar in Dundee and asked the barman for Stevie's home phone number. The guy said that he shouldn't give that number out, before Denny said it was either that or he would cut his balls off when he came to Scotland. The barman quickly gave him Stevie's number. He dialled and Stevie answered it in his usual gruff voice which could often sound like a growl at times.

"Is that you Stevie? This is Denny from over the water. I need a big favour pal. Are both Levi and Bohdi around? If so can you get them to Edinburgh airport for a flight that will be arriving in about four hours and here is what I need from them."

He gave him a description of the guy that would be arriving off the four o'clock flight from Munich. He said he wouldn't have any luggage and he would be favouring or holding his left shoulder. If they weren't sure then tell them to bump in to his shoulder, but I want them to follow him and here is the most important part. I need the registration of the car that picks him up.

"I'll take them down right away as they have been off their classes. It seems that they always have an excuse for not attending. It would be sensible for me to wait on them and bring them back, as I can't let them loose in Edinburgh as that wouldn't be fair on the city. As soon as they give me the information then I will phone."

"One last thing Stevie. It looks like I will be coming to Scotland to settle a debt and I was wondering if you know anyone who could procure a few things for me and my men. To start with four sniper rifles, four hand guns and two way radios."

"For fuck sake are you proposing to start a bloody war Denny? As it happens I know someone. He can get you anything and I mean anything. If you are coming over then try and give me a week's notice and I can introduce him to you. However, I want Levi and Bohdi kept as far away from you as possible. Agreed?"

"Agreed Stevie, but you know what their like. Oh, and thanks for sending them over to the wedding. They were a revelation, even although I was going to either shoot them a few times or set my dogs on them. Couldn't make up my mind. Speak soon."

In a couple of hours Denny and Tomaz arrived back, and Denny told Tomaz to go home to the lodge. He found it strange that Tomaz had never mentioned him setting fire to the farm. He told Willie he needed to speak to him about Helen's shooting.

Willie had said he would make them something to eat and would be out in a few minutes. Denny was sitting on the steps when Willie handed him what looked like a sandwich of sorts and a cup of lukewarm tea. Denny thought it would be good to have the girls back.

"Can I just tell you Willie, that Felix gave me the name of the guy that shot Helen and where he drinks about. It was the same person with whom I had a run in when he was poaching in the forest several years ago. He still has all his sycophants hanging around him, and is a total loser, but we need to have a word with them all soon and persuade him to hand himself over to the police. Remember Willie, I can't have you going off on one and injuring this guy. As I said before, he won't get away with it."

"Yeh okay, but it's maybe wise that I am not with you when you pay him a visit."

Denny had told him to go and phone Gertie and he would speak to Helen when he was finished. He knew that he would have to stand the men at the Town house down, so he went to other house phone and phoned Gunther.

"Gunther, can you get over to the men and stand them down and I will see them tonight in the same place at seven o'clock. Tell them not to be late."

When he had managed to speak to Helen he knew she was down cast. She told him that she and the boys were missing him and asked when could they come home. He knew there was no point prolonging all this, so he told her to get Jinty to drive them back tomorrow night. Helen had said she was so glad.

After they had finished speaking, he had no sooner put the phone down when it rang again. It was Stevie giving him the information he needed. Levi had also told him that the man that picked him up was quite tough looking and was giving the guy a hard time of it. Denny had thanked him and said to thank the boys for their efforts, and he might see them soon.

When Denny had walked into the same bar as they had previously met in, everyone was sitting there including Karl and Gunther.

"Men, thank you so much for looking out for my family, I really appreciate what you did. I know it must have been boring, but before I give you what is due to you, I have a favour to ask. In a few weeks or months, will you be willing to do it again? This time however it will be on the estate?

Karl and Gunther looked at each other wondering what the hell Denny was saying.

The men were nodding their heads, so Denny handed them their envelopes. There was silence when they looked inside. One guy had his hand on his forehead not really believing what he was seeing, before he spoke.

"I know you said you were going to pay us a bonus, but this is incredible. We wouldn't have to work for many years with this amount, and to be honest we would all agree that we didn't have to do very much."

There was more nodding of heads.

"I told you before, knowing that my family were safe was of paramount importance to me, so you all deserve every deutschmark. Gunther will contact you soon."

As they walked out, Denny did the same as before and handed the barman a wad of cash. When they were out Gunther said, "What is happening here Denny, I thought this was all over?"

"If you both could be over at eight o'clock tomorrow morning I will explain everything. See you then."

Denny walked away while Karl put his head in his hands and said, "What have we got ourselves into brother. This is crazy. I don't think my brain can handle this."

"Let's wait and see what he says tomorrow Karl."

Denny had driven to the hotel the guys had booked into, and when he went in he met the owner and handed him a large envelope and shook his hand.

"All traces of these men have been obliterated Mr. Foggerty. I will pay more care as to who I book in to the hotel in future."

Denny just nodded and walked out.

When he got back to the house he quickly got Arno and Udo and walked into the forest. He never gave the area where the killing had happened a second glance. He was just happy to have two of his pals beside him. After a while, even although it had started to rain, he sat under a tree and put his arms around the dogs. His sixth-sense was almost non-existent now, but his brain was still in a turmoil. He wondered if he was now addicted to killing, or he was becoming immune to its effect. He was tired, so very tired and the thought of having to go over this again in Scotland was starting to drain him.

"Okay my Hounds from Hell, I'll race you home."

Knowing full well they were probably just laughing at him. Denny took off at speed, knowing he shouldn't do that, however twice Udo stopped to cock his leg and Arno had sat down for a time to scratch his ears. Denny coming in a miserable third place when they got to the house. As he sat on the steps blowing out of his backside, Willie came out and sat beside him.

"You're not as fit as you used to be brother. Next time you decide to race the dogs then include me as I know it will only be the dogs that will beat me."

Denny grabbed Willie and within minutes they were wrestling in the mud on the forest floor. Just letting out steam. It went on for about ten minutes before they lay there laughing and when they eventually looked up, there was Tomaz standing on the middle of the steps. They couldn't believe it when he spread his arms out and just let himself fall on top of Denny and Willie from a height.

"What was that about you little Czech nut case," said Willie. Tomaz lay there covered in mud, but laughing.

"Tomaz, please tell Yuri that there will be a meeting tomorrow morning at eight o'clock."

"You don't half like a meeting brother. Don't you?"

"It's a very crucial meeting Willie, and I need your complete backing. Tomaz, where the hell is Ottar?"

Tomaz made signs that he was with his dad and turned his hands up to ask if that was okay. Denny just nodded and told him not to get too attached as he was an old dog. Tomaz put his hand on his heart and smiled. Denny couldn't help but smile back. He turned around to see Yuri and his dad, along with Ottar walking from the lodge.

"Denny, it was time I repaid your hospitality. So, I am going to cook us all a lovely meal tonight as the girls are away and it is always my sons who seem to be looking after me. Is that okay?"

"Sounds good Artem. At least it will be better than Willies's cooking."

"I heard that you bastard Foggerty."

Artem had made a lovely meal of chicken casserole, and after the five of them had finished they sat with coffee and biscuits. Everyone reminisced about their lives and their aspirations for the future.

Artem spoke to Denny and said that he was surprised that he had very little aspirations for the future. Denny was quiet for a few minutes.

"Artem, the way I am, I only live for the next day and if I wake up the next morning then it's a bonus. After what I have to say tomorrow, then maybe you'll understand me more."

When everyone left, Denny went inside and phoned Shonagh.

"Hi Denny, I have no doubt that this is not a social call. How may I help you my handsome ex- colleague? Maybe one of these days you will be phoning me to tell me you still 'fancy' me or how my health is, or just to hear my dulcet tones."

"Bloody hell Shonagh, has Jack managed to give you the orgasms you have been craving or are you now a willing participant in the Edinburgh drug scene."

"Neither you 'dickhead'. What is it that you want. Hang on. Oh no, did they come for you Denny?"

"I'm afraid they did Shonagh, but we were prepared and now the worms are feasting on their flesh. However, I need some information, and I need an answer as to whether you are coming over to see the neuro surgeon I mentioned."

Denny gave her all the information that Stevie had relayed to him. He asked if she could try and find out who the car was registered to. She pondered over this before saying the best person to find this out would be Tommy and she would speak to him in a few days when he was back off holiday.

"I will phone you as soon as he gets back to me. I have been putting a lot of thought into your offer, and as my pain is getting a bit worse, then I would appreciate if you could organise for me to at least speak to the guy."

"No problem, my bonnie Edinburgh girl and I have a funny feeling I will be seeing you sooner rather than later."

"One last thing Denny. Do you think you are turning into a serial killer?"

"Not sure Shonagh, but if I am then it would be a serial killer who only kills evil people. Not sure how that works."

Denny had said goodbye and put the phone down and made a note to ask Maria to contact the hospital for Shonagh. He never heard Willie coming back with the dogs, minus Ottar of course.

"Think we should try and get some sleep brother as the girls and the twins will be back tomorrow. Hopefully, everything should be back to normal."

"I doubt that very much Denny after another of your legendary speeches. I must go and conserve my energy as Gertie will have been missing the tender loving touches of the Love Master."

"Are you for real McLeod? It has only been a few days for God's sake."

Willie just shrugged his shoulders and walked to the annex.

As he lay in bed, Denny realised how much he missed Helen lying beside him, and promised himself he would tell her that tomorrow night. His sleep was troubled more than normal. Col and Finn were prominent in his dreams. At about three in the morning, he sat back against the headboard with sweat all over his body. He got up and dried himself off before lying back on the bed. What started to go through his mind was how he could look the twins in the face without wondering if they would ever find out that their dad was a mass murderer. Even although he was always trying to tell himself that it was all justified. He wondered if he deserved Helen and the boys.

He was up early and started to get the dogs out for their morning walk. Willie came out at the same time and suggested he walk with him. Neither of them were in the mood for talking, so they just walked taking in the morning scene and all the noises coming from the forests. Eventually, Willie sat down and asked Denny to sit with him.

"Denny, I know this will be a crucial time for you over the next couple of months, but I am worried that all this killing is getting out of hand. Don't you ever think we could be caught at some point, and then what would happen? I'm a bit worried as to what you are going to say at this bloody meeting. I think I know what you are going to do. Do you think there is any other way around it?"

Denny just shook his head.

Willie just stood up and started walking home. Denny thought he had better just leave him alone with his thoughts. He knew Willie wouldn't be happy when he told everyone at the meeting what his plans were, but if they weren't up for it then he would do it himself. Nobody was going to try and kill him and get away with it. Nobody.

When everyone had arrived for the meeting Denny stood in front of them.

"What I am about to say might come as a bit of a shock to some of you. More to the point, what I am going to ask some of you to do, I have no right to ask, and if anyone doesn't want to, then feel free to say no. After what we have been through, you may have thought that it is all over. It not. It's just starting."

They all sat still, some with their head in their hands, wondering what Denny was going to come out with.

"I am not going to live my life looking over my shoulder. Wondering if there is a bullet with my name on it. I am going to take this fight to them. Please, don't be naive to think that they won't send more people to try and finish the job they started. Within the next few weeks or months, I will have all the information I need as to who is trying to kill me and I am going to end it once and for all. Please, don't think the worst of me as I am not happy that this has to be done. Okay, please listen. I am one hundred percent sure that these people are from Scotland, and I intend to take their little war to them. I'm neither sure who they are or where they are in Scotland, but as I said before, that information will be with me soon."

"Artem, could you be so kind and make us all some coffee and biscuits while we ponder over what I have just said."

Denny walked in to the kitchen with him as he wanted to speak to him alone.

"I'm sorry that I am putting a lot of pressure on your sons Artem, but I really do need them for what I am about to carry out. However, I know they worry about you, so if you feel I shouldn't ask them for their help then I won't"

"Denny, you said that all this would probably be happening in weeks or months so don't worry about me. I might see the weeks out, but not the months as I will be dead by then. My condition is getting worse, a lot worse. However, please don't mention this to my sons, and you have my permission to ask them, as this estate is the best thing that has happened to them. I have lived a hard, but fulfilling life son, and at my age I hope you will say the same."

Denny just put his hand on Artem's shoulder, gave a little squeeze and smiled at him. He walked out and a few minutes later Artem came out with the coffee and biscuits and the men's mood changed slightly.

"As you are all finished, well except for Tomaz as usual, here is my plan. I would like it if you and Tomaz would come with me Yuri, as well as you Karl. Willie, you and Gunther would stay behind to protect everyone here. The most important job for you pair. The planning for this operation would be second to none, I promise. We will have help over there, but they wouldn't be helping by lifting a gun. Before you ask Willie, there will be friends of Gunther helping with the forests, as well as the protection of the estate."

"Denny, I speak for Tomaz when I say you can count us in. I know that it won't be easy, but we trust you."

Tomaz just sat there nodding with his arm around Ottar.

"I don't know how Gunther feels, but I will come with you Denny. I've always wanted to visit that beautiful country of yours. Maybe not in these circumstances, but I'm in. Do you know how many people we will be up against?"

"At this stage I haven't a clue, but when we are ready I propose to telephone them to say we are coming."

"What the fuck are you thinking about Foggerty. Letting them know when you are coming?" said Willie.

"Willie, I want them to be at their strongest when we hit them, so that there are no surprises for us. Remember, no loose ends pal, so I want them all in one place so that we can eradicate them all, and I mean all, from this earth. Trust me it will all work out, plus I can't have the Love Master away from Gertie for any length of time. God forbid."

The atmosphere was a bit strained as they all looked at one another. However, it all changed when Tomaz pointed to Denny and then Ottar, indicating he wanted to take him a walk. Denny nodded and as the pair of them were walking towards the forest he wondered if the wee man Tomaz knew what he was getting himself in to.

"Please, go away and think about what I propose to do, and if you have any doubts or questions, then see me tomorrow. Tomorrow we start getting back to normal on the estate. It's been neglected for a while. Yuri, I would like to speak to you."

"Yuri, I would like for you and Tomaz to accompany me to a bar one night as I have found out who shot Helen, and I need to give him a bit of encouragement to hand himself over to the police. You up for it? It's really for their protection not mine."

"Not a problem Denny. I take it there will be limited force?"

"Not sure. Let's see how it 'pans' out."

Denny left it at that and walked in to use the phone. When it was answered, Maria asked him straight out if all the danger was now past.

"Maria, the people that came for me are no longer a threat, but I must speak to you at some point, as I have to tie up all the loose ends I left back in Scotland. It will be brutally hard on everyone on the estate, but it's got to be done."

"Oh Denny, why does it have to be like this. You and Helen had a great life before all this blew up. Why are people so evil?"

"Maybe I'm not the right person to answer that question Maria. However, I will speak to Helen please, after I ask a favour from you. You will remember Shonagh from the wedding, well I would like her to be examined by the top neuro surgeon in the hospital in Munich. She is experiencing advanced pain, and I would like to help her if possible. I know the guy will be busy which suits my purpose so the end of the year would suit me and Shonagh. When I arrive in Scotland I will need a lot of ready money, which I want to be as untraceable as possible. Please let me know what you can do, and about an appointment for Shonagh. Also, not a word about this to Helen. If you could put her on then that would be great."

He told her how he had missed her and the boys and to get packed up to come home anytime she wanted. She sounded excited so he said goodbye and put the phone down.

He shouted on everyone that the girls and the boys would be back in a few hours.

"Willie, I need to speak to you in private please. Let's go into the dining room where we won't be disturbed."

When Willie had sat down, Denny went to the antique dresser and opened a drawer. He brought over some documents and handed them to Willie.

"What's all this Foggerty? You know I'm not very good with forms and papers."

"Willie, I will go over them with you, but please don't 'piss' me off by arguing about them. These are bank documents in your name, both for the DK bank in Munich and the Bank of Scotland in Edinburgh. Please don't balk at the figures."

Willie looked at the bottom line on each document and put his head in his hands and let the papers drop to the floor.

"Brother, putting both the amounts together nearly makes me a fucking millionaire. What is happening here? I'm just an ex-jailbird from Helmsford, now I could bloody buy Helmsford. If I do that do you think they will call me sir?"

"Bloody doubt that time bomb."

"Willie, I want to make everybody I love secure in life, and rest assured this money doesn't tie you to the Albach Estate. Do what you want with it. Gertie will be looked after as well."

Willie got up and gave Denny a hug. Not the usual hug that leads to them wrestling, but a genuine brotherly hug.

"Thank you Denny. Thank you from the bottom of my heart."

"Your welcome pal, but I'm sure you were going to cry just now, weren't you?"

That was when the wrestling match did start. Right there on the dining room floor. The phone interrupted their 'playful' fight. It was Ian.

"How is everybody over there? We've been worried. What happened?"

"Ian, don't worry, they did come for us. Five of them, but we soon sorted it out. We killed four of them and took the fifth and stuck him on a plane back to Edinburgh."

"Are you bloody mad Denny? You let one go?"

"I sent him back to Edinburgh as I had people watching for his flight to arrive and most importantly who picked him up. Getting the car registration was the main aim, and at this moment in time, Tommy and Shonagh are working on finding out who owns it. Then I can work out my plan to come to Scotland and wipe them out."

"For fuck sake Denny, have you lost it? You don't know who you are up against. You should know there are a lot of very hard men in Scotland. This is madness."

"Ian, I have explained to everyone that I can't carry on with my life just looking over my shoulder every moment of the day. Don't worry there will be four of us."

"Sorry, Denny this must be a bad connection. For a minute I thought you said there would be only four of you."

"That's all I need Ian. My plan is complicated, but workable. Oh, and your brother won't be with me. He will be staying at home to look after the estate."

"Denny, if there is anything I can do to help then you only have to ask. You know you could be on a one way journey to meet your pals in Hell don't you?"

"It has crossed my mind, but I have so much confidence in my plan and my own ability, that I am sure I will be having another talk with you by the end of the year. Have confidence my friend. Please get Neala to phone Helen tonight for a catch up. See you soon."

When Ian came off the phone he put his head in his hands and sat down. Neala asked him if he was alright.

"Neala, I can't believe what Denny is going to do. It's like he is going to try and win a war virtually single handedly. I'm not sure if he's mad or not."

"Ian, if there is one man that can take the war to the enemy, then it's Denny."

"It's just that he is so casual about it. He asked for you to phone Helen tonight if possible in our conversation."

Ian walked out the door and went and sat by the harbour outside Scroggies. The lights from the building work on the far side of the harbour lit up the water which gave off an eerie glow. He wondered if he would ever see Denny again.

In the middle of the afternoon, they all stood and watched the jeep with Jinty at the wheel coming up the track. When it reached the house, Helen didn't wait until Jinty had switched of the ignition before she jumped out and ran up and into Denny's arms. After smothering him with kisses she started hugging and kissing everyone else. A long hug was reserved for her little hero Tomaz. He certainly was enjoying it. Jinty and Gertie came up with the boys and Denny hugged them close and gave them lovely kisses on their foreheads.

"I will go with Gertie and make something for you to eat."

"Don't bother young lady, I will make everyone a meal. You go and hold your babies with your husband," said Artem.

Jinty walked up to the veranda and threw her arms around Yuri.

"I have been so worried about you and Tomaz. I had visions of losing you both."

Then the tears started flowing. Until a booming voice said," Hey, stop that bloody blubbering Thomas. You know that I can't stand it."

"Just because you're a heartless bastard Foggerty, it doesn't mean that we all are."

"That heartless bastard saved us from losing our lives Jinty. Believe me," said Yuri.

Jinty dried her eyes and very slowly walked over to Denny, put her arms around his waist and held on to him. Like tomorrow would never come. He bent down and whispered in her ear.

"Thank you for looking after Helen and the boys Jinty."

"Thank you Denny for looking after my two boys. You do know I love you, don't you. My beautiful big giant from Durma."

After the lovely meal prepared by Artem, Denny announced that he wanted the estate to get back to normal. He then walked the dogs, and after everyone had gone home, Helen had said they should have an early night after the boys went down to sleep.

When they were together she did her usual slow strip of taking her clothes off teasing Denny. Tonight, Denny didn't need any encouragement. He picked her up, put her on the bed and removed her panties. They both realised that there was to be no foreplay tonight, and they were soon enjoying each others body. Helen had thought she had never felt Denny as 'hard' as he was tonight. After several hours of making love in their favourite positions, they were totally spent, then fell asleep as their heads hit the pillows.

The next day felt good for Denny. He knew it was just a lull in the storm, but he was going to embrace it no matter how long it was going to last. They were all just about to head into the forest when Willie pulled Denny aside to speak to him.

"Denny, have you noticed how Ottar's health is starting to deteriorate?"

"Yeh I have brother. I phoned Otto a week ago and he told me just to let things play out. He said that Ottar would let us know when it was time. However, I think it's Tomaz that's keeping him going, but it will be hard on him when it's time for the dog to go. We know he is a very old dog for his breed, but let's not wish him away."

For the next few days, it was all about work and Denny had deliberately organised it so that he was working with Tomaz. One day they were sitting eating their lunch, so Denny thought he would broach the subject of Ottar with Tomaz.

"Tomaz, sit still and don't move a muscle. I know you can talk, you haven't fooled me for sometime now, but this time please just listen, and don't try and give me any of your 'crap' sign language. You have spent a lot of time with Ottar, and I am sure you will see that he is getting very old. So old, that I don't think he has a lot of time left running through these forests. So, when his time comes he will know, and when he goes you can be upset, but life goes on. Okay?"

Tomaz couldn't accept the reality of what Denny had said, so he just turned his head to the side and nodded. Denny just grabbed him and gave him a quick hug, before telling him lunch was over and they had work to do.

It was two days after that Denny got a phone call from Felix telling him about the bar that the guy that shot Helen, drank in. Denny knew where it was as it wasn't far from the Hoffman's shop. He asked if Felix could phone him tomorrow night if the guy was in. Felix had said that wouldn't be a problem.

It was getting colder each day they were working, and Denny thought how cold it would be when he eventually went to Scotland. He knew that Yuri had been used to adverse weather while on operations in the army, but he doubted that Karl and Tomaz would have experienced anything like a severe winter in Scotland. When they finished work that day, Helen had told Denny that Felix had phoned and could he phone him back as soon as possible. He told Yuri and Tomaz to go and shower, and after eating they were going with him to the town. Denny phoned Felix and he was told that the person they wanted to speak to had went in to one of the bars in the town. He had his usual entourage of sycophants with him. Denny thanked him.

Within the hour they were heading to meet Felix near the bar in question. When they got there Denny had asked him where they were sitting and was there a back door to the place. Felix told him and explained where the back door would bring him in about.

"Right lads, this is what I want to happen. You two go in to bar and sit down between the 'scumbag's girlfriend and the next guy. Tomaz, if there is a big heavy guy there then you sit beside him and have one of your knives ready. You will probably get abuse from the guy who is just a mouthpiece, but I will then come in from the back door. Also, no names. They should know mine, but I don't want them knowing yours. Oh, and no violence unless it is absolutely necessary. Are we clear?"

They both nodded and headed to the front door of the bar. When they walked through the door they noticed a few old guys sitting opposite the bar, and the people they were there to speak too were sitting in a small 'snug' room, just through from the bar. It was obvious that the guy they wanted was holding court, while playing up to his girlfriend. Denny was right about the heavy guy being there, along with a smaller guy who didn't look particularly happy to be in the company.

189

They never gave the barman a glance, just walked forward and sat next to them where Denny had asked them to. They sat in silence just looking at them all. Until, the 'main' guy started to shout.

"Get the fuck out of here, this is private. Remove yourselves or me and my friends will do it for you. Do you know who I am?"

"I know who you are you 'scumbag'," said Denny as he walked through from the back door.

As Denny sat down beside him, the guy paled.

"I presume you know why we are here, don't you?"

There was no response so Denny thought he would take the lead.

"I see that your faces have all healed up from the last time we met, and you, well I hope your vagina wasn't too sore every time you went for a 'piss' was it? Here is what is going to happen."

It was then that the girl started to scream at Denny. No change there then he thought. He put a finger to his lips shushing her. The big guy looked like he was going to make a move at Denny.

"I wouldn't if I were you pal, as my little friend there has a knife at your ribs and one word from me and you're a dead man. Or, he might just decide to stick it into your heart just for the sake of it."

Tomaz removed the knife and pretended to take it over his own throat while never taking his eyes of the guy, who had decided the best course of action was to stay still.

"Okay, I will explain it all to you now. This cretin here shot my wife thinking it was me, because I rearranged his face of few years ago while he was illegally poaching on my land. As I did your face also big guy. So here is the story 'scumbag'. You will go to the police station and give yourself over to officer Meyer, and tell him the truth. Nothing less. You will probably get ten years in jail, and I will make sure you will be in real fear of bending over the sink in the showers to wash your face. How does that sound to you?"

The female started her shouting and screaming at him, but Yuri had enough of her and grabbed her by the back of her head and smashed her head on the table. She sprang back and was lying prone on the back of her seat with her teeth smashed and her nose spread over her face. It wasn't a pretty sight.

"Sorry big man, but I just can't stand 'gobby, loud' women and also, I have a headache."

Denny thought so much for no violence then. The small guy at the table started to make a move for the door, but Denny caught him by the arm. He could see that the guy had wet himself, so he turned to him and said.

"You can go pal, and you were never here. If I hear that you have mentioned this to anyone, I will set my dogs on you, and they love ripping people's balls off. You okay with that?"

The guy started to cry, and Yuri thought that Denny was going to explode. Instead, he threw the guy out of the 'snug room' taking a table and chairs with him. The guy bolted out of the door.

"What's it to be then?"

"You have no fucking proof that I shot your wife have you?"

"That's the thing you bastard. I don't need proof, because you are going to the police, yourself right now, and confess that you were on my land to shoot me. If you deviate from the truth, I will come for you and if you think the beating I gave you last time was bad, then you won't waken up from the next one I give you. Honest. We are going to leave you now and there will be no mention to the police of our little tete a tete. We bid you goodnight."

As they walked through the bar the barman was lifting the phone, presumably to call the police. However, Denny grabbed it off him and smashed his face with it. As the guy lay prone, the old regulars stood up together and wandered behind the bar to fill up their glasses from the optics. Probably not for the first time.

They sat in the car for a while not uttering a word, well Denny and Yuri anyway.

"Do you think he will go to the police Denny?"

"I think he will Yuri, but I don't think he will tell the truth. His kind never does, but I hope I get a phone call tomorrow morning from Officer Meyer."

They drove home and Jinty was waiting for Yuri. Denny could see by his face that Yuri just wanted an early night, but he just shrugged his shoulders and wandered off to the shooting lodge with her.

Since the incident, Denny had wanted to spend more and more time with the twins and Helen had often caught him rolling about

191

the floor with them. She was so glad their worries were over. Well, the next few months would try their relationship to the limit.

Next morning, Denny was just back from walking the dogs when the phone ran. It was Officer Meyer telling him that the guy who had shot Helen had walked in to the station and confessed to illegally hunting on the estate and may have inadvertently shot a person by mistake. Although he couldn't be sure.

"Officer Meyer, I am coming down to the station to tell you exactly what happened, so please keep the guy well away from me."

He grabbed the bag with the jersey that Helen had been wearing that day and shouted on Willie. He told him what was happening and said to get everyone out working after breakfast. Denny took off at breakneck speed down the track and when he got to the station he ignored the 'jobsworth' that was telling him he couldn't park there. He didn't even bother closing the door, just marched into the station and asked for Officer Meyer. When the officer came through, he could see the mood that Denny was in, so he asked him through to his office.

"I can tell by your mood that you are not happy with what the culprit has told us Denny. If it had been my wife I would feel the same. Do I believe him? Never. I have had too many run ins with him and his gang over the years, and it's always his father that pulls strings to get him off. Let's sit down and we will go over the scenarios."

They talked for about half an hour before officer Meyer said something relevant to Denny.

"Denny, can I say that if this case goes before judge Klein then we may have a problem."

"Why is that?"

"Well, it is a well known 'secret' that this guy's father, and the judge are the best of friends. Many people have speculated that whenever his son gets off with his crimes, then money changes hands."

Denny then opened the bag, brought out the blooded jersey and put it in front of the officer.

"What is this Denny?"

"It was the jersey my wife was wearing when she was shot. Mine. A cream jersey with a bright red stripe through it. Have you ever seen an animal that looked like that Officer Meyer? One of my sons could have been strapped in a harness to her chest. I would be mourning one dead son now."

"Why didn't you present this evidence to me when I was up at the estate?"

"For the simple reason I know how corrupt the law can be at times, and if necessary I will present it at the court case. Thanks for your candour officer Meyer, but you know I could never let him get away with it, don't you?"

"That's what I am afraid of Denny."

As Denny walked away he turned around.

"How about you and Officer Schmidt come over to do your own thing in the forests next Wednesday. Does that suit? Oh, and can you get me information on this guy's father."

"I will try and do my best, but it will have to be off the record mind you."

Denny just nodded.

"By the way Denny, what was your occupation before you took over the estate?"

"Police Detective."

Denny just smiled and walked away.

He drove back far too fast as his sixth-sense was playing up. Nothing serious, but he had an inkling of what was going on. When he got to the house he shouted on Willie, as it seems nobody had gone out to work, and when he came out he told him he was going to take Ottar a short walk and to expect the worst.

"For fuck sake your not going to shoot him are you?"

"No need Willie. Just be on hand when I come back please."

Denny went to the kennel and Udo and Arno never moved, but Ottar really struggle to get to his feet. Denny could see he was in real pain. Just standing with his head drooped. After he shut the door, Willie walked over and gave Ottar a hug, although Denny thought the dog didn't know who Willie was. Denny started to walk very slowly towards the forest whereby he found a tree to sit under. Ottar lay down beside him with his head on Denny's lap, where he could look at the big house. Denny put his hand on Ottar's chest where he could feel the dogs heart. The beat of his heart was getting slower and shallower until Denny couldn't feel anything at all. Ottar was gone. End of an era.

"Well, my beautiful boy it's been an honour and a privilege to have lived with you, and I hope you have felt the same."

Denny bent down and kissed him on the head.

After a few minutes he rose, picked Ottar up and walked back to the house. Willie was waiting for him, as was Helen. He expected Helen to be in tears, but she just kissed the dog and said she would cry later in private.

"Willie, can you please go up and get Tomaz."

Willie ran up, and within minutes of him reaching the lodge, Tomaz was speeding down the track. When he got near Denny, he stopped a few yards from him. Unable to believe that was Ottar in his arms.

"Come here Tomaz, and give your pal Ottar a kiss, don't be afraid."

By then Yuri and Artem had appeared and just stood watching Tomaz. It was then that he pointed to his eyes, pleading to Denny for the tears to flow. Denny just gave him a nod and the floodgates opened. Artem walked over and held him tightly.

"Helen, can you get a nice warm blanket to wrap Ottar in. Tomaz, no more tears please and go and get two spades from the equipment store as you and I will bury him."

Denny had suggested there was a lovely area just up from the back of the house where he thought Ottar would like to rest in peace. Helen had thought that would be nice and Tomaz just nodded his head. As they dug the hole, Denny had said he wanted it deep and covered with large stones to deter foxes. When they were finished he asked everyone to stand in a silent prayer. That set Tomaz off again before Denny shouted at him.

"Tomaz, there are two more dogs to look after, which one are you going for?"

Tomaz looked at Denny and put up one finger on each hand. He was going for both of them. Denny smiled and then gave him a hug. Denny then went and got the dogs out and walked them up to the grave. They knew, and Arno had walked forward and lay down with his head on his paws just looking at the grave. Udo had refused to go anywhere near the grave, no matter how much Denny had tried to coax him.

"Okay, everyone we will have something to eat and then we have to get back in the forests, they won't look after themselves. Willie, it's you and me along with Udo down in the South valley and Tomaz and Yuri with Arno up North. I need to know if you see any sign of foxes, dead or alive."

It was a very sombre breakfast, with only Willie asking Denny what had happened at the police station. Everybody looked at Denny, but he just shook his head, letting everyone know to drop the subject. Denny had asked them to wait on him as he had a phone call to make.

"Otto is that you? It's Denny, I've got some bad news for you. Ottar passed away a few hours ago. He was at peace when he went."

"Thanks for letting me know Denny, and I am so glad he passed away in the place he loved the best. At least you have his sons with you. I spoke to Maria about your little problem and how you had sorted it out. How did the dogs perform Denny?"

"They were unbelievable Otto. Remind me to tell you about them when I see you next."

"Let's go you lot, we have a lot to catch up on. Still wear your rifles and have your radios on your waist bands. Tomaz you are in charge of Arno today, so you had better do a good job. Hear me?"

Tomaz jumped up and walked over to Arno and put his arm around his neck. Just waiting for Denny to say they were off. It was good to see.

"Artem, please look after the girls and my boys. Don't take any nonsense from the girls. My boys can do what they want."

The day seemed long for Denny, and it was dragging for Willie as well. He had said so after Yuri had radioed Denny about finding some dead foxes. Youngsters by the look of them. Denny thought he was going to have words with this Albescu, but he was trying to get his head around everything else at the moment, and now this. He didn't think his head had enough room for all the rubbish that people were throwing at him. It was about that point that Denny radioed Willie and called a halt to the work for today. He knew he needed to lie soaking in a hot bath and get an early night. Losing Ottar had taken more than he thought out of him. When he got back to the house, he told everyone just to go home and he would see them in the morning, but he needed to speak to Willie.

"It's to let you know that I had an interesting conversation with Office Meyer earlier. It appears that the father of the guy who shot Helen is in 'cahoots' with one of the judges and there is a chance that this guy might escape justice."

Willie just sat there not quite able to take in what he had said.

"Are you telling me that 'scumbag' might get away with it. One of my nephews could have been killed for fuck sake. I told you we should have found him and slit the bastard's throat, leaving him for the wolves up in the North valley. We could still do it, couldn't we?"

"It would be a bit obvious now brother. However, I did give you my word that he won't get away with it. I'm going for a long soak and go to my bed. Today hasn't been a very pleasant one, and I fear there are more of these days to come."

That night Helen had been very emotional over Ottar. Several time she woke Denny with her crying. All he could do was hold her tight. At about two thirty they were both woken up with the dogs giving out some small yelps and loud whinging. Helen had asked Denny what was going on. He knew immediately.

"The dogs are grieving Helen. They are missing Ottar. I'm going to lie with them for a while. Will you be okay?"

"I will be fine and please give them a hug from me."

Over breakfast, Denny told all the men about what was said at the police station, albeit out of earshot of the girls. They all looked a bit stunned, especially Tomaz who just sat shaking his head. Denny could see his anger starting to come over him, so he quickly assured everyone that the guy would not get away with it. He would get his head around it, but he told them not to worry or think about it until the court case.

"Yuri, I wonder if you could come with me and show me where Albescu the fox poacher lives. It couldn't have been very nice seeing those carcasses of young foxes yesterday. I am just about fed up of people bringing their evil on to my land, but then again I might have brought my evil on the first time I came here. I plan to get rid of all the evil on the estate and to exterminate all the bad people who think they can ride roughshod over me. I

196

didn't initiate the violence, but sure as hell I am going to retaliate, and they will wish they had never heard of Denny Rey Foggerty."

"That was some speech brother. Later, I am going to write that down and keep it for posterity."

Denny threw a bread roll just missing him, but Arno grabbed it before Udo knew what was going on. All tensions were lifted when Gertie came out of the house and tripped over Udo who had been lying just outside the French doors. The coffee pot and cups went flying. Udo knew that he had better make himself scarce, so he took off jumping down the steps, before running to the nearest tree, looking back at Gertie, and defiantly cocking his leg against it. Everyone was trying not to laugh as she stood at the top of the steps cursing him in German. They all helped her to clear up.

"Please listen everyone, I need a concerted effort from you all over the next week. The streams are being clogged up with fallen debris and you all know how vital the water is to the animals. We can all finish a bit early as Yuri and I are going to see a man about a dog, sorry, a fox. Okay Yuri?"

Yuri nodded and then they all rose and started to walk to their work. Denny had said that Willie would be working with Tomaz, and he was to try and not to shoot him. Tomaz was still a bit down so Willie had told him they would play tricks on the other pair with their radios. Tomaz had laughed. Throughout the day, Willie was making animal noises into the radio. Tomaz couldn't help but laugh. The radio crackled.

"Willie, your last animal impersonation sounded like a bloody T Rex for God's sake. Please let us know if you are under attack from prehistoric animals down there. If you are, then they can have you."

Willie had turned round to see Tomaz laughing his socks off. He had thought Tomaz was a precious wee soul, but there was always that little streak of danger about him. He thought he would rather have him on his side than against him though.

It was Tomaz who heard it first and cupped a hand behind his ear and started poking Willie and pointing. There was a motorised vehicle in the forest over to the West. Willie immediately got on the radio and contacted Denny.

"Get over there and we will come from the North. Don't take any chances. My sixth-sense is not telling me of any danger to us. Be quick."

Tomaz grabbed Udo around the neck and pointed to where they were going. They all took off with Willie trying to outrun Tomaz, but after a while he was lying a poor third in the race. After a while they met Yuri and Denny coming down from the North.

"I can still hear it but it's faint. However, I would know the sound of that engine anywhere. It's that bastard Albescu. He would often run his old Mini Moke along the track that ran past our farm. Presumably to go poaching on your land Denny," said Yuri.

"Let's go over to where he lives tonight pal and see what is going on. I suggest we take some coats and hats with us as a bit of a disguise as I don't want anything happening to him tonight."

"It's likely that he will be drinking in the small village a couple of miles from our old farm."

As they started to walk back, the first snowflakes of the year started to fall. Denny thought that was an ominous sign considering he intended to pay Scotland a visit some time soon. After they had all eaten Yuri had appeared at the house where Denny was waiting for him. They both took an ATV and headed over the hill to where the farm had been. When they got to the top they stopped and looked at the burnt out shells of the buildings. Denny gave Yuri a few minutes for reflection. Afterwards Yuri just shrugged his shoulders and told Denny they needed to keep going as the light would fade soon.

They crossed a bridge just down from the farm. He never knew that this river existed or where it flowed to, but it certainly was fast flowing. Denny kept that fact in the back of his mind. After a few minutes they could see the lights of the small village getting closer.

Yuri stopped before they got right into the village and pointed out a dilapidated house which belonged to Albescu. Denny thought it was nothing more than a 'shithole.' How anybody could live like this beggared belief.

"Okay, Yuri lets get our scruffy clothes on. We will park the vehicles here. Hopefully they will be safe for the length of time we will be here."

After donning an old coat and hat each, they walked to the centre of the village and the only bar. It wasn't quite as bad as Albescu's house, but it was heading that way.

"Just follow my lead Yuri. I have been taught by the master, Felix. No trouble tonight. I need to know what this 'animal' is like."

As they walked through the doors, Albescu was instantly recognisable. He was sitting drinking what Denny thought was vodka or some clear alcohol. His singing wasn't being appreciated by the clientele, but Denny thought he looked like a bully, and wouldn't think twice about exerting violence on anyone who objected. They sat at the next table, but after a while they wished they hadn't as the odour that was coming off him was rank and overpowering.

Albescu kept looking at Denny as if he recognised him, before he asked him if he had seen him before. Yuri quickly intervened and said they had been traveling all over looking for work and Denny couldn't speak as he had been a mute since birth.

"Everybody, we have a 'dummy' here. Never spoken a fucking word in his miserable life."

Nobody laughed except him.

"Albescu here is never without work or money. I trap foxes on that rich bastards property, giving me money for the vodka each night."

Yuri grabbed Denny's arm as he felt he was going to confront him. Eventually, he felt the tension in his body starting to ease. They sat for a couple of more minutes before the stench was beginning to make them nauseous. Anyway, Denny thought he had seen enough. When leaving the table, he deliberately bumped into Albescu's table spilling some of his vodka. Immediately, the Romanian got up and grabbed Denny's arm. Denny mouthed that he was sorry and took ten deutschmarks out of his pocket and slowly put them on the table pretending to show fear.

Albescu shoved him away, pocketed the money and then started to shout, "You see everybody, they are all frightened of me and the next time that 'dummy' comes in here I will kill him."

Yuri and Denny left the bar with Denny starting to laugh.

"Why did you bump into him you stupid bastard Denny. You could have started a fight and then the plan would have been ruined."

"Firstly Yuri, I needed to find out if he had any strength about him, which he hasn't. He's just flab. Secondly, I'm a rich bastard Yuri and thirdly, what plan?"

This made Denny laugh even more which unnerved Yuri a bit.

"Denny, I would like to speak you sooner rather than later about our 'trip' to Scotland. There are certain things I want you to explain to me. Just when you can please."

"Will this week be okay for you pal?"

Yuri nodded, and they started to take off their old coats until they realised how cold it was getting, so they thought better of it. The snow was getting heavier, so they hightailed it towards the farm and then over the hill to the house.

Jinty's car was parked outside, and they walked into the kitchen looking for a hot drink.

"You here again Jinty? Let me ask you this. If Yuri didn't live here would you be up as often?"

"Listen Foggerty, do you remember you said I wasn't to do my usual straddling of you while all that nonsense was happening. Well, it's over so here goes."

Denny had wished he had kept his mouth shut, as Jinty provocatively walked over to him, lifted her skirt leaving nothing to the imagination and straddled him.

"Right Denny, I'm not moving until I get my kiss. Make your mind up."

Just then Helen walked in and shouted at Jinty to get off her husband.

"Helen Fraser, I am trying to get him excited, as I think he must be neglecting you in the bedroom stakes."

"Trust me you little 'trollop' our love life is great thanks. So, get off him."

Denny picked her up by the waist and walked over to Yuri and planted her in his lap.

"Is she like this with you Yuri?"

"Yeh she is, but when she sits on my lap it's for real."

Jinty's face was a picture as they all started laughing. As Yuri and Jinty were out the door, Denny didn't realise what was happening when she ran back, grabbed his head and gave him a long kiss on the lips.

"Get out Thomas. I'll never know why I have you as my best friend. Now beat it."

It was then that Willie came in with a glum face on him.

"What's wrong with the Love Master tonight then?" said Denny.

"That's just it brother, the Love Master can't perform his moves this week. A whole bloody week. No pun intended. Life really isn't fair. What do you think?"

Willie wasn't quick enough in ducking as Helen hit him square in the face with the tea towel she had thrown.

"What?"

"Oh, and just to cheer you up I have told the two police officers they can come over next Wednesday for a day in the forest. Remember, your in charge pal."

"That's it Foggerty, I'm leaving this place."

Willie walked away looking as miserable as sin.

Denny knew that day would come, but he didn't know when.

Later at night, Denny and Helen sat outside on the veranda. They were drinking tea, and generally just chatting about the boys and life on the estate with a blanket wrapped around them. The future never came up. The snow was coming down harder, so he turned and looked at Helen.

"Helen, have you ever thought about living elsewhere?"

"What's brought that on? To answer your question then no. I take it you have been thinking about it."

"Helen, I feel that the estate is closing in on me at times, but to allay your fears, I would never leave here, but what I was thinking about was buying another estate or large house with extensive grounds in Scotland. You know I think it is one of the most beautiful countries in the world. Yes I am biased, but I took a train trip up North to the Highlands once and the scenery I saw was absolutely breathtaking. My thoughts were that we could spend several months a year there while still living here."

"I can see it in your eyes Denny that you seem keen, so maybe we should sit down and work out the possibilities at some point.

However, I have a funny feeling that there is a lot more to happen before we can even think about this."

She looked at Denny, but he couldn't make eye contact with her.

They were both exhausted, and decided they would be better in their bed than sitting out here.

After walking the dogs, the next morning, Denny wondered if there would be any chance of much work getting done. There had been a bit of a snowfall during the night, which made it slightly tricky working on any banking at the streams. Everybody turned up on time, although Willie still had his surly face on.

"What I would like to speak about over breakfast is that smelly bastard Albescu. So, if you have any thoughts on what we should do with him then please speak up. Tomaz did his usual and drew his finger along his throat. Willie didn't seem very interested, and just suggested they shoot him. However, Yuri came up with an idea.

"As you know, he always has to come over the small bridge in his vehicle to get to the estate, so lets stage an accident that makes it look like he toppled off, full of vodka of course. The swollen river would do the rest. The difficulty being that we may have to beat him unconscious first to make it happen. I'm sure there will be a few minor details to work out, but I know it will be viable."

"Sounds like a fair plan Yuri. I like the idea that we make it look like an accident, as I don't want this estate coming into disrepute."

"That's a laugh Foggerty, considering we have just killed four people, and your proposing to lay siege to Scotland."

"What a miserable bastard you are this morning McLeod. Just because your not getting sex for a week. Get a grip man. If you end up coming with us to 'lay siege to Scotland' as you succinctly put it, then the Love Master might be out of action for about six to eight weeks. How does that sound?"

Willie lay back in his chair with his head in his hands.

They all wandered into the forests without must enthusiasm. Denny felt that everyone was feeling flat, but he reckoned it was because of the weeks previously, when they were all on a high. Now it was back to normality. Denny thought he would work with Yuri today and it would give them a chance to speak about Scotland. As they sat under the cover of some branches for lunch, Denny had said he would tell Yuri everything he could, but at present that wasn't a great deal.

"To be honest Yuri, I don't know who or how many people we will be up against. I have the suspicion that someone is not happy that I blew up one of his drug running boats, and ended up killing four of his people. I wasn't in a good place with the whisky at the time. Should I have got involved? My brain tells me yes, but my gut instinct is not so sure. We won't have the manpower, so when we engage them, then it will be a 'cut and run' tactic. I plan to make people disappear and put the frighteners on everybody else. Soon, I will have all the information I need to make the start of a plan, and I will include you in it, but unfortunately, until we get there, we won't have the full picture. There is one thing Yuri, I won't let any harm come to you, Karl or Tomaz. Myself? Well, I can't guarantee anything".

He went on to ask Yuri where he thought his future lay. Where he could see himself in five years or so.

"To be honest it has crossed my mind recently. I'm not sure about my relationship with Jinty, as I feel I'm being rushed a bit by her. She is a lovely girl, but I have been used to being on my own for most of my life. I also have to think of my dad and Tomaz. I love working here, but there is no room for advancement is there."

"Take your time with Jinty. She is a great girl and all her flirting with me is just her way of coping. She is still a shy person and would run a mile if I came on to her. Slowly wins the races Yuri. Please don't worry about your dad as we know he is very ill and probably won't be here on this earth for very long. As for Tomaz, well I'm generally a good judge of character, and I honestly think that that little 'bugger' will come good. He will surprise us. Advancement? Well, how do you fancy learning more about the forest. How we could develop it into one of the biggest nature reserves in Europe. There may be an opening coming up for a Forestry Manager soon."

"What are trying to say Denny? That's Willie's title is it not?"

"Not saying anything Yuri, but I know things will change over the next few months. The Albach Trust must change, and I will have to change with it. If you want to learn more, then I will get Otto over to teach you the things he taught me. Trust me, he is a very knowledgeable person and makes it all interesting. Have a think about it and get back to me. Also, your thoughts on Scotland please. Oh, when its time to let Helen and Jinty know about Scotland, do you want me to tell Jinty?"

"Just leave it Denny, it will be better coming from me."

Nothing much was spoken about in the afternoon, and Denny was quite glad as there was enough going through his head. He knew that Officer Meyer would get back to him soon and he didn't think it would be good news. What he really needed was a sit down with Maria to put over all his thoughts to her. He was thinking she might be in for a surprise.

When he got back to the house and hugged his sons, the phone ran. It was Miss Glover.

"Good afternoon Denny. I hope that you are all well and my two boys are thriving. I really need to speak with you. Let's hope you enjoyed yourself on your short visit to the island. You may not have heard, but there was grave news not long after you left, as we were all told that Mike Stewart had decided to commit suicide. What possessed him to do that I'll never know. Since you left I have done a lot of soul searching with regard to your offer of me coming over to help you with your project for the estate. I feel if I don't accept your offer now, then I will regret it. Oh, and by the way Miss Bryant thanks you very much for your offer, but she feels she has a lot of unfinished business here on Durma. My biggest concern Denny is where I would live. I would prefer to be near you all, as I obviously wouldn't know anyone over there apart from yourselves

"Don't worry about that Miss Glover. There will be a new two bedroom bungalow waiting for you by the start of next year. Just at the bottom of the estate. If that is okay? I have so many plans for the estate, and I would like to speak to you about them to see if you are up for the challenge."

"Of course, Denny if I can help the estate in any way then I would be happy to. Am I up for the challenge? You bet I am. I really thank you for what you are doing for me. Is Jinty behaving herself?"

"Silly question Miss Glover, I will speak to you soon, and I have somebody here to speak to you."

"Denny, before you go, can I please ask you to call me Gladys."

"It would feel a bit strange calling you Gladys, but I will try my best. Here is Helen and take care Gladys."

Denny handed over the phone to Helen, who by the look on her face was wondering who the hell Gladys was.

Denny thought that was another piece in the jigsaw. When Helen came off the phone she looked happy, and it was then that he had decided not to tell the girls about Scotland until the last minute. He wanted life on the estate to be as normal for the next few weeks.

As he was sitting outside just watching the snow fall he knew had to sort things out. One at a time he told himself. The first being Albescu. The snow falling incessantly was good for their plan as they needed the river to be swollen. Within a couple of nights, that Romanian bastard wouldn't kill another fox on this earth.

Next morning, over breakfast, everybody seemed down. Even the girls, although Jinty had managed to drive through the snow to see her lover boy. Denny wondered how it would affect her if Yuri ever decided to end it. At the moment she seemed happy.

"What the fuck is wrong with you all? Are you all trying to imitate McLeod here. You look quite happy Artem, but it seems you are the only one."

Just then they heard a vehicle coming up the drive. Slowly they all lifted their rifles and held them ready in their laps. Denny was quite impressed. When Denny looked out he recognised it was Otto and Lina. He went down the steps to meet them, shook Otto's hand and gave Lina a hug. She had a large bunch of wild flowers in her hand.

"Nice to see you both."

"And you Denny. As you can see we are here to see Ottar's grave if that is okay?"

"Of course, remember Otto he was your dog and you spent most of his life with him. Helen and Tomaz are looking after his grave. Before you go up, can I ask you for your help. One of my men is keen to learn more about the forest, and I really don't have a lot of time to teach him. So, I was wondering if we could impose on you to come over for him to learn. Just as I did."

"Not a problem Denny."

Otto walked over to the dogs, and commanded them to come with him to the grave. Arno was up for it, but Udo just took off into the forest. Otto just smiled, with Lina wondering what was going on. Denny could see them standing over the grave and Lina walked back on her own as Otto must have said he wanted a minute by himself. Helen and Gertie came out with the boys and greeted them. In no time at all Lina had the boys in each arm. Looking very happy.

"Denny, you were going to tell me how the dogs performed during you skirmish."

"Come over here away from girls Otto."

As they sat at the far end of the veranda, Denny told Otto about the dogs.

"Bloody hell, that couldn't have been a pretty sight my friend? How have they behaved after that?"

"Neither up nor down. The only thing being that Udo won't go near the grave as you just witnessed."

"Don't worry about him Denny, he will come round."

Denny told Otto about the incident with Tomaz and Ottar on the steps when Willie wanted to shoot them both. Otto burst out laughing. Denny then told him about his plans for the estate, and the buying up of forestry land throughout Germany. Also, his idea of buying an estate in Scotland.

"That is massive son. I hope you know what you are getting in to, but I'm sure you will have done your research. If there is anything I can do then please just ask, but maybe you and Maria should be sitting down and discussing this".

Denny agreed with him and promised he would phone him soon to come over for Yuri.

Chapter 9

After Otto and Lina had left, Denny then went up to the men and said they were going to participate in a camouflaging exercise which will be needed when they go to Scotland. He said that Karl would be over to explain what they had to do, but they were to take it
seriously, as it could save their lives.

"Bloody hell Foggerty, we're now going to be playing hide and seek in the bloody snow. It's freezing out there."

"It will be even more colder in Scotland pal as you well know, and just because you won't be with us, doesn't mean you should take it half heartedly. Right, let's take a walk in to the forest to see what areas we need addressing."

As they walked together the mood seemed to lighten a bit with Tomaz being the butt of their jokes. Although, Tomaz wasn't really getting it at times. The wind was starting to pick up and it was difficult seeing at times, but that was all good for acclimatising themselves for the job in hand. Denny knew it would be difficult for them, but knew the wilder the weather the better. He was determined to get the four people going to Scotland trained up to the maximum.

When they were walking back, Denny had asked Yuri if he could work out a training program for the four of them over the next six weeks. Just physical fitness, based on the training he experienced in the Czech army. Yuri had agreed, and said he was glad Denny had wanted this, but had said the training would be brutal.

The rain was mixing with the snow now.

"Yuri? I think we should head over to see about that Romanian bastard tomorrow. That river should be high and flowing powerfully. What do you think?"

"Sound by me Denny, but I think we should take Tomaz with us as I think it could be a three man job."

"All good Yuri, but it's maybe better that he leaves his knives at home as this is supposed to be an accident."

Yuri wondered if he would ever get used to how calm Denny was when he was about to murder someone, or did Denny consider it a murder? When Denny got back to the house Gertie had shouted on him that he had to phone the police station and speak to Officer Meyer. He knew what he was going to tell Denny, so it came as no surprise when he said that the judge for the court case would be Judge Klein.

"So, we're pretty much screwed aren't we? Okay, I will have to resort to Plan B and that might be a bit messy for some."

"Denny, please don't do anything stupid will you. I really do realise how you are feeling as I would be, but you can't jeopardise your freedom over a scum like him."

"Well, I trust you my friend, so what I will say to you is that I will do everything in my and the Trust's power to exact revenge on them, judge included, if he gets off with it. Remember, I was a Detective back in Scotland, a bloody good one at that, and I know how people got rid of bodies. Will I put them in the ground? Let's wait and see. One thing Officer Meyer, nobody, and I mean nobody, will ever get enough evidence to convict me. Looking forward to seeing you and Hans on Wednesday. Take care."

Denny put the phone down. He went to the folder he had been given on the guy's father and read it from cover to cover. He fell asleep sitting on the chair before Helen woke him up with a kiss. He was a bit startled, but grabbed her and pulled her down on to his lap and started kissing her. He felt it better to get all the kisses in now before he had to tell her he was going leave her for God knows how long.

They were interrupted by the phone, and Helen reluctantly went and answered it. Denny could hear the conversation, and then heard Shonagh's voice. Eventually, Helen shouted it was Shonagh and asked him to come to the phone. He asked Helen if she could give him privacy, which she found to be a bit strange, however she knew better than to question him.

"Hi Shonagh, It's nice to hear from you. How's your arm? You and Jack still okay? Sorry for the questions, but I always think about how you are."

"I'm sure you know this is not a social call, don't you? I have the information you asked for. The car is registered to the Ruthven Estate, which is just below the Cairngorm National

Park. Probably about a couple of hours from Dundee. It is owned by the Right Honourable James Robertson MP. I can't get a lot of information on the estate, but one of my colleagues up there has said that over the last few years there has been a lot of activity in and around the big house. A lot of comings and goings. He did say that there has been a lot of talk about the local sergeant being in Robertson's pocket, but only hearsay. The MP is not a well liked man, even among his own constituents, but especially among his fellow Peers in Parliament. He has an office in Edinburgh and sometimes stays over, but he does spend a fair bit of time in Aberdeen and Dundee, but only rarely at the estate. Not sure I can give you much more Denny."

"That's been great Shonagh. I really appreciate it. One last thing though. Do you have his office phone number?"

"Why would you want his phone number Denny? Are you going to meet him or what? For God's sake."

"Shonagh, stop being 'gobby' and give me the number. It's all part of my plan."

She gave him the number and he said his goodbyes. He phoned her back immediately and started to give her kisses over the phone when she answered.

"I know it's you Foggerty, so get lost as these are false kisses."

He put the phone down and laughed.

He thought that another piece of the puzzle had been solved.

Denny had waited until everyone was waiting to start work including Karl, before speaking to them.

"Okay, folks please listen to me. In preparation for us leaving for Scotland, I have asked Yuri to put us through a rigorous training program each day for us going to a windswept, freezing, but beautiful Scotland. I want us to be as fit as we can be, as I don't know how long we will be there, and I have a feeling that at some stage it will end up a test of endurance. Karl is also going to teach us a bit about surveillance and concealment, so during all this if you have any thoughts or questions then you must say. It may be too late when we are over there."

"Willie, as you and Gunther are staying here then you don't have to participate okay?"

"What are you trying to say Foggerty. I bet I am still fitter than you lot, even after you have been training for a few weeks. You up for the bet brother?"

"I will take your bet pal with the forfeit still to be agreed. It will be fun taking it from you. In fact, I will make it easier for you. I'm backing Tomaz to beat you in any contest we agree on."

"The only way he will beat me is if I have two broken legs. End of story."

Yuri had told everyone to take their tops off, as they were going for a run. Even with the snow coming down, and when he shouted then everyone was to hit the deck and lie face down, until he said it was okay to get up. Karl looked like he had stepped into Hell, except it was snowing there.

Off they went at speed with Willie laughing at them. The dogs were loving it and every time they went to ground, the dogs did as well. Yuri took them up the hill on the North trail towards where his farm used to be. The hill was absolutely brutal, and Denny hung back helping Karl along as he thought he might end up having to carry him. After half an hour, Yuri shouted that they were to get back to the house by any means and as fast as they could.

Tomaz and Arno took off into the forest, but Denny knew he had to run with Karl, while Yuri ran as fast as he could to try and beat Tomaz. He failed miserably. Before Karl and Denny got back, Tomaz was sitting on the steps drinking a cup of tea and eating one of Gertie's scones.

"How did you do that you little bugger? I would have scratches all over my face trying to run through the trees, and stop feeding Arno your scone for fuck sake," Denny shouted.

Tomaz just put his arm around Arno's neck and smiled. This time his smile was a bit different thought Denny. Tomaz was changing. He wrapped Karl in a blanket, and the girls came out with a welcome mug of coffee for everyone.

"Right, everyone we have work to do so let's go. Willie, get your arse out here as we're going to do some work. Seeing as your supposed to be the Forestry Manager, how about you being in charge of the work from now on. Oh, and girls please don't let Karl die. We need him."

By the look of Karl, he thought the girls would have a job on their hands.

Work that day was cold, and everyone was just going through the motions. Even the dogs were feeling it. Later, when the rain came down in a torrent, Willie called a halt to the work, citing the fact that not even the animals and birds would be out today. Karl was gone when they got back, so Denny went in and phoned Maria.

"Hi Maria. It's been a while since we've spoken. I was wondering if you could do some work for me please. It is very important to me, so I was wondering if you wanted to pop over and speak to me tomorrow or I can come over there?"

"Of course, I will come over tomorrow at about four o'clock, and it will give me a chance to see the boys as well."

"Thanks Maria and be prepared for not liking what you will hear."

The rain never let up that night, but he went and told Willie that the two officers would be here in the morning, and he was to keep checking on them throughout the day, but Denny felt that he wasn't paying much attention. On leaving the annex he wandered up to the lodge, stopping for a few minutes at Ottar's grave. When he knocked on the door Artem answered, and he got a bit of a shock how failed he looked. Artem asked him in, and Denny asked where Tomaz was. Out 'training' was his reply. Denny smiled. He knew he was going to win his bet. Artem made some tea and asked Denny if they could have a chat.

"Denny, I hope this isn't too morbid for you, but as you will see by my condition, I fear the end isn't far away. I came to terms with it a while ago, so I have no fear of dying. What I would really like is for to be buried here in the forest as it's such a lovely place, but only with your permission."

"Does both your lads know what you want Artem? You can choose a spot where you would like to lie, and it will be okay with me. Remember, I did say to you that your boys are now part of this family, and I promise they will be well looked after for the rest of their lives. No matter where they end up."

"God bless you Denny. I will die a happy man knowing that. Well as happy as I can be."

They chatted for a while before Tomaz came in. Soaking, sweating, but looking happy.

"I've got a wager riding on you pal, so you had better come through for me."

Tomaz got down and started to do press-ups. Whether he was having a laugh or trying to impress, Denny just smiled and said goodbye. The rain had started to go off, so he knew that visiting Albescu had to be tomorrow night. When Yuri drove back from seeing Jinty, he would speak to him.

That night in bed, Helen had asked him what was all the secrecy on the phone was about, and why did he have everyone out 'training' in atrocious conditions. He felt that the time for telling her was near.

"I will tell you soon Helen, but please don't worry. Also, Maria is coming over tomorrow at four o'clock to speak to me about estate work, but I think it could be just to see you and the boys."

Karl was the first to appear, so Denny went into the equipment room and brought out four camouflage coats and told everyone when they arrived that breakfast would be a bit later as Karl wanted to give them a lesson in concealment. Wearing their coats, they wandered in to the forest where he gave them a demonstration where you could hide yourself and people would just walk right past you. Everyone had a shot at trying it out, however Denny struggled due to his size, but Karl had said he would show him another way at some point.

Willie shouted to everyone that breakfast time was over, and they were starting work. Denny just looked at him and laughed. Willie was actually taking the initiative. By two o'clock he called a halt to the work which gave Yuri the chance to tell everyone except Willie, that they were running back at speed. When they got back to the house Denny was in front with Yuri close behind him. Tomaz's training the previous night must have taken it out of him as he struggled.

Yuri and Karl's training was to be relentless over the next few weeks, with Tomaz ending up the star pupil, but Denny never mentioned anything to Willie about it.

Maria came bang on time and to be honest, Denny knew long before she appeared as she was driving her dad's car, and the noise from the engine was unbelievable. When she got out she gave Denny a long hug, and then went to see Helen and the boys. They were crawling about the lounge and Maria was soon on the floor interacting with them.

Denny gave her and Helen a while to speak about the boys, but he was keen to get on with the meeting. Helen could see he was itching to speak to her, so she didn't keep her too long and said that after she spoke to Denny, she should come and have something to eat with her and Gertie.

Denny sat with her in the lounge and started to tell her about all his plans for the estate and also his intentions to expand into Scotland at some point, if the right estate came along. She was both surprised and impressed, and she suggested leaving all that with her and she would write up a report on all the possibilities. She knew about the impending court case, so she would organise for a lawyer to represent him.

"That would be great Maria, but I am glad you are sitting down for the next part. As you know we have had to deal with people coming over to my home to harm us all. We put that to bed, but Maria, this is not over. These people will come again and again, until they have finished the job, and I have no intention of looking over my shoulder all the time. So, please don't judge me on what I am about to say. I am intending taking the fight to them in Scotland. I have done my homework and planning, and I am confident of a favourable outcome. What I do need is a considerable amount of untraceable money deposited in a bank in Edinburgh and one in Dundee. I need a new genuine passport for one of the lads and one not so genuine for another lad that will get him to Scotland and back. I'm sorry about that. There will be four of us leaving in a few weeks, probably after the court case. I will leave you with two folders. One is on the father of the guy that shot Helen, and most importantly one on the person that sent people over to kill us. Please get me as much information as possible."

By this time, Maria was sitting with her head bowed.

"Denny, my life was easier before you owned the Trust, a lot easier. I applaud everything you are wanting to do, except you waging war on Scotland. It's my intention to visit your beautiful country, but hopefully before you raise it to the ground."

"Oh, before you go Maria I need to speak to you urgently about getting some houses and a couple of classrooms built on the land at the bottom of the drive. The houses are for friends wanting to live and work on the estate. The classrooms are for the teaching of the underprivileged kids we talked about a few minutes ago. How about we speak in a few days?"

"Denny, I am going to eat with Helen and Gertie now, before my head explodes."

She gave him a hug and went to the kitchen.

It wasn't long before Yuri and Tomaz came down to the house, ready for going to see Albescu.

"Tomaz, please leave your knives here will you."

The look on Tomaz's face was one of disbelief. How did Denny know? They quickly went over the plan, which was simple. Abduct him and drown him. Willie had walked out and asked what was going on.

"We're just going for a talk with the fox poacher Willie. Don't suppose you want to come?"

"I won't bother pal, as I have a lot of loving to plan for."

As they headed off on their ATVs, Willie sat on the steps watching the lights disappear. He started to think about how much he really knew about Denny. He loved him like a brother, but it bothered him how indifferent he was to murdering people. Okay, he himself had pushed Scottie's head under the water, but there was not a day gone by where he had questioned his action. Over the next few months, he had to do a lot of thinking. If it meant a few hard decisions had to be made. Then so be it.

He looked up and saw Helen looking out the window watching them go. He wondered how long she would put up with his way of life.

When the three of them got to the top of the hill they stopped and gave another look at the old farm. Denny thought it would be prudent for the other two to have a last look. Tomaz wasn't hanging around as he throttled his ATV, and set off to the village. The sleet was being driven into their faces, and it was then that Denny noticed that Tomaz was only wearing a short jacket. He made a mental note to speak to him before they headed of to Scotland.

Tomaz made a sign to stop when they got to the bridge. The river was on flood and lappingjust underneath. Perfect thought Denny and turned to see Yuri giving him a nod. They switched their lights off when they entered the village and parked behind an old ruin of a cottage near the bridge.

"Listen folks, we have talked about our plan before. It has to be simple. Abduct Albescu, take him to the bridge and drown him, but it has to look like an accident by him. What do you think Yuri?"

"It's probably best if I go in to the bar and see if he is there, but I would bet money on it that he will be. I need to see if there is an exit from the bar to the yard at the back and see where his Mini Moke is. That is crucial to the plan."

They walked quickly keeping to the shadows of the houses. There wasn't anybody going out in this weather, and when they got to the bar Tomaz and Denny were starting to go around the back.

"I don't think anybody will recognise me, unlike the big mute giant that spilled his drink. What do you think Denny?"

Denny smiled and walked with Tomaz to wait for Yuri giving them a heads up.

As Yuri entered the bar, he immediately saw Albescu sitting next to a door at the far end of the room. He was worse for wear with the drink. He stood at the bar and waited until the barman could take his eyes away from a grainy television screen at the far end of the bar, before he came and asked Yuri what he wanted to drink. Yuri ordered a vodka and stood looking around him before asking where the toilets were. The barman just pointed with his thumb to the door next to where Albescu was sitting. He realised that nobody could see the door from where they were sitting at the bar.

He left his drink sitting and walked to the toilet. The stench from the poacher was worse than he had remembered, and even while trying to get the door open he felt he was being immersed in the rancid smell. Yuri quickly walked past the two cubicles trying not to breathe for fear of vomiting. Three rusted bolts were keeping the door secure, but he had no problem sliding them back. When he got out he started breathing deeply to try and get some fresh air into his lungs, but the putrid smell was still in his nostrils.

"Bloody hell, Yuri you don't half stink. Is he in there? By the smell of you the answer is yes."

Yuri explained everything to them, and Denny suggested that they quickly go through the door where he would knock him out and drag him out the back door.

"He is such an arrogant bastard that Tomaz found his keys in the vehicle over there. If we are ready then Tomaz will get the Moke started and we will be back soon."

They walked through the back door and in to the toilet. This had to be quick. Denny nodded to Yuri who pulled the bar door open. Denny slipped through, grabbed Albescu by the throat rendering him incapable of saying anything, before giving him two massive punches putting him out for the count. They dragged him through the door, along the toilet floor and out the back.

Tomaz was waiting in the vehicle with the engine running. They lifted Albescu into the passenger seat and Denny and Yuri got in the back and told Tomaz to floor it. As they headed towards the bridge, Yuri held on to Albescu to stop him falling out. Tomaz skidded to a halt

on top of the wooden bridge where they all got out. It looked like Albescu was coming to, so Denny started punching furiously. Tomaz had never seen Denny like this and felt very afraid.

"For fuck sake stop Denny, this is supposed to look like an accident."

Denny came to his senses, and they all moved the poacher to the other side of the vehicle, and started pushing it until it was teetering on the edge of the bridge. One last mighty push and the vehicle went in to the water. All they could see was the top of the vehicle as it floated down the river.

"Right, lets go," shouted Yuri.

"I'll be a minute boys. Don't worry I'll catch you up."

Denny needed that minute to let his evil smile come over his face.

They didn't waste any time in heading back, and when they arrived, Denny had suggested they use the hose at the back of the house, to wash themselves down to get rid of the smell.

Willie walked out and said," Well, half the animals in the forests smell better than you lot. I trust you had your 'wee talk' with the poacher, and I presume he will never bother us again?"

"No, he won't Willie. Yuri a word please. My old friend the sixth-sense has been playing up and unfortunately it has been all about your dad. I really shouldn't say this, but he spoke to me a few days ago about his health. He said he was in a lot of pain and didn't expect to live more than a few weeks. I said he could be buried on the estate, so please take your time and the three of you can choose a spot."

"I thank you from the bottom of my heart Denny. I've been expecting it, but it's a struggle getting through to Tomaz, he just shakes his head and walks away."

"I'll say goodnight to you all and see you in the morning."

When he went in to the bedroom Helen was still awake lying in bed.

"I hope your going for a shower Denny, as your not getting in to bed smelling like that, and while your at it, open the window and throw your clothes out. When you do get in, please don't think you're getting near my body."

When he came out of the shower he was hoping she may have changed her mind, but she was lying there breathing heavily. He sat in the chair just looking at her sleeping. He knew he had been neglecting her and the boys again, but things were getting on top of him, but he couldn't take his eye off the ball. He slipped in to the bed and tried to get some sleep before his nightmares started.

When he opened the curtains in the morning he got a bit of a shock, as here was a police car with two people sitting in it. There was a knock on the main door and keys being used to unlock it. In came Willie, and Denny went down to greet him.

"What is happening brother? Have you been rumbled about your trip to talk with the poacher?"

"Calm down, Willie do you know what day this is? No? Well, it's the day you will be looking after our two police officers who will be spending their time in the forests, doing their own thing."

"Oh no Foggerty. Tell me I am having a nightmare, and I will wake up anytime. Why me?"

Denny went out and told the officers that he wouldn't be long as he had the dogs to walk. After a twenty minute walk he came back and asked them if they would like to come up on to the veranda, where the girls would be serving breakfast soon. Denny had bought a fire pit to sit on the veranda as mornings and evenings could be chilly at times, so the two officers had commandeered their seats next to it. When everybody started to arrive, they were very hesitant when approaching the house with the police car sitting outside. Denny explained to everybody why the officers were there, which seemed to settle everyone down.

"I will need to speak to the two of you when we return from your work. William will be looking after you today, and rest assured you will be secure, as you will have a dog each, and William will be within hearing distance of the dogs barking. He will explain more after breakfast. Unfortunately, my men and I will have to leave you as we are on a fitness kick, as forestry work can be gruelling at times."

The men took off and they were virtually sprinting before they got to the end of the trail. The officers looked impressed, but they wouldn't have been if they knew what the fitness regime was really for. After breakfast was finished Gertie and Helen came out and handed them a packed lunch.

"Mrs Foggerty, you are both so kind. With this hospitality you will struggle to keep us away."

Willie's face turned to a look of despair, and Helen thought she heard him growling, or maybe that was one of the dogs.

"Right, if your ready I will take you to your areas. There are always dangers in the forests so be alert. The dogs will alert you to danger by barking furiously. Don't ignore them. I will come as quickly as possible. Don't go too near the river banks, as at this time of year they can crumble under your feet."

As they walked out, they met the men running in. Willie's face lit up like beacon. Here was Tomaz, way, way behind them blowing out of his backside.

"I will take any bet you want Foggerty. If I can't beat your useless wee man, I will even give up sex for a month. Sorry officers."

When Willie was out of sight, Tomaz sprinted past everyone laughing his head off. When they sat having their breakfast, Denny had said they weren't to let on about Tomaz and they were to keep up the pretence every time Willie was around. Denny had told the men that today would be a quick breakfast, as they were falling behind with the work. It was then that Helen walked out, put her arms around his waist and gave him a big hug. She then walked away leaving Denny to wonder what was going on.

The work in the forest was hard today and Denny could see that Tomaz was probably missing having one of the dogs around him.

"You missing Ottar pal?"

Tomaz just nodded his head and then turned away.

"Do you think that you will have a dog of your own at some stage of your life?"

Tomaz just stared at him, before nodding and then mouthing Ottar.

"That would be nice pal. Let's see what the next few months bring."

Willie was just pottering about the house and gun room when he heard Udo barking furiously. He knew it was him as each dog has a particular bark. He grabbed his gun and ran at full pelt to where he left officer Schmidt. He could see Udo up ahead, but he had to stop to gather his breath. He thought this wasn't good, but it was only Tomaz he was challenging so he would be fine. Udo was standing looking over the edge of the banking barking furiously.

Willie walked forward and peered over. Here was the guy waving and shouting that his leg was trapped under a branch that had been washed down. Willie said he would try and scramble down further along the banking. Udo was still barking.

"Udo, shut the fuck up will you?"

Willie realised he shouldn't have spoken to him like that, and motioned for him to come into him. Willie praised him and rubbed his ears before trying to get down the banking. Finally, he came to the guy. He could see what the problem was, so he bent down and lifted the branch off him. He asked the guy if he felt alright, before giving him a lift up the banking.

"I feel such a fool Mr McLeod. I was sure I saw a rare flower on the other side of the stream and got too near the banking. It is only my pride that is hurt, but I would appreciate if we could keep this between ourselves, as I would love to come back here."

"Fine by me pal, but please don't let it happen again, or I will have to report you to the big giant who owns the estate."

Willie walked away laughing. The officer wondered if he was supposed to laugh or not.

Everyone met up at the house, where there was a bit of a struggle to get a share of the fire pit, which Gertie had kept going all day. Helen brought out coffee for them all, and after they had finished, Denny asked Helen, Gertie and Jinty, who had appeared, out from the house as he had an announcement to make. The officers headed back. After thanking everyone for their hospitality.

"I'm sure you all know by now that there is a fitness challenge between me and my brother. Whoever wins will have the bragging rights for ever. I have nominated my champion, and that is Tomaz."

Tomaz immediately got down started to do press ups. However, he fell on his face after five, but turned his head away from Willie, looked at Denny and winked. Another smile came across Willie's face.

"We have however, to still agree on a forfeit for whoever loses. What my proposal is, although I don't know if Willie will go for it as he is a bit of a woose."

"Anything Foggerty, anything."

"Okay, I will continue with what I was about to say. Whoever loses will strip naked, run along the track to the forest, along the estate boundary, and then run back up the track with everyone, and I mean everyone standing watching."

Willie's face paled. He couldn't say a word to start with.

"Right, Foggerty I accept your bet, but if 'mighty mouse' there loses you will do the forfeit with him. Agreed?"

Denny walked forward and shook his hand with everybody clapping and cheering.

"If you lose Willie, are we going to see something special or are you going to say it's the cold weather. I hope it's you Willie, as I've seen Denny's naked body often enough. Although to be honest, it is something to behold," said Jinty.

"Enough Jinty," shouted Helen.

Chapter 10

The phone was ringing, and Denny got a bit of a shock when he answered it. It was Jean Scougal from Durma.

"Hi Denny, I hope you don't mind me phoning you, but I have spent a lot of time thinking about your offer of me coming over to live and work with you on the estate. So, I have decided to accept. I spoke to both Gladys Glover and Neala, and I know they are keen to come over, so if you still want me then just let me know when I can come."

"I'm so glad to hear from you Jean. Of course, we would love to have you over. However, the job description I gave you may have changed. Please keep this between us, but there may be an option to be more involved with the boys here on the estate. I can't say for definite, but there will be a job of some description and good accommodation waiting for you. Although, it may be a few months yet. Speak soon. Now I'll put you on to Helen and Jinty is here as well."

He shouted on Helen and Jinty.

He still couldn't help feeling slightly guilty that he had put a bullet in to her son's head. Not for him, but for her as she had lived such a hard, hard life. Surely she must know by now he thought.

After a while Helen and Jinty came out, and said it was nice to speak to Jean. She was excited about her coming over, as was Jinty.

Denny took the dogs and wandered in to the forest. He walked further than he intended, before sitting down with Arno and Udu. They were lying either side of him, and it seemed a competition to see who could get the closest to him. He truly loved his dogs. In fact, he often preferred them to people. There was nothing complicated about them. They never talked back. Walk them, feed them, but most importantly give them as much love as you can. It was as simple as that. Unconditional love.

Unlike his dogs, his life was far too complicated and wondered if it would ever change. He knew his sortie to Scotland would change it for ever, but he had to get it right. Keep it simple, and make sure he would kill them all, and most importantly, no loose ends this time. He wondered when this was all over if he would still have a relationship with Helen. Would all his demons disappear this time? Unlike the last time. All this made him make his mind up that there would never be any killing at his hands, unless his extended family, and only his family have their lives threatened. He ran everything past the dogs, but wasn't sure they were listening to him as they were too busy enjoying having their ears rubbed.

His decision making over the next few weeks was crucial, and he decided to tell Helen what was about to happen sooner rather than later. She was beginning to suspect something was about to happen, so it wasn't fair to keep it all under wraps.

In bed that night, he felt she wasn't as receptive as she usually was, although they had made love several times. He felt she wasn't as vocal when she had climaxed, as she had previously. He thought that his own lovemaking was like he was just going through the motions. Two people with too much going on in their overcrowded heads.

In the morning their was no cuddling in from Helen. She got up and quickly showered saying she needed to see to the boys. This was the workers day off, but he felt the way Helen was feeling, he would be as well going out in to the forest to do some work. His heart wasn't in it, but at least he had the dogs with him enjoying themselves. After a while Arno gave out a low growl. He looked around to see a young fox standing on the other river bank. He was standing with his nose held high trying to get Denny's scent in the morning air.

Denny walked to the edge of the banking and stood still.

"Well, my little one, I hope you and your like will have a long and fruitful life, without that bastard of a poacher," he said.

He decided to head home as he was becoming melancholy, something he thought he was incapable of.

When he was just about home, he heard a car coming up the drive. He eventually made out it was Officer Schmidt. He got out holding a letter.

"Good day to you Denny. I have a letter from Officer Mayer, and he sends his apologies that he can't deliver it personally.

However, he said to give him a phone call to speak about it, as it isn't the news you were hoping for."

"Don't worry Hans. There are corrupt legal systems all over the world, and Bavaria is no different. I have already told Officer Myer that if the decision goes against us, then the guy and his father won't get away with it. The judge as well. Too many people are angry about what went on."

"Nothing violent I hope Denny. My colleague has told me that you were a police Detective back in Scotland, and you had buried a few bodies in your time.

Denny looked incredulously at him before bursting out laughing.

"I think that discussion was lost in translation. Come away in, and I will tell you about my experiences in Scotland, assuming its okay with you."

Denny thought Hans was running up the steps, and he then sat next to the fire pit. Gertie came out and asked if they wanted coffee and cake. Denny didn't get a chance to answer as Hans had said he would love it. Denny laid it on strong for him without giving anything away, and after an hour Hans had looked a bit pale.

"Your job here is a walk in the park in comparison. So, let's hope it stays that way. However, if you fancy a challenge, I will definitely put a good word in for you, but should that happen, then promise me one thing will you. Toughen up, as you will need it. Please thank Officer Mayer for asking you to give up your time to come and see me. I will call him tomorrow, but please give him a heads up, that I am not a happy guy knowing that there is every chance of that bastard getting off lightly."

They said their goodbyes and it was then that Willie came out from the Annex.

"What was 'PC Plod' wanting Denny?"

He handed the official letter to Willie, who after reading it, asked what he was supposed to be seeing.

"The judge for the court case is best mate with the guy's father, and there has been talk of money having been paid to the judge to make sure his son either gets off with it, or is given a paltry sentence for his offences. So, I might have to think about plan b."

"There wouldn't have to be a fucking plan b if you had listened to me in the first place. This guy nearly kills your wife, and he will probably get away with it. It's still not too late to snatch the bastard and feed him to the wolves, like I had suggested in the first place. You need to listen to me more often pal."

"You finished Willie? Remember, you were the one that thought I was getting too used to killing people. It would be a bit obvious if he disappeared now don't you think."

Willie screwed up the letter and threw it to where the dogs were. They quickly started to tear it apart with Arno getting the biggest part, and stood there growling towards Udo telling him to back off.

"I'm sure it said I would have to bring that letter to the court on the day."

"Tell them to fuck off will you. It's a good job I won't be coming to court that day, or I would just finish the job, right there and then. I don't think there would be enough 'polis men' there that day to stop the Time Bomb. What do you think pal, should I just go for it?"

"I really hope that Gertie's time of the month is over, so that the Love Master can get some relief, as well as all the nonsense out of his head."

Denny went into the house and phoned Maria. He told her all about the judge and the guy's father, as well as his thoughts on what the conclusion would be.

"Knowing you Denny, you will have another plan running through your over complicated brain. However, no matter the outcome, don't you think you should just let it lie? You're going to risk everything by trying to extract your revenge on him."

"I take your point Maria, but you know I won't let him, his dad or the judge away with it. Can you ask the Trust's lawyers to look into the criminal record of the guy who is up on the charge, to see which judge he had at the time of his offences and what he received in the way of sentencing. Also, what were the judge's finding on the day, and by whatever means necessary, the judge's personal bank records around these times. Please don't say it can't be done, or how difficult it would be Maria, because I have had it done myself while working in my time with the Edinburgh police. So, no 'crap' Maria, please."

Denny thanked her for her help and said goodbye

He wasn't going to wait to phone Officer Meyer, so he phoned the local police station where Officer Meyer picked up.

"Thank you for sending Officer Schmidt over with my letter. It was a great source of amusement between my dogs, who had great fun in ripping it in to tiny bits. Which shows my contempt for it. However, I don't hold anything against you Officer Meyer, unfortunately you are only a pawn in a corrupt system. I will give you a heads up however, and that is I have already instructed the Trust to bring its power down on the judge and the guy's father. As for the guy himself, there is no shortage of people here on the estate willing to extract their own justice on him should it not be a very fair outcome. I'm sure that when you were enjoying your time in my forests, you were a bit unnerved by the eerie wolf calls coming from the North valley when the light was fading. You could easily lose your way up there, and never be seen again.

"I don't know what to think or say Denny, as it looks like it's going to get messy. It is my hope that the guy gets what he deserves, but like you I have my doubts. No matter what happens, I hope we can remain friends, and rest assured if he was last seen in the North valley, I won't be looking too hard. Let's see what the trial brings us my friend. I bid you farewell."

Denny put the phone down, smiled and thought he had just made a friend for life. It was just a matter of waiting now. However, everything seemed to be on hold at the moment.

He quickly phoned Maria again and asked her to book a flight to Edinburgh for him for tomorrow. He went indoors, and asked Helen for a chat.

"Helen, I'm sorry to spring this on you, but I'm off to Scotland for a few days. I have some business to look in to."

"What fucking business Denny? Don't bother answering me as no doubt it will be one of your clandestine meetings, or your phone calls. I bloody know there is something going on, but I don't know what. You're playing me for a fool Denny, and I'm not liking it. You know what Denny, do what you bloody well want, you usually do."

She walked away cursing to herself. Denny knew he couldn't tell her anything, but it was getting harder for him to try and hide what was going to happen in the near future. That night she had slept in a separate bedroom, and hardly spoke to him when Gertie and her served breakfast for everyone. When the girls went inside Denny asked everyone to pay attention to what he was about to say.

"I will be away for the next three or four days men. I am off to Scotland on a recce for when we eventually head over there. Willie will be in charge, and I apologise for not pulling my weight in the forest. It is apparent to me that I need to get the lay of the land before we arrive. Sorry that it is short notice, but I make no apologies for what I am doing. It may keep us alive. Our little challenge will take place when I get back, so Willie it's maybe best if you concentrate on a fitness regime rather than a love making regime. I'm sure Gertie might be glad of the break."

Tomaz got on the floor and did his usual pretence of only managing a few press ups before collapsing.

"By the look of your so called champion big man, I will look forward to humiliating the both of you. Now, I suggest you go and get ready for what Bonnie Scotland will throw at you."

As the men went off to work, Helen walked out with a face like thunder, and sat with the boys near the fire pit. She never looked at Denny. He wandered over and picked up Col. She never made eye contact with him.

"Helen, can I ask you a few questions. Please answer me truthfully will you. Do you still love me? Do you love your boys? Do you love living here?"

"Of course, I bloody do. What stupid questions are these?"

Denny's temper rose very quickly, and he said," Well, let me tell you something Helen. Everything I am doing is to protect us from the people who will still want to see me dead. Did you think that after the last episode that it was over. Helen, your not a stupid woman, yet it seems that you have just stuck your head in the sand. I love you and the boys more than life itself, and I will do anything to protect you. I really can't tell you what is happening, to protect not just you, but everyone around us. So, get off your fucking high horse Helen will you. Oh, and another thing is that the court case for the guy who shot you will be coming up in two weeks, and at the moment it's a bloody mess"

"Denny, why didn't you tell me about it. I thought it was a random poacher?"

"Why didn't I tell you? Simple Helen, you can't handle it."

Helen could see he wasn't far away from losing it, so she didn't say anything else. They just sat there in silence while playing with the boys, until Denny said he needed to go and pack and gave Col back to Helen.

He realised that it would have to be warm clothing as the news on the radio had said, Scotland was experiencing low temperatures and snow. He took the opportunity to lie down on the bed as he was still raging, and his head hurt. He must have drifted off, and was awoken when Helen came in and lay down beside him. They lay there entwined in each others arms until the phone interrupted them. It was Maria telling him the flight time for tomorrow, and how much money she had put into an account in the Bank of Scotland in Edinburgh.

"Maria how are you coming along with all the information I requested. Especially the folder on the Member of Parliament. I could have done with it for my trip."

"How about I meet you at the airport tomorrow for a coffee and a chat?"

"Sounds good Maria, but I don't want our chat to be 'heavy' as my brain would struggle to cope with it"

"Don't worry, I won't give you too much hassle, promise."

Denny finished packing and went down stairs to play with the boys, to wait for the men coming in from the forests. When they finally arrived back there was nothing to report, so Denny told them he would see them in a few days, and told Willie he would need a lift to the airport early tomorrow morning.

"Can I have a word before you go Yuri please. I haven't seen much of your dad. How is he keeping?"

"Not good Denny. I fear it will only be a few short weeks before he goes. I know he is in a lot of pain, but he tries to hide it. Tomaz is doing his usual, by trying to ignore what is happening. Unfortunately, there is nothing anybody can do about it."

"I'm thinking we should be contacting the undertakers in the town Yuri, just to give them a heads up. What do you think about getting some morphine to ease the pain."

"Probably best Denny, although he refuses any medication as he wants all his faculties about him at all times. Neither Tomaz or my dad need know about the undertaker though."

Denny said he would go with him when he got back from Scotland. He assured Yuri he was only going over to try and see locations and get his head around his plan, and he reassured him there would be no intervention on his part. Purely surveillance.

Denny and Helen had decided on an early night after the boys had gone to sleep. Denny was a bit surprised when they had started to make love, as he felt Helen was getting a bit rough, especially with her thrusting while she was sitting on top of him. It felt like she just wanted to climax and get it over with. He didn't know why she was like that, but he supposed things hadn't been great between them lately. When he was on top and making love from behind, he slowed everything down with long gentle strokes and tried to give her as many orgasms as possible, with Helen being very vocal. It always put her off to sleep afterwards.

As there had been very little sleep as normal, he got up and showered before checking on the boys. He felt he needed to walk with the dogs before he left, so he got them out and walked, and walked with them, finding areas in the forests that he had spent virtually no time at all in. After a couple of hours, he turned for home and decided to race the dogs. He stood there with Arno and Udo either side of him.

"Now listen you pair. You don't start until I say 'go'. No cheating, as I feel this could be my day when Denny will be the winner."

The dogs hadn't got a clue what he was on about, and just stood looking at him. It was then that Denny cheated and took off. He was twenty yards away before shouting on the dogs. They caught up with him within seconds, and Denny started to laugh uncontrollably while running. Every so often, the dogs would stop and 'cock' their legs up against any available tree. As they were nearing home, Denny put in one monumental effort to try and beat the dogs, but he knew they were just playing with him. It was about four hundred yards from home when the dogs spotted Helen on the veranda and took off leaving Denny puffing in their wake.

"You should give up Foggerty. You should know by now that the dogs love me more than you."

"Bloody looks like it, doesn't it. Traitors."

Denny walked up to her and gave a big hug and kiss, and said it was time to leave for the airport after another shower. She just nodded. Willie was waiting for him when he came down. Helen was at the top window and gave him the merest of waves. Denny started to get a bit angry now, at how people were ruining his life. This was the start of the end of their lives, although they didn't know it yet. Denny allowed himself one of his evil smiles. His enemies would see it soon enough.

Willie and Denny didn't say much during the car ride to the airport. As Denny got his luggage out he turned to Willie and said," I love you brother, and that will never change no matter what happens."

As Willie drove away he wondered what Denny was on about. Surely, he didn't know what he and Gertie had been talking about. He put it out of his mind. Denny watched the car drive away and wondered when the time came, as it surely would, what he would do without Willie. There was no point in worrying about it just now.

When he walked in to the terminal, he could see somebody waving frantically. It was Maria. When they met up, Maria had suggested they go to a small coffee shop where it would be more private. Once they had ordered, Maria was straight to the point.

"I have here the folder you requested Denny. Having looked at it, I can only suggest that you tread very carefully. This guy has very influential friends in the British Government, which means the police force as well. I'm not saying he is a very likeable person, but he may be a difficult person to bring down. Do you know why he sent people to kill you Denny?"

"Maria, I can only think of one thing, and that he was somehow connected to an incident back on Durma where I came from. It involved drugs, and the people that died were selling their drugs through the island. I have a strong feeling that this guy is the head of the operation, so I intend to cut off the head of the snake. I'm not stupid enough to think that he is fully in charge as I don't think he has the power to send four guys to their deaths in trying to exterminate me and my family. There must be somebody else there pulling the strings. It won't matter anyway, as they are all going die."

"Denny, when you speak like that you send a shiver up my spine. When is this going to end?"

"Soon my 'kleine'. Put your faith in me, and please pay Helen some visits when I'm away the next time".

It was time for Denny to go for his flight, so they got up and hugged. She whispered in his ear.

"I wonder what our lives would be like now if we had still been together Denny?"

"Who knows Maria, but that was another lifetime away."

As they walked their separate ways, Maria suddenly stopped and shouted," Will I ever see you again Denny?"

Denny just smiled, turned and walked away. Maria felt a tear run down her cheek.

Before going to the gate for his flight he went to the telephone booths and phoned Stevie.

He eventually answered.

"Morning Stevie, how are you and the family? Still running around with that pack of wolves of a gang? I need something to ask of you. I will be at Edinburgh Airport in about three hours, and I need to buy a four by four jeep to get me through your snow covered roads. It needs to be as hush hush as possible though. I'm coming over to do a recce on the places we will be visiting when we come to kill some people."

"Bloody hell Denny, I take it you got rid of the last lot of 'crap' that came for you. Okay, forget about buying a car, as I have a jeep at my work. It's not new, but it will get you anywhere you want to go. It's not registered to me, so I will get Levi or Bohdi to put some false plates on it as they seem to collect them like other folk collect football cards. Let me know when you arrive, and I can tell you where to pick it up about. Neither of the boys have a driving license, but that doesn't seem to stop them. They will get the train back to Dundee. If by chance you get into any trouble from the law, then ditch the jeep and give me a call."

Stevie wondered what the hell he was getting himself in to, although he had no intention of getting on the wrong side of Denny.

"I appreciate your help more than you know pal. I trust we can still rely on Andrew supplying us with the equipment we need, as it could be within a month that we will be back over?"

Stevie had said everything was in place, just as Denny had said the last call for his flight had been announced.

As Denny walked down the aeroplane, he tried to memorise the faces of the people on the flight, although there was a lot of empty seats. He knew it was just a futile gesture, but he had to start getting in to a state of awareness. Nothing would happen over the next few days, but he wouldn't take any chances.

The flight was cold and bumpy, with a guy snoring next to him, until he moved seats. He was glad when he was walking through the terminal at Edinburgh looking for a phone. He eventually found one and contacted Stevie who had told him the jeep was in a small private car parking facility just outside the main entrance. All expenses had been covered.

It didn't take long for him to get to know the vehicle and he was soon travelling in to the City. He had been doing a lot of remembering from his time there, and where the best place he could find a quiet hotel. He had no intention of going to Robert Trapps' Hotel or contacting Shonagh. He even told Stevie that if Levi or Bohdi saw him in Dundee, they were to stay away from him or else.

Denny, drove through to Leith, where he knew there was a lot of nondescript hotels. Many a businessman had taken his secretary to one, when he was supposed to be working late. He chose one which looked a bit dated, but looked clean. He would hate to bring bed bugs back to Helen. That would put her in an even worse mood.

He insisted that he had a room with a window that looked out on to the main street. It was his intention not to use the jeep in town and get any taxis that were available. On the flight he had read, and reread the file on Robertson the MP. The guy had rented office accommodation in York Place, not far from Princes Street, so Denny decided that would be his first port of call.

He lay down and went to sleep for an hour. When he awoke his tiredness had gone. York Place wasn't that far so he decided to walk. When he arrived, he looked at all the name plates on the side of the doors until he found Robertson's name. He quickly pressed the bell and a lady answered on the intercom, asking who was calling. Denny asked if it was possible to speak to the Right Honourable Robertson. She advised him he was in London, and only saw people on a Monday and Tuesday. He thanked her, walked over the road and looked up at the first floor window. Here was a guy in a pin stripe suit speaking on the phone. He needed to find out if he actually saw people on these days, but he would find out for real at some other time. No hurry. If that was the guy up there he was after, he would let him live for a little while longer.

He knew he had plenty of time to get to Dundee. He needed to check a couple of places out in the town. It was strange driving up the A9, as certain places brought back memories. Some he would rather forget. The jeep handled beautifully in the conditions, and even with a good covering of snow he remembered how beautiful a place this was. It was getting a bit dark when he parked up in the centre. Stevie had given him information that Robertson had often been seen eating and drinking with some of his cronies in a restaurant called The T-bone Steak House in Union Street, and then moving on to the Hawthorn Bar at the bottom of Hilltown. He tended to splash his cash among those that would suffer him apparently.

He knew roughly where these premises were, so he wasn't long in checking them out. It was only a case of finding out about the exits, but he doubted anything would go down here as there would be too many people hanging around. On walking back to the car, he kept looking around, fully expecting to see Levi and Bohdi, as these 'buggers' could appear out of nowhere. When he got back to the jeep, he leant against it and looked around. It wasn't that long ago that his life was in danger in this city. Mostly through his disregard for his drink problem, and his indifference to killing people. That was in a different time, so he wasn't going to dwell on it.

On the journey back to Edinburgh the snow was falling heavily, and he thought how that might cause them a problem when they came over. The jeep was handling the conditions with ease, and he was glad the hotel had a small car park at the back, so it would be out of sight.

When he went into the hotel, the lady behind the desk asked him if he would like coffee and sandwiches brought up to his room. He said that would be nice, and thanked her for her kindness. He phoned Stevie from his room and asked him if he knew where the Ruthven Estate belonging to Robertson was.

"Everybody knows where that Tory bastard's estate is. He's a disgrace to Scottish politics."

After his little rant, he told Denny how to get there, but warned him the snow would be deep up there, and to be prepared.

"Thanks for that my friend. We really must meet up soon. It's not the same just speaking on the phone."

"That would be great Denny, but let's try and make it before you start killing people. What do you think?"

"Might be a plan Stevie. Take care."

After eating, Denny stripped off, got under the covers, and within no time he was asleep.

Next morning, he tried to have a shower, but it was just a couple of hoses over the taps, however the water was hot. Breakfast was just bacon and eggs, but he was famished and accepted seconds from the owner's wife. He reckoned the Scottish air had given him an appetite. While he sat with a pot of coffee, he spread out a map he had bought in the city on the table. He reckoned it would take him a couple of hours, just as Stevie and Shonagh had said. It might be more prudent to head off as soon as possible.

Just as he came down stairs, the owners wife came from the kitchen and handed Denny a thick blanket, a thermos with tea and a packed lunch.

"I don't know where you are going son, but what I do know is, it will be snowy, so you have to be prepared."

Denny gave her a hug and thanked her very much.

As he drove he was formulating a plan for when he got to the estate. He would memorise every tree and blade of grass around it. The journey was long as the snow was driving at the windscreen. Which meant that he had to reduce his speed. When it wasn't snowing he looked at the scenery and thought what a

233

lovely part of Scotland this would be to live in. The hills were spectacular, and it seemed like he was forever driving along side a river.

He knew by his watch that he was getting close. At a turn off he saw a sign which said 'House For Sale'. He didn't know why, but he turned off the road and drove up a dirt track which seemed to run parallel with the road. The jeep was slewing all over the track, but the four wheel drive was holding firm. At one point he thought that he was lost, until a house light appeared out off the blizzard that was just starting.

He parked next to an old tractor and was walking to the house when the door opened. There stood an older guy with a shotgun aimed at Denny.

"I would hate for you to shoot me on a night like this," said Denny.

"I would hate to shoot you son, as I would have to dispose of your body, and by the size of you it would take some effort. State your business or be off with you."

"How about I tell you over a cup of tea, as I am getting a bit cold standing here."

"Are you anything to do with the Ruthven Estate and that bastard Robertson?"

"Just the opposite my friend."

The guy studied him for a minute before he lowered the gun and motioned for Denny to come in. As Denny walked in, a woman came and said that he looked cold, and to go and sit by the fire. Within a few minutes, she came from the kitchen with tea and home baked scones for the three of them. To Denny she looked like what everyone would want their granny to be.

"Right pal, your time is up. What are you doing here?"

"Alasdair, mind your manners please."

"No, he is quite right Mrs?"

"My name is Davina, and this is Alasdair. Our surname is Blair."

"My name is Daniel Rey, and I would like to leave it at that if it's okay with you?"

They both looked at each other before Alasdair nodded as if to say fine by them.

"All I can say is that I have a score to settle with Robertson. I won't say anymore just in case I get you into trouble."

"No more than we are already in Daniel, but if you want to elaborate tomorrow morning then fine. If not, then no worries son."

"I'm afraid I won't be here in the morning folks, as I have taken up too much of your time already, and I must be heading back."

Davina walked to the window and drew the curtains back. There was total white out.

"You're not going anywhere in that, Daniel. You can stay here tonight, and don't worry there will be a snowplough along first thing in the morning, as it's stationed in the next village.

Denny walked to the window and couldn't believe his eyes. He was looking over the Ruthven Estate. What a vantage point he thought.

"Can I ask you a personal question, and you don't have to answer if you don't want to. Why are you selling up?"

"We are being harassed by men from the estate, who continually make offers on the house. The offers are derisory, and every time they come their attitude is aggressive. They once said that it would be a shame if the house burned down in the middle of the night. There are comings and goings at all times of the night with what sounds like wild parties. It is Alasdair with his gun that keeps them at bay."

Denny thought for a minute, before he asked them how much they wanted for the house. When they told him how much, Denny quickly offered them double what they were asking.

"Are you having fun at our expense Daniel, as I am not laughing son," said Davina.

"Trust me folks, that amount of money is neither here nor there to me. Please give me your bank details and let me use your phone to call my company."

They just nodded, still in a bit of shock and pointed to the phone. Denny went and phoned Maria.

"Maria, please do as I ask and do it quickly."

Denny gave her all the details that Alasdair had handed to him on a piece of paper.

"Please phone your bank first thing tomorrow, and I urge you to accept my offer for your sanity. I will be gone early in the morning."

The Blairs were a bit awestruck, but they cautiously thanked Denny for the offer for the house. Davina said she was off to get another bed prepared and start the tea.

Denny and Alasdair sat beside the fire chatting about anything they could think off. However, Denny wasn't prepared to divulge more than he thought he should, for everybody's safety. Alasdair had offered him a whisky, and after giving a small laugh, he declined his offer. Davina had made a lovely meal, and afterwards Denny had asked them if they minded telling him everything they could about the Ruthven estate.

Denny went to bed that night content knowing that another piece of the jigsaw was in place. He thought that this was a very large jigsaw though.

What woke him the next morning was someone banging on the door. He jumped out the bed and put some clothes on. When he got in to the living room, he saw Alasdair standingpointing his shotgun out of the open door. He heard two men of foreign nationality raising there voices to Alasdair. Denny knew he didn't want to be seen as it wasn't in his plan. He went and stood behind the door.

"I have already phoned the police Mr Blair, and they said they would be here shortly. Meantime, will I get your other gun?"

"Yes, get the gun son, so that we can shoot these two bastards where they stand."

Everything went quiet, and Denny heard the crunching of footsteps in the snow which had a slight crust on it. He went to the window, and after a while he saw the guys appear at the entrance to the track where they crossed the road and walk to the estate. Alasdair handed him a pair of binoculars and walked in to the kitchen. Denny decided he would give this estate the once over, but he wasn't going too deeply in to it. He hid behind the curtains just in case they had their own eyes on the house. Things change and there was still a few weeks to go.

Davina shouted that breakfast was out. When he went through, he witnessed a mound of scrambled eggs and bacon, with toast and butter.

"Just to let you know folks, I am hanging around here until you have phoned your bank. Meanwhile, after we eat can you show me the extent of the property Alasdair please."

After breakfast and bang on nine o'clock, Davina phoned her bank in Edinburgh. She came off the phone a very happy lady and smiled at Alasdair. She gave Denny a huge hug, and thanked him so very much. Alasdair shook his hand and thanked him as well.

"Okay, Alasdair I think I would like to see the whole of the property now and don't leave anything out please."

As they walked around, Denny thought what a bonus this place was, although he had to make sure that it was kept a secret, as to who was going to move in. Alasdair pointed out as much as he could, and it wasn't until he was almost finished that he came out with the most important part of all. He had showed him that there was a field next to the estate that was his, and had been used in the past for grazing when they had cattle. They had stopped using it due to the hassle they were receiving from the men on the estate. It was also pointed out to him that the track at the back of the sheds led to an old quarry where some old farm machinery had been dumped, but it was said to Denny that it was now a very deep and wide hole.

Denny asked if Alasdair would mind if he could be left to wander the property for a while to see how it was going to fit into his plans. When he finished he walked back in to the house and firstly asked them what the old well was for. Davina said it was an old well that had dried up a long time ago, with only a small amount of water in it, but it was very deep.

"Right folks, here is what is going to happen. The money I have offered you is to include everything, and I mean everything. On an agreed date, you both pack a bag with all your personal stuff, get into your vehicle and drive to where you have planned never looking back. As soon as you are away, my men and I will occupy the property. Don't try and contact me or this house ever again after that. Please just enjoy your money and the rest of your lives. Agreed?

I will be leaving now, so I suggest you paint 'sold' on your sign in a few weeks. Not before, as they will feel it's okay to still come up and try and intimidate you anytime they want, so keep your gun handy. However, I will make sure they regret it. Trust me."

Denny started to get ready, and it was then Davina walked over and hugged him with tears streaming down her face.

"Davina, no disrespect, but Daniel doesn't do tears."

She jumped back slightly, but Denny smiled, said his goodbyes to Alasdair, but before he walked away, he asked if he had an old flat cap he could have. Alasdair went one better and gave him a cap plus a balaclava. Denny walked to his jeep, knowing he would never see either of them again.

As Denny drove down the track he saw the yellow snowplough heading down the Dundee Road. He turned right and headed towards the entrance of the estate taking in every detail he could. The house was bigger than he thought. It must have at least seven or eight bedrooms. There were trees around the sides and back with only a small piece of grass between the trees and the house. The double doors on the front looked solid as did the windows. Some of the upper rooms, which he thought must be bedrooms, had small French doors leading to a small balcony.

He needed a closer look, so he slipped on the balaclava, flat cap and drove up the estate drive. They mustn't have had anybody keeping an eye out, as he got nearly to the front door before somebody came out to challenge him. Denny quickly got out and spread his map over the bonnet of the jeep. The guy that came out could only point his gun at Denny, and was shouting something in an accent he couldn't make out.

"Sorry, but I am lost, can you tell me if I am on the right road to Glen Well? Really sorry to bother you."

The guy was getting more and more agitated, and his gun was being used to try and poke Denny.

It was then that Denny thought he would up the anti, and started to shout at the guy. He knew that the guy couldn't afford to discharge his gun, as that would bring attention to the estate. As he raised his voice even louder, two other men, armed with rifles came out the front door.

"What is going on," shouted one of them. This guy had the most ridiculous hairstyle Denny had ever seen. His head was shaved along each side, with a middle parting on top, leading to a crazy looking pony tail. He obviously had some authority.

238

"I came in here looking for directions to Glen Well, and all I get it is a bloody gun pointed at me, what is happening here," said Denny.

"You have no right to be here as this is private property, now I suggest you leave before I make you leave."

There was then that a shout came from the hall. Denny could only see it was a tall thick set guy. He was obviously telling his men to sort the problem. Just then all eyes went on to a grey van that was coming up the drive. Denny had seen this before, and knew it was drugs. A police car was next to come up the drive.

When the officer got out, Denny had seen his type before. His swagger was to make up for his lack of height.

"Right, everybody stay back as I will handle this. Who are you and what do you want?"

"I only came in here to ask for directions as I was lost, and ended up with a gun stuck in my face. This is a bit frightening for me."

"Okay, where are you looking for?"

Denny told him and the officer said to keep going up the main road for about fifty miles.

"Now I suggest you get in your car and get lost, other wise I will have to lock you up for trespassing."

"Don't worry I'm going, but what I will say is that as a police officer, you should know the laws of the countryside. There is no trespassing law in Scotland."

As Denny walked to his jeep, he turned around and stared at everybody standing there. The last thing he saw before driving off was 'ponytail' putting his arm around the officer as they started laughing about something that was said. They were cocky, too cocky.

Denny had gained quite a bit of information during the brief time he was there, but knew he needed a lot more, so that would be where Karl would come in.

Although the snowplough had been down the road it was still pretty treacherous in places. As he was driving, he wondered if coming over in a few weeks was the best plan, but if he left it too long then he ran the risk of Robertson ordering another hit on him. The roads were getting better as he neared Dundee, so he started to make good time. Although he was tired, he never felt more alive. Knowing, that in a few weeks, he would launch an all out attack on the bastards that had tried to kill him.

Through Dundee, it was only another hour until he was sitting in the car park at the back of his hotel. When he went through the front door, the owners wife came out from reception and asked him if he was alright. She was worried about him when he didn't come back the previous night. Denny reassured her he was fine, and had got caught up in the snow, causing him to look for a bed and breakfast. He told her he would be away first thing in the morning, and asked her if he could use her phone for a local call.

"Hi Stevie, I intend to fly back tomorrow morning so where would you like me to leave the car. It's at the back of the Leith Water hotel, and I will be getting a taxi to the airport."

"Just leave it there pal as Levi and Bohdi, or at least one of them, will go down and pick it up. Leave the keys at the reception please."

"Thanks Stevie, and can I say I would have struggled without that jeep of yours. Much appreciated."

"Pleasure pal. I think."

The following morning, he went down stairs and after breakfast, he went to settle up for his stay. The owners wife came through.

"Please, don't think I have been rude, but I never asked your name," said Denny.

"It's Nisbet son. George and Martha."

"Well Martha, I thank you for your hospitality. Please don't argue about the amount of money I am giving you for my stay."

He went into his money belt and handed her enough cash to make her eyes bulge.

"Are you sure son, this is a hell of a lot of money for a two night stay. In fact, any length of stay."

"Martha, your welcome and can I ask you if you know of any other small hotel near you that is as nice and quiet as this."

"That's not a problem son, my brother has the same size hotel just a street over."

"Okay Martha, in a few weeks myself and three friends will arrive in Edinburgh, and we will need four rooms, but I will phone you to confirm. It will be only for a few days, but I will be paying you for a couple of months, as I don't know how long our business will take. There will be no names or questions as to where we are working. To put your mind at ease, the only thing I will say is that we will be the good guys."

Denny had decided to walk to the centre, before getting a taxi. He picked up his holdall and started to walk out the door.

He gave a little wave, while not looking back. Mrs Nisbet had to hold on to the reception counter, as a strange feeling had come over her, making her feel faint, as she watched Denny walk out the door.

There was a bitter wind blowing as he started to walk to the centre, which reminded him to get winter survival clothes ordered off this guy Andrew that Stevie knew. When he got to Princes Street he found a phone box and called home. Gertie answered and immediately put Helen on. By the tone of her greeting, he knew she was still hurting, and he told her he would be home in a few hours, and told her to get Willie to pick him up at the airport at two o'clock. He knew she wasn't going to say much more, so he said goodbye and hung up.

He found a bench where he sat for a while, before the cold was getting too much. He hailed a cab, and when he got in he couldn't believe it. It was the same guy who had brought them to Edinburgh when they had left for Bavaria. This wasn't in his plan, but thought he could use it to his advantage.

The cabbie recognised Denny right away and started to ask him about what he was doing in Edinburgh. One look from Denny, and the guy quickly remembered he should have kept his mouth shut. They drove in silence to the airport which was a bit unnerving for the guy. When he pulled up at the terminal, Denny didn't move, which made the guy worse.

"I'm going to ask if you will do something for me. In a few weeks, myself, and three other men will fly in to Scotland. Two in to Glasow and two to here. Are you available to pick us up? Obviously the flight times will be far enough apart, so that you can use one car. You know I will make it worth your while. Remember, it must be you who picks us up and there will be no asking any of us, who we are or why we are in Edinburgh. Also, should anyone ask where you dropped us off about, give them a location far away. Are you okay with that?"

The guy could hardly speak as his mouth was so dry. Eventually he managed a reply.

"Don't worry, you still have a note of my number, but if I don't answer, then do not give your details to anybody else. Please phone back until you manage to get me. If anybody does ask me where I dropped you off about, then I will direct them to a couple of council estates that they will be lucky to get out off."

As Denny got out, he handed a wad of cash to the guy that he probably wouldn't make in a month. Denny just walked on never looking back. The guy gave out a large gasp of air, while holding tightly on to the steering wheel. This was only the second time he had met this guy, and twice he felt scared. There was no way he was going to let this guy down. Whoever or whatever he was.

Denny was early for his flight, so he headed for something to eat, for what airport grub was worth. He started to go over everything that had happened over the last few days, knowing he would have to speak to the men about it, especially Yuri. After trying to digest what resembled food, he fell asleep. When he awoke, he was so angry with himself. That had been a schoolboy error, and he must never let that happen again as his life could depend on staying awake and alert.

When he walked to the departure gate, he was constantly watching for people that might be interested in him, but he supposed he was just being a bit paranoid. The flight was just as rubbish as before. Always plenty of turbulence to keep you on your toes.

When he walked in to arrivals Willie was waiting, looking suitably bored as usual.

"C'mon Foggerty. If we hurry up I might get a bit of loving this afternoon, before I look after the dogs."

Denny shook his head, and when he got to the jeep he put the seat back and drifted off to sleep. He was awoken by the sound of machinery when they were nearing the estate. It was the houses and classrooms being built. Denny hadn't paid much interest in what progress they had been making, but he reckoned it would only be a few months until they could be occupied. He thought he might phone Ian and Neala tonight. Helen could phone Gladys Glover as well, but unless she cheered up it wouldn't be a very riveting conversation. He wondered if he was being too hard on Helen, however life over the next few months was going to be hard for everybody.

When he got out of the jeep, the dogs came running to him. At least they still loved him, until Helen came out of the house, whereby they bolted to be by her side. She walked down the steps and gave Denny a half hearted hug, sarcastically asking him if he enjoyed his 'jaunt' to Scotland.

"My 'jaunt' as you refer to it was fine thank you, but if you are going to make sarcastic comments to me, then I would rather you didn't speak at all. I will be speaking to Ian tonight, so I thought you might like to catch up with Neala. Giving Gladys Glover a call might be an idea as well."

Denny walked away from her and went to hold his boys. As he sat with them in his arms he knew his plan for Scotland had to work, or his purpose in life was gone. If his existence was causing people to be in danger, then he would walk away from everything and everyone, including his boys.

He walked up with the dogs to see how Artem was holding out. Seeing him like he was came as bit of a shock to him. He was sitting by the stove wrapped in a blanket. His face was drawn, and he looked so thin. When he saw Denny he gave a forced smile, while grimacing through pain. Yuri had been right about it only being a few weeks before he would go. Yuri walked through with a coffee for the both of them, and he sat down opposite Artem. Denny told him about how he found Scotland this time. How beautiful it was, and how kind the Scot's people were.

"Denny, it sounds a wonderful country, and although I will never visit it, I sincerely hope my sons do."

A coughing fit stopped him talking, and he then brought blood up into a hankie. Denny started to do all of the talking, and occasionally Artem tried to laugh or at least a smile.

He said goodbye to Artem, and said he would pop up in a couple of days to see how he was. Yuri came to the front door to show Denny out.

"Yuri, I see what you mean about your dad, I never thought he would go down as quick. Maybe we should go to the undertakers tomorrow afternoon. What do you think? Also, I want to speak to you and Tomaz, as well as Karl, in the morning about my trip to Scotland, but you will have to get Tomaz to come to terms about his dad sooner rather than later."

"That sounds like a plan, and I will be sitting down with Tomaz tonight, to try to get through to him about dad when he comes back from his training. He's taking it very seriously Denny."

"So, he should be Yuri as I don't fancy running about in front of a crowd with my 'tackle' swinging about. Tell him to keep going."

Denny was so very tired. Sleep looked like it was never going to come back anytime soon, so he thought he might have to do with power naps whenever he could. Not ideal, but it was all he could do at present.

He went into the big house and asked Helen if she needed help with boys, but she said both her and Gertie were fine. Denny wandered over to the chest of drawers and took out a bank book and put it in his inside pocket. He went down to speak to Willie.

"Hi brother, I hope I am not interrupting your love making session or did Gertie give you the thumbs down this time? I thought you might be waiting to hear how I got on in bonnie Scotland."

"I'm struggling to come to terms with it all Denny. I know that we had to protect ourselves the last time, and I would do it again in a heartbeat, but ultimately we are still killing people. Okay, I won't be with you in a few months, but how many of you are coming back? It makes me shudder brother."

"I take everything you have said into account, but do you want us looking over our shoulders every minute of the day. Sorry Willie, but I can't do that. Wondering if my wife and boys will be safe. Wondering if you and Gertie, as well as all the men will be safe. I know it is my fight, and I have told everyone that they are either in or out. If they are out, then I have no problem with it. They are not beholden to me."

Willie sat back in his chair and shut his eyes.

"You know I will have your back in any fight that comes along pal, but I thought I would just put my thoughts over."

"I need to see both you and Gertie about an important matter tonight, so if you could come up for a bit of supper at eight that would be great. Helen should be there, but I'm not sure as she seems to have fallen out with me."

"I've noticed Denny."

He walked up and in to the kitchen where Helen and Gertie were preparing food for the next few days. He told Helen that he had spoken to Willie, and that he wanted to speak to him and Gertie over supper at about eight o'clock tonight. He thought he saw Helen's head give the slightest of nods. It was best that he removed himself. Helen was bad enough now, but wait till he told her about the 'siege of Scotland' he thought. It didn't bear thinking about.

He thought a short walk with the dogs would be in order, but Willie had already seen to them, so it was only the company he needed. The dogs weren't complaining. While he walked, he wondered if his thoughts on buying an estate in Scotland were too ambitious. That was for another time, if he was alive after his trip.

Supper at eight was a bit strained, so it was only a bit of chit chat with Helen contributing very little. Denny went to his jacket and took the book from his inside pocket, came back and sat down.

"Gertie, Helen and I would like to give you a wee present. I'll say the same thing to you as I said to Willie, your sex mad boyfriend. Please, don't argue about the figures you see on this form, and for fuck sake no tears. If you don't understand what the figures mean, then Willie will explain. Willie was looking a bit curiously.

He handed Gertie the book, and by the look on her face it was going to be up to Willie to explain what it was all about. She looked and better looked, before Willie took the book and pointed out that Denny and Helen were giving her a tremendous amount of money as a present. It still wasn't really sinking.

"Mr Denny are you trying to tell me that you and Miss Helen are giving me all this money. Why? I have some money saved up and you pay me well."

"It is something we both want to do Gertie, as we love you as one of the family. With what Willie received as well, you could travel the world and never see the same place twice."

It was then that tears started falling down her face.

245

"Travel the world Denny? What makes you think we want to do that?"

"Just a thought brother. You never know."

Willie didn't know what to think.

"Right, I'm out of here, but before I do, can I ask the three of you when you last spoke to Artem? To be brutally honest with you, Artem is dying, yes I did say dying. He may only have a few weeks to go."

Helen put her hand over her mouth in shock. Gertie and Willie just looked at each other.

"I'll leave you with that thought. I'm off to bed, after kissing my boys."

When Helen came up to the bedroom, Denny was just getting a change of clothes for work next morning.

"You don't have to do that Denny. Just stay here tonight."

"I'm not sure that is the best idea Helen. You are so up and down with me, and I can't handle that. Everything I am doing is for everybody else. Not me. I know that some of the things I am doing seem a bit clandestine, but I have been trying to explain to you, with little success it seems, that for everybody's safety it depends on me keeping the information in my head. Mine. What are you not understanding about that?"

He walked past Helen without looking at her. He stopped at the door.

"By the way the court case is at the end of the week. I thought I would tell you in case you think I am keeping it from you," he said sarcastically.

When he was gone, she sat on the bed and cried. She didn't know what was happening to their relationship. Was she being too hard on him, she really didn't know, but her head was getting as mixed up as his. She knew she loved him with all her heart, but there was too much going on with him, and she felt he was going to drop a bombshell sooner rather than later. No matter what it was, she felt pangs inside the pit of her stomach just thinking about it. She didn't know how she was going to get through this. The court case was going to be hard for him, and she prayed that he wasn't going to kick off in court and be arrested. She thought life was just a bloody mess at the moment.

246

It wasn't that long ago that she was so happy on her wedding day. Maybe tomorrow will be better.

She crept though in the morning to the room Denny had been sleeping in, but he was already up and away. Sadness slowly came over her, and there were more tears. She wished she was like Denny emotionally at times. Their love making was suffering, and she knew when she was on top and making love, it was as if she wanted to satisfy herself as quickly as possible, and to hell with him. Yet, he was always very gentle and careful with her, making sure she enjoyed every minute. It was just a case of getting on with it she supposed.

When the men arrived next morning, Tomaz was missing.

"Where is he Yuri?"

"Last night's talk didn't go great Denny. He was really upset, even though my dad tried to placate him. He took off into the forest and only came back a few hours ago. I'll speak to him again tonight."

Denny jumped up knocking over his breakfast. Nobody dared say a word. Yuri knew where he was going, but he didn't follow, as he saw the look on Denny's face. It looked evil he thought.

Denny strode up to the cabin. He didn't bother knocking and burst in to their living area.

"Excuse me Artem, but I have business with you son. Stop your fucking snivelling Tomaz. You know too fucking well that your dad is dying, and there is nothing anybody can do about it. Especially you pal. Now, you have exactly five minutes to get in to the shower and wash as you stink. Fucking hurry up."

Tomaz took off at speed, and it was exactly five minutes when he stood in the living area in front of Denny. When Tomaz made for the door Denny shouted at him, and asked if he had forgotten something. Tomaz looked around, but a vacant stare appeared on his face.

"How about you give your dad a hug, before I boot your arse."

Tomaz ran to where his dad was sitting and gently squeezed him. Artem looked over his son's shoulder and gave Denny a slight nod.

"Right, lets go."

As soon as they were out the door, Denny grabbed him by the scruff of the neck, and frogmarched him down the path to the big

247

house where everyone was still sitting. Denny dragged him in to the middle of the men. Helen and Gertie quickly went inside and shut the doors.

"Have a good fucking look at all the men, have a look will you. We are all in this together, and we rely on each other to stay alive. You can't even come to terms with reality. How long have we all known that your dad was dying, but you chose to bury your head in the sand. It was you who wanted to go to Scotland, and now I am not sure if I can rely on you. How long were you going to sit bubbling in that chair. Until your dad died, while we worked and prepared ourselves. You will have to fucking toughen up Tomaz or else your out. Go and work with Willie today as I don't want to see you for the rest of the day. Yuri, take us on a bloody hard run pal. Willie you don't have to come with us."

As the men took off Tomaz was at the back, but Denny didn't know if he was keeping up the pretence, as Willie was standing watching them. When they got back, even Denny was feeling his muscles. It was then that the girls came out with packed lunches for everyone. Denny felt that he needed to get rid of the tension on the estate. It was then that he thought about the challenge. He would make it a bit of a party affair, a bit of a release. He realised that the preparations for Scotland had been going on for far too long. All his fault.

When the men finished work Denny had asked them to gather around the fire pit. The girls came out with coffee and biscuits for them, before he asked them to go inside and keep away from the windows and door. They knew not to ask why.

"Right men, let me take time out to tell you about my jaunt, as my wife called it, to Scotland. The first thing I am going to tell you is that the weather was brutal, a lot harsher than here. The snow was two or three feet high where we are going, and the wind was bitter. I have managed to procure a property which looks directly over the estate which we are going to take out. So, you won't be lying in a ditch covered with snow. Well, not all the time. There is a lot of preparations in place. Will it be difficult? Of course it will, but no more than I have planned for. Can we do it? Sure, but we will have to be ruthless enough to keep ourselves alive. If we get caught by the authorities, then we will never see daylight again. It would be up to each individual as to whether

248

they put a bullet in their brain if that happens. Any questions at this stage?"

It was Yuri who spoke up.

"I presume you will tell us where we are going when we get to Scotland, and not before. Will we have all the equipment, including transport that we need? Most importantly though, do you think we will be ready."

"We need to keep up the fitness, as well as learning all about surveillance from Karl. The next few weeks will be intense, and each off us will have to get in the right frame of mind. Do you hear that Tomaz."

Tomaz nodded his head furiously, while trying not to feel embarrassed in front of everybody.

By the look on the men's faces there was a lot of nervousness and Denny felt they needed a distraction from going to Scotland.

"Helen, you and Gertie please come out will you. I think we have taken our mind off the most important event that is going to happen on the estate. The challenge between my champion Tomaz and William McLeod our Forestry Manager, the self proclaimed master of all things involving love making. Although, I have always suspected that Gertie would have a different view. Let's make it Sunday, and if the girls are up for it, then let's make it a party. Yuri, please make sure Jinty will be over, and your dad better be here to see his son crowned champion. Helen, can phone the Town House and see who would like to attend? What do you say everyone?"

A cheer went out, and everyone was smiling.

"Hey Foggerty, you had better not get carried away with yourself asking all these people. I'm not sure they will be keen on seeing you running stark, bollock naked, along with your 'broken down champion' who is vertically challenged."

Tomaz immediately got down on the floor, and did his usual pretence of falling flat on his face after just five press-ups.

"After seeing that Foggerty, you can ask half of Zwiesel if that is the best your champion can do. Don't worry Gertie, nobody is going to see my Adonis like naked body on Sunday, except you later on."

Everyone was just laughing, as Gertie just put her hand over her eyes.

249

"I promise we will put on a party that will raise everyone's spirit and Gertie and I are going to make a trophy for the winner and also the loser. I don't know what, but what do you think Gertie.

"I think we are going to make it a beautiful time, and I have an idea for the trophies, so leave it with me."

"Just do what you want Gertie, as I will be lying back watching these two losers doing their forfeit. Trust me."

As the girls walked away, Denny could see them chatting away putting ideas to each other.

"Okay, everyone let's go. We have work to do. Karl, I will meet up with you at the end of the day to discuss the logistic of where we are going. I need your ideas, although not having seen the area, I appreciate it will be difficult. Tomaz, please choose which dog you want beside you today, and you had better look after him."

The look on Denny's face made Tomaz choose Arno quickly, and he started off to work with Willie.

"Keep your eye on Willie, Tomaz, as he might 'accidentally' drop a log on your foot, as that's the only way he will beat you on Sunday."

Willie never looked back, but just gave him a hand gesture over his shoulder.

As Denny walked with Yuri to where they were going to work, his head was about full to bursting with everything that was coming up. He was bored with his life at the moment. He wanted it to be just him and Helen along with the boys. Walking the dogs, and having playful fights with them. Sitting on the veranda with Willie and Gertie, with everybody talking rubbish at times. Laughing at the boys exploits that day. He wondered if that was too much to ask. Then, the thought of attending court on Friday brought him back to reality.

Willie tried his best to get into Tomaz's head by telling him how he used to be the Scottish Hill running champion for three years in a row, before he ended up in Bavaria. How he could do one hundred one-handed press-ups before breakfast. Tomaz didn't believe a word of it and did his usual of doing five press-ups before lying puffing on the floor of the forest. Willie just laughed at him, almost pitying him having to show of his 'tackle' to everyone on Sunday.

Denny sat down with Karl at the end of the day, and told him as much as he could. Several times Karl just nodded his head, but at other times he was shaking it.

"Why the shaking of the head Karl? What's the problem?"

"Not a massive problem Denny. It's difficult to visualise the area where we will be, and we don't know what the house is like inside, but there is one thing we need and that is white camouflage clothing for the snow, as well as the usual Operational Camouflage Pattern. That shouldn't be a problem for anybody who knows what they are doing, as there is still a lot of surplus after the War. You just have to know where to get it from."

"What I will try and do is draw you a plan of the house and grounds, with as much information as possible. You can ask me about the drawing, but please remember it was seen from high up. As to the gear we need, my pal Stevie has assured me he has a friend who can get us anything. What I do need, is for both you and Yuri to give me a list of what we are going to need, right down to the last detail."

"We will have all the details for you within the next couple of weeks, but one question before I leave. Are you sure about Tomaz?"

"To be honest Karl, if Yuri hadn't been coming with us then I would have had my doubts, but I am certain he will come good. If he fucks up, I will shoot him myself."

"That's good enough for me Denny."

Just then Karl drove away, and Denny shouted on Yuri not to make any supper tonight, as they were coming down to the house for something to eat, and he would come up to get them when it was time. Yuri just waved. When he walked in to the house, he asked Helen if she could make enough supper for Artem and his sons, also to phone Jinty and see if she would like to come over.

"Jinty? Your getting soft in your old age Foggerty, or is it that you have missed tormenting her?"

"Certainly not the first part Helen."

Although the dogs had been out all day, Denny took them away and gave them training on looking after everyone on the estate when he wasn't there. They loved the intensity of it, and

251

he wished he was able to take them with them. If he intended to live part of the year in Scotland, as well as here, then he would have to speak to Maria about bypassing customs, for them as being stuck in quarantine wasn't an option. Just something else to be stored in my brain he thought.

When he got back, he fed the dogs and left them to wander outside, but knew they would be lying as near to the fire pit as they could get as soon as he was out of sight. After a quick shower he did his usual and lay on the bed. He knew there would be no sleep, but at least he would be resting his body. An hour later he got up, dressed and walked up to the lodge. When he walked in he could hear Artem in discussion with Yuri.

"What's happening folks?" asked Denny.

"It's this stubborn old bastard Denny. He said he didn't want to come down for supper, as he would just be a burden to everyone."

"Son, I can hardly walk to the toilet, never mind walking to the house. Just leave me here will you?"

"Not an option Artem. Go and get your 'glad rags' on please."

Artem wasn't going to argue with Denny, so he got Yuri to help him with a clean shirt, and sat down again.

"Right, Artem here goes. Your coming with us whether you like it or not."

Denny stooped and picked him up, with Yuri putting a blanket around him. Denny felt that Artem was just skin and bone. As they walked down the path, Denny stopped and turned round to see Tomaz dragging his feet, and lagging behind them. Denny knew it couldn't have been easy for him to see his dad like this. He just gave him a glance and nodded for him to get in front of them. When they got up to the top of the steps Denny asked Artem if he wanted to sit by the firepit, or go and eat inside. Artem just nodded to the fire, so Denny just instructed the dogs to remove themselves. Reluctantly they did.

"Helen, we have the Czech contingent here to see you."

Helen came running out and immediately went and gave Artem a gentle hug. She thought Tomaz looked a bit left out, so she gave him a hug and a kiss on his cheek.

"Never forget Tomaz, your still my hero and always will be."

Denny watched as Tomaz put his hand momentarily over his eyes as if he was embarrassed. Although, he thought this might be another moment of pretence from him. Willie and Gertie arrived, and it was only a few minutes later that they heard Jinty's car coming up the track. When she got out the car, Denny got her attention.

"Hey, Thomas do you know that your car has more than just first gear, don't you?"

"Piss off Foggerty. It's nice to see you too."

Denny slowly and menacingly walked down the steps, put her over his shoulder with her shouting and swearing at him, and thumping him on his back. He walked up the steps and plonked her down beside Artem. She held Artem gently, and gave him a kiss on his cheek. It was nice to see a smile come over his face. Denny wondered what it must be like to know that you have only a short time to live. He thought if it happened to him, then he would not put his family through it. He would end it himself.

"Remember Tomaz, no feeding the dogs with cakes."

Although he thought he would need the eyes of a hawk to catch the little bugger. Helen had got the record player out, and the sound of different types of music was being carried through the cool evening air. Denny wondered why they didn't play music more often, but there was a lot of things they should be doing more often. The fire was roaring, and everybody was singing to the songs, even although they weren't sometime singing the right words. He knew it didn't matter as long as they were all happy.

When the food came, it was a feast fit for a king or possibly Artem. Denny saw him just pick at his meal, but nobody said a word, as he was smiling all the time. Denny stared at Tomaz, with the expression being 'don't you bloody dare feed my dogs cakes'. Tomaz stared back and waved his finger at him as if to say, catch me if you can.

The eating and singing went on for several hours and only ended when Artem fell asleep. Jinty said she would need to get back, and then gave everyone a kiss, especially Artem, on the forehead as he slept. Well not everyone.

"Have you left anybody out with your kisses Thomas?"

"Don't think so Foggerty, unless you mean your smelly 'dugs'."

Everyone just laughed, but she crept back up the steps, grabbed Denny in a headlock, pushed his head back and gave him a beautiful 'smacker' on the lips. She knew she had to run, so she jumped in the car and sped off down the track. Denny had been a bit put out with this as he had been caught out by Jinty again. Even more so when he turned round to see Udo and Arno getting tucked in to a large cake each. Tomaz wasn't waiting. He leap over the rails, and landed like a cat on all fours on the ground. He stopped, wagged his finger and took off towards the lodge.

Denny walked over, picked up Artem and carried him up the trail. When they were in the house, Yuri had told Denny just to put him in his chair beside the fire, as it was easier for him to get to the toilet.

"Thank you Denny, you have made an old man very happy. I've never seen him smile and laugh as much in a long time. He is happy knowing that when he goes, Tomaz and I will be among friends."

"Not friends Yuri, family."

When Helen and Denny went up to the bedroom they took one of the boys each, changed them and read them a story. Afterwards, the boys were put in their cot. Denny started to take his clothes off, but he noticed that she wasn't even bothering to look at him. Instead of stripping naked for bed, Helen had put on a pair of panties and long tee-shirt, which was a statement to Denny. Don't touch my body tonight. He just kept as far away from her in bed that was possible that night.

Chapter 11

When the sun rose the next morning, Denny just lay and looked out the window. He knew his life wasn't playing out the way he wanted it to. He turned, and just looked at Helen who was still sleeping. God he loved that girl, but he was making her life hell at the moment. He couldn't help it though, so he shouldn't be beating himself up about it. He heard a car coming up the drive, and when he looked out he saw it was officer Meyer. He thought it strange, so he quickly dressed and went down stairs. When he opened the door he gestured for the officer to come in.

"Please come in my friend. Sit down, and I will make us breakfast."

When Denny came back with tea and toast he enquired, "What brings you up here at this early hour. I certainly hope it's not bad news. I don't think I could handle it."

"Just a bit of a social call Denny, but it also gives me a chance to speak to you about the court case on Friday. How are you feeling about it? Have you been giving it much thought?"

"To be honest, I have given it very little thought, as after speaking to my solicitor, who is probably the top guy in the Albach Trust, we both know he will get away with it. You are the third person who thinks the same."

Denny just sat and stared at the officer. A stare that made him extremely uncomfortable, even frightened.

"Do you remember when I told you that he might get away with it in court due to a corrupt judge, but he will pay for it with his life. Well, that still stands, but don't worry about it. Nothing will change my mind. Remember, we will remain good friends, and I can assure you that you will not have to come and arrest me. Are we good?"

It was then that he gave one of his evil smiles. The officer almost spilt his tea, and thought he might have to leave.

"I will be in court that day Denny. A police presence just in case something kicks off, but if you do then please give me the nod, as I might have to leave the courtroom with a bad stomach."

It was his turn to smile, but it wasn't anything like Denny's evil grin.

"When this is all over, I would like to see you and Officer Schmidt back over here pursuing your interests. It will only be a few months before we will be greeting our old school teacher who will be in charge of looking after the children when they arrive. It would be nice if you both meet her."

"It would be our pleasure Denny. I bid you good day. Until Friday."

Denny sat on the steps with his coffee watching the police car heading down the track. He knew he couldn't kick off in court, as he could be locked up which would scupper his plans for Scotland. He thought he might make a few phone calls after work, basically just keeping in touch with folk. Something he wasn't very good at.

The same scenario was being played out this morning. All the men arriving, and going on their training regime before breakfast, and work. He was getting so fed up now. He wanted to get to Scotland, and kill the people on the Ruthven Estate. Come home, and not have another worry in his life. Like that was going to happen he thought.

While the men went on their brutal run, Denny went upstairs, and walked into the bedroom where the twins slept. Helen was already there attending to the boys. He went over and picked up Fin, who had already been changed. He saw Helen trying hard not to look at him.

"I can see you trying hard not to have a 'wee peek' at me Helen Foggerty. It costs nothing for you to look at this big hunk of a husband you married only a few months ago. Would you like to come and give me a little peck on the cheek if nothing else?"

Helen was very hesitant, before she slowly went and sat in his lap, with Denny holding Fin in his arm. He held out his cheek for her to kiss, and when she leant forward, he turned his face, and kissed her fully on the lips. She started to laugh, which was music to his ears. He went and put his son down, and even although she started to strip off and walk towards the shower, he knew it wasn't going to be today that he would end up making love to her. Her body had never lost it's beauty from the first time she had stripped off, and ran in to the sea on Durma. She was going to make him wait though. Ah well. He thought how strange the female species was, but he had thought that many times before.

It was just a wait for the men to come back from their training. After breakfast, he asked Helen and Gertie to come out and sit with everybody. When they were all seated, Denny thought it was time to tell everyone about what would happen at the trial. When he was finished Yuri said," Are you joking with us Denny? You're saying he is going to get off with it, with no real jail time?"

"I'm afraid so Yuri. A corrupt judge will be letting him off. However, I have already told officer Mayer that if he does, then it will cost him his life. Don't worry folks, I won't be getting locked up anytime soon."

"Do you think it was wise telling the police officer what your intentions are brother.?"

"I was just telling him the truth Willie."

"Mr Denny, can I say something?"

"Of course, Gertie, carry on."

"Well Mr Denny, if you had did like I suggested, and got me one of these pistols, I could have went down, and shot him a few times. What does everybody think?"

Everyone erupted in laughter, and started to applaud her. She stood there imitating firing a pistol, which made everyone laugh even more.

"Don't ever lose that one brother."

Willie was sitting cringing. Helen grabbed Gertie by the arm and dragged her inside, even although she was still firing her imaginary pistol.

"Willie, you and I will work together today. Karl, I suggest you have a break from training us for a few days. Have time off, go home, and work out any plans you have for our trip. Any little detail that might help us to get over the finishing line. Can you tell Gunther I need to speak to him about selecting several men to replace us on the estate while we are away. When he is choosing though, please tell him he has to be one hundred percent sure that they are trustworthy around Helen and the boys, as well as Gertie. Remembering, that Jinty and Maria might turn up at any time. I'll see you on Sunday for the 'Big Challenge', and try your best to persuade Ada and Gisela to join us on this momentous occasion, when Willie's pure white naked body will be on display, and dazzle us all. Sunglasses will be permitted"

"In your dreams Foggerty. Bring everyone you know, as it will be you laughing on the other side of your face. The mighty Willie McLeod will prevail."

While Denny, and Willie were working, he told him his plan for Scotland. He told him he wanted as many of the enemy, for want of a better word, to disappear mysteriously at our hands. If it looks like an accident then great."

"Have you put a lot of thought in to where you can dispose of the bodies Denny. I haven't seen the area, and I'm sure there is a lot of wilderness that people can disappear in, but how many bodies are we talking about?"

"I reckon they must have about thirty people on the pay role Willie, so I reckon we have to eliminate at least ten of them. I have an idea how to get rid of the rest, but it all depends on timing. I know they have a drugs lab under the house, with vans coming and going. I saw it while undercover in Edinburgh. Maybe if there is a 'big man' up above, then he will give me a hand. You just never know."

Willie started to laugh.

"Did you really see it Denny, or was it through a whisky haze, and if your looking for divine intervention, then your fucked pal."

Denny threw himself at Willie, and as usual they were busy laughing while wrestling each other, until Arno started to bark at them furiously with his teeth up. They then knew it was time to stop. The vision of the guy with his throat ripped out, and his scrotum hanging off, was enough to know when not to mess with the dogs. Willie grabbed Arno around the neck and brought him in to his side, which surprised Denny, but Arno loved it.

"Would you miss us all, even the dogs, if you weren't here brother?"

"Of course I would, but what are you trying to say, that I'm going to leave?"

"I would never dream of it pal, God forbid."

Denny smiled, and started to heave some fallen branches away from the path.

Willie wondered if his brother had more than just a sixth-sense. Surely he wasn't able to read his mind. Although nothing surprised him about Denny. Absolutely nothing.

After work Denny, went and phoned Ian and Neala. Ian was just coming out the bath, so it gave him a bit of time to speak to Neala.

"How are you and the baby Neala? How has the pregnancy been for you?"

"I won't lie to you Denny, it's been hard. I have days when I have no energy, and feel I could sleep all day. However, I make myself get up and get on with things, and thankfully the sickness is getting less and less. I can't remember if we told you or not, but we are having a little boy. Although the way he is kicking, he doesn't feel that little. How are you all over there?"

"That's great news Neala. I am so happy for you. Helen will be so excited when she hears the news. We are all good over here, the only couple of down sides are that Artem, Yuri and Tomaz's dad, has only a few weeks to go as he has the cancer. Also, I have to go to court on Friday for the court case of the guy who shot Helen. I'm sure Ian will have told you how it's going to play out, however the end game will be that the guy will lose his life."

"Denny does life not mean that much to you, as the casual way you talk about taking people's lives is so cold, and it is just a way of life to you, and you don't care. I presume you have thought about how the twins would react if they ever grew up and find out about you."

"Neala, your right, I don't care if the people I despatch to hell are evil. I never lose any sleep over it. Oh, and my boys will never find out from me, and if someone else says anything then God help them. I will put Helen on now, and I will speak to Ian when the pair of you eventually stop talking."

Helen came through and started to speak to Neala. She was so excited to hear the news of the sex of the baby. Helen asked her if she was looking forward to coming over to stay. Neala had said she couldn't wait, as the island was beginning to close in on her. She needed a new challenge in her life. As soon as the house was finished they would be over. Helen had told her in confidence that her and Denny hadn't been getting on too well. It seems he has something to sort out in Scotland. Neala knew exactly what it was, but it was obvious that Denny hadn't told her, so she wasn't going to divulge that information. Ian came through, so she said goodbye, and passed the phone to Ian so that he could speak to her.

After a while Helen had passed the phone to Denny.

"Evening Denny, I hope you're well son. There is so much I could ask you, but I'm scared of the answers. Firstly, I will tell you my news. We have provisionally sold the house to a lovely couple from the mainland. They have two nice kids, which will be good for Durma. My boat will be sold within a few days, so it's just a waiting game now before we get over there."

"I passed your new house the other day Ian, and it looks really good. I have a feeling that when you eventually get over your brother may not be here. Just a hunch, but it's just that he is going through the motion, and some of the things he says, well its like he is trying to tell me something."

"Bloody hell Denny, I really thought he was settled at last, but it doesn't look like he is. Do you want me to have a word with him?"

"Nah, you're fine pal, as I'm sure he will tell me in his own sweet time. I'll go and get him for you."

"Before you go Denny, are you still coming to Scotland to wreak revenge on the people that tried to kill you?"

"I sure am, pal. Everything is falling into place. Keep watching the news, but It will be a while before all hell breaks loose. Oh, and just to say I am in court on Friday for the guy that shot Helen."

"Please, do me a favour my friend. Don't do any thing to the guy, while you are in court."

"As if Ian."

Denny said cheerio, and thought it will be nice to see the pair of them again, unless he was face down in the Scottish snow with a bullet in his head.

After Willie came off the phone, he asked if he could have a word with Denny. They went outside, and sat next to the fire.

"Denny, I know that you will be heading to Scotland for your little crusade in a few weeks. So, can you tell me what will happen if none of you come back?"

"Willie, don't you fucking dare trivialise what I am going to do. You know why, yet you make stupid remarks about it all the time. I often feel like putting my twelve bore in your 'gob,' and pressing both barrels. It would give me peace. Do you really think I want all this nonsense, but I am willing to listen to you for another way round it. No, I didn't think so. So just fuck off and leave me alone. Oh, and for your information, Maria has everything in hand. Good night."

Denny walked in and lifted the phone. He phoned Shonagh. It took a few rings before she eventually picked up.

"Hello Shonagh, I hope I am not interrupting anything between you and Jack. You know you need to keep your man happy."

"No, Denny I was just out of the shower. Before you make any more remarks, Jack and I are no longer an item. We haven't been for a few weeks now."

"What the hell has happened Shonagh? You both seemed happy enough when you were over here, and when I spoke to you last."

"You know why Denny. I told you the last time we spoke. He tries hard in the bed, but he never seems to fulfil me. Unlike someone did a long time ago. I just get so frustrated at times."

"For God's sake Shonagh, you will have to get over the brief encounter we had. You can't keep dwelling on it. Yes, it was a nice time, but nothing could come from it. You're a lovely looking girl, and there will be loads of men out there who would love to be in a relationship with you."

"That's the problem Denny, they're not you. Anyway, what is it you're after, as I'm sure your not asking after my health."

"Actually, I was my bonnie girl, but you have suddenly put me off my chain of thought. Bloody hell Shonagh, have you got any more surprises for me."

There was a pause on the line.

"Well, to be honest Denny, there is. I intend to leave the police force just as soon as you return to Bavaria after your sortie here. I hope to come over for my examination with the nerve expert, and I will take it from there. Maybe I will travel the world. You never know."

"Hell Shonagh, I really was just asking how you were, and you come out with all this. It sounds like you haven't been happy for a long time. In all honesty though, if your not happy in your relationship then get out of it. Life is too short, and you don't get another shot at it. I need to go now Shonagh, but I will put Helen on as she would love to speak to you. Also, there will be a very slight chance we will see you when we arrive in Scotland, but I really want to keep you out of this. Be safe."

After passing the phone to Helen, he went upstairs and sat watching his boys. He thought how determined he was not to have them grow up without a dad. He thought back to how much his own dad was such a big influence and comfort to him while he was growing up.

He could still hear Helen on the phone, so he decided to have an early night, as there was no point in waiting for her, as he would be lucky to get a good night kiss from her, never mind the chance to make love to her. He knew that once he told her his Scottish plan making love might not be an option. It was late when she came to bed, did her usual and slept as far away from him as possible. Once he told her his plan, he knew that their relationship would take a downward spiral. It was just something that he had to put out of his mind.

Friday came round quick enough. It was eight o'clock in the morning, when a plush looking car drew up at the bottom of the steps. Denny went out to see who had arrived. A suited gentleman introduced himself as Jonas Schneider, a solicitor from the Albach Trust. Denny asked him in, and Gertie popped her head out of the kitchen, and said breakfast wouldn't be long, which surprised the solicitor a bit.

"Would you mind showing me this magnificent house Mr. Foggerty. I have heard about it from various people."

"Not at all Jonas, as long as you call me Denny. Let's go."

While they sat having breakfast in the magnificent dining room, Jonas had commented on what a beautiful estate this was, and what a lucky guy Denny was.

"Thank you Jonas for your kind words, and I do appreciate you coming to see me here, rather than just at the court today. I know, as you do, what the outcome will be today so don't be disappointed if the guy doesn't get convicted. I fully expect him to get off with it, as I am sure you know he will. Please, don't lose any sleep over it. I won't."

"Denny, trust me, I have several investigators working on the judge's history where his decisions have been highly questionable. We have also looked in to the guy's father and it makes some interesting reading. It appears he has been offering some large bribes to several contractors who have won some big contracts all over Germany to use his products. We can't tie everything in at the moment, but my investigators are like bloodhounds, and when we do get all the information, then the judge and the guy's father will be finished. Possibly jailed."

"Well, that's a win in my book Jonas, but I can see by your face that your wondering what I am going to do to the guy when he gets off with it. I think it best if I just say he won't get off with it. Maybe in court he will, but he will lose his life at some point."

"I was told to expect that answer, and Maria has told me to pass on this message, that you must behave yourself in the court room."

Denny started laughing as Helen walked out with the boys. Denny introduced Jonas to her.

"I'm very pleased to meet you young lady, although I wish it was under nicer circumstances. Can you please tell me the exact nature of you injury."

"Better still, I will show you."

Helen wasn't shy at opening her shirt and showing him the scar. Although, Jonas did get a bit of a fright when Tomaz suddenly appeared at his shoulder. Tomaz was pointing at Helen's scar and gesturing that he was the one who had 'patched' her up.

All the men were getting ready to go to work.

Willie got the dogs out, and Jonas had asked if he could meet them, as Otto had told him all about how fine dogs they were. Denny asked Willie to send them up the steps, but first they found a convenient tree to cock their leg on. He could see Tomaz walking forward, and suddenly he motioned for the dogs to go and protect Denny. They bolted up the steps and stood in front of Jonas with their teeth bared. Tomaz was laughing.

"To say I am frightened Denny, is an understatement. Are they going to attack me?"

"Don't worry, they will, but only if I tell them to. You're safe. Tomaz, you little bastard, I will boot your arse when I get back."

Tomaz dropped to the ground and started his pretence of press-ups, but this time Willie shoved him down, and stood with his foot on his back.

"Have a look Foggerty, as this is what's going to happen on Sunday. Trust me."

Jonas looked a little bewildered, but Denny wasn't going to make him any the wiser. Denny said it was too early for the court, and suggested they sit outside at the fire and have another coffee.

"Maria was explaining to me that you had big plans for extending the forestry side of the estate. Both here and abroad, and you will be over in Scotland looking over estates that might be for sale. When will you be going."

"Soon Jonas as I wanted to get this court case out of the way. Plus, we have the father of one of my workers who is terminally ill, and lives on the estate, and it's looking like he won't last a few weeks, so I won't go until he passes. It was just then that Jinty came up the driveway. She saw Jonas, walked over, and sat on his lap with her arms around his neck. He was mortified.

"Where did you get this good looking guy about Foggerty?"

"He is actually a solicitor for the trust Jinty. He is representing Helen in court in a wee while."

"Ah, maybe I should not be flirting with him then, but if I need someone to represent me, then you're the guy pal."

She gave him a kiss on the cheek and walked away in to the house.

"What just happened there Denny?"

"Don't worry Jonas, she is a lovely girl, but I would never tell her. I think it's best that we head down in to the town now."

They were just about to head off, but Denny had asked him to wait as he ran in to the house, and came out with a carrier bag.

"Don't worry Jonas, it's not a gun. It's evidence."

Jonas looked at him, and thought this might be one of his more interesting court cases.

When they arrived at the court building the car park was nearly full, but Jonas managed to find a space near the front door. When they went in, there was a clerk taking everyone's names and the details of what case they were there for. The clerk said that they were running late as judge Klein hadn't turned up yet.

About fifteen minutes later, a small insignificant man walked through the large front doors. Jonas whispered that this was their judge, Klein. Denny couldn't hold back.

"Well, it's nice of you to get out of your bed and grace us with your presence judge."

"Do you know who you are speaking to young man."

"I know only too well who and what you are, and as your holding the proceedings up, I suggest you get a move on."

"If you were in my court room or chambers, I would have you arrested."

"Well, I am not, so bugger off, and stop wasting my time."

The judge walked away with a face that looked like he was ready to explode.

"Well, that was a good start Denny. You're going to make me earn my wages today."

Denny burst out laughing.

"C'mon Jonas, no matter what we say It's not going to change the outcome is it, and as long as I don't get arrested I will be in your debt. I think we should go in now."

As they walked in to the court room they were shown where to sit. They noticed the defendant wasn't in. Eventually the door opened, and in he walked with his dad by his side and sat down facing the judge's bench. The judge was nowhere to be seen, so Denny was out of his chair, and slid in behind the two guys without them noticing. Their solicitor hadn't arrived yet.

"You are going to get away with this today, because your dad's pal is corrupt, but as soon as you are out of this court room, you're mine. Nobody tries to kill me, and it ends up with my wife being shot. I promise that everywhere you look I'll be watching you. I know where you live, and I'll know if you move. I will know every time you go for a piss. I am the ghost you will never see. Good day you scum."

The clerk of the court saw where Denny was sitting and asked him to go back to his seat. Denny went back to where he had been sitting, and gave the father and son one of his evil smiles. They quickly turned their faces away.

When the judge finally came in he sat down, but noticed Denny sitting with his solicitor. He started to bang his gavel furiously, while asking for police presence. By chance it was officer Meyer who walked down to the front of the judge's bench.

"I want that man taken from this court room, and escorted out of the building officer."

"Your honour, this man is my client for the prosecution, and may I point out that anything that happened before these proceedings has no bearing on this case. If you want I could ask for a mistrial and pass it to the Law Society with all the relevant information, and let them wonder why public money is being squandered," argued Jonas.

"Who are you? Name please."

"My name is Jonas Schneider, representing Mrs Helen Foggerty from the Albach Trust."

"Then why isn't she here, and I don't see anything about the Albach Trust in my papers?"

Jonas was about to say something, when Denny put his hand on his arm, and stood up.

"She isn't here because she is too traumatised, after being shot in the chest by that scum sitting there."

"May I ask who you are?"

"Me? My name is Denny Foggerty, and I own the Albach Trust, yes you heard me, I own it. Every square centimetre of it."

"I should have had you arrested for what you said to me in the foyer."

It was then that Jonas had stood up, and said that you can't arrest somebody for telling the truth about somebody being late. Everyone could see the judge was rattled, not that it would make any difference.

The proceedings started off with everyone giving their names, until Jonas stood up.

"Your honour, this is highly irregular, that a man of Mr. Wagner's age, which I believe is twenty four, has to have his father sitting next to him. So I would ask the court to remove that person to the public gallery."

"Mr. Schneider, I gave permission for that to happen, so just leave it at that."

"I'm sorry your honour, but this is highly irregular, so if he is not removed to the public gallery, I will be calling for the Law Society's investigators to look into this trial, which is already turning in to a farce."

The judge waved his hand at the guy's father, and he walked to the public gallery, taking a seat at the back. He told Jonas that he wanted this trial to be over, so he wanted to hear the accused story on the day of the shooting.

Everything that came out of the guy's mouth was a lie from start to finish. When it was time to cross examine the guy. Jonas gave him both barrels.

"Everything you have told us is a pack of lies Mr. Wagner."

Just then the judge tried to intervene, but Jonas told him he had the right to cross examine the accused without interference from anybody.

"You have just told us that you were out showing your girl how to fire a rifle. Then you have said you were out hunting with your girl, and that's when you say the gun was accidentally discharged while aiming at an animal on one of the trails. All this contrary to what you first said at the police station. You have just said it was getting dark, yet I have five witnesses who will swear in this court that it was only mid-day. Jonas then shouted at him.

"You are making this up as you are going along. I put it to the court that you are lying through your teeth Mr Wagner. You went out that day with the sole intention of shooting my client here. Due to an altercation that happened in the same forest several years ago. Please look at me Mr Wagner, and tell me I'm wrong."

The guy just sat with his head down, as Jonas went and sat beside Denny who whispered," nice one Jonas"

It was then time for the council for the defendant to cross examine Denny. Jonas could see by his body language that he was out of his depth.

"Surely Mr. Foggerty, you have to admit, no matter what time of day it was, this was no more than an inexperienced rifleman, aiming a pot shot at what he thought was an animal through thick foliage, with his rifle accidentally discharging."

Denny turned round to see the judge nodding his head.

Denny slowly rose holding the carrier bag in his hand, and threw it at the judge, who instinctively ducked, although it landed in front of him on his bench. He started banging his gavel wanting the police to intervene. Jonas quickly told the judge, that what he had in front of him was evidence that the accused could not have mistaken for any animal.

"Have a look at what's in the bag will you, and tell me how somebody wearing the sweater, could be mistaken for an animal. For fuck sake, it's a cream sweater with a bright red stripe on it. Have you ever seen an animal like that. It is my sweater, and that scum sitting there tried to kill me, but nearly killed my wife instead, as she just slipped it on to bring me my lunch. You know what though, we know all about you Klein, and what the outcome of this trial is going to be, so just get on with it. I am getting bored."

"I am now going to end this trial by giving my judgement, and I'll decide what sentence is appropriate. Mr. Wagner, I find you guilty of reckless discharge of a fire arm, and I am going to fine you three hundred deutschmarks, and order you to pay compensation to Mrs. Foggerty of the same amount. Case closed."

Denny stood up and slowly started to clap his hands while looking at the judge.

"We were told this case would go like this. Corrupt to the hilt. Please, tell your pal sitting up in the public gallery if he tries to pay compensation to my wife, he will have me to deal with me. Got it?"

"I will see you in my chambers Mr Foggerty, and will decide what to do about your insubordination."

"Oh, go and fuck yourself you corrupt bastard. If we go to your chambers, then it will only be me coming out."

Jonas stood up and walked Denny out of the courtroom, with the judge still banging his gavel on his bench. When they got back in Jonas' car, Denny burst out laughing, with Jonas lying back wondering what had just happened.

"Well, that's a story for our grandkids Denny, as sure as hell my colleagues won't believe it."

"Thank you so much for your help Jonas. Without your calming influence and timely interjections, I would probably be locked up just now. As a way of showing my appreciation, why don't you and your family come over next Saturday for lunch, and a walk through the forests, and meet my extended family. I'm sure the kids would love it. Nature at it's best."

"What a lovely gesture. You know you don't have to? I accept your offer, but one thing I have to ask you, will your dogs be around? It's just that my daughter will want, and try to, put her arms around them, and having met them this morning, are you sure that would be wise?"

"Jonas, they are the most loyal dogs you will ever meet. When I introduce your family to them, then they will protect all of you with their lives. They will love the attention they get from your family, but please tell your kids, they are not for taking home."

They both laughed, as Jonas headed back to the estate. They shook hands, before Denny got out and waved him away. He knew he had to go and speak to Helen about the outcome of the trial. He sat down on the big seat next to the fire, and shouted on her to come out for a minute. She walked out from the dining room.

"Helen, please come and sit down beside me for a minute. Don't worry, I won't try and put my hand up your skirt, or inside your blouse, although that would be lovely. Where did these days go Helen?"

"I take it by your flirting, if that's what you call it, that the trial didn't go as you wanted it to?"

"No, it didn't Helen, but it went exactly as we were told it would."

He went on to tell her what had happened, and his offer to Jonas and his family, which Helen thought would be nice to meet other people. She told him that she was glad a horrible time in her life was over, and there would be no repercussions from him. He feigned surprise, which she took with a pinch of salt.

"Foggerty, why is your hand creeping up the inside of my leg under my skirt?"

"Bloody hell Helen, I can't seem to control my hands when I'm around you."

"I know Foggerty, but keep them under control until tonight. You never know what might happen."

As she walked away, he thought a smile had come over her face. It was a start.

He went inside, brought the twins out and started playing with them. He lost all sense of time, before two mad dogs flew up the steps and started licking the boy's faces. Col started to cry, but Fin was loving it. Helen came out, wondering what all the commotion was about, and shouted at Denny to get his bloody dogs out of the way as Col was getting upset.

"Oh, I see they are my dogs when they are causing a problem, but yours when they are cuddling in to you."

"Too right Foggerty."

It was then that the men came along the trail from their work, and Denny indicated that they sit for a while, so he could tell them about the court case. Gertie brought out the coffee for everyone, and a bag of cakes for Yuri to take up for his dad.

"Well folks, the shambles of the court case was as we expected. The guy lied through his teeth, and the judge was as corrupt as we were told he would be. He was fined a paltry three hundred deutschmarks, with the same in compensation to Helen, which I told him to stick up his arse. Both the judge and his father are being actively investigated by the Trust and will be brought to account. However, I have yet to decide what will happen to the guy that shot Helen."

"I fucking told you Foggerty that we should have shot him long ago. Mind you, we maybe should have bought Gertie a pistol and gave him a fighting chance by having her chase him through the forest. Probably his heart would give in never knowing when she would get lucky and manage to hit him."

They all laughed.

"I agree with you Willie, but I suggest we leave it to the trust to do their bit first. Denny will think of something as well," said Karl.

Denny looked over at Tomaz, who seemed to be breathing heavily, and looking very angry. He caught Yuri's attention, who looked at Tomaz and clouted him over the back of the head.

"I suggest we keep our thoughts to ourselves as we have a big day on Sunday, unless you have chickened out William."

Just then, Tomaz started to run around the veranda, imitating a chicken.

"Sit down you little wimp. William here will show you how to be a champion, and let me tell you, I will never tire of telling you about it. Bring it on Foggerty, and I might even be the Love Master to Gertie all night, probably just stopping when it's time for this little jog of yours to happen."

"Okay, it will be eleven o'clock for the race, and party time after that. Food and drink, as well as music and dancing. Oh, I forgot, and humble pie for William here."

As the men left laughing, Denny shouted to Yuri that he would come up for his dad at ten thirty, and he wouldn't be taking no for an answer. Yuri just gave him the thumbs up. Denny needed his time with the dogs, so he walked away in to the forest. It was cold, so his mind wandered to the weather in Scotland. He had to find a way to turn it to his advantage. It was obvious from when he drove up to the big house, that they seemed blasé about their situation. It was getting colder as he walked so he turned back, much to the disgust of the dogs, who were just starting to enjoy themselves.

When he got back, he immediately phoned Karl and asked about the possibility of him getting white camouflage gear over to the estate for next week.

"Who is it all for Denny?"

"The four of us Karl, as there is supposed to be a heavy snowfall within the next ten days. It would be good if we could practice with the same gear we will get over there."

"No worries Denny, it will be here in a couple of days."

"Oh, I meant to say that I need to speak to everyone, including Gunther, just before the big race. Are you confident about Tomaz winning pal?"

"The only way he will be beat is if he breaks a leg. Denny, I have never seen anybody so fit and fast, but he mustn't get too cocky."

Denny spent the next couple of hours helping Helen with boys and tidying the place up, but Helen had told him not to go in to the store room at the back of the house, as she and Gertie were making preparation for Sunday. He thought that was fine by him. When it was starting to get late, he told Helen he was going up for a shower, and heading to bed. It had been a long, and eventful day for him. He was tired.

Due to the noise from the shower, he never heard Helen coming in to the bedroom. He walked through towelling himself, only to see her lying naked on the bed.

"No teasing you, or foreplay tonight Denny. I want you inside me now. Forget finishing drying yourself. I know it's been a while, and I only want you to stop making love to me when your exhausted. Got it?"

Denny was a bit taken aback by this, but found he was hard immediately, so he threw the towel away and joined her on the bed. He didn't waste any time, and quickly entered her. She was very receptive, and kept moving her hips to the rhythm of his thrusting. After about two and a half hours of strenuous love making in various positions, they were both exhausted. They didn't bother going under the sheets, as they were sweating from their exertions, so they just lay back, held hands and fell asleep. Sometime during the night, they must have crawled under the sweat soaked sheets, as they were clinging to their bodies when they awoke.

"Don't think that this is going to happen every time Denny. I know you are holding something back from me. Something big, but I have been neglecting you, so I thought I would help you out this time. Don't get used to it. Until you tell me your secret, you are on rations, so get used to it."

Denny just nodded, and walked away. He knew that once he did tell her, he could be celibate for a good while. After showering, he went to get the dogs out. He heard, rather than saw Jinty coming up the drive, so he waited to let them out. When she stopped and got out, he asked her if it was safe to let the dogs out now she had switched off.

"I'd rather run you over Foggerty."

Denny started to chase her along the track with Jinty screaming like a banshee. He caught her with ease, and then cradled her in his arms, before starting to walk back. She kept looking at him wondering what he was up to.

They were nearing the steps when Helen walked out.

"Is there something I should know about you pair?"

"Yeh, he is a bloody 'dick head' Helen."

"Tell me something I don't know Jinty."

Denny didn't put her down, instead he walked to the dog kennel, opened the door and threw her in. He knew by the squeals that she was getting slobbered over. He strolled away before Helen came running down, and let her out.

"I'll get you back for that Foggerty."

"You probably have already Thomas, as I will have to give the dogs vaccinations now that you have been in there with them."

"Drop dead Foggerty will you."

"Maybe sooner than you think young lady."

Helen and Jinty just looked at each other, wondering what he was on about.

Denny decided to walk up to see Artem, and met Yuri coming down the track.

"How's your dad today Yuri?"

"Probably a bit worse Denny, although if you are going to see him, he might tell you he feels great. Not long for him now Denny."

As he got to the cabin, he decided to look through the window. Artem was sitting at the fire, but he could see his face distort in pain at times. He walked through the front door, and a lovely smile came over Artem's face. Tomaz came through and gestured to Denny that he was making tea, and did he want any? Denny nodded.

While Tomaz was out of the room, Denny asked Artem how he was feeling, who turned to see where Tomaz was, before shaking his head, whispering that it would be soon. Tomaz came in with the tea, so the subject was changed.

"What do you think of Tomaz's chances tomorrow Artem?"

Artem said he thought it might be fifty, fifty which immediately riled Tomaz, who stood there with his arm up in the air as if he was already the champion.

"Listen wee man. Karl has told me that if you run the race as you can, then you will be a certainty. However, he did say that if you got too cocky then you might lose. This is not for me pal, but your dad sitting there. Tomaz walked over and held his dad, and didn't seem to be letting go until Artem gave a small gasp of pain.

"Tomaz, please go gently when hugging your dad. Don't get upset, just be careful pal. You want your dad to see you lifting the trophy don't you?"

A smile appeared on his face. Denny knew then that Tomaz wouldn't let him down. After he finished his tea, Denny told Artem he was off, and would be here for him at ten o'clock tomorrow. He decided it would now be ten o'clock as he reckoned that Artem was a proud man, and he wouldn't want anyone from outside the estate seeing him being carried down to the house. Artem was starting argue.

"Listen, you old bastard, I will be here at ten, and drag you down, never mind carry you down if I have to. Don't bloody to argue."

Tomaz just laughed.

When he got back to the house, Gertie and Helen were hard at the preparations for the Challenge. He wasn't bothered, that if by a miracle Willie won, he had no problem of getting his kit off and running around the estate, but he wasn't sure about Tomaz. Too late for him now. He was going to spend time with the dogs, until he realised they were gone.

"Helen, where are the dogs?"

"Yuri walked in from the forest after checking the safety of the run for tomorrow. He and Jinty have taken them for a romantic stroll in the forest."

"Jinty Thomas out for a romantic stroll? She had better not be jumping his bones in front of my dogs. They could be scarred for life, and it might take me an age to detrain them to get the image out of their heads."

"Give her a break Denny. Life wasn't easy for her with that bastard Scottie. I think it's only now that she is getting over that time. Come and see what she has brought over for tomorrow's occasion."

When Denny walked in, he couldn't believe the spread that was laid out on the large dining room table. The girls had done everybody proud. He knew he was very lucky that way. It was then that he knew he had to up his own fitness regime, so he went in, changed and started to run the route. It wasn't long before he realised how hard this was going to be. The long straight wasn't too bad, but he tried to jump the gully at the stream, only to end up half way over, soaked up to his knees. The immediate climb to the cairn was brutal, and he struggled big time. He lay back against the cairn, and shut his eyes, and must have drifted off.

He was woken by two dogs jumping all over him. He saw Yuri and Jinty waving from the North trail. They came over, and sat down beside him.

"Extra training for me from Monday, Yuri. I feel wiped out with just that short run. I need to get fitter for my other little jaunt to Scotland."

"Another bit of time away Foggerty? Is that why Helen is in a mood these days? What is it this time? C'mon, you can tell your pal from Durma. Maybe, we can all go over at some point to Scotland, so that I can show Yuri all the sights in God's country."

Denny looked at Yuri, who gave a slight shake of the head. Enough to say that he shouldn't mention anymore.

"Just business this time Jinty, and yes it would be nice. Let's wait and see though."

Yuri showed Denny the two small stones on the top of the cairn. One had a T and one a W scratched in to them. Tomaz and Willie had to take the appropriate one when they reach here, to prove they had not cheated in any way.

"Time for us to go Denny, as Jinty is cooking a meal for the four of us tonight."

"Best of luck with that Yuri. If I don't see you in the morning, then I will call the doctor and tell him we have an outbreak of food poisoning on the estate."

Jinty jumped on top of him, and pinned his arms down by his side. Denny started to shout help, over and over, as she straddled him.

"Your smelly 'dugs' are standing at the back of me with their teeth bared, aren't they Foggerty?"

"They sure are Jinty. Remember, you called them smelly, so I don't think they are very happy with you anyway. Plus, you are pinning me down."

"Get them to back off Denny. I feel like I am going to wet my pants. Please tell them to relax."

"You're not 'peeing' over me Thomas. So it's your turn to relax and back off. You're fine now, as they are away"

Yuri had enjoyed the charade as he sat back against a tree, wondering if this scenario would ever change. Probably not.

Yuri and Jinty walked away hand in hand, but Denny couldn't resist winding Jinty up one more time. He whistled to the dogs, who went crazy and started yelping at the top of their voices. Jinty grabbed a hold of Yuri, who wasn't fazed and started laughing.

"Foggerty, you're an arsehole, do you know that?"

Denny just gave her the thumbs up, with an exaggerated smile. He thought he saw a smile starting to break over her face, but she was turning away by that time.

Denny sat back against the cairn. He wondered if his life would change when he got back from Scotland. If he got back from Scotland. Too many doubts were beginning to form in his head. He knew, that when he got over there his sixth-sense would kick in. Or he hoped it would. The view over the forests was absolutely mesmerising. Surely, he couldn't let all this go. He knew he had to get this trip to Scotland spot on. Everyone else would play their part, but it was up to him to make sure everyone came back safe. No pressure there then. Time for home now, as he was maudlin.

As he walked back there were some flurries of snow, and he knew that soon there would be a heavy downfall. He hoped it would keep away until the 'Challenge' was over, and also for Jonas and his family coming over. When he got home he phoned Officer Meyer, and Hans Schmidt.

"Officer Meyer, firstly please excuse me for not using your first name, but have I ever asked you what it is?"

"It is Leon, Denny, but officer is fine by me."

Denny then explained about Jonas, the trust's solicitor coming over next weekend with his family, and does he think that he and Hans would be interested in teaching his kids about the birds and fauna in the forest.

"It would be an honour and a pleasure Denny. I know the way the shift patterns work we are both off, but I will ask him tomorrow and get back to you. It will also give me a chance to speak to you about the travesty that happened during your time in court."

"Don't worry Leon, it was as we expected. Remember, if you are across next week, Gertie's culinary skills will be on show. If you both have a partner, then it would be nice to meet them. Please give me a call anytime to confirm."

He then stoked one of the fire pits, before bringing more logs from the store, ready for tomorrow. The boys were crawling about the lounge with their mother trying to entertain them. Denny joined in with games, trying to be the daft daddy, and succeeding according to Helen.

"Anything I can help you with for tomorrow darling?"

"Firstly, if you're trying to sweet talk me into bed, then you can forget it. Yes, you can help me by staying out of the way. Gertie and I have it all under control. Why don't you go and speak to Willie, as it's going to be a big day for him tomorrow."

Denny thought it would be a good idea. After knocking several times on the annex door, he walked in to find Willie asleep on the sofa, so he went through, put the kettle on, and rummaged about for some of Gertie's biscuits. When he brought through two teas and biscuits, Willie was still out for the count. He kicked him on the way past, wakening him. Willie didn't know where he was, except here was Denny drinking tea and eating biscuits. When he came too fully, he asked Denny what he was doing.

"Can I not come in and see my pal now and again, oh and by the way your tea is on the table there. Sorry no biscuits for you pal, as you have to watch your weight for the big humiliation, or should I say challenge tomorrow. Are you nervous Willie? Having to get your kit off in front of all these people."

"Get a life Foggerty. I am going to enjoy the spectacle of you running around, showing your 'tackle' off to all the ladies. Yuri has told me what the course will be, and I am more confident than ever that I will be the victor."

"Good for you Willie, I like confidence in a person, however I hope we will still be brothers when it's all over."

"The way you're talking, do you know something I don't Denny?"

"Not at all Willie. However, changing the subject, it is my intention to be in Scotland as soon as possible after Artem passes. It should be the coming week according to Yuri. I was with him earlier and he wasn't good. Poor guy. I need to speak to you about us leaving, and you will be in charge. Speak soon, and if there is anything you want to speak to me about, then no worries."

As Denny went away, Willie thought that there it was again. Did he know what he and Gertie had planned? He knew Gertie wouldn't say anything, not even to Helen. Nothing surprised him about Denny. If anybody could go to Scotland, wage war on an enemy with virtually no men, and come back alive then it would be him. At least he prayed that would be the outcome.

Denny was at a loose end, so he shouted to Helen that he would take the boys upstairs for a bath. She said that was fine and would be up shortly. When she did get up, she got a bit of a shock. Here was Denny and the boys in the bath together.

"Denny, I know it's a big bath, but bloody hell."

The boys were loving it though. Denny was playing with their toys, and there was a lot of laughter.

"Aren't you coming in mummy? It's been a while since we were in the bath together. I promise I'll behave in front of the boys. Well maybe."

Helen finished off washing them, then started to change them for bed. When Denny got out he dried himself, and told Helen he would take the dogs for their last walk before settling them down.

It was going to be a big day tomorrow, so Denny went upstairs early, as he really needed the sleep. He was soon starting to drift off, but knew his bad dreams weren't far away. Next morning came soon enough, but Helen had told him to lie still, as she and Gertie had work to do, but she would give the dogs a short walk. He must have drifted off for an hour, and after showering went down stairs. When he walked out the main doors, he was taken aback. There were banners everywhere. Equally sporting both Willie and Tomaz's names. There were decorations, and balloons festooned everywhere. Music was already being played with the volume on low, ready to be belted out when the party started.

Four fire pits were already burning, although Denny wondered where the other two had came from. He could see this turning in to an uplifting day, with hopefully a lot of laughter. He saw Jinty fixing a banner, so he went over to her, and put his arm around her.

"I take it you stayed at the lodge last night Jinty. How is Artem?"

"Here was me thinking that you were asking after me Denny. Artem is failing by the day pal, as I'm sure you will have seen on your visits up there. I'm not worried for Yuri, it's Tomaz that we will have to be careful with. He can be very precious at times."

She was about to cry, until Denny held her tight, and whispered there was to be no tears yet. He gave her a big kiss on the cheek.

"You do know I love you like the sister I never had, don't you?"

She grabbed him, and tried to squeeze the life out of him, until he broke away from her grasp. He wandered over to the dogs, let them out and then shouted.

"Cmon, you pair, this is the day I am going to run the legs off you."

Denny took off sprinting as fast as he could, while continually shouting at them.

"Is that the best you can do? I haven't even started yet. C'mon my boys. We need to be faster. Get a grip will you. You will never beat me."

Willie and the girls stood wondering what the hell he was doing. Was he losing it? The dogs were just toying with him, and they all carried on until they were out of sight. By the time he came back he felt a bit wiped out, making a mental note not to challenge the dogs at running again, although, he knew he would never stop challenging them. He loved doing it. He wondered if the dogs thought he was quite right in the head. He didn't care.

"Hey, Foggerty how about you going up for another shower, as I can see you've been sweating and no doubt hugging the dogs. You have to go up and bring Artem down. We want to make a fuss over him, and our guests will be here soon anyway."

Denny had enough energy left to run up the stairs, and jump in the shower. When he came out he felt exhilarated, regretting that Helen hadn't come in with him.

He went up to the cabin. Yuri and Jinty were getting Artem ready, but Tomaz was nowhere to be seen. Yuri nodded his head to the back of the cabin. As Denny wandered to the back off the building, he looked out the window to see Tomaz doing his stretches. It was nice to see the lad taking the challenge seriously. When Tomaz came in, Denny asked if everybody was ready and picked up Artem. He swore he felt a lot lighter than a few days ago.

When they got to the house, Helen and Gertie had positioned a large cushioned seat next to one of the fire pits, with an uninterrupted view of the challenge course. He was soon being plied with a plate of bacon and egg rolls, although they knew he would only pick at it.

Next to arrive was Maria, with somebody else in the passenger seat. Maria came up the steps and introduced her friend as Jenni. They had been friends from early school days.

When coming over in the car, Maria had said to Jenni that, deep down she wouldn't mind if Denny's champion lost, as it would give her another chance at seeing his sculpted body again, as well as other things.

"Were you two an item, Maria? C'mon tell me all about him."

After Maria had finished, Jenni was hoping that Denny's champion would lose as well.

"Don't even think about it Jenni. He is very happily married, and Helen is such a lovely girl."

Next was the Hoffman brothers and their partners, Ada and Gisela, who all made a fuss over Artem. Willie was conspicuous by absence. Denny asked Yuri, Tomaz and the Hoffmans, if he could have a word them all. They went into a room just off the dining room.

"Please take a seat where you can lads. This wont take long. I have an envelope for each of you, and I would like you to accept what's in it without argument please."

When they all opened their envelope, there was stunned silence. Tomaz was poking Yuri, wondering what was happening. This has nothing to do with the Scottish trip, not blood money, as I can assure you, we will all be sitting here at Christmas, by the fires. It was Gunther who was first to speak.

"Why Denny? Why all this money? This will set us up for life. You have done so much for us already."

Next, it was Yuri who said he couldn't believe that this was happening. Karl was just sitting shaking his head. Denny could see that Tomaz was a bit lost, so he told him that he was a very rich lad, but if he lost the race, then he would take the cheque back. There was a bit of nervous laughter.

"Try and forget what has just happened lads, as there is a party to enjoy. Let's go."

It was Jinty that shouted at them when they came outside.

"Where the bloody hell have you lot been?"

"Just talking race tactics my little angel," said Denny.

"And it takes five of you to do that. My arse. Trying to hide from doing any work more like."

It was half an hour before the race was due to start, and Willie still hadn't made an appearance. Denny went to his door, knocked several times, but still no answer.

"Right Wille, if your not on the start line in thirty minutes, I will declare the challenge null and void, and you will have to pay the forfeit. Let's be having you.

There was still no answer, so he walked away. It was then that Helen turned the music up, and everyone was starting to get in the party atmosphere. They sat around chatting until, ten minutes before the start time, Willie walked up the steps. Everybody started to crack up laughing. He was wearing an old pair of faded, kaki, demob shorts, and a vest that had seen better days. Denny was almost on the floor laughing, and thought only Willie would come out dressed like that. Tomaz was laughing, and trying to hide behind his dad, so that Willie wouldn't see him. It was Jinty, who stood up and started to applaud him for his brass neck. Everyone joined in the applause.

Willie started to stretch, until Gertie shouted.

"William, your 'balls' are hanging out the side of your shorts."

Everyone was in stiches. Even Artem was laughing, in between bouts of coughing. Each of the girls taking it in turn to check on him.

"Foggerty, let's get this show on the road. I can't wait to be crowned champion. What's the hold up?"

"Just waiting on one more person arriving Willie. Hang on, she is coming up the track now."

They all looked out, and started to cheer and clap, as Frieda started to wave her walking stick.

Willie couldn't believe it.

"Anybody else Foggerty? What about the 'polis' you had up here the other week?"

After Frieda got settled beside Artem, Yuri asked for the music to be turned down.

"Right everyone, I will explain to you all what the route is going to be for the two contestants. Whoever wins, will be crowned the Albach Estate champion. This title will be held for life, and no arguing. Next year, unknown to our hosts Helen and Denny, I propose to have our own Olympics when we will all join in. A loud cheer went up, with continuous applause.

Denny looked at Helen and smiled. She gave him a beautiful smile back. He nodded at Yuri, as if to say yes.

"Right, Tomaz and Willie get to the start line. Absolutely no cheating mind, or there will be consequences. When I decide what they will be. I will say one, two and then I will fire the gun."

Denny wasn't quick enough in realising what Yuri had just said. When the gun went off, he lunged over to stop Frieda from toppling off her seat, and he thought that Artem's heart was going to pack in with fright. The dogs went ballistic. They were barking, snarling and took off after the runners, until he whistled on them to return. Yuri looked at Denny and mouthed that he was sorry.

Tomaz was running behind Willie, imitating his long strides, pointing at his shorts and laughing.

"Hey, you little bastard. Stop mucking around. You're too cocky. Get bloody moving," shouted Denny.

They were just coming to the end of the trail with the long climb to the cairn ahead. Willie thought he was keeping pace with Tomaz. Until the shout came from Karl.

"Now Tomaz. Get bloody moving."

All of a sudden, he took off at blistering speed, which not only surprised everybody, but it must have left Willie in shock. Tomaz must have been watching Denny running with the dogs, but as he couldn't shout he kept punching the air. After collecting the stone from the cairn he stood with his arms in the air, and let out a frightening guttural cry. Some of the guests were a bit put out with this, but Denny knew he was just imitating the dogs. Possibly in honour of Ottar.

When he was half way down, Willie was only half way up and struggling as everyone could see. Frieda was standing now and roaring encouragement to the pair of them by waving her stick in the air. Artem was clapping his hands willing his son on. Tomaz didn't disappoint him. After passing Willie, it was like Tomaz had moved up a gear astonishing all the guests, and he took off down the South trail before turning back on himself. When he came round the last corner he sprinted like his life depended on it to the finish line.

When he went through the tape he immediately ran up and hugged his dad who had tears in his eyes. Tomaz then ran and jumped on Denny, who caught him and gave him a big hug.

"Thanks for that my wee champion. I now know that I can rely on you when asked."

It was then that Maria shouted.

"That's a bit unfortunate Denny. Jenni was so looking forward to seeing you parading in the nude. Actually so was I, again. Maybe the next time."

"No luck Jenni and Maria, my wife is standing over there."

It was then that Willie came round the last corner, with a face as red as a beetroot. The guy was struggling. Everyone was clapping and cheering him in. By this time Tomaz was sitting on the steps eating a large cream cake and drinking tea. Denny thought that Willie's legs were going to give in, but all credit to him as he managed to finish the course. He climbed the steps and just collapsed in to a chair, sweating profusely.

Denny thought he would give him a bit of time, so he went over and turned the music up. The party had started. Everyone was enjoying themselves, and Jinty got Yuri up to dance much to his embarrassment. Denny noticed Helen sitting on her own, so he went over and asked her if there was anything wrong.

"It's such a bitter sweet moment Denny. Here we all are enjoying this lovely day, but I can't stop thinking about Artem. We know, and he knows he is going to die very soon, but it's the knowing part that I can't handle. Why does anybody have to know that they are dying. Why do we just not wake up one day when our time comes. It's because of illnesses Denny. They just prolong the inevitable. I'm sorry, I know that at some point soon you are going to drop a bombshell on me, and it will really hurt me Denny. I make no apologies for that."

"I won't lie Helen, that what I will say will be difficult for you. Not just you but a few other people. You have to trust me that I'm doing this for us all. My life lately has been pretty miserable at times, and I can't go through life living like this. I promise that in a couple of weeks I will tell you all about it. As for Artem, then just look at the way he is enjoying himself. Laughing and singing. Why don't you go and get him up to dance?"

"Dance? Are mad Foggerty? How can he dance?"

"Easy Helen. Lift him from the seat, hold him, and sway to the music while tapping your feet."

Helen walked over to Artem, just as Neil Diamond was starting to play. She curtseyed in front of him and asked if he would like to dance. He started to shake his head until Tomaz lifted him up. Helen put her arms around his waist, and they slowly swayed while singing to the song. After the song finished, Tomaz helped him back down. Artem put his arms out to give Helen a hug and a kiss on the cheek. Everyone was enjoying the music, but Denny walked over to the record player and turned the volume down much to the annoyance of Tomaz. He had just asked Jenni to dance with him.

"Stop booing me you lot. There is an important matter of a forfeit to be done. A bet is a bet. This is where Mr. William McLeod, formerly of Helmsford and Her Majesty's prison at Peterhead will run 'butt' naked along the trail to the end and back. I think we will allow him to keep his boots on. What do you say?"

Everyone started to clap and cheer, as Willie was trying to hide behind Gertie.

"Can we please have you to the top of the steps William. Right next to Frieda as her eyesight is beginning to fade. At your leisure I would like, sorry no we would like you to discard your clothing."

"Before I do this, can I just say to you men that you're a bunch of bastards. I have been 'stitched up like a kipper'."

The men all clapped, cheered and shouted Willie's name. He then walked over and shook Tomaz's hand and said well done. This was it for Willie. He slowly stripped with everyone cheering. Stood at the top of the steps, then slowly walked down and started to walk to the end of the trail. It was then that the unbelievable happened. Tomaz stood up and took his clothes off and ran after Willie while waving his arms like a 'loon'. They all stood wondering what was happening. Artem was laughing, and said Tomaz used to do this when he was a young boy and got excited.

It was then that Frieda stood up and while waving her stick shouted, "Go on my boys. It's been along time since I've seen two bodies as white as that, but I'm not complaining, although you could do with a little more down below lads."

Denny couldn't believe what was happening. When they were almost back, Willie put his arm around Tomaz's shoulder as they walked the final bit smiling. After they dressed, Denny announced that the presentation would now take place. They all gathered together near the front doors.

"Ladies and gentlemen, before we carry on with the festivities, I would just like to say on behalf of us all, a massive thank you to our three beautiful girls for organising this great occasion."

A big cheer went up and the girls all curtseyed.

"Now, I would like for them to bring out the prizes for the contestants. The winner's prize will be presented first, now that you have got your clothes on Tomaz. Not sure if Jenni will want to dance with you after that exhibition though."

Helen came out with a cake with a marzipan figure of a runner bursting the tape and presented it to Tomaz. He put it down and gave her a huge hug, but it wasn't like he was letting her go.

"Hey, wee man, put her down, as you don't know where she has been."

If looks could kill then Denny was a dead man.

"He gives better hugs than you Foggerty, trust me."

Then Jinty and Gertie came out carrying a cake with a large 'penis and balls' on it and presented it to Willie. Tomaz mysteriously produced a knife from somewhere and cut a large bit off the penis, before making a break for it.

"Okay folks, lets have a party and let's get tucked into the cake."

It wasn't long before everyone was enjoying the cake. Until Denny had turned round to see Arno and Udo with their muzzles covered in cream, devouring their share with Denny shouting.

"Tomaz, you little bastard, I told you not to feed the dogs, didn't I. Where are you?"

Tomaz was nowhere to be seen.

When Tomaz came out of hiding, none of the girls were safe. He never wanted to stop dancing. Both Maria and Jenni were exhausted with his attention, and at one point Jinty had went and rescued them. Although, deep down it had been a long time since they had so many dances and they loved it.

The time came for everyone to go home. It had been such a lovely day, and everyone had thanked the girls for their hard work and had helped with the clearing up. Eventually, it was only Helen and Denny, as well as Willie and Gertie sitting around the fire with a tea in their hands.

"It was nice to see everyone having a good time wasn't it. Even although some of it was at my expense."

"Don't worry, Willie you were my hero, and tonight your Gertie is going to give you a lot of loving."

"If his body holds out Gertie, but please don't come running for help when his body seizes up with cramp."

They said goodbye and before they got upstairs the phone rang.

"Evening pal, it's Stevie here. Just to let you know that I hope you aren't intending coming over to see us soon, as we have had one of the heaviest snowfalls in recent years. Roads are impassible with lots of villages cut off. Three feet of snow is the norm where you intend to go. The reason I am phoning is for you to maybe revise your plans. Both Edinburgh and Glasgow airports are shut down, and they are predicting this weather could last for a month."

Denny's heart just sank. All the planning had just went up in smoke. He knew that he would have to speak to the men and get their thoughts. This wasn't good, but he needed to get his brain around it.

"Thanks my friend. I need you to do me a favour though and that is, when you see any change in the weather then please let me know. It doesn't matter if it takes a turn for the worst after that. We need to be in Scotland as soon as it's viable. Please give Andrew a call, and tell him we will definitely be needing the gear, and if he wants the money I can transfer it to you for him."

"Don't worry about Andrew pal. He's a good guy and your gear will be there when you need it. I'll keep you posted with regards to the weather. Cheers."

He had no sooner put the phone down when it rang again. It was Shonagh.

"Have you been watching the news Denny? If so you'll have seen we are under a lot of snow. Worst in a long time. The snowploughs are even struggling, so whatever you have planned, then you may have to think again."

"Yeh Shonagh, I have just had a call from my pal in Dundee and he says it's very bad up there. I wonder if you could do me a favour if you can. I have provisionally booked rooms in two small discreet hotels in Leith for when we first come over. If I call you with the names and addresses, can you get cash to them so as they will keep the rooms for us. Please give them far more money than they would expect, and I will transfer money into your bank account. No arguing from them or you. Understand?"

"You sound like my existing boss with your requests Denny."

"Yeh, but I bet he isn't as much fun on stakeouts is he?"

He hung up.

Shonagh thought she would have to try harder to get this guy out of her head. Deep down, she knew that wasn't going to happen.

Chapter 12

Next morning Denny looked out the window early. He thought how bare it was with all the banners and flags down. With nobody there. Although, he suddenly realised Tomaz was sitting over by the far side of the veranda with both dogs. He didn't want to waken Helen and the boys, so he dressed and went down stairs.

"Tomaz, what the bloody hell are you doing here at this ungodly hour."

He mouthed to Denny, that Karl had said to him that he was to take him out running to get fitter. Denny just looked at him and couldn't help smiling. He suddenly heard a window being opened, and saw Tomaz putting both of his hands over his eyes, before turning his head away. When Denny looked up, Helen was leaning out of the window, asking what was going on.

"Hey Mrs. Foggerty, you trollop. Could you not have put something on before hanging out the window? Tomaz, is embarrassed. We are going to do some training if you can manage the boys. Won't be long."

"Okay, please don't be long as I want us to have a family day today, and tell my wee champion to get over it as he has seen these 'big boys' before."

Denny went in laughing and changed his clothes, shoes and thought to himself that he was going to see what Tomaz was made of. It had been agreed that they would do the same route as yesterday.

"Right Tomaz, here are the rules. There are no rules. Don't be upset if I leave you standing."

Denny would come to regret saying that.

"Let's go wee man."

Denny cheated and started to run before he said 'go'. Tomaz didn't move. He couldn't for laughing. Denny was half way along the trail when Tomaz started the chase. He had caught Denny before the trail ended, and as he passed him he started to run backwards showing off, before he turned and sprinted with the dogs to the top and stood at the cairn with them. Denny wasn't even half way up when he immediately stopped.

Tomaz suddenly started howling. The dogs were howling as well. Denny thought he had seen and heard a few scary things in his life, but this was equal to any of them. It was then that the wee man took off down the trail never even giving Denny a backward glance when he passed him. What a bloody strange wee man this was he thought.

When Denny managed to finish the course, Tomaz was sitting on the steps with his arms around the dogs. Willie was walking up from the annex.

"Not so easy was it Foggerty, and that's without you being stitched up like I was. This little bugger is scary, but I will tell you one thing. If you have to run for it when you go to Scotland, he will be miles in front of you all."

"There will be no retreat Willie. There will be no loose ends when we are finished. Trust me. Our little war has been put back anyway. Bonnie Scotland has beat us, as they are locked down with heavy snow. Worse than normal."

"What is going to happen now then Denny?"

"I have a lot thinking to do, but how do you fancy a trip to a bar tonight Willie?"

"You going back on the whisky Denny? I'm not sure that would be a good idea."

"No, I was going to pay the guy that shot Helen a visit. He will be thinking he got away with it. I'll phone Felix to see if he can let me know if he is in the bar. You up for it? However, no violence Willie. There can't be."

"Count me in pal, I could do with a change of scenery."

Denny and Helen spent most of the day with the boys. He had forgotten how much fun it was. Both their moods were lifted. It was after tea that Felix had phoned back to say that the Wagner guy hadn't went near the pub yet, but he would have a few drinks and wait just in case. However, he had just seen his dad, and that corrupt judge going in to one of the posh restaurants before he had walked along.

Denny took his chance, shouted on Willie who came running out and both headed off in to town. They parked along the road from the restaurant. When they got to the large front window, here were the pair sitting toasting each other as a waiter had brought the first course. Denny told Willie to follow his lead as they entered. Denny just kept on walking and sat down at the table with Willie occupying the other seat.

"Get out of here as this is private. I'll have you ejected if you don't."

"Listen you pompous arsehole. You will sit here and listen to what I have to say and if you say another word I will throw you through this window. Got me? Even as we speak my lawyers from the Trust are sifting through your judicial career as a corrupt judge. They have gone back years and found all the corrupt sentences you have handed out and all the kick backs you have received, including from this guy. They have bank records and witnesses who have now come under the umbrella of the Trust

"As for you Wagner, well they have looked in to your bribery to gain municipal contracts. Companies have handed over all the relevant information to them. So here is what I am thinking. I think you are both fucked. What do you say my brother?"

"Well and truly, and I think the fraud police will be knocking on their doors soon. Let's go."

As they stood up, Willie tipped their plates of soup into their laps. Denny started to laugh.

"Willie, do you fancy going to the bar where Wagner's son sometimes drinks in?"

"Sounds like fun pal, let's go."

They knew it would be along shot, but when they walked through the door they saw Felix sitting in the corner. He nodded to the back room and walked out with Denny passing him a wad of cash as they passed each other. It was the same barman that was hit by the telephone previously. Willie asked for two coffees, but the barman said they don't do coffee in here. Whereby Willie grabbed him by the throat and said, "You do now, and I'll know if you have spat or pissed in it. If you have then you are a dead man. Now fucking hurry up."

The barman wasn't long in bringing them two cups of coffee and Willie had stood smelling it for a few seconds while looking at the barman. He gave him a nod and walked with Denny through to the back room. Nothing had changed. Wagner was still holding court with the people from before. Willie and Denny sat at the table beside them.

"Good evening folk. I just thought I would introduce you to my homicidal maniac of a brother from Scotland."

"Which of these lowlife was the one who shot my sister in law Denny."

Denny pointed to Wagner who had started to shake.

"I don't want my brother here to snap your neck, as I have been saying that I want to be the one who does it. However, there has been a bit of an argument about it. So at some stage we might just toss a coin for it. Don't worry as it won't happen tonight, but it will be a night when you are on your own and you won't expect it."

"Brother, can I ask you who this ugly female is with the nose that is spread over her face and the teeth and jaws wired to look like something out of a horror movie."

"This scum's girlfriend, who is the one who keeps egging him on, but maybe she will suffer after he has left this earth. Who knows, but it would be nice."

Denny got up and pulled the chair back of the young lad who he was sitting next to.

"Nothing has changed I see. Your still pissing your pants."

As they walked through to the bar, Denny saw the barman lift the phone. He didn't notice Denny coming around the bar listening in as to who was on the phone. The police.

"Denny grabbed him and smashed his head off the gantry. Didn't you learn from the time before? Willie, remind me to see if I can purchase this bar so that we can have a better sort of clientele in here. Like these gentlemen here. Help yourself to the drink lads. This idiot will be out for a while."

For being elderly they couldn't half move. Denny walked back in to the back room.

"By the way Wagner. I just spoke to your dad to tell him that he and his corrupt pal are going to jail for a long time for judicial and municipal fraud. I wonder if they will survive. Doubt it. What do you think?"

One of Denny's smiles came over his face.

When they were heading to the car Willie stopped and asked Denny, "Denny, why the hell did you ask me here tonight? You don't have to keep showing me what an evil bastard you can be at times. I know."

"Maybe I'm just a little bored at present Willie. I have let my work ethic drop a bit, as well as my fitness which you experienced today. My head is constantly aching with what is going to happen in Scotland. I'm not worried, but what I am concerned is that my sixth-sense seems to have deserted me and I will need it back soon. I feel we all need a break from the estate, and did I tell you I am thinking of buying more forested estates over Europe. Scotland being of special interest to me."

"No Denny, you have never mentioned anything, but with all that is going on with you, why have you never came to me. We could have talked about it? Stop trying to be this super human being. Just try and be Denny Foggerty. Loving father, husband and occasionally loving brother."

Denny laughed at the last part.

Next morning, he got all the men together before breakfast, with the girls out of the way.

"Men, I have news regarding Scotland. We won't be going for a little while. Apparently they have been locked down due to snow and Arctic temperatures. I gave a lot of thought about it last night and I can't say I'm not disappointed. I really want to get this out of the way. For you guys as well. I will be advised as soon as there is a thaw on the way, and we will get into Scotland and wait if need be, at least we will be there."

It was Yuri who was next to speak.

"It is what it is Denny, so don't worry about any of us. If you get word and we have to go immediately then I suggest, that as from today, we get ourselves as fit as possible. What does everybody think?"

There were nods all round.

"I think you should all 'piss' off and start your new regime by running the route that me and our wee champion ran the other day. I will sit here with a couple of bacon rolls with coffee, waiting for you come in. However, I am willing to take a bet from anybody that they won't beat Tomaz. No takers? Wise men."

The men jumped up and started to run. Tomaz wasn't messing about this time. He took off with the dogs beside him. When they were half way up the incline, Tomaz was at the top with his arms around the dogs doing his usual howling, setting the dogs off. This totally freaked Karl out, he was scared. So he

292

decided he wasn't going anywhere near the cairn, and just turned and started to run back. When they were coming back Tomaz came sprinting in with the rest a fair distance behind. However, he immediately turned and ran back to where Karl was. He was struggling, but Tomaz kept encouraging him to get him back.

After getting something to eat, they headed in to the forest to work. Karl had told Denny that he was off to his shop as he was expecting the camouflage gear to arrive today. Denny told him to hide it when he arrived over with it. Out of the girl's prying eyes.

Denny thought he would benefit from some decent sleep tonight, however that was not going to happen. After eating and seeing to the boys, both Denny and Helen decided to go to bed early. They were both woken up in the early hours with loud banging on the door. When Denny ran down, Jinty came in.

"I think you had better be quick, as it's not looking too good for Artem. I'm going back up."

Denny went and banged on the annex door. Willie opened up.

"Willie, it's Artem. Can you get Gertie to come and stay with the boys please?"

Helen was waiting at the door wondering what was happening. Denny told her and she waited momentarily, until Gertie came to look after Fin and Col. Denny went and let the dogs out to sit on the veranda and look after the house. While Gertie went upstairs, the three of them ran to the lodge. When they went in Artem was lying in his bed with Yuri and Tomaz standing either side of him. Yuri just said that it would be soon.

"Tomaz, please hold your dad's other hand."

Reluctantly, he slowly lifted his hand and started to stroke it. A few minutes later Yuri felt his pulse and just shook his head.

"He's gone."

Tomaz looked at Denny with a plea of 'can I please cry.'

Denny just nodded at him, and the wee man broke down, which set off Helen and Jinty. Helen went to comfort him, but he just bolted out the door in to the forest. Helen was about to go after him.

"Leave him Helen. He will come back when he is good and ready."

Denny went to the door and whistled on the dogs. They bounded up, and he told them to go and look after Tomaz. They took off with their noses to the ground. Denny and Willie helped Yuri put Artem in a body bag they had been given by the undertaker. Who, Yuri would phone at a more sociable hour. Denny would phone both Karl and Gunther and ask them to come up so that everyone could help dig Artem's grave. They all sat around the fire drinking sweet tea that Jinty had made, although his death was hardly a shock. The conversation was light hearted and everyone at times was talking a bit gibberish. When the light broke through the window, Denny said he was off to try and find Tomaz.

He had a rough idea where he would be, and when he got to the end of the trail he looked up to see Tomaz sitting at the cairn with his arms around the dogs. No doubt keeping them warm. When he got up to the top, Denny sat down and put his arm around Tomaz.

"Look at that beautiful sunrise son. I've not seen the sun as red and so bright as that in a long time. I think that must be your dad lighting up the sky. What do you think?"

Tomaz looked up at Denny and nodded.

"C'mon wee man. Let's go and see everybody and no more bloody tears."

Tomaz again nodded and wiped his eyes on his sleeves.

"Tomaz, at some stage of your life you're going to leave here. It might be a long time away, but you will. You will meet someone, have a family and want to spend the rest of your life with them, probably not here though. Trust me. Right, this time I am going to beat you home."

Denny knew he was going to stop saying that to either Tomaz or the dogs as he was last as usual. Tomaz walked him up to the lodge where the girls made a fuss of him.

"Helen, Willie, I think it's about time we left them to grieve in peace. Let's go and give our boys a hug and be grateful for small mercies. Willie, when did you last hug your nephews?"

Willie just put his head down.

Everyone showered and sat outside to have something to eat, although it was a pretty sedate affair. It wasn't long before the undertaker arrived with the coffin. It was nothing fancy, just as Artem would have wanted. They waited until Karl and Gunther arrived. Yuri and Tomaz came down to help carry the coffin to the house. Everyone was helping carry the coffin, although it wasn't heavy and wouldn't even be with Artem in it. They left the undertaker to dress the body while they sat in the living area. When he was finished he came through, and asked for help to put Artem in the coffin. It was then sealed up and the undertakers job was done. He said a few words and walked to the door. Denny followed him out and handed him a bundle of cash, which the undertaker was going to argue about, until Denny just shook his head.

"Yuri, I hope you don't mind, but I have paid the guy. It's the least I can do for you and Tomaz. As well as Jinty."

She walked over and gave him a hug. Yuri gave him a nod.

Helen had phoned Maria who had said she would like to come over to the burial if Helen would give her a time. When all the men had assembled, they walked with picks and spades in hand to where Artem had chosen for his grave. After they had started, Helen, Gertie and Jinty had walked up to see where Artem had chosen to rest. The grave would be positioned so that he would be looking over the valley to the West. He would see some beautiful sunsets. It would be protected from the elements by a copse of trees.

The men took it in shifts to dig the grave. However, Tomaz was working so furiously that he refused to be replaced by some of the men. Denny knelt down, grabbed him by the collar and hauled him out, before pointing a finger at him. It took them a few hours to get the hole deep enough so that no animal would try and dig the body up. Even though it was in a box they would give it a try. After they had finished, they put a tarpaulin over to stop any snow or water getting in.

"Yuri, that's as much as we can do pal. We will leave it up to the three of you to decide when you would like him buried tomorrow. As soon as you all have decided, please let us know as Maria is wanting to come over tomorrow."

"We will Denny, I'll pop down and let you know. Thanks to you all for your help and your kind words. My dad was so happy knowing that we are part of this lovely family. Bless you all."

That started all the girls crying again. It was time for Denny to leave. He took the dogs away and just wandered the forest. He wondered about his own mortality. A few years ago he was killing

295

himself with alcohol, and some evil people were trying to kill him. He missed his parents, especially his dad, and wondered what his life would be like if either of them was still alive. Today brought back memories of the first time he attended a funeral with his dad. A hole had been dug and the coffin, for want of a better word, had arrived and the guy was despatched to the earth. Surely there must be a better ending to your life. He knew that he wanted something better. To go out on his terms.

When he got back the three girls had been out in the forest picking wild flowers for a wreath for Artem. Denny was lucky that he had the three girls around the place, but at some point soon there would only be two maybe even one.

"Yuri has been down and asked if we would all like to be at the grave side at eleven tomorrow morning. I told him that would be fine, and I have contacted Maria. We are preparing a small spread for after the burial."

"No worries Helen. If you want me to look after the boys at the grave, then not a problem."

"Gertie and I will be fine, as I think you and Yuri might have your hands full with Tomaz."

He left the girls to it and went to see Willie. This time he just walked in, and after five minutes of idle chitchat he asked him if his kettle was broken. Willie started to moan as usual, but got up and made two teas, and surprisingly enough, accompanied by biscuits.

It wasn't long before they were laughing and joking which was something they hadn't done in a while.

"Denny, if you didn't live here then where?"

"It's a no brainer Willie. There is only one place and that is Scotland. That is why I am actively, along with Maria, looking at some estates there at the moment. What about you?"

Willie just mumbled something about a big world out there, and didn't say much more.

Next day, the time that everyone was dreading was nearing. Karl and Gunther were already there. The five of them, plus the boys, headed up to the grave site. Denny was pleased that nobody had gone over the top with dressing up, as that wasn't Artem. Maria came speeding up the track and shouted on them to wait. When they got to the grave, the men walked to the lodge and met up with Yuri, Jinty and Tomaz. Jinty left while the men started to lift the coffin.

It was then that Yuri nodded to them. Yuri and Tomaz were in front, Willie and Denny in the middle and Karl and Gunther at the back. They walked without saying anything. When they got to the grave, Yuri had laid out rope to be used as cords to lower the coffin in. It was a bitterly cold day, but that didn't matter to anyone.

Yuri asked the men to all take a cord and Denny could see the hesitancy in Tomaz, so he put a hand on his shoulder and gave him a slight nod. When Artem was eventually lowered in to the grave, all the men threw the cords in. Jinty walked forward and handed the wreath to Tomaz to throw in beside his dad. It was a good job that Denny was beside him as everyone got a bit of a shock when he tried to throw himself in beside his dad. Denny grabbed him and pulled him back from the edge of the grave.

"His spirit was gone a long time ago son. Be strong," said Denny.

"I would like to say a few simple words about my dad. He had a hard life bringing us up on his own after my mother passed. We never had very much, except his love for us, but that was enough. He was a strong man and bore his illness with humility. He accepted what he had and just got on with it. We love you dad. See you sometime."

It was then that Maria said she would like to sing a folk song which she thought Artem might have liked. Yuri nodded.

Nobody realised what a beautiful voice Maria had. It was when she had finished Denny had looked up the hill to the North.

"Surely not. Are my eyes playing up. What does everybody see on the crest of the hill?"

"It's a stag Denny, but I think my eyes are deceiving me also. I think it looks white, but it can't be, can it? "said Yuri.

They stood there transfixed at this magnificent beast just standing looking at them. Tomaz grabbed a hold of Denny's arm. He knew he was a bit scared.

"I think he might have heard Maria's beautiful voice and came to investigate, or he just wanted to say goodbye to Artem. No matter, we have all been blessed."

Before they started to fill the grave in, they all took a bit of dirt and threw it on the coffin. Sending Artem back to nature. They then stood in their own silent prayer. The men worked tirelessly to fill the hole in as a small flurry of snow had appeared. When they got back to the house the girls handed them all a towel each, and told them to shower in any bedroom they wanted.

The meal, although lovely, was a very sombre affair. Denny could see that Tomaz was agitated. So he played him a bit by asking everybody if anybody wanted to take the dogs out. Tomaz took off and within minutes the dogs were out and following him along the track.

"I've got a funny feeling Yuri, that Tomaz will leave us at some point. I'm not often wrong with my feelings."

"I hope so Denny, he needs to get out and see the world a bit, but his lack of speech worries me a bit."

"I wouldn't worry about that Yuri. Trust me."

Yuri just gave him a quizzical look.

Karl and Gunther said their goodbyes, as did Maria after Yuri gave her a hug and thanked her for singing today. Yuri thanked the Hoffmans for their kindness and hard work.

When Tomaz came back they could see he had been crying. Helen said that he should stay in the house tonight, as she would get him to help with boys.

"Remember, they need changed and bathed later, so if you are not up for it, I will do it all myself as their dad is useless at changing nappies."

She hid her smile at Denny. Tomaz was eagerly nodding his head and pointing to himself.

"Remember, you little bugger, those boys are my nephews, so you had better look after them."

A broad smile appeared on his face, and he gave Willie the thumbs up.

Helen asked Denny and Willie to keep him occupied.

"Tomaz, how about we take the dogs, walk into the forest and assess where we have to concentrate the work on, but I need your input remember."

Again the perpetual nodding of the head.

Just when they were about to leave, Willie came out.

"Hey, wee man when you get back how about you helping me to clean out the store room?"

This time it was the thumbs up.

When they got to certain parts of the forest, Denny started to tell him about what work he wanted done and asked for his opinion. Denny thought it was amazing how Tomaz could gesture enough to get his thoughts over, although Denny had to ask him a few times what he meant. This was only to keep him busy.

When they got back, it was nearly time to eat, so Helen said she needed to give the boys some playtime before they ate. Tomaz was right in there and took the boys off her, went into the dining room and started playing with their toys. The boys were loving it.

After they ate, Tomaz had helped Helen with the changing of the boys, though he was a bit reluctant with the dirty nappies. When the boys were put to bed, Tomaz gestured that he wanted to go up and sit beside his dad for a while.

"Carry on son, and maybe call in at the lodge for a change of clothes."

It was a quiet and early night for everybody. Today had taken its toll, especially Tomaz. When Helen had looked in on him before they retired, he was sound asleep.

It was later than normal when Denny woke so he thought he would get the boys and give Helen a break. He was in for a shock when he went in to their room. They weren't there. He ran along the corridor and told Helen. Panic was just about setting in when they heard movement down stairs. Denny flew down the stairs with Helen right behind him. As he pushed the lounge door open, they saw Tomaz sitting on the floor having great fun with the boys. There was such relief for both of them.

He told Helen that he needed to make a few phone calls and went into the dining room. He didn't know if it would be too early for the Blairs at the cottage near the Ruthven estate. It only took three rings before Alasdair answered it.

"Good morning my friend, this is Daniel Rey here. How are you both. I didn't want to phone you, but the good old Scottish weather has prevented us from getting over. We really needed to be there by know, however we are hoping to come at the first sign of a thaw. I take it you are still getting visits from the estate?"

"Good morning Daniel. Don't worry about us, we are just looking forward to getting away, and yes we have had a few visits, but nothing since the heavy snow. There are a few things I would like to speak to you about. In all the turmoil I can't remember if I told you that all the fields at the back of the barns belong to you. They go on as far as the eye can see. Also, there is another entrance to get up to the house. About a mile and a half back down the road, there is a small forestry track which leads up to the fields I have just mentioned. You can't be seen from the estate when taking that road, although I think it will be pretty overgrown, but I have all the tools in the shed to enable you to clear it."

"Alasdair, that is bloody great news, and I thank you for that. Give Davina my regards and you'll get a phone call soon. Stay safe."

When he came of the phone, he felt that another very big part of the jigsaw was in place.

The men were starting to gather outside, waiting to go on their daily training regime. Willie stood there with the rest of them.

"What's happening Willie. Surely you can't we training with us today? Bit of a shock there pal."

"The challenge was a bit of a wake up call for me. Plus that night I wasn't at my best when Gertie and I were in the throws of passion, so it was her that was having to do all the work."

The men just laughed, with Willie wondering why. Another shake of the head from Denny.

Denny felt down while working that day. He was working with Yuri, and was trying to give him snippets of information, as to where they were going in Scotland. It was difficult for Yuri, not having seen the place. Later in the afternoon he watched a police car coming up the track. When it stopped, both Leon Meyer and Hans Schmidt got out.

"Good afternoon Denny. Hans and I were just doing our rounds so we came up to see when we should turn up on Saturday. Oh, and one other point I should mention. Young Wagner has been causing a lot of problems in the town over the last few days. Drunkenness, brawling, even driving under the influence of drugs. He seems to have lost the plot."

"Can we say ten o'clock here officers. Breakfast first though when you arrive. I think there will be two kids, who I'm sure will be eager to take in what you say."

Hans said it was fine by him and Leon nodded. They then headed off.

Denny walked away smiling at the thought of Wagner losing it. When he walked in to the house, Helen asked why they were here. He explained it was to sort out a time for Jonas and family coming over. He asked her if she was remembering, and by the look on her face it was a no. Denny went down and told Willie about Wagner.

"Best news I have had in a while Denny. Let's hope he completely loses his marbles."

Saturday morning came soon enough. He watched as Jonas' big fancy car came up the track. His wife and two kids stepped out, and as they all approached the steps, Denny told them to come up. Jonas introduced his wife Sofia, his daughter Emelia and son Sam. Willie was sitting there so Denny introduced him as his step brother so as not to confuse the Albach ownership to Jonas. Helen and Gertie came out with the boys and Sofia was gushing all over them. Everyone from the lodge came down and more introductions were done. They were just waiting on the officers arriving before breakfast was served.

When they were all gathered, Denny explained about Hans and Leon's expertise in the forest and would Jonas and Sofia be okay to let the kids go in to the forest with them. Denny said he could vouch for them. The kids, who were nine and ten were desperate, so the parents said that was fine by them.

After a beautiful breakfast, Denny suggested that Leon and Hans start their little trek while the weather was holding up. He saw that Emelia was asking her dad something. Denny knew right away what she wanted.

"Tomaz, can you go and get the dogs out please."

When Tomaz opened the door the dogs bounded up and stood either side of Denny. He could see that Sofia wasn't sure.

"Would you like to give my dogs a hug Emelia? What about you Sam? Please come over here. You are perfectly safe. Try and give them a scratch behind their ears as well."

The kids walked forward and after a little bit of hesitancy, they had their arms around the dog's necks.

"Tomas will go with you to be in charge of the dogs, and though he can't speak he will be able to gesture to you. However, you must do as Leon and Hans say please.

As they all walked out Jonas said, "I never thought I would see the day when I would let my kids wander in to the forest with two strangers, two dogs and a young lad who can't speak. It's like something out of a dark fairy tale."

"You mean two police officers, two of the most loyal dogs you will ever get, and as for Tomaz I would put my life in his hands."

"Police officers Denny? You are full of surprises."

Everyone sat around the fires talking about the plans for the estate, before Denny suggested that he would like to show Jonas and Sofia some of the estate and Helen would show Sofia the house when they got back. Gertie suggested that Helen would love to go with them, and she would look after the boys.

They walked talking, until they came to Denny and Helen's favourite view. Sofia immediately put her hand over her mouth in wonderment. Denny suggested they sit for a while. It was then that Sofia said, "This is one of the most beautiful vistas I have ever seen, and you both get to see this anytime you want. I am so envious."

It was then that Denny asked them to stay perfectly still.

"Have a look just over there and you will see a family of foxes on the prowl. We had a big problem with a guy who was poaching them."

"What happened to him Denny," asked Sophia.

"He met an untimely death Sophia, and good riddance to him."

Jonas looked at Denny, but saw on Denny's face that he shouldn't ask how.

Helen pointed down the valley, where the officers and the kids were. Tomaz was sitting on a small rise with the dogs, watching over them all.

"What's the story with Tomaz, Denny?"

Denny told him about how he had such a tough life and about the accident that had left him a mute. Although, he said he wasn't one hundred percent convinced that he was a mute. He said that they had buried his dad a few days ago, but he was a beautiful young lad, although a bit precious at times.

"Denny, why did you say Tomaz might not be a mute? Is there something you know that everyone else doesn't? "said Helen.

"I'll speak to you about it sometime Helen."

They wandered back, and Gertie met them with the coffee pot and cakes. Willie was sitting over by the boys who were having their mid morning nap. Helen took Sofia in to see the house. She told Helen it was stunning. When they came back out and sat down, Sofia got the shock her life as the dogs bounded up the steps and stood with their teeth bared.

"Tomaz, what have I told you about that. Stand the dogs down. Now."

They could see the kids and Tomaz laughing hysterically. When Sofia composed herself she asked if the dogs would have attacked.

"No Sofia, they have been on high alert since they left, making sure everyone was safe. They would have if your kids were in danger. Don't worry, they are like that with Fin and Col as well. It's just Tomaz's little joke. Your laughing now Jonas, but you weren't when it happened to you. I would trust them with my family's life."

When everyone came back, the kids were loving hanging around the dog's necks Although, there was a nervous smile on Sophia's face.

"Listen kids. Maybe when or if you come back then we can go on a trek and see if can see the white stag if you want. I told your dad about the legend when he was here before, so I'm sure he will tell you about it. Did you enjoy what Hans and Leon were teaching you?

They nodded enthusiastically with cake in their mouths. The Schneiders thanked Leon and Hans very much, as did Denny and Helen before they departed. It was time for them to go and Sophia gave Tomaz a hug for looking after her kids. As usual, it was up to Denny to tell Tomaz to let her go.

"Right, Emelia I warned you that you couldn't take either of the dogs home. So say goodbye to them."

She gave each one a hug and kiss, with a slobbery lick to the face in return.

Denny and Helen waved them away, and then Helen asked for Denny to sit with her a while.

"Denny, what were you saying about your thoughts on Tomaz not being fully a mute."

"Helen, I honestly think that it is an unwillingness to speak rather than an inability to. He can get the dogs to do what he commands, but if you watch him it looks like he is whispering in their ears. If you can whisper, then you can talk. I seriously think it needs something traumatic to physically happen to him before he comes out of it. I have almost caught him out twice, but he is a clever wee bugger, so I don't know what is in that head of his."

"Remind you of anybody my husband?"

They sat for a while, before Denny said he needed to walk the dogs again. This time there would be no challenging them to a race. He couldn't wait to be walking along the trail with his boys and dogs together.

"When are going to tell me what is going to happen Denny?"

"Soon."

When they woke up the next morning, Denny knew there was something different. He looked out the window and there it was. At least three feet of snow in places.

"Quick, Helen let's get the boys changed, fed and in to their wet suits."

It was only when she looked out herself and seen the snow, did she understand his excitement. He dressed and ran down to the annex and banged on the door. Willie opened it with a rifle in his hand, wondering what was happening.

"C'mon brother, we will see you outside in half an hour."

When Willie's eyes focused and saw the snow, he was as excited as Denny. Tomaz came running down and went to get the logs for the fires. Denny let the dogs out and they went mental. Running around try to catch their own tails and yelping. Helen came down with the boys, gave them to Denny and went back up to get changed. Gertie came out with just a very short dressing gown on which wasn't covering much, with Tomaz's hands covering his eyes again. She was going to start breakfast, until Willie shouted.

"Bloody hell, Gertie go and put some clothes on as at some point you will be rolling around in the snow with the boys, plus Fin and Col as well," said Willie laughing.

Yuri and Jinty had heard all the laughing. Mainly from Willie and Denny who were intent on trying best each other with a snowball fight. As they wandered down they were bombarded with snowballs from all the men and took cover behind a large tree.

"Right you lot. I'm bringing out the boys, so it's snowmen now instead of snowballs."

Tomaz was throwing snowballs at the dogs, who were catching them in their mouths and then shaking their heads with the cold. It then seemed to be a competition as to who could make the best snowman. All working furiously to be the biggest and best. They kept looking at Tomaz, who seemed miles better than the rest. At one point Jinty was bent over trying to gather up snow when Denny hit her a beauty with a hard packed snowball on her backside.

She started to run about holding her 'butt,' screaming that she was going to end his sex life by cutting off his genitals. When she turned round, Denny and Willie just pointed at Tomaz. She ran and jumped on Tomaz, who landed on his back with Jinty starting to cover his face with snow. When she let him up, he had a look of disbelief on his face. Denny and Willie just shrugged their shoulders and smirked.

Throughout the morning, they built snowmen in the image of the people they didn't like. Wagner, Albescu and Scottie. They constantly pelted them with snowballs. However, Jinty was a bit hesitant in throwing at Scottie's image, until Tomaz ran and took the head off with a flying punch sending it rolling away. Jinty and Helen burst out laughing. Willie then ran in to the kitchen and brought out Gertie over his shoulder and threw her in to the deepest drift he could find. She jumped up and shouted, "No loving for you tonight William McLeod. Maybe even longer unless you get in to the kitchen and bring out the hot orange juice I was preparing."

Willie reluctantly trudged inside, and brought the juice and rolls out. The twins were loving rolling about with dogs and Denny. Everyone was having such a good time. A happy day. It

305

only stopped when they were all getting a bit cold, so they sat around the fire on the veranda. Tomaz wasn't giving up yet as he whistled on the dogs and the three of them took off, trying to plough through the thick snow. Denny thought the dogs wouldn't need much exercise later. The hot orange juice and rolls had done the trick and the fun carried on until early afternoon, when everybody was too tired to carry on. Except Tomaz and the dogs, who looked like it was only the end of round one for them.

Denny phoned Karl that night and told him he needed the camouflage clothing over in the morning even although there would be no work due to the snow.

Everyone was assembled on the veranda next morning. Karl had said that he had the gear in his car and asked Denny where he wanted it.

"Everybody grab a bundle and get up to the lodge once the girls are inside and Jinty has left for work. Find your size and after eating we will change up there and head along the North ridge for some training."

The men took their training seriously, and after a full day being taught, Karl said he was reasonably happy. However, he wanted to try out an exercise the next day and told Denny what he wanted to do.

They were all keen to participate in the exercise the next morning.

"Willie, we are going after breakfast to the south trail, and I want you to come and find us. We will be hidden, disguised, whatever you want to call it. Lets see what your powers of observation is like. Remember, no dogs and no guns."

"Okay Denny, I will play your little games and I have no doubt I will find you all very easily. So don't be disappointed when I do folks. Are you sure I can't bring my rifle Denny?"

Denny shook his head in disbelief at his brother. Not sometimes, but most of the time he wondered what was going on in his head. When the men left, Willie was in no hurry to go looking for them, as another bacon roll was polished off.

Eventually, he walked to the South trail, hoping for any obvious signs as to where they were hiding. After half an hour, he just about had a seizure when Tomaz burst out from a drift yelling. Willie grabbed him and pinned him down in the snow telling never to do that again. Tomaz was beside himself with laughter. Willie walked on and was just passing a large tree when Denny rose from a drift at the back of it, picked up a stick and touched the back of Willie's head.

"Bang. Your dead brother."

Willie had to hang on to the tree to compose himself, only for Yuri to jump from the snow covered branches, giving Willie another big fright.

"Right, that's it. I'm heading home before my heart gives up. Get lost the lot of you."

"Willie, you still have Karl to find."

"He's probably hiding in the trees somewhere so he can bugger off too."

As they walked back with Willie, who wasn't in the best of moods, they could see him cautiously looking around for Karl. It was then that Karl, who was in a large drift by the side of the trail, slid his arm out along the ground, and grabbed Willie's ankle. That was it for Willie, he took off screaming, before shouting and swearing at them. Complaining that he had been stitched up again.

When everybody was back and heading home, Denny heard the phone and went to answer it.

"Good day Denny. It's Stevie here. They are talking about a thaw coming within the next ten days, so if you need to get over, then I suggest you do it within that period. However, it appears that another storm may be heading our way in a wee while. Up to you pal. The airports are clear, but only just, and the roads at the moment are passable with care. You did say you wanted to get here and wait if need be. If the weather changes then I will let you know."

"Thanks Stevie, you've been an absolute God send. I'll phone you when we are ready to come over. I presume I can rely on you to provide me with your jeep? Please let me make a payment to you for it."

"Nah, no need for any payment. I don't know what you are going to do over here, but I want you to lose the jeep when you are finished with it. I've told you before that it can't be traced to me. Look forward to seeing you pal."

Something was going on in his head, but couldn't fathom out what it was. He sat down for a minute. Suddenly, he knew. It was his sixth-sense returning. Thank God for that. He smiled.

When the phone rang again it was Helen who picked up. She shouted on Denny, saying it was officer Leon Meyer to speak to him.

"Hello Denny. I have some news for you. It is pretty awful really. I told you about young Wagner causing havoc in the town. This time it's devastating. While in a state of drugs and alcohol, he took out a gun and shot his girlfriend dead, and critically injured one of his young pals. He injured a couple of officers in the shoot out. They say he started on some heavy drugs and couldn't handle them. He is in a mental institution in Fussen. It could be this week that his dad will be arrested for fraud, so I'm not sure he can handle it, after the news of his son. The judge has been ordered to surrender his passport, and not to leave Zwiesel. It's all happening at once Denny."

"You're a good friend Leon letting me know. However, would it surprise you if I said I couldn't give a fuck about the three of them. I hope the young lad who was shot pulls through. He always seemed to be frightened of Wagner, and only hung around him under peer pressure I suppose."

"I had a feeling that would be your answer Denny, but who can blame you. I'll keep you posted."

"Leon, let me say I think you are one of the good guys, and I think both you and Hans would be good additions to what we have planned for the estate. Although, I think you and your wife, assuming you have one, should come over for supper when I come back from my business trip to Scotland. "

"Both Hans and I are married, and it was just unfortunate that our wives couldn't be there at the weekend. Thank you for your offer, and I hope to see you when you get back."

He then went down and told Willie.

"Bloody hell brother. I didn't really expect that, but a bit of justice for Helen though. Are you going to tell her?"

"I don't think so, as knowing her, she would feel sorry for him. Do you fancy a trip to Fussen pal?"

"To do what?"

"I fancy going to the institute to just gloat at the bastard. How about it?"

"I suppose I should come and see what the inside of a mental institution looks like. After all, living and working here will drive me there anyway. Count me in, if you can get permission, but only the men get to know about it. Okay?"

"I'll let you know Willie."

The news from Stevie and Leon had cheered him up, and with his six-sense coming back, he felt there was light at the end of the tunnel.

Now there planning to be done for Scotland. He phoned Karl and asked if they could have a talk on what his thoughts were on the drawings of the estate he had given him. Karl said he would be up in the afternoon. As it was the shop he phoned, Denny asked to speak to Gunther.

"Hi Gunther. Can you try and pick five reliable men to look after the estate when I am away. We can meet in the same bar if that suits you. Remember, they must be the best you can get."

"I'll get back to you tonight Denny. Leave it with me."

Right, thought Denny. Its Jonas next.

He asked to speak to Jonas after being put through to his secretary.

"Hello Denny, how can I help you?"

"Strange request Jonas, but I was wondering if you could manage to get permission for two people to get in to the institute at Fussen to visit an inmate."

"I take it you have heard the news about Wagner then? What you are asking is highly irregular Denny, but I will see what I can do, and I will have to give them a good reason."

"Tell them that I want to make amends, and see if I can help him in any way."

"Knowing you Denny, that must be the lamest excuse ever. However, they might just go for it as long as they don't find a gun on you when you're searched. It might be a few days before they get back to me. Speak soon. Oh, and my daughter has been asking if she can get a dog. Not any dog, but one of yours."

This had made Denny smile. In fact, all the recent news had made him smile. Maybe the Big Man up above might be wanting to be in his team. Then again maybe not.

309

There was too much filtering through his head and went inside and shouted on Helen.

"C'mon Helen. Let's sit here and phone everyone back in Durma. They need to be kept up to date about coming over."

They phoned Ian and Neala first getting the good news that she was feeling much better and finally enjoying her pregnancy. The sale of the boat and house was imminent, and they just had to give the house buyers an entry date.

Next was Jean Scougal. She seemed so excited, and couldn't wait to come over and start her new life as she put it.

Finally, it was Gladys Glover, who wasn't that excited about her own accommodation, just the classrooms.

Denny had told them all that their houses would be finished before Christmas, but as soon as they were over they had to choose their own furniture and wall décor etc, but that could be delivered within a couple of days. They would stay at the house until that was done.

Karl had arrived early, so they sat next to the fire with coffee and cake and went over all the scenarios that may come up with the estate. Karl had said it was a bonus that the trees that surrounded the place came up nearly to the building itself.

"What do you think these small windows around the building would show us Denny?"

"That's easy Karl. I'm a hundred percent sure they are manufacturing drugs in the basement. Bloody drugs seemed to have followed me all my life."

"I take it you want everyone disposed of Denny?"

"No loose ends pal. There must be no mistakes on my part. Trust me."

Karl had said that he was still going over his own ideas. There was a bit of fine tuning still to do, but he would be ready.

He told Helen he had to meet a few people about his thoughts on expanding his interests, and might be out for a couple of nights. Helen didn't believe one word of it.

Gunther had phoned and asked if tonight was too soon to meet the men, but Denny had said that would be great, and Willie and him would meet everyone at seven o'clock at the bar. He knocked on the annex door and told Willie about the meeting. It was not a problem for him, and he would be ready.

310

As they drove down to the bar, Willie was questioning what was the purpose of getting these men. Denny told him that he didn't want a repeat of the previous incident, whereby they might send more people over.

They walked through the back with only a slight nod to the barman. Gunther greeted them and introduced them to the men. On looks alone they seemed capable, but looks could be deceiving.

"Okay, men my name is Denny, and this is my brother Willie. We are from the Albach estate, as I'm sure Gunther has told you. He will have told you why you have been asked here. Some of you have helped me out in the past, and it's good to see you again. I need men who will help to look after the estate and keep my family safe for an unknown period. You will be required to do forestry work as well. Willie will instruct you on what is required, which hard work is part of it. However, the main part is keeping my family and Willie's partner safe, as well as anybody who is on the estate at any time."

One of the men interrupted by asking him how they were to protect the family.

"By any means necessary, and if that means putting a bullet in the perpetrator then so be it. If you have any problems with that then please leave now.

Nobody moved.

"I take it you have all fired a rifle at some point?"

There were nods all around.

"All the guns will be registered to the estate, and each of you will have a license to use them. You will carry them with you every day you are there whether working or not. I know they are talking about more snow at some point, but I expect you over at the estate, even if you have to dig your way over."

One guy asked what would happen if he did have to shoot someone.

"I have checked with the police and also the top solicitor minds in the Albach Trust and they have said it won't be problem. Trust me. You will be introduced to everyone over there soon. One other point. If you decided to put my extended family in danger, or abuse them in anyway, then my brother here will put a bullet in your brain, and he never misses. My extended family include my two dogs. Willie will then take your body, and put it up in the North valley to be eaten by the wolves."

Just then, a young lad started to laugh, and asked if he was joking.

When he looked around he saw that no one else was laughing.

"Willie, am I joking?"

"You never do pal, and can I just say that if any of you fuck up, then I might only wound you and stake you out in the valley. Or I might just let the dogs rip your genitals off. Death by dog. Interesting."

"If you are all in, then please say now. You will be working for us as soon as we leave here. Gunther will have your phone numbers, and he will tell you when to get yourselves over to see what the estate layout is like, and meet the people you will be protecting. My friends and I are going for a short trip on business.

"Are you all in?"

There were nods all around.

"Good. Here is the money you will be paid each week. Gunther will see to that. There will be a large bonus at the end if my family is safe. Some of you will know about that from a previous time."

Denny then handed an envelope to each of the men. There were gasps as to the amount, as there was the last time.

"We'll be seeing you."

He nodded to Gunther, and as he walked through the bar, he handed the barman his usual wad of cash. The guy gave him his crooked forefinger to his brow sign.

"Do you think you'll be all right with looking after everyone Willie? I hate to put this on you, and to be honest I would rather have you with me in Scotland. However, if I had to trust the lives of my family with anybody, then it would be you pal."

"Just come back in one piece Denny will you. No heroics please."

Nothing else was said until they got back.

"I'm taking the dogs for their last walk Denny. I need to clear my head."

He watched Willie walk away, and he knew it was more and more likely that he would walk away from this place. By God he

312

would miss him. He wasn't going to dwell on it now. There was too much to work out.

He walked up to the lodge to speak to Yuri and Tomaz, but Jinty was there. She could see by his face that she needed to make herself scarce.

"Right lads, I have had a phone call from my pal in Dundee. He says that there will be a thaw of sorts, over there within ten days, so I am planning to go sooner rather than later. Are you still up for it? Yuri I will be telling Helen tomorrow night what we will be up to. Do you want me to tell Jinty at the same time?"

"Just leave it to me to tell Jinty pal, but I think our lives will be hard for some time to come."

Denny just nodded and left the lodge. He knew this was going to be the hardest thing he would ever have to explain to Helen. He would make the people, who caused all this, suffer.

When he walked in he said to Helen that he would like to speak to her tomorrow night once the boys were tucked up in bed. She eyed him suspiciously.

"Is this the bombshell you're going to drop on me Foggerty. Where my life is turned upside down again?"

He couldn't answer her. She was right. Was this all about him. Surely both Jinty and her will see why it has to be done. Then again it is Helen and Jinty. He was 'pissed off' with his life at present, so what was another thing to bother him. After collecting the logs and stacking them next to the fires, he trudged upstairs, kissed his boys and fell into bed. He never heard Helen come in to the bedroom. At least she had slept beside him. Next morning it was him that got the boys up, changed them, ready for Helen to breast feed them.

He decided he would spend time with his family today, not do anything else except think and plan. He looked out when he heard the dogs yelping. It was Tomaz taking them for a walk. He shouted his thanks out of the window, and asked him if he could look after them all day. Tomaz gave him the thumbs up. God knows what Tomaz would get up to with them.

The phone rang. When he answered it, it was Jonas telling him he had received a call late last night from the institute, saying that they had given permission for two people to visit on Thursday, for one hour only.

"Great work Jonas, and I promise there will be no guns. Honest."

"I would love to believe you Denny, but there is a little doubt at the back of my mind. If you need anything else, then just give me a call."

The rest of the day went just as Denny wanted. Plenty of time with the kids and Helen. Also enough time to sit, relax and work out all his plans in his head. Unfortunately, the day passed too quickly. He saw Jinty arriving and going up to the lodge, so he hoped Yuri had remembered that they agreed they would tell the girls about Scotland at the same time.

When it was time, Denny asked Helen if the boys were settled, and could she come and sit down so that he could speak to her.

"Let's get it over with Denny. I'm sure I am not going to like what you're going to say. If I walk away from you, then too bad."

Denny started to raise his voice, but trying to keep his anger in check.

"That's typical of you Helen. Lately, you have been thinking the world is against you, and everybody owes you a favour. Well, just sit and bloody listen. Then you can walk away from me."

Just then there was a commotion coming from the path at the lodge. Jinty was coming first, shouting, with her finger being pointed at Yuri. Her face was bright red with anger. Denny could see that Yuri was trying to hold his temper in. That was it for Denny. As Jinty was heading to her car, Denny leaped down the steps, grabbed her by the arm, and dragged her up and pushed her down in the seat next to Helen.

"Right, you pair better listen and listen good, as I don't want any arguments."

"Foggerty, I have finally found the nicest guy ever, and because of your inability to let sleeping dogs lie, there is a chance I might lose him."

Denny suddenly blew his top.

"Listen Jinty Thomas. If you interrupt me once more with your big gob, I will personally drag you down the track, while literally kicking your arse, until you are off my land. You then won't be coming back on it. Ever."

Jinty's face went from red to white immediately. Helen gestured for her to keep quiet.

"Okay, let me tell you what is going to happen, and most importantly why. It wasn't that long ago that men arrived on this estate, hell bent on killing us all due to something I thought I was justified in doing in another life time. Are you listening Helen? They were going to kill us all. That means you, me and our beautiful boys sleeping soundly upstairs."

Helen put her hands over her ears, before Denny went and removed them.

"Why do you think we sent you to the town house. Did you think it was a game we were playing? These evil people came, and we killed them. Did you get that the pair of you? We fucking killed them to protect everybody here on the estate. Jinty, your man that you were gobbing off to, was a massive part in our success."

She looked at Yuri, and started to cry, before Denny shouted at her to stop.

"Don't you bloody dare tell me about sleeping dogs. Are you both that stupid to believe that everything is fine. That these people won't come back again, and try eliminating us."

Denny stopped to let his words sink in.

"I'm not looking over my shoulder every moment of my life. Worrying if my boys will be safe growing up. So I made a decision that I would go to Scotland and wipe the fuckers out. This time there will be no loose ends. I asked, not told, Yuri, Tomaz and Karl to come with me. However, if they didn't want to, well that was fine by me, but like me, they didn't want to be looking over their shoulders either."

A longer pause this time from Denny.

"Helen, do you remember asking me about my 'clandestine' phone calls to Shonagh in Edinburgh? Well, she was gathering a lot of intelligence for me, along with Tommy. I also have been speaking to Stevie in Dundee, who has been helping me with various things that I won't go in to. A few good people who want to help us. Even Levi and Bohdi have been helping us. God help us with that one. My trip to Scotland was all about gathering information. We have prepared to the best of our ability, and we will be leaving within ten days, so please prepare yourselves. One thing I would like to say, and that is, we don't like killing people, but these people are evil and if it means keeping us all safe, then we will do so, with such ferocity that they will think the devil is waging war on them. While we are away, Gunther has organised for several reliable men to work and protect the estate. Willie will be in charge of everything, under instructions to shoot anybody who steps out of line. If you speak a word to anybody about this, then somebody could die."

Denny sat down feeling quite mentally drained. At last, everything was out in the open.

"Is there anything you two would like to ask me?"

He could see that they had been holding hands. They just shook their heads. Helen went and held Denny. Jinty was crying as she hugged Yuri, but making sure that Denny couldn't see the tears flowing.

"One last thing. I promise, we will all be safe."

Now with that out of the way, he could speak relatively freely while all the girls were about. He went down, and asked Willie if he could speak to him. He told him as much as he could about his plans, and when he had finished he asked him for his honest opinion on what the outcome might be.

"You have put a lot of thought and planning into this brother. A few things will be difficult. One, is that you are intending to try and make people disappear, but there has to be a plausible reason why they disappear. They have to be well hidden if you have killed them. Whether it's buried or burnt, but you need one large incident which will look like an accident that will get rid of a big proportion of them. As many accidents as possible, before somebody suspects something. Also, you must have a reason to be where you are going. I would suggest that you are there for winter survival training. Both you and Yuri should know a bit about that. That's about as much advice as I can give you pal, and I will be praying for you all. Everything here will be fine."

Denny thanked him before giving him a hug.

"Oh, by the way, Jonas called me to say that we can go and visit Wagner on Thursday. You up for it?"

"Try and stop me pal."

It seemed like a large weight had been lifted from Denny's shoulders. He would spend the next few days playing with the boys, and paying as much attention to Helen as he could. He phoned Gunther and asked him if he and Karl could bring the men that they had chosen over tomorrow night at about seven o'clock. He wandered in and told all the girls that the men were coming, could they meet them, and also put a bit of supper on for them. They were okay with that.

He wandered up to the lodge to speak to Yuri and Tomaz.

"Lads, can you please go in to Zwiesel, and buy whatever clothes and footwear you will need for our trip. Tops, trousers and underwear. Remember, it will need to be thermal. Most of it won't be coming back with you. Our winter gear will be there for us, plus all the arms and accessories we will need."

He looked at the expression on Tomaz's face, before saying, "Don't worry wee man, there will be plenty of knives to choose from."

A big smile came over his face. He knew he needed to speak to Karl and Gunther, but tomorrow night would be soon enough.

When he eventually got to bed, All Helen wanted to do was cuddle him all night, which was understandable. Next morning she got him aroused, only for Col to start screaming his head off. Denny thought that night time might be better. He decided to keep his fitness up, so he went to get the dogs. Tomaz appeared, and gestured that he wanted to go for a run with Denny. As they took off, it might have been his imagination, but he felt lighter and a bit more supple. They heard a shout, and here was Yuri trying to catch them up. Eventually the three of them headed up the hill to the North valley. When they got to the top they stopped, and Yuri and Tomaz looked down on their land, with the buildings now piles of ash.

"Do you miss it lads?"

"No, not really Denny. I often think back to some of my early memories, but to be honest, later in life there were some bloody awful times."

Tomaz indicated that they should sprint for home. No doubt for his breakfast knowing him. Denny started to howl, setting the dogs off. Tomaz then started, with Yuri following him soon after. If anyone had seen and heard them, then it must have been a scary sight. On the run home, Denny felt Tomaz was holding back, until the last few hundred yards, when he just stepped up a gear.

After breakfast, he firstly phoned Maria, and told her to get the passports for Tomaz and Yuri over within the next few days as well as cash for everybody. Also, money to be deposited in the banks in Edinburgh and Dundee.

"So it's on then Denny. What did Helen say to all this? More to the point, do you really want to do this, my big Scottish friend."

"Bloody hell, don't you start Maria. As you can imagine Helen wasn't very happy, but she understands why I am doing this. I hope you do too."

"Denny, as long as you all come back safe and sound, I will be happy. Although, there are a few reservations rolling about in my head. Speak soon."

Denny walked in, and asked Helen if she would like to speak to Shonagh after he was finished. She said she would love to.

Denny phoned her, and it was answered on the third ring.

"Bloody hell Shonagh, are you ever at work? No wonder the Edinburgh Police has gone down hill since I left. Did you get the hotels sorted out, as it may be only a few days before we will be there."

"So, the time has finally come Denny. It's been a long time coming. Will my beautiful country ever be the same again? Yes, the hotels are ready, and the owners know it has to be discreet. I showed them my warrant card, so they think it is a police matter. So all is well. Oh, and by the way, it's a wonder you can remember any of your time in the force, due to the whisky. Tommy and I still wonder about what you did with the car you were issued with?"

"Ah, the car. Now there is a story my bonnie girl. We might call in on you when we all arrive, but I can't promise as you know. I might phone you on an occasion, to see if anybody has been reported as a missing person up where we are going. Nobody from where we are going will know about you, so you don't have to worry about anything. Love you Shonagh see you soon."

"Get lost Denny Foggerty."

Next was Stevie. When he answered, he was using his gruff voice.

"Having a bad day pal? It sounds like it."

318

"Hi Denny. Your fine pal, it's just that my wife has been nipping my head all day. What can I do for you?"

Denny told him the date they would be coming over, so if the jeep could be left in the hotel as before then great. He asked him if there was anyway he could get all the gear to the small farm overlooking the Ruthven estate. Which he pointed out now belonged to him.

"That's a pretty tall order Denny. However, I know two reprobates that would be excited about doing it."

"Thanks Stevie. No need to ask you who the reprobates are. How about we meet up for a coffee in Dundee, when we are able to get up to the Ruthven estate?"

"Sounds like a plan pal, as long as I'm not expected to shoot anybody."

The phone went dead, and Denny started to laugh.

Throughout the day, while waiting for the meeting with the men, Denny was getting a bit agitated. He didn't know why, but he hoped there wasn't going to be any doubts creeping in to his head. Otherwise, people would lose their lives.

Just before seven o'clock Denny heard two vehicles coming up the track. It was both Karl and Gunther bringing the men up. When they all got out, Denny asked them up to the veranda for something to eat. When seated, the girls came out with a lovely spread. Denny introduced all the men to them. They were very courteous to the girls.

After they were finished Denny started to tell them everything about the estate and what work was involved daily.

"I apologise that I can't tell you how long you will be over here, but it will be weeks instead of days. The girls will feed you each day and each night you will take it in turn to stay over in the lodge. If it's your turn to go home for the night, then you will be here at seven o'clock each morning. No later. You will carry your rifle to your work each day. There will be no random shooting, unless you think my family could be in trouble. Then shoot to kill. Also, if by chance you see a white stag, and you take a pot shot at it, then Willie will put a bullet between your eyes. It will only be a few days before you start, so I suggest that you go with Karl tomorrow to the Outdoor store in Zwiesel, and he will advise what clothing and footwear to buy, and it will be charged to my account.

The men sat looking at each other, wondering if this could get any better. The dogs were just wandering about. It was then that the cocky lad who didn't believe Willie when he said about them ripping people's genitals off, started to say something.

"Are these the dogs you were saying would attack somebody's 'balls'?" They seem quite timid to me."

All the men were looking at each other, and wondering who would have the pleasure in showing the guy how 'timid' the dogs were. However, Denny was getting a bit fed up of this charade. Tomaz was pointing furiously to himself, before Denny turned to Willie and nodded. Willie walked over to where the dogs were, and gave them the command, pointing to the young lad. All hell broke loose. They ran at the guy while knocking over cups and plates. Even jumping over the tables. No stopping them. They then stood either side of the lad with the usual display off teeth and growling. They had their mouths only a few inches either side of his face, and he must have felt the heat off their breaths. The guy dropped his cup in to his lap. He was petrified and shaking.

"Don't ever call my dogs timid. They will be with you and Willie in the forest every day. Get to know them, as they might save your life at some point."

Just then Helen came out, as she had heard the commotion.

"Willie McLeod, look at the bloody mess you have caused getting these dogs riled up. Leave the young lad alone. Look at him, he's terrified. All these cups and plates broken."

Willie couldn't believe he was getting the blame for this.

"Can you please get the dogs off," shouted the guy.

Denny nodded at Tomaz who went forward, grabbed the dogs and whispered in their ears. Helen saw this and looked at Denny who gave her a slight nod. It was then the dogs couldn't wait to run to Helen for a cuddle. Some of the men just shook their heads, wondering what was happening.

"If you need to ask me anything, then now is the time to say. Otherwise, I will see you in two days."

As they walked away, it looked like the young lad might need help, but Denny had hoped he would have learned his lesson.

That night in bed, Helen was constantly wanting Denny to make love to her, and she to him. He was hardly getting his breath back, before she was trying to get him hard again. It wasn't that she wasn't getting satisfied, but the more she got the more she wanted. After three hours, Denny was feeling a bit spent, so he had to say to her that he just wanted to go to sleep. He thought it might not go down well, but she eventually just cuddled in to him. He wondered if all this would be happening if he wasn't going away.

The next day, he called all the men together for a meeting. They used the lodge, as there was the possibility of the girls hearing something they wouldn't like. Karl had come up earlier, as he would do each day until they left. When Denny told him to replenish his clothes at the Outdoor store, Karl had said he had his own and wouldn't need anything.

"Okay, men this will be our last meeting before we leave, so let's get it right. No point being over there and realising we should have thought about something before we left. Do we understand about the concept of 'cut and run warfare'? We will be seriously outnumbered as far as I could see when I was over there. However, people going missing or having a believable accident, will certainly go in our favour. Can we get rid of them all by this way? Not a hope in hell.

Everything is in place over there to give us the best possible chance. Our equipment will be the best that money can buy. The four of us will be living on a farm, which overlooks the estate, and our excuse for being there is that we are in Scotland for winter survival training. With the purpose of starting a training camp in the Highlands. We will stay in an Edinburgh hotel, until we know the conditions are right for us to move further North. Tomaz, in the event of any of us getting a wound of any kind, then you will attend to it. Okay?"

Tomaz just nodded.

"I can't really tell you about the estate, as you would need to see it, but Karl has a rough map to work to. So, hopefully he has a few ideas from day one. Any questions?"

It was Yuri who spoke up.

"Denny, Willie came up with a relevant point with regards to getting rid of any bodies. You got any ideas?"

"Yuri, when you see the farm, you will realise the number of places a body could be hidden. However, too many bodies going missing will attract suspicion from the estate, as well as the law. Remember, the estate has the local police in their back pockets. There is a small village about two miles away where we can get provisions, and if we have to get a decent meal every so often, then there is a small hotel and bar called the Stag's Head just outside the village, but we don't want to advertise our existence."

Karl was next to bring up a question.

"Denny, I'm going straight to the point with this. What happens if you are killed?

"Then you get the hell out of Scotland, and you must never look back. Got it?

"Right, if there is nothing else, then I suggest we go down for something to eat."

Chapter 13

As the men walked down to the house, Denny could see the mixed emotions on the men's faces. Karl was thinking about everything that had been brought up. Yuri? Well he just wanted to get on with it, while Tomaz was wondering what was on offer for breakfast. After breakfast, they all went their own separate ways.

He went in and shouted on Helen, and asked if she wanted to go for a walk in to the forest, through the snow.

She jumped at the chance, with Gertie saying she would look after the boys. They walked hand in hand, until they sat down under a large tree. That was when she broke down. As much as Denny hated tears, he couldn't get on to her. She just cried and cried, with Denny just consoling her with an arm around her shoulder. He couldn't begrudge her the tears.

"Denny, I am so scared that something will happen to you, and the boys and I will never see you again. I couldn't handle that. I'm sorry, I know you can't stand tears."

"Helen, I can understand your worry, but I promise nothing will happen to me. I will end this once and for all. We will soon be living as a normal family, but you must be strong, not just for the boys, but everyone around you. Oh, you mustn't forget my dogs either."

This brought a wee smile to her face. She gave him a long lingering kiss.

"I've got something to tell you."

He went on to tell her everything about Wagner. He left out the part of Willie and him visiting the institute tonight.

"What makes people do that Denny?"

He thought he was the wrong person to ask that, so he just said he must have mental health problems.

"Daniel Foggerty, you know how much I love you, and would sit here forever with you. However, my arse is freezing, so can we please wander back?"

"Helen, you know me. I could always massage it for you?"

"You're right Foggerty. I do know you. Let's just walk."

"Helen, I will be away in a few days, so lets try and be nice to each other, or at least civil."

When they got back it was just a waiting game for Denny, until it was time for him and Willie to go to Fussen. He told her they were going to have a meeting with the men who would be guarding the estate. Denny thought how easy it was to lie to people, when you had been an alcoholic.

Maria arrived over with the passports, money and money belts. She went in to see everyone, especially the boys. When she came out she headed for Denny and gave him a big hug. She never said anything, just got into her car and drove off.

When it was time to go, Willie was sitting outside beside the fire waiting for him.

"Willie, can I just ask you something? Have you got any guns or knives on you?"

"No brother, just my bare hands, and you know how lethal they are."

"We are just going to gloat, and try and make his life as miserable as possible. Plus trying to get through three inch thick glass might even be a struggle for you."

"You think?"

The car drive was pretty quiet, with only Willie moaning at Denny for twice getting lost. Fussen was just a quiet nondescript town, with very little life about it. Not many people were going about. What they were approaching was just one soulless building. When they got there, they just sat in the car and looked at it. It was one ugly block of concrete, peppered with bar covered windows. Even for the two of them, it was a depressing place. If you didn't have any mental problems going in, you would when or if you came out.

"Hey, Denny are the bars on the windows to stop the inmates getting out, or us getting in?"

Denny could only laugh.

As they walked to the main entrance Willie said, "All that is missing is a moat filled with crocodiles pal. Not even guard towers with guys holding machine guns. What's going on"

"For fuck sake McLeod, stop letting your imagination run away with yourself."

"Just saying pal."

As they got to the door, they were let in by a guy the size of the gable end of a 'public toilet'. He just asked for their names, without a smile cracking his face, before nodding for them to enter through the first door. It looked like they had another two doors to go through. It was then that two guys came out and searched them. Willie wasn't too happy to have his inner legs searched. After the two guys walked away, the pair of them were left waiting for about ten minutes. It was then that a man with a white coat on, opened the third door and asked them to come through, where they were to take a seat at a desk over by the far wall.

"Hey Foggerty, this is getting a bit scary is it not? I'm worried."

It was then that the smell of disinfectant hit them. Not the usual household cleaner, but strong industrial strength sterilizing wash. Denny hoped they wouldn't be long in this room as he was starting to feel nauseous. A young woman came into the room, and sat down beside them.

"Okay gentlemen. Sorry for the delay, but we have had a bit of a problem with an attempted suicide not long ago. I will just ask you a few quick questions, and we will take you to see the patient. Mr Daniel Rey Foggerty is it, and you work on the Albach estate near Zwiesel?"

"Nope."

"Sorry, I thought I was addressing Mr Daniel Rey Foggerty."

"You are, but I am not employed by the estate. I own it. In fact I own the whole Albach Trust. Every single bit of it. Sorry, I'm not trying to be flippant. This is my Estate Manager, William McLeod, who happens to be my adopted brother, as well as a pain in the arse at times. I thought all this information was given to you by Jonas Schneider?"

The woman immediately read her notes again, and her face turned red.

"I'm so sorry Mr Foggerty. I didn't pick up on that. Please accept my apologies."

"I wouldn't worry about it miss. He likes to brag about it at times."

"Brother, you are no longer in my will. I would rather have the dogs in it than you."

Fortunately, they were both grinning as the woman didn't know what to think.

Mr Foggerty, Mr McLeod, there will be a superintendent through immediately to take you to see your patient.

"Thanks', that is very kind of you."

She didn't know if Denny was being polite or facetious.

After another lengthy wait, two people walked through one of the inner doors. This time a man and a woman. It was the woman who spoke first.

"Good evening gentlemen. I hope you haven't been kept long. Please follow us along the corridor. Before you get to see Mr Wagner there are conditions. You might struggle to communicate with him, due to his mental state. On no account must you antagonise him in any way. If the warden, who will be in his room with him, thinks that the visit should be terminated, then he will. There will be no banging on the glass, or making gestures of any kind to him. You will be allowed one hour, no more, with him. Is that understood?"

"Bloody hell, you must have him wrapped up in cotton wool for God's sake. This being the guy that shot my wife and killed his girlfriend, along with critically injuring one of his friends. It appears that he is getting better protection than they did. However, we accept the rules, and we will stick by them. Won't we William?"

"Of course brother. So if we can be shown to his visiting window, then that would be good. Thanks for all your help."

"Doctor Andros will take you along, and I will come back when your time is up. Until then gentlemen."

"Excuse me Dr Andros. Do you ever get used to the smell in here?" asked Willie.

"What smell sir?"

As they walked along the corridor, Denny couldn't help contemplating what the chances of getting out of here were. Probably nil. They could see two seats placed at a window. The glass must have been shatter proof, and at least two inches thick. When they were sitting, they couldn't see anybody. Until they saw Wagner, securely tied up in a straight jacket. The room was large, and he was just walking back and forward, from one end to the other. He had a blank stare on his face, and his eyes were like two small black holes in the snow. The attendant was just walking with him.

When the attendant saw them, he motioned for them to sit facing the glass, and to speak into the grill in the middle of the glass. He sat Wagner down and said he was going to sit over at the far wall to give them privacy. Wagner didn't recognise who was sitting in front of him. Every so often a small dribble would run from the corner of his mouth. After about five minutes of Denny and Willie just grinning at him, they thought there was a flicker of recognition on his face.

"Denny is it you or me that is going to tell him that this white walled room is going to be the only place he will see for the rest of his life. I think I will leave that up to you. What do you think?"

"Well brother, I think I would like to tell him that this place is as good as it gets for him, seeing as his little pal died from the gunshot wounds that this coward inflicted on him."

They saw that there was more recognition on his face. Denny looked over at the attendant, who seemed intent on reading some sort of magazine.

"Maybe, I should tell him about the arrest of his father and his pal the corrupt judge. How long do think they will get? Probably ten to fifteen years when they will suffer a lot of abuse at the hands of some violent prisoners. Should I tell him or not Willie?"

Willie couldn't help it, but he put his head below the level of the window and laughed. The attendant couldn't see him, but Wagner could. It was then that the drool from his mouth was starting to get worse. He started to rock in his chair, before eventually managing to throw himself against the glass, smashing his forehead and nose, with blood spraying everywhere. Willie got a bit of a fright, but Denny had been anticipating it. Wagner was trying to kick the glass, before the attendant ran across and pinned him to the floor.

"Have you had enough Denny. I think I don't want anymore of this 'crap', what do you say?"

The attendant had managed to subdue him, and pressed a buzzer for help. Four men came running along the corridor, and Willie had joked that they were coming for them.

They just walked to the front reception, where they were met by the same woman who had first spoke with them.

"I'm sorry it had to end like this Mr Foggerty."

"I'm not. Please try and keep him locked up. Should he manage to escape, then I will hunt the fucker down and rip his inners out, before finally killing him. Now, get these fucking doors open."

They both went and sat in the car, listening to some music, when Denny's evil grin came over his face. Willie didn't like to see it.

"Hey Foggerty, we surely are a pair of evil bastards. What do you think?"

Denny just burst out laughing.

Nothing was said on the way home, mainly because Willie had fallen asleep, which suited Denny.

After he had kicked Willie awake, he noticed that Helen was waiting at the main doors. She looked worried. He headed up and asked her what had happened.

"Denny, everyone up at the lodge has gone down with a sickness bug. Jinty came down so far, and shouted on me. They are all in their beds, with sick buckets next to them."

Denny thought that he was cursed again. All this preparation and planning was going down the drain, unless what they had was just a twenty four hour bug. He knew he couldn't dwell on this, but just carry on as usual. He walked to about twenty yards from the lodge before shouting on someone. Jinty appeared at the door with not a 'stitch' on.

"Jinty, please tell Yuri and Tomaz not to come near the house, as well as yourself, until you are all clear. Drink loads of water, and we will see you all soon. Oh, and I suggest you put some clothes on Jinty."

"I am burning up Denny. The sweat is running off me."

"Okay, but Jinty I am worried about the animals in the forest getting frightened, seeing that lily white body of yours. Although it's blending in with the snow right enough."

As Denny started to walk away, he heard the door slamming. He went down and told Willie that they would have to look after the new men together, and that Gertie was not to go in to the lodge, but it she wanted to give them some food, then she was to leave it at their door, but rap loudly. Just so that any animal would not come calling.

Denny was up early next day, although at one point he thought about waking Helen up to see if she was up for a bit of love making. When he had looked over, she was sound asleep, so he thought it was a shame to wake her. He made breakfast for him and Willie, who had wandered up looking still half asleep. They sat next to the fire.

"Not a good start to your plans pal, is it? Let's hope they will be fine tomorrow. How do you want it to play out with these men today? I trust the dogs are going with us?"

"I am not playing it out anyway Willie. You are going to knock them in to shape anyway you want. Although, we should split them up, but seeing as Yuri isn't here, then I suggest you take us all together to work, and if I need a bollocking for something that is not your way, then do it."

"With pleasure pal."

Helen popped her head out the door and told it was Jonas on the phone for him. Denny had been expecting this call, but not as early.

"Good morning Denny. Sorry for such an early call, but I have a busy day ahead of me. It seems that you and Willie caused quite a stir at the institute last night. When you left, apparently Wagner was going ballistic, and even when the men finally let him up, he kicked off again. They eventually had to restrain him on a bed. I had a call from the administrator ten minutes ago, asking if I could ask you what was said last night between you to make him kick off like that. The girl at reception is still a bit put out about what you said to her."

"Hi Jonas, I appreciate your efforts for getting us in to see that scum. You can go back to the administrator, and tell him that we were only conveying our best wishes, and hoped he would get well soon. As for the girl at reception, I only told her the truth. She needs to toughen up though. Anyway, how's that lovely family of yours?"

"Denny, I wish I could believe you. I really do. Yes, my family are fine, with my daughter still on at me for a dog. See what you and your dogs have started. Anyway, I believe you are away on business for a few months, although I never had you down as a businessman Denny. Hope to see you when you get back."

"I never said what type of business Jonas. Cheers."

Denny thought it was time for dog walking, before the men arrived. When he opened the kennel door, the dogs were jumping about, ready for another day in the forest. It was then that two vehicles came up the track. Karl and Gunther. He would walk the dogs while the men were served breakfast by Gertie and Helen. When he got back, he explained about Yuri and Tomaz. He let them know that Willie would be in total charge, and it was time to work.

During the morning, Denny was really only there observing the men to see if they came up to standard. He thought Willie was being a good taskmaster, but equally a good teacher. At one point he sat down against a tree without thinking.

"Hey, Foggerty just because you own the bloody forests, don't think you are getting out of working. Now, get up off your arse, and get on with it."

The men just stood looking at Denny, wondering if he was going to say anything.

"Sorry boss. It won't happen again."

Keeping as straight a face as he could.

He was impressed with the men, even the young cocky lad who hadn't been too sure about the dogs. He kept a wary eye on them when either of them came near him. After a good productive day, the men walked back to the house. When they were sitting around having a coffee waiting to go home, Denny had a word with them.

"All right men, give me a few moments of your time. How did you find the work? It was a bit taxing, but that's what it's like when your working outside. The snow hasn't helped either. Has anybody got anything to say or ask? Tomorrow, we will stop a bit earlier, if the boss allows it, and you can show me what you can do with a rifle."

Nobody said a word, and they just enjoyed their coffee. After they left, Denny asked Willie if he had reservations about any of them. Willie had said they had all worked hard, but he would wait until tomorrow to make a judgement on them. That was good enough for Denny.

It was then that they saw Jinty walking from the lodge. Denny was incensed.

"Jinty, what the fuck are you doing. It's only been half a day, and your going down to the house. Bloody well get back. If you feel you need fresh air, then get wrapped up in blankets, and sit out at the back of the lodge, now beat it."

"I feel a lot better Denny, honest."

"Get lost Jinty. Gertie and I don't want your germs. If you get any closer, I will turn the high pressure hose on you forcing you back to the lodge. As Denny just said, beat it."

"I'm bored lads."

"Too bad, get lost. Let's see what your all like tomorrow."

Denny thought he had better put the travel arrangements back a few days, so he went in and phoned Karl.

"I think you are being sensible Denny. The travel alone will be tiresome, and you don't want to be arriving not being at your best. Mistakes could be made. Please keep me updated as to what you are thinking."

Willie got up without saying a word, and went in to the annex. Denny thought that Willie could be so strange at times. He had never told Denny about his upbringing or really not much about his life in general. Denny wondered what life would like when he and Gertie left the estate, which wasn't far away. They would be hard to replace as workers, but especially as good friends. Helen would be devastated when she eventually found out. Still, he couldn't think about it just now. When, not if, he came back, he knew it would happen. He went in for supper.

The next few days were hard for Denny. He needed to get to Scotland. It was all weather dependent, both here and there. He couldn't concentrate on very much, except Helen and the boys. The target practice for the men went well for everyone, except one guy. Willie told him he couldn't 'hit a cow's arse with a banjo'. The guy was the only one that didn't laugh.

Denny had told them that every second day they would go out for a run to keep fit. Much to the disgust of Willie. All of them in the lodge were fine next day, but Denny warned them of their personal hygiene, especially when they were at the house. On the morning of the second last day, Denny told the men not to have breakfast just yet as they were going out for a run with Tomaz.

They seemed keen at first, until the run started in earnest. Denny had told Tomaz to take it easy on them. However at the start, Denny had shouted that if any man could beat Tomaz, he would give him an extra weeks wages. Willie was just going along for the sake of it. The young cocky lad was the nearest to Tomaz at the end, but he was still a fair distance behind. Another two struggled in, before collapsing on the steps. They waited, and waited, before Willie appeared, half dragging, half carrying the last two. When they got to the steps Willie said, "Hey Foggerty, were you amused by all that?"

"Yeh, just a little bit. Right lads, breakfast is about to be served."

Nobody, except Tomaz was keen.

The phone rang, and Helen had shouted on Denny to come and take it. It was Stevie.

"Good morning my friend. What can I do for you?"

"Morning Denny. Just a bit of advice. By the end of this week Scotland will be under another blanket of snow. So, if your coming, then 'get your arse in gear.'

"Thanks pal. It won't be tomorrow, but the day after, so can you please organise Andrew."

"It's all sorted, and the jeep will be waiting for you at the hotel, but be warned, that if this snow does hit us, then getting around will be very difficult. See you."

Denny then organised a meeting with everyone for tomorrow night, after Karl and Gunther had dropped the men off in Zwiesel, and then returned. Denny told Willie, and had then the unenviable task of going in and telling Helen.

He asked her to come and sit down next to the fire with him. He could see by her face that she had an inkling of what he was about to say.

"Helen, we will be away in two days. Definitely. I'm not going to say sorry, as this has to be done. I was upfront with you the last time about how dangerous this will be, but I'm still telling you that we will all be safe. We will be leaving early in the morning, as there is to be a lot of snow covering Scotland just after we arrive. At times, we will be out of touch as the telephone service is not great where we will be. So don't worry. If by chance there is an emergency, then hopefully we can still contact Shonagh. She can then contact you."

As expected, Helen started to cry. Denny put his arms around her, and hugged her gently. He didn't care about the tears this time, as he understood how she was feeling.

"Denny, I'm sorry for crying, but I can't help it. I've struggled since you told me previously. Deep down, I was hoping that it wouldn't happen, but I knew I was kidding myself on. Let's make it the best time we can tomorrow with the boys, please."

"Sounds like a good plan Helen. Remember, you have to be strong. I know that Willie will be in charge of the estate, but you will be running this house, as both Gertie and Jinty will only be there to help you. You will all be perfectly safe with the men I have employed, and Gunther and Willie, are sound."

"Yeh, but they're not you Denny."

As she walked away, he went indoors and shouted on Jinty. When she came out, Denny asked her if he could have a word. When she sat down, he could see by her face that she was worried as to what he was going to say.

"Don't look so worried Jinty. I just need a little talk with you. You haven't done anything wrong. Well not yet anyway. I can understand that you want to spend as much time with Yuri as you can. However, you still have the business in town, as well as the house. You did talk about expanding the shop and employing more people, but you are never there, so at some point it could go 'belly up'. It's great that you and Yuri are getting on well, but you can't go around all the time just fluttering your eyes at him. There is a balance in life, and you have to embrace it.

"Denny, I have found lately that my life has been a roller coaster, and I find it has been difficult for me to comprehend it all. I'm taking in what you are saying, and when you all come back, things will change, but I can't even think about it just now, as I'm too emotional."

"I would like if you can be here for each other when we are away. It could be weeks, or even months, but I am going to tell you something in confidence that mustn't get back to Helen. When we do get back, there will be changes. There will comings and goings. I know we talked about Jean Scougal starting her clothes alteration shop next to the bakery, but that probably won't happen, so have a think about extending your house, which would be ideal for you, and hopefully Yuri.

"I'll look in to it Denny. I'm sure the bank would be agreeable to a loan."

"Jinty, at times I wonder what is going on at times in that head of yours. Everything would be paid for through the Bank of Denny Foggerty."

"Not sure I am getting you Denny?"

"Bloody hell Jinty. Me, Daniel Rey Foggerty, will be paying for it all. Jinty, I know you are a just a girl, although a bit of a 'hairy arsed girl', from what I saw the other day, but what is it you are not getting?

There was a bit of a pause, before the penny dropped, and she punched him on the arm.

"I've got you now Foggerty, and thank you so much, then reached over an gave him a hug and kiss."

Just then Helen walked out.

"Oh, not again. What is it with you pair?"

"Nah, your fine Helen. I'll leave him to you. Oh, by the way Denny, the punch was for you looking at my arse, you pervert."

She walked across to Helen, smiling.

Denny was going through the list of things to do in his head, when he knew he had to phone Maria. It took ages for it to be answered.

"Good morning my beautiful fraulein. May I have a word with you?"

"Of course you can, unless it's you trying to get me in to bed again. Although they were lovely times Denny."

"Nothing like that you hussy, although you're right, they were lovely. Anyway back to business. Do you remember the bar we were in when you got a bit of a hassle when I first came over? It's where Wagner held court over his sycophants."

"I know the place you are on about pal. What about it?"

"I would like you to buy it for me, not try, just make the owner an offer he can't resist and I'm serious."

"For God's sake why Denny."

"I don't like the barman Maria, so I can then sack him. Speak when I get back."

When the call was disconnected, Maria sat back in her chair and started to shake her head. Nothing was simple since that man came to Bavaria. She had to get their time together out of her mind, before getting back to work.

Denny then went upstairs and with Helen's help, started sorting out his clothes for the trip. She took clothes away and washed them, and hung them up to dry. When she came back up stairs, he asked if the boys were sleeping. When she nodded, he walked forward and started to take her clothes off. She wasn't waiting either, and started to undress him in a hurry. Denny just threw her on the bed, and got on top of her, quickly entering her. Denny had never known Helen to climax so quickly. When they were both satisfied, they dressed and headed down stairs. Jinty was sitting with the boys, and gave them a sly grin.

When Denny walked out, Tomaz and Yuri were sitting outside.

"I take it that Willie has told you about our departure date?"

They both nodded.

"Any second thoughts lads?"

"None what so ever Denny. We both have been thinking about it, and we are more convinced than ever that it is a just cause. The people we are up against should be wiped off the face of the earth. A few months ago we could have all been killed. So let's go for it."

"What about you Tomaz?"

He just gave the thumbs up, but this time turned them upside down, with an evil grin on his face. Denny knew he was in good hands.

That night Helen just hugged him. He just slipped out of the bed early, and got his two boys and took them down stairs, and sat holding them while sitting on the veranda.

"Well boys. I don't tell you enough, but I love you more than life itself. To the moon and back. Daddy is going away for a while, so be good, very good for your mum. She will be crying sometimes, but it's nothing that you will have done. She will just need your cuddles and kisses to get her through this."

He had just given them a cuddle and a kiss, when Helen walked through the door and came and sat with them. Today, they really didn't want to be interrupted, as they just wanted to play, play, and play with the boys. The only interruption was a call from Shonagh telling him the same thing about the weather as Stevie had said.

"Thank you Shonagh. We will be over in Scotland tomorrow, although I doubt we will see you. I will have to wait until you are over to see about your shoulder to catch up with you. I am looking forward to that. Take care."

The men arrived soon after, and Denny had told Willie to forget about the runs in the mornings. It wasn't what they had signed up for, and wasn't fair. He reminded Willie that he would be on the airport run tomorrow, with him giving a nod of the head. Denny spoke to the five men and shook their hands.

"When I come back. If any of you want to accept my offer of working for the Trust, then please let me know. I did say that it probably won't be here, but the Trust will be venturing in to other business ventures all over Germany, especially the forestry industry. If you are prepared to travel or relocate, then there will be opportunities for hard working people. However, it will be on condition that my family and friends will be kept safe."

"Tell me Mr Foggerty please. What are the chances of them being put in danger?"

"Very slim pal, but you need to be on high alert from now. I won't see you till I get back, but Willie will be in charge, as well as Gunther. Good day gentlemen."

One of the men had turned to the guy next to him, and asked him quietly if he thought Mr Foggerty looked evil at times. The guy had just nodded his head.

The day was what he had hoped for. Just the four of them. Jinty and Yuri were spending time with each other, and Tomaz had decided he would go out working with Willie and the men. Although, Willie had thought it was more to do with him thinking he was in charge of the dogs.

After the men had went home, Denny had called a meeting of the men in the dining room. He went over every detail again and again so that there would be no mistakes.

"Yuri, here is the name and address of a café, near to where my old flat used to be. My friend now lives in it. There will be only about a short time between our flights, plus the taxi drive from Glasgow, so we will see you at the café. Remember, please keep your eyes and ears open at the airport, and keep the conversation in the taxi to a minimum. I will give your descriptions to the guy, and the firm is called Thistle Cabs. When Karl and I get picked up, I will pay the guy. Is there anything else I have missed?"

Nobody said anything.

"Right lads. Contrary to what Willie thinks, I am going to phone the guy who is behind all this. His name is Robertson, and he is an MP for the Lothians and Borders. Primarily I need to find out why he was, or is, so intent on killing me. You should be able to hear him on this speaker, but it is important that he thinks there is nobody else here, so please keep quiet."

Denny lifted the phone, and dialled the number in Edinburgh. His secretary answered and asked who was calling. Denny told her that it didn't matter what his name was, just put Robertson on the phone. She started to say that she needed a name, before Denny raised his voice and said, "Listen you little 'arse wipe'. Get him on the phone, as he will definitely want to speak to me."

It was about a minute before he came on.

"I don't know who you are, but you can't speak to my secretary like that. Now state your business, as I am a busy man."

"I will gladly state my name and business. My name is Foggerty. Daniel Rey Foggerty, and my business is to put a bullet in your brain. Does the name ring a bell? This is a courtesy call, to ask you a question, and to tell you what is going to happen to that miserable life of yours. Firstly why have you been try to kill me?"

"Well, I had only one sibling and that was my brother. You shot him on the Isle of Durma. Shot him like a dog. However, it wasn't my idea to send men over to your estate to try and kill you, it was one of my employees."

"The one that runs the Ruthven Estate I presume, and your brother being one of the guys that were distributing drugs through the isle I lived on? Me shooting everyone at the boat that night, was only me doing the world a favour."

"What do you know about the estate Foggerty?"

Denny had detected a little tremor in his voice.

"It's Mr Foggerty to you scum. I have been up there, and I have no interest in what your business is. My sole interest is

337

coming to Edinburgh on my own, and putting 'a lump of lead between your eyes,' okay?"

"I could get Radovan to send down the men, all thirty of them, to protect me. You would be hard pushed to get even near me. So I am not worried. You could end up dying in the country you were born in. How does that sound Foggerty."

"You will never know I am there, although I will give you something. It will be after the next snowstorm you are expecting over there. Then you will be visiting your 'shit hole' of a brother in Hell. Give him my regards. Watch your back."

Denny put the phone down. He looked at the men for a reaction, but none was forthcoming. It was left up to Willie.

"Blood hell pal. Thirty men? That won't be an easy job of getting rid of them. Half a dozen maybe, but you can't get rid of them all, and make it look like an accident each time. At least you know how many you are up against. I don't think they will send anybody down from up there, just to protect Robertson. I'll bet that this Radovan will be the main guy, but I would try and find out as much as you can."

It was then that Karl spoke up.

"Denny, to get rid of that amount of people, you need a bit of a disaster to happen. Fire, flood, or even an explosion, when they are all congregated in the house. I have been thinking, but it's a long shot, so I would rather see the place before I could be sure. Although, looking at your sketches, I think it could be feasible."

"Okay, men I thank you for your time, and you don't know how much I appreciate you coming with me. Let's make it a wicked war for them. I'll see you all tomorrow. Yuri, can I speak to you please."

When they all left, Denny asked Yuri if he thought that Tomaz would be all right at customs and on the flight. He told Denny that, although this was his first flight, he would be fine as they had went over it time and time again. That was fine for Denny.

He went in and phoned Shonagh.

"You just can't get enough of me Denny, can you?"

"Shonagh, in another time, probably not. Right, I know we are pressed for time, but I have found out about who the boss is up at the Ruthven estate. His name is Radovan. Sorry, but that is as much as I can give you. Any chance?"

"I am going on night shift just now, so if I can, then I'll make a few phone calls. Either way, I will phone you when I finish shift at six tomorrow morning."

That night, Helen had wanted Denny to make love to her like it would be their last. He wondered if she knew something that he didn't. At two in the morning, he had to tell her he needed sleep, so they just drifted off together. He was up early and went to get the dogs. When he opened the kennel, he turned round to see Tomaz behind him. Denny knew he wanted to walk the dogs as well, so he just gestured with his head along the trail. Denny took the dogs and Tomaz to where his favourite view was. They sat there with an arm around each of the dogs. Denny looked at Tomaz. Surely, he wasn't going to let this young man down, but during conflict you can never be sure. They just got to the steps when the phone rang. It was Shonagh.

"Morning Denny. I've got some information for you. Not a lot, but its better than nothing. The guy you were asking about is Radovan Popa, a Moldovan. He came in to the country four years ago, and was soon on the police radar, in regard to his involvement in the drug scene. Edinburgh was a busy place for his drug distribution. He narrowly escaped conviction a year ago, due to the timely intervention of our mutual friend Robertson. He is quite a tall and burly guy. His next in command is a guy called Balan, who has the worst hairstyle you could ever imagine. Radovan is barely seen outside, and if there is any retribution to be carried out it is always Balan, although it does say, that he won't do it without his men around him. Bit of a coward apparently. Sorry pal, I have nothing else for you."

"Thank you Shonagh, I have actually met these guys, albeit informally, when I was up at the estate, but you know what my bonnie girl, they don't have long to live. You have been a bigger help than you could ever know. See you soon."

She put the phone down, and thought about what it must be like to have so little regard for a human life. She had once held a gun when on a police operation, but she really didn't like it. Yet, here was Denny coming over to squash humans like they were just bugs to him. A cold feeling went up her spine. Not for the first time when she thought about this man. Maybe he wasn't human after all.

All the men going to Scotland had an early breakfast. Gunther would be over with the men soon. He would be in charge, until Willie was finished with airport runs. Denny looked up and saw Helen putting a lamp in the window. He motioned for her to open the window. When she did, he asked what the lamp was for.

"I will light it each night, so that you will always be able to find your way home."

"Please, come down with the boys as we are heading off."

Even although Tomaz and Yuri were leaving slightly later, Jinty was sitting on Yuri's lap in tears as usual, until he shouted at her.

"Sorry, but we are not all like you, you hard hearted bastard."

Helen came down with the boys, and Denny gave her a big hug, with a gentle squeeze and kiss for the boys. She went to Karl and gave him a hug. Jinty strolled over and gave Karl a kiss. She then walked to Denny, held him tight, looked into his eyes and said," Bring them all home please."

"That's a promise Jinty, believe in me."

Helen just stood there and shouted, "See you soon young Foggerty."

"You sure will young Fraser."

As Denny was sitting in the car, he couldn't believe that this day was finally here. Willie wasn't in the mood for talking, so the conversation was between him and Karl. The traffic was bad, and the journey seemed to last forever, and wasn't helped with Willie blasting the horn at everybody. When they got to the drop off point they got out of the car with their holdalls. Willie came round and grabbed Denny, as well as Karl.

"I'll be waiting for your phone call to bring you home. Give them hell."

As Denny and Karl walked away, Willie wondered if he would see either of them again. There was always something going on in his life since he met Denny Foggerty. Just some peace and quiet would be nice.

The airport was absolutely packed. This wasn't good for Denny trying to keep an eye on people, until Karl told him to relax as he was becoming paranoid. He knew Karl was right. He had told Robertson that it would be a while before he was over. He had thought that Robertson was stupid enough to believe him.

After they had checked in, Karl had told him to shut his eyes for thirty minutes, and he would be awake and alert. Denny was tired as Helen hadn't given him much chance of sleep last night. A while later he got a dig in his ribs from Karl telling him it was time to board. He couldn't believe he had been asleep for over an hour.

When on the plane, he had done his usual and checked everybody out while walking down the aisle. When he got to his seat he stood and looked up and down, much to the amusement of Karl. During the flight, he got to know Karl better, as they had never really had a meaningful conversation at any time. He felt it was okay to tell Karl about his chequered life. Although, Karl had raised his eyebrows a few times, but had thought he was glad he was on Denny's side. They had both refused the offer of food, as they would wait till they got to Edinburgh.

Denny knew that Yuri and Tomaz would be at the airport by now. He would feel easier when they were all sitting in Edinburgh.

When they arrived and walked out the terminal doors, Denny spotted the taxi driver waiting for them. The guy gave them a wave, and went and opened the boot for their luggage. After they got in, Denny just sat there looking at the snow flurries hit the windscreen.

"Is this the snowstorm starting that was expected?"

"Looks like it Mr Foggerty."

"I've told you before, there is no Mr Foggerty, just Denny."

"Okay sir, sorry Denny."

Karl was just laughing in the back. Denny thought he would have to give this guy a break at some stage.

"I presume you know where Luigi's café is pal. Please take us there, as we are both a bit peckish."

The café wasn't far from where he used to live. Shonagh now owning the flat. The snow was getting heavier, and Denny was hoping that Yuri and Tomaz would get here.

It didn't take long for the taxi driver to get to the café. When they had stopped, Denny went into his money belt, took out a sizeable amount of money and gave it to the driver, who was just about to argue, until Denny glared at him.

"I take it that you are off to collect our friends now? Please make sure you get back before the snow gets much worse. The taller of the two has been instructed to pay you for their fare. Remember, none of us got dropped off at the café."

The guy headed off, delighted about the amount of money he would be making from these people.

Denny and Karl went into the café and sat down. People would probably call it a greasy spoon café, but many a time he would eat in there when he was struggling after a day on the whisky. They didn't recognise him, and if they did, they just ignored him, which suited Denny. It was coffee after coffee, while waiting on the taxi to arrive. They thought about going out for a walk, but the snow was getting heavier, so there was no point in getting wet.

Denny was beginning to get a bit irritated, but Karl had said they would be there when they could.

"Denny, for God sake would you just settle down. We need you with a cool, calm head on you. Yet, right from the time we hit the airport, you have been nervously worrying about things that you had no control over. Get a grip man."

It was then that the guy behind the counter shouted that he was closing up, as the snow was getting heavier, and they had to make sure they could all get home.

Denny thought that was all they needed. Just then the taxi they had been waiting on arrived. Yuri and Tomaz got out. The taxi owner said he would wait for a phone call to take them back. Denny went around the taxi, and opened the door. The guy looked a bit frightened, until Denny shook his hand.

"You have been a massive help pal. We will definitely be needing you when our business is finished here. You're a good man."

As the four moved off, the guy sat visibly shaking. Who or what had just shook his hand. This was the part he hated about dealing with this man. The money was unbelievable, but he never slept for a couple of nights after his dealings with him.

"I take it you haven't eaten yet Yuri?"

"No I haven't, but this one here just couldn't help himself with the chocolate that was on sale. I had to stop him, before he had a sugar high."

"Lads, the snow is coming down hard so let's try and get under cover and get some heat in to us, and food for you Yuri."

Denny asked them to follow him, and after half an hour, he arrived at an entrance to some flats.

"Before we go in, let me tell you who lives here. It's my old sparring partner from my time in the police force. Her name is Shonagh, and I wasn't going to come here, but the weather has forced my hand. Please treat her will respect, as she has been a God send, with all the information she has gathered for us."

As they climbed the stairs, Denny was apprehensive about doing this, but they would leave if the snow stopped at any time. When they got to a door, Denny produced a key and opened it, while putting his finger to his lips telling them to keep quiet. He thought she might be away to start her shift. When they got in to the living room music was playing. He hoped she wasn't entertaining anybody, but the door to the hall was ajar and the bathroom door was open. With water being run.

He told the men to wait in the living room, and not to worry if they hear a scream. Denny then slowly walked along the hall, before pushing the door to the bathroom open. He could see Shonagh clearly behind the shower curtain. She was singing to the music from the living room. He then crept to the shower and quickly pulled the curtain back.

Shonagh let out a loud scream, and Denny could see she was a bit shocked to say the least.

"Denny, what the fuck are you doing here, you gave me such a shock."

"What I am doing here, is looking at a lovely naked woman with a beautiful body. What do you think?"

"Bloody well get out Denny, and more to the point, how did you get in?"

Denny produced the key, and then told her she should have had the locks changed ages ago, as her security was rubbish.

"Hurry up and wash your touché Shonagh, as I have some friends in the other room waiting to meet you."

When Denny left, she had to hold on to the taps for a minute. All she could think about was Denny being here. She started to get a really warm sensation between her legs at the top. Then she put one of her hands down, and slowly started to touch herself, until she suddenly realised what she was doing. It was this man that had a profound effect on her. Why did it have to be like this. Always Denny.

When she entered the living room, the men stood up, and Denny started to introduce them, with Yuri and Karl shaking her hand. Tomaz however, put his arms around her and held her tight. It was after a minute that Shonagh asked, "Is he always like this?"

"Every time Shonagh. Leave her be, Tomaz."

Reluctantly he did.

"Can I ask you a favour Shonagh? Yuri and Tomaz haven't eaten today, so is there any chance you can rustle something up for them, but please be aware that Tomaz would eat a horse if you served it up to him."

"I've got a dozen eggs there, so how does scrambled eggs and toast sound."

Denny started to laugh and said, "That sounds about right just for Tomaz."

The men started to laugh, which broke the ice a bit.

After the men had been fed, and everybody was sitting with a coffee, Shonagh said, "Do you men know what you are getting in to?"

They just nodded, with Tomaz gesturing to see if there any more toast, until Yuri told him to settle down. Denny kept looking out the window to see if the snow had stopped.

"You can all bunk down here if you want Denny. I have plenty of blankets."

"Thanks, but no, Shonagh. We need to get to the hotels tonight. Snow or not."

While they were just waiting, Karl asked Shonagh when she had first met Denny. She looked at Denny who just gave a slight nod.

"We were seconded to the same station in the Edinburgh police, which seems another life time away. We worked undercover a lot, to try and take down a drug ring. We did, mainly due to Denny, but to tell you the truth, he worked every day under the influence of whisky. He was given charge of his first big undercover operation arrest, which meant we all had to wear a gun. Unfortunately, so were the suspects, and I ended up getting shot in the shoulder. Denny has organised for me to come over to see a specialist at the end of the year. Loads of other things I could tell you about him, but I won't."

Yuri asked Denny if he had anything to add to all that.

Denny had been looking out the curtain and said, "Nothing, other than she should have ducked. Let's go, the snow has stopped."

After gathering up their holdalls, this time Shonagh gave them all a hug. Yuri had to drag Tomaz away from her. When the men had thanked her and left, it was only Denny standing there. She hugged him like she might not see him again, but she knew to hold back the tears.

"See you when you come over. Oh, by the way, you still have a lovely body on you."

He smiled and walked out the door. It was then that the tears started.

The snow was about a foot deep, with the sky getting darker, ready to drop more on them. The walk was longer than Denny remembered, and their feet were getting wet, but they plodded on until they came to the first hotel, the Leith Water hotel. When they all trudged in Martha recognised Denny immediately.

"Come away in lads, you look wet and cold. Sit yourselves down by the fire. I'll bring tea and coffee right away. Martha was true to her word, and they were soon drinking mugs of steaming hot coffee. Tomaz's eyes lit up when she brought a big plate of chocolate biscuits through.

"I've phoned my brother to say you have arrived, but there is to be no signing of any register. He is fine with that, as am I. The name of the hotel is the Scotsman, and my brother's name is Jim Meikle. He isn't married. At present, he is getting the rooms warmed up for whoever is going to stay."

"Thank you Martha. Your being very kind. Just to set your mind at peace, here is my warrant card."

Denny quickly opened it, and closed it just as quick, with the men wondering what was going on. Martha left looking a bit more satisfied.

"Where did you get that?" asked Karl.

"Shonagh left it lying around. She will never miss it, as she is on desk duties. Don't worry. Here is the story lads. As from tomorrow we must be alert, very alert. Yuri and Tomaz will go

345

round to the Scotsman, and Karl and I will come round after breakfast. We will then work out our next steps. Please take these wooden wedges which I made for each of us, to put under our doors, just in case somebody tries to put their shoulder through it. As soon as it's feasible, we will be heading North. Let's try and get a good night's sleep."

Denny was up most of the night, looking out the widow at the snow coming down hard. At about three o'clock he decided to turn in, as they wouldn't be going anywhere tomorrow. After breakfast, and before going to the Scotsman, he went to the car park at the back and started to clear the snow of Stevie's jeep. The back door opened, and out came the owner George. He had two small spades and brushes as well as several travelling rugs.

"I don't know where and when you are going son, but you're going to need these at some point."

Denny thanked him, and then used one of the brushes to clear the snow off the jeep. He noticed that Stevie had left him with a full tank of petrol. He hoped that when all this was over, he would get to know Stevie better. He stopped what he was doing. His sixth sense was telling him that something wasn't right.

On entering the reception, Martha was on the phone. She just put her hand up, indicating for him to stop a minute. When she came off, she had said that she had been speaking to a young girl, who had been asking if they had any unexpected guests over the last couple of days. She said she was working for the Government, but she didn't believe a word she was saying, and she told her no. Her brother Jim had received the same phone call, and he had told the girl that they had no guests at all with this weather.

Denny had thought it had been Robertson's secretary just trawling through the phone book, and asking the same question to each hotel. However, he needed to speak to the men, and quickly.

Karl and Denny had gone to the Scotsman, and went into Yuri's room. Tomaz was already there, so Denny told them about the phone calls. Nobody said a word until Karl spoke.

"Let's not worry too much about this. It is obvious that he was a bit spooked by Denny's call. I don't believe for one minute, that the guy running the show on the estate, will want to send any of

346

his men down to Edinburgh. So, he has probably told Robertson to make these calls, and when he finds nothing, he will think he has been worrying for nothing. We shouldn't be deviating from our plans one bit."

"Agreed Karl. So we will head off tomorrow, but until then let's just pretend to be tourists. I will show you Edinburgh. Well, as much of it as I can remember from through a whisky haze."

They headed to the centre of the town. Tomaz seemed to be walking with his mouth open all the time, no doubt in wonderment at the beauty of the city. Denny suspected he had never seen many places in his life. None as grand as this though. Denny had taken them to eat in a familiar café in George Street, and told them to soak up the culinary delights of what Edinburgh had to offer, for tomorrow they would be eating store bought food. Denny kept looking at the wall clock, and just about twelve forty, he suggested they walk back to Princes Street.

When they were leaning up against the garden's railing, a massive boom went out. The men hit the deck. They were looking around them, as to what had just happened. Denny stood holding the railing laughing his head off. When they got up, there was still a confused look on their faces.

"Don't worry lads. This is just a tradition that has been going on for a long time. There is a canon up on top of the castle battlements, that is fired at one o'clock each day. Nervous lads? I trust you got a fright?"

They just looked at Denny, shaking their heads, not impressed.

As they walked back, they couldn't help looking around them. Denny thought that they needed to get out of Edinburgh. The men were ready for, and needed action. The day was long for them all, but it was just a matter of waiting it out. Denny went and phoned Stevie.

"I'm passing through Dundee tomorrow pal, and it would be good if we could meet up."

Stevie suggested the Hawthorn Bar in Hilltown, where he would make sure they would get a coffee. Denny knew where that was, and suggested ten o'clock in the morning, as they didn't want to leave before the snowploughs were on the road.

Next to be phoned were Alasdair and Davina. When Alasdair came on the phone he seemed a bit nervous.

"Don't worry Alasdair, it's Daniel here. You can leave the house mid- morning tomorrow. We won't be long in arriving after that. One thing I was going to ask you was, do you have any other guns in the house other than the shotgun?"

"There are two other nearly new single shotguns in the rifle cabinet in the hall. They will need a bit of cleaning, but there is plenty of ammunition in the drawers. I wish you all the best in your endeavour Daniel, and it's been a pleasure for Davina and I to have met you. Look after yourself son."

Denny came off the phone thinking what a nice couple they are. However, he would never see them again. For them, it might be just as well.

Back at the hotel, Denny spoke to George and Martha, and told them they would be leaving after breakfast, but he would pay them enough to keep their rooms available for several weeks, and Yuri would do the same with Jim at the Scotsman.

"Denny, your friend the lady police officer, paid us a very large amount of money the other week. More than we could have imagined."

"They must be paying her too much money Martha. I will have to ask her about that, but I will see you all right tomorrow morning. I insist."

Denny had a restless night, and was prowling around the bedroom from the early hours. He knew that the killing was about to start, and he had to get his head round it. He had been so focused that he hadn't thought much about Helen and the boys. However, he would give them a call tonight, but he would tell her that it would be him that was to do the phoning, not her. Otherwise, she would never be off the phone.

There wasn't much conversation between him and Karl at breakfast the next morning. They had just finished, when the two from the Scotsman walked in.

"Morning men. Yuri did you pay Jim?"

"I did Denny, after a bit of an argument, but I explained that we were on a special ops exercise, and total secrecy about us was paramount to the success of our mission. Sounded good. What do you think?"

"Good enough for me pal. If you can wait for me in the car, I will only be a few minutes."

Just then, Martha and George walked out with several bags of food and handed them to the men. They walked out and Tomaz started up the jeep.

"Martha, George I don't know if we will ever meet again, but I have a funny feeling we will be back for a night or so. I am going to give you this cash, and no arguing please. This is for you both to forget we were ever here. Got it?"

The way Denny said it, they could only nod. When he went out the door, they just held on to each others hand under the reception desk.

"Now I see what you mean Martha. What, or who is he?"

When they started up the road to Dundee, there were just flurries of snow, but when they crossed the Forth Road Bridge it was getting heavier, which wasn't a good sign. The men loved seeing the bridges, and the scenery in general.

"Did you say you were thinking about buying land here Denny?" asked Yuri.

"Yeh, I am Yuri, but it's finding the right place. You will have seen that there are forests everywhere, but it's finding the right place. I don't want to develop an estate from scratch, just enhance it."

After about an hour, Dundee was getting closer, so Denny had told them that they were meeting Stevie for a coffee in the centre of town, but on no account were they to think of this as a 'jolly'. This was business.

As they sat waiting an e-type Jaguar pulled into the car park. Out stepped this suave guy with his collar and tie on, meaning that he was ready to talk business. This had to be Stevie.

Denny got out, walked over and gave him a hug.

"Pleased to meet you Stevie. Nice to put a face to a name pal. C'mon let's go inside as the snow is getting heavier, and I can introduce you to my men."

When they were inside, coffee and biscuits were brought through, as they sat chatting. Mainly about why Denny and his men were over here. When Denny told him about what had been going on he could see that Stevie was getting a bit angry.

349

"I knew that Robertson was bent, but drugs is the lowest of the low. He deserves everything he gets, but I presume he will be nowhere near the estate?"

"Nah, he will be ensconced in his little concrete tower in Edinburgh, full of his own self importance. Don't worry though, they will be having another by-election soon."

They had been sitting for about forty five minutes, when Stevie had suggested they head off as the snow was starting to get heavy, and the sky was black with snow clouds.

"Right Denny, I know you have been itching to ask where your gear is, so I have had Levi and Bohdi pick it up and stored somewhere safe. Unfortunately, these two buggers have gone off the radar, so it wont be tomorrow that you will get the gear, but hopefully the day after. I paid Andrew, and he thanks you very much for the trade."

Denny asked him how much he was due, and when Stevie told him, he ran across the road to the Bank of Scotland, returned with Stevie's cash, as well as cash to replenish both his and Yuri's money belts.

"Well Stevie, I don't know if we will ever meet again, as life has a way of jumping up and biting you in the bum. However, let's hope so."

"It's been a pleasure Denny, and I hope the next time we meet is under happier circumstances. Not during one of your skirmishes into our bonnie country. Oh, and by the way, remember to get rid of the jeep. On no account do you give it to Levi and Bohdi. See you."

Stevie walked away, as the men got into the car and drove up North.

The snow was going to be a hindrance for them as the roads got narrower. The further North they were getting the heavier it was getting. It was making life difficult to see through the windscreen.

"Remember men, as difficult as it is to see through the snow, try and find anything that could be of an advantage to us".

Denny couldn't see the edges of the road, so they weren't making very good progress. After a couple of hours they came to the village of Kingmore. Denny had passed through it when he was last here, and had noticed a general store where they could get their provisions. They were glad to get out the car, and Denny had told them it would only be another half an hour to the cottage.

Just about fifteen minutes later Denny saw a sign that said, The Stag's Head Inn, Hot Food. He pulled on to the track leading to the white building. He told the men to get out as they were going for a hot meal. Their eyes, especially Tomaz, lit up. As they walked in, there was a lovely looking, welcoming lady behind the bar. She was very elegant and introduced herself as Maggie. Short, silver hair. She had a roaring fire going, although there was nobody in.

"Excuse me Maggie, but is there any chance of a meal with coffee?"

"Of course there is lads, but I only have scotch pies with 'tatties' and 'neeps' if that will be alright?"

"That will be fine, although by the look on the lad's faces, they are not sure what to expect, so don't bother trying to explain it to them."

Maggie told them it would be about half an hour, so they should just sit by the fire and warm up. As they were sitting in the armchairs, Denny had said depending on how long they were going to be here, then they would do this on an occasion, giving the impersonation that they were tourists.

A beautiful young girl came from the kitchen, and set a table in the small dining room. Tomaz was absolutely smitten. She smiled at him, and he smiled back, with Yuri telling him to close his mouth. Denny knew right away that this could be a problem. The looks from Yuri and Karl confirmed what he thought.

When the girl came out with the coffee mugs, Maggie had shouted to them that Tallulah was a mute, but she could get by with her own self taught sign language. Tallulah came through with the meals for Yuri, Karl and Denny. She then went back for Tomaz's plate. When she came back with it, everyone just looked at their own plate and then at Tomaz's. Not one mince pie, but two, and heaps of 'tatties' and 'neeps resembling the hills round about. She put her hand on his shoulder when she left the table. They all knew this could turn in to a difficult situation.

"If I am being nosy then just tell me to go away, but I was wondering where you come from lads. We don't often get visitors at this time of year, and especially in this weather."

"No your fine Maggie. We have come up from Edinburgh on a winter survival course which I run. We seem to have picked the right time. The weather is perfect for it. Do you own the hotel Maggie?"

"I just run it for a friend. I often think it's a tax dodge for her. It's fun in the summer, but the clientele has gone down since the arseholes moved in to the estate. Unfortunately, with the takings down, my pal is thinking of selling up, so that would be me out of a home and a job. Ah hell, here comes some of the arseholes I was talking about."

Denny looked out the window and saw a four by four coming up the drive. Now that Maggie was back behind the bar, he spoke to the men.

"Let's finish our meal and get out of here, with no hassle, okay."

Tomaz was sitting at the bar trying to communicate with Tallulah. They were getting on well, until three men from the estate came in and one shouted.

"Hey boys, we have two dummies tonight."

Denny immediately pressed his foot down on Yuri's foot, and shook his head.

"We are here for food and beer. Get us something, and make it quick."

"You can get beer, but there is no food left," said Maggie.

"There must have been food for this lot, pointing to the men, yet none for the men from the estate? What are you playing at you stupid bitch. You should remember who we are."

It was then that Denny held up his hand to the other men, and walked slowly up to the bar. He sat next to where the guy was standing.

"Listen to me you lowlife. I think you should apologise to these two youngsters for calling them dummies. They can't help it. Just like you can't help being ugly. As for calling the owner a bitch, I think you will find that you will no longer be welcome here."

"I say sorry to no one, so you can fuck off."

Denny turned to the men who all gave a nod. He grabbed the guy by the back of his neck, and smashed his face off the bar, with blood pumping from his nose. Maggie jumped out of the

352

way and grabbed Tallulah to protect her. Denny dragged the guy out the door, before unceremoniously throwing him in to the snow. His two friends started to get up, but Yuri and Karl just shook their heads at them. Then Denny came in.

"I suggest that you two go and get your so called friend, and you can all get the fuck out of here."

After the men had left, Denny had apologised to Maggie, before asking to speak to her in private.

"Maggie, I may have a small problem with one of my men and Tallulah. You know, the one with the big appetite. Not a big problem, but it could cause us a bit of a disruption, however when we have finished our mission, I will gladly leave him with you. Here is a phone number you can get me on. I have bought the house on the hill, which used to belong to the Blairs. So please write it down and give it to no one. Also, if your pal ever decides to sell this place, then phone this other number. A girl called Maria will answer, tell her what it all about, and she will know somebody who would be interested in buying it."

When Denny first came up here, he had a feeling that this could be a special place to live. However, he had bigger priorities than that.

"Okay, lads let's go. We will be there in about ten minutes. We might have a problem getting up the track if there is a lot of snow on it, but with the off road gear and our combined weight, we should be okay. Be on alert."

"You do know Denny, that we are likely to get a visit from the guy whose face you just smashed," said Yuri.

Denny just nodded.

A few minutes later the big house on the estate came in to view. Denny suddenly slowed down, eventually coming to a halt.

"Look at the building on the hill on the right, which overlooks the estate. Is it my imagination or are there lights on?"

It was Karl who interrupted him.

"Maybe, the couple who were due to leave haven't, or maybe it's just a mistake from them leaving a light on."

"Trust me Karl, my sixth-sense is telling me neither. Get yourself ready lads."

Denny saw the entrance to the track and although it was difficult, he 'gunned' the jeep between the trees. The vehicle, slewed from one side to the other, before getting over the slight rise at the top. There was an off road vehicle sitting outside the front door. Denny drove the jeep over to one of the outbuildings. When they got out the wind was howling, so he reckoned they probably wouldn't have heard their vehicle.

They chose a couple of small iron bars, a large stone and walked to the door. Denny put his finger to his lips. He walked in to the living room, where two men were busy rummaging through cabinets and drawers. They turned round looking shocked, before the taller of the two started to speak in a heavy Eastern European accent.

"You get out of here. This house belongs to the estate now. Get out or we will throw you out."

Just then the men came through the door and the 'gobby' guy's face went pale.

"Who was it that told you that the house now belonged to the estate you 'shit hole'. I was under the impression that I had bought this land from the Blairs. I think you must be getting mixed up. Now get out of my fucking house you scum, and if I see you up here again I will shoot you. Please convey this to your boss, whoever he is."

The men started to manhandle them out the door, when the guy that was doing all the 'yapping', turned and pointed his hand at Denny and said, "You will regret messing with Radovan. Trust me."

Denny grabbed his wrist and snapped it like a twig, and for good measure, twisted his arm and pulled it down, smashing his elbow, The guy let out a scream. As the other guy got in to the passenger seat Yuri, waited until one leg was still on the ground, before slamming the door. Just to be sure he slammed it again. The guy tried to scream, but for some reason, nothing came out. Strange for having a leg broken in two places. Probably delayed shock Yuri thought. The other guy turned the key, and between them managed to turn the car, and head down the track. There was a lot of screaming coming from the car now, before it was heading in to the estate.

"Tomaz, come in here please. There are guns in that cabinet in the hall. Some might need a bit of cleaning. Make sure they are okay to fire, by taking them to the outbuildings, where you

will find a couple of bales of hay. Fire the guns in to them."
Everyone else, get the food in, and I will start a fire. After you
have put the food away, have a look around the house, and see
what are the best vantage points in case we get visitors, although
I have a feeling we will be getting a visit from the police
tomorrow. Should be fun."

The men got their kit out of the car, and Denny told them that
they would have a bedroom each, as he was going to sleep on the
sofa. He wanted to be near the front window, to see if anybody
might approach. That night was just a case of settling in and
getting sleep, but before that Denny had asked the men to sit
down, and give him their thoughts on how to proceed with their
plan.

It was Karl who spoke first.

"Denny, it is all reliant on the gear arriving to make us safe
and secure. There is nothing we can do, except wait, but
meantime check out the whole of the farm, just in case there are
any surprises in store for us. We have to decide on who will be
doing what job."

It was Yuri next to speak.

"At least there are two of them out of commission after today,
but if there are supposed to be another twenty eight, then I'm
afraid we are up against it. Make no mistake. I am agreeing with
Karl, that we have to exterminate them on a grand scale. How? I
haven't a clue. Maybe we should throw snowballs at them."

They all started to laugh.

"Let's sleep on it, as it's been an eventful day," said Denny.

The morning light couldn't come fast enough for him. As he
had been lying on the couch all night with everything going
through his head. He agreed with the men that killing thirty
people was no mean feat, but there had to be a way, but what?

Tomaz had gotten up early, and started to make breakfast for
everybody. Over breakfast Denny had told them they had to find
the other entrance to the farm, as they didn't want the jeep to be
seen coming and going. They all cleared the table, put on their
boots and coats, and headed outside. The entrance had to be over
by the trees, so they strolled over and spread out. Eventually,
Tomaz started waving and the men ran over to where he was
pointing.

"Bloody hell Denny, there it is and if the snow wasn't there we would have noticed it before. It looks pretty overgrown, but nothing we haven't handled back home."

"Well done Tomaz, and your right Yuri. Tomaz, get into that shed over there and see what tools Alasdair Blair has left us."

Tomaz ran over, and threw himself at the door with his shoulder taking it off it's hinges.

"Oh, for fuck sake Tomaz, I only meant for you to open it."

Tomaz stood pointing to the door, as if to say 'it's open'.

They went in and found a cache of tools including chain saws, axes, and hand saws. All perfect for the job in hand. Denny then asked them to try and take the concave top off the well, just over by the barn. It wasn't easy, as it seemed to have been mortared around the rim. Yuri ran to the shed, brought back a hammer, and started to break up the mortar. After a while, the top started to move, and they managed to get it off. The smell that was emanating from it was awful, and they had to stand away from it, holding a hand over their noses.

"What the hell has been in there," asked Karl.

Tomaz thought he was going to throw up.

"It doesn't matter as it might come in handy for us if we have to get rid of anyone. Let's get the lid back on."

They had no sooner finished, when they heard the roar of a four by four coming up the track. They ran to the house, grabbed the shot guns and put them just inside the door. They all wandered back out, when the vehicle drew up.

The little, jumped up excuse of a police officer that Denny had encountered previously, got out. There was a guy sitting in the passenger side. He obviously didn't recognise Denny and started to mouth off.

"Right, yesterday I received a complaint of two assaults up here, so I am about to charge you all. I want your names, now."

"Firstly, I own this land, and I would like to know who the person in the vehicle is."

"He is from the estate, and I asked for his assistance today, just in case anything kicked off."

Denny didn't say a word. He just opened the vehicle's door, grabbed the guy and frog marched him to the top of the track. He then threw him as far as he could, with the guy sliding down the snow on his back to the bottom, before he took off slipping and sliding towards the estate.

"You can't do that, I am the law around here, and that will be another charge levied at you."

"Ah, shut the fuck up you snivelling little rodent. You are on my land making false accusations against me. The people yesterday had broken in to my home, yes my home, and were threatening to me and the men that have paid handsomely to come on my survival course. If you really are a police officer, then you would know I can use as much force as I need to protect my property and my life."

The officer was about to remonstrate with Denny, until he picked him up by the front of his tunic, lifted him until his feet were off the ground and choking from Denny's grip. He was then carried around the car, where Karl opened the door, and Denny threw him in.

"I will get a squad up here tomorrow to have you all arrested."

"No you won't, as you would have to explain your connection to the estate. You wouldn't want to do that, and remember, everyone around here knows you are on the 'take' from the estate. Now get off my land before I shoot you, if I had a gun."

"Well, this has been an eventful couple of days. I wonder what tomorrow will bring," said Karl laughing.

They got the chain saws, and axes, before starting to hack there way through the trees and bushes. The going was tough after years of neglect, but they kept at it until lunch time. Karl was continually looking down the road to see if the gear was going to arrive.

"Don't worry Karl, the equipment will be here. Two lads I know will not let us down."

"Did you say lads, Denny?"

"I did Karl. Two lads that you've never met the likes of before. It's hard to describe them, but what I will say is, don't be surprised about anything they say or do. Best if I don't say any more."

Karl just looked at him, wondering who the hell was coming with the gear.

Progress was good, and they could actually see the main road, but they still had a way to go.

As the light was fading, Denny called a halt for the day, and everyone cleaned all the tools, ready for the mornings work. As he wandered in to the barn he wondered what was under the large tarpaulin in the corner. When he investigated, he found bags of concrete and lime. Obviously Alasdair had been intending to build something, but had never got round to it. Something switched on in his head, but he would leave it until it was needed.

Denny's sixth-sense was trying to tell him something, but what.

An hour later, Denny jumped up from the seat beside the fire, and told the men to get their guns and be ready. He looked out from behind the curtains to see two headlights on a van of some sorts slewing up the path.

"I am going out first, so get yourselves moving when I shout, with your guns ready, okay. As Denny walked out, the security lights came on, although they weren't great. The van drew to a halt a few yards from him. He shouted, and the men came out with the guns aimed at the windscreen.

"Get out of the fucking van, and put your hands up. Any sudden movement will cause you to be blown apart."

The two guys got out, and when the driver came round and they stood together, Denny looked down to see the old, manky baseball boots they were wearing.

"Bloody hell. It's Levi and Bohdi. It's been a wee while lads."

There they stood, each with a white camouflage tunic on, along with a camouflage cap, grey tracksuit bottoms and their baseball boots..

"All right lads? Last time we met you Mr. Denny, it was going to be death by dog, now it's death by shotgun. Are your dogs around," asked Levi.

Bohdi immediately started to look a bit scared, just in case Udo or Arno sprang out from somewhere.

"Put the guns down lads, and let me introduce you to Levi and Bohdi. Two reprobates from Dundee, although I don't think that anybody here could better them at shooting."

"Or getting the girls Mr. Denny. I'm like a babe magnet since I lost my virginity. They can't get enough of me."

"Shut the fuck up Bohdi. Nobody wants to hear about your three pumps and a squirt."

That set Denny off laughing. It's like they had never been away.

"Right, can you get all the gear out the van, so that we can wipe it down."

"What do you mean wipe it down? Have you been driving around in a stolen van," asked Denny.

"Technically, we have only borrowed it Mr Denny. You see it belongs to Davie Rae, grocer, butcher and drunkard. He will never know where he left it, as he likes the 'drink' too much, a bit like you used to do pal. Anyway, it's his own fault for leaving the keys in the ignition, and please help yourselves to all his stock. Anyway, is your kettle broken? If not, I could murder a 'brew,' so two sugars and milk for us both."

The men just stood there wondering who these young upstarts were.

They all helped to empty the van, before Denny told Levi to hide the van under the large tarpaulin in the barn.

"Can't stay too long pal, as we have to get back, as we know of a party that has been organised. Plenty of young nubile girls. Do you like that word, nubile Denny?"

Denny shook his head before saying, "The pair of you are going nowhere pal. Have a look up the valley."

When Levi turned, and looked up the valley, he could see that the sky was absolutely hanging with snow clouds heading their way. To say he was disappointed was an understatement, and he shouted on Bohdi.

"We can forget the party brother. See what's coming down the valley."

Bohdi was crestfallen. It was like the end of the world was nigh.

"Right, lads let's get in and see what Andrew has procured for us."

"What does procured mean Mr. Denny?" asked Bohdi.

Denny just looked at him, and headed in as the snow started in earnest.

"Get the bags open and lay out everything we have. Karl, you be the judge if we have enough please."

As they were going through the gear, Karl held up two pairs of smallish camouflage trousers, and two arctic sleeping bags.

"Right you pair, is there anything else in these holdalls that I don't know about. I trust that I have paid for these, so tell me now."

"Well Mr Denny, seeing as you are this billionaire sort of guy, we thought that you wouldn't begrudge two impoverished young lads from Dundee a few items."

"A few items? There are more?"

"Well, you see it's like this. Our baseball boots are okay most of the time, but in the snow they can be a bit slippery, so we asked Andrew for a couple of pair of boots each. Oh, and we have a rifle hidden in Davie's van. We told Andrew you would be fine with it."

Denny thought that they had some nerve, but nothing about this pair surprised him. He looked over at Karl, who started to distribute the guns and ammunition to the men, as well as their clothing and boots. When he gave Tomaz his knives, it was like Christmas had come early for him. A big beaming smile creased his face. Karl was just about finished the last holdall when he said, "Bloody hell Denny, look what your pal has left us as a present."

Karl held up two grenades much to everyone's surprise.

Denny looked over at the young lads, who were drinking their tea.

"Okay you pair, I will ask you this once, and if I find you have lied to me, then I will shoot you and drop you down the well. Have you taken a grenade?"

"Mr Denny, I swear on the bones of the lassie I was jumping on the other night, that we don't have any grenades," said Bohdi.

Denny looked at them and noticed that they had diverted their eyes a bit.

"Okay, but you have been through the holdalls to find out what was in them. Haven't you?"

"Just checking the inventory, to make sure you are a satisfied customer pal."

Denny left it at that, as he was never going to get the better of them.

They sat in the living room in the warmth of a roaring fire, basically getting to know each other. Levi and Tomaz were really getting on and making up their own sign language, even laughing at times. Denny just sat there amazed at them. It was late when Levi looked over at Denny.

"Mr Denny, you have an arsenal big enough to take out a lot of guys, but it depends on how you are going to do it. Remember, with a gun you can only take out one guy at a time. You have a great vantage point up here, but there is a lot of open space round about you. You going to tell us what is happening here, as Bohdi and I could help?"

Denny looked over at the men, looking for their approval. They all nodded, so Denny told them everything about himself, and how he had met the men.

"The bastards came over to try and kill you? Bit much that. I won't ask where you dumped the bodies. Can I say though, that you must have been an evil bugger throughout your life, but I take your point, that it's all been for the greater good. A few more questions before we bed down in the van, and the van it will be, as you lot will probably snore, just like Romeo here. Anyway, I have to ask how that fit wife of yours is, and of course the bairns. Also the lovely lassies, Jinty and Maria?"

"They're all good, and Jinty is now living with Yuri, and Maria is going steady."

"No disrespect Yuri, but did Jinty not have a Scottish boyfriend, who wasn't welcome at the wedding?"

Tomaz just drew one of his knives across his throat.

"Looks like we will have to looks further afield when we get over there Bohdi. Let me tell you something Denny, to get rid of that amount of men you need one thing, and that is explosives."

"Over where?" said Denny.

They picked up their kit and went out the door laughing.

Denny had thought today had been a bit of a circus, so tomorrow he would work the men hard clearing the track, and he would rope the young lads in to helping them.

As Denny lay on the sofa that night he thought about yesterday, when he was looking out the window over at the estate, and had made a little silent prayer to the Big Man up above asking if he could give him some help. Maybe a bit of divine intervention, and then Levi and Bohdi turn up. Even the Big Man had it in for him.

Chapter 14

It was about two in the morning. Denny was just trying to get some sleep when the front door creaked. He jumped up, grabbed his gun and shouted, alerting the men.

"Show yourself now, or I will blast you through the door."

Levi appeared through the door with his finger to his lips.

"There are a couple of guys trying to get up the track, although they are slipping and sliding about."

By this time, everyone was up and dressed with their guns in their hands, all except Tomaz who had his knife belt on.

Denny pulled Levi in, and asked him about Bohdi. He had said he was lying snoring, but he had put the rifle next to him in case he woke up.

"Okay lads, you all know what to do. They will be despatched to hell tonight. Yuri, you and Tomaz go out the side door and circle round the front. If possible, I want this to be done quietly. Karl, you and I will meet them at the door. Levi, when I tell you to move, run back to the van, and if he is still sleeping, then get the gun, and point it out the back window. Don't fire it unless we are in danger."

Denny switched off the outside light, took Levi outside, before telling him to make a run for it. He looked around the gable end, and could just see the guys scrambling up the track. They were struggling due to the heavy snow fall. Denny whispered to Karl, that he wanted to take a slight risk, and would only have a hand gun in his belt at his back, but to keep him covered. They stood just inside the door, switched on the security lights and waited until they lit up.

Denny walked out with Karl at his back. Two men stood about two or three yards from them. He could smell alcohol coming from them. They both had hand guns. One of them was the guy whose face he smashed off the bar at Maggie's place. The fact that they hadn't opened fire, made Denny believe that they had been driven to do this by alcohol.

"I see your not so brave now that there is a gun pointed at you, are you?"

"I see that you are more ugly than I thought, and your nose job hasn't helped. I have a feeling that Radovan would kick your arse if he knew you were here."

"He doesn't know, and he doesn't tell us what to do."

Those were the last words the guy would utter, as Tomaz and Yuri were standing behind them.

Tomaz slit one of the guy's throat, and Yuri plunged his knife in to the other guys neck. They all quickly stepped back, as there was a lot of arterial blood spraying around. Denny lunged forward and grabbed their guns in case they accidentally went off.

"Quickly, let's get the lid off that well, but I need to find out how much water is in it. Karl, before we drop them in, please drop a stone down and try and gauge the amount of water by the sound of the splash."

They dragged the bodies over to the well and took the lid off. Levi and Bohdi started to come out of the van, until Denny roared at them to get back in. Karl dropped his stone into the well, before he turned to Denny, and said he never heard a splash.

"Right lads, get the bodies in, and I want the bags of concrete from the barn over here pronto. Levi, Bohdi get out, and start bringing the bags over with rest of us. Tomaz, go and see if you can find a hose and outside tap."

There were plenty of bags, so they just kept tipping them in, until Denny called a halt. Then Tomaz came walking over with a hose, which had to be attached to a tap somewhere. Yuri put the hose in to the well and turned the nozzle on.

"What's your plan for this Denny."

"I'm hoping to cover the bodies as much as we can with the concrete, before pouring the bags of lime in after the concrete has set, although the lid should have a good enough seal on it to keep the smell in. Bohdi and Tomaz, get down the track and with a couple of branches, sweep the footprints away as best you can. Yuri, when you feel that there is enough water in, we will put the lid on, and tomorrow we will pour the bags of lime in, but we need to hose the blood away at the front door. Hopefully, there will be more snow to obliterate any trace of them being up here. Although, I don't think they would have told anybody, just in case it got back to their boss."

As Denny started to walk back his evil smile came over his face, scaring the hell out of Tomaz.

"If everything is cleaned up, then we should try and get some sleep. Levi you and Bohdi get your sleeping bags, and you can sleep on the living room floor, and no arguing."

Denny wasn't worried about the men, it was the young lads that concerned him. When they eventually fell asleep, they weren't having the best of dreams.

Morning came soon enough, and over breakfast Denny had asked everyone what their thoughts were on last night. The men just shrugged their shoulders with the lads copying them. Denny knew he had to get Levi and Bohdi back down the road to Dundee, as quickly as possible.

As they sat eating, they could hear music and shouting coming from the estate. When Denny slightly opened the curtain, a bullet came through one of the small panes at the top. They all hid behind anything they could, in the living room. After a few minutes Denny got up, and carefully looked out again. Yuri looked out from the other side. All they could see was a single guy at one of the balconies, pointing his gun randomly, but wasn't firing it. He was staggering around, and Denny had assumed he had been drinking with the two guys that are now in the well.

Everyone sat on the floor with Yuri saying it looked liked a one off incident, with the guy not knowing where he was aiming. While sitting down on the floor Denny made a decision. Whether is would be the right one or not, would be determined later. Levi got up, looked out the window, ran through to the hall, and picked up one of the rifles with a scope on it. Denny shouted at him.

"Mr. Denny, please, all I need is one shot at the guy. You know I could shoot a gnat's 'dick' off at five hundred yards."

"Shooting a human being is a whole different ball game son. You and Bohdi are working with us today. It will be hard, but if your brother has had any experience in the woods it will be a dawdle for him. So go and get the boots on that I paid for, and we will get out as soon as I am back from the big house on the estate. I'm going to confront the big boss. When I am down there, Karl you and Yuri open the windows and if anything happens to me then put a bullet in Radovan's head, as well as his side kick with the stupid pony tail. Afterwards, we have to get on with that trail."

Denny put his boots and coat on and asked Tomaz to take one of his knives, and remove the bullet from the ceiling beam. The men prepared themselves, as Denny started walking purposely down the track. They watched him cross the road and walk in to the estate, and manage to get right up to the front door, before someone with a gun came out and challenged him.

"I want to speak to the boss, and make it quick, as it's cold out here."

"What do you want?"

"Are you fucking stupid? I want to speak to the boss, and not just the guy just standing inside the door with a gun," Denny shouted.

The guy backed in to the house and after Denny hearing a lot of shouting the guy with the pony tail appeared at the door.

"I am the boss, why are you on the estate? We have work to do here, and you are disturbing us."

It was then that Denny really started to shout.

"Your not the fucking boss, so get him out here now, as this is inconveniencing me. Get a move on."

He too backed in to the house. Again another wait. Eventually, a tall stocky guy with a scar running down one cheek came out. Denny knew it was Radovan. Standing behind him was the police officer from the other day who started to say, "That's the guy who assaulted two of your men Radovan."

"Shut up you little prick, as I want to speak to the boss, not his little monkey."

Denny thought there was a little smirk on Radovan's face.

"Why are you here?"

"I'll tell you why. One of your men fired a bullet through my window up there this morning, just missing my head. So what do you have to say."

"How do you know it was one of my men?"

"Simple. I saw him do it, and this is the bullet which came into my house."

Denny went in to his pocket, with 'pony tail' producing a knife."

365

"Listen 'dick head,' if you are going to pull a knife on me then you had better use it, otherwise I will stick it up your arse. Literally."

Radovan told his man to back down, whereby Denny tossed the bullet to him.

"Why are your men causing problems in this valley? Why can't you just get on with your own business, and leave others to get on with theirs. Just leave me and my men alone. We will be gone when the snow finally clears, and if any of your men come to my property looking for trouble, then I will meet them with force."

"My men won't trouble you again, but remember we have thirty men here, well we did up to this morning. Two have disappeared. You wouldn't know anything about that do you?"

"Not a clue pal," said Denny as he walked away.

"I didn't get your name?" shouted Radovan.

"No you didn't."

Denny strode back to the farm. At least he didn't get a bullet in his back he thought. He had put it in their minds that they were legitimately here, and they would be leaving soon. When he got back in the house, he told them what had been said.

"Not sure that they will believe it if any more of their men disappear. What do you think Denny?"

"You could be right Karl, so let's try and make any more fatalities or injuries look like accidents. With the two injured guys, and the two others stinking up the well, then that could be them down to about twenty six. Not bad for a couple of days work. Right lads let's get some work done. Levi, Bohdi, you will be with Yuri and Tomaz today and you will put in a shift like everybody."

"Don't suppose we're getting paid for this pal?" asked Bohdi.

Denny just glared at him, before Bohdi looked away. The going trying to clear the other track was hard, so Denny had told Tomaz to make everyone a tea or coffee every hour and a half. The men worked tirelessly, and it wasn't long before they were nearly at the bottom. It was then that Denny heard the noise of motor engines.

He ran down and looked up the road. Here was a convoy of vans towing caravans coming down the road. There must have been at least a dozen. Denny stopped the first van and asked them where they had come from. The guy said it would be better if he should ask the guy at the very back.

The convoy slowly passed, but the last van never slowed down. He was about to turn back up the track until he heard the sound of horses hooves. Surely that can't be right he thought, until he walked to the middle of the road and looked in to the distance. He thought his eyes were deceiving him as a beautiful gypsy caravan was slowly coming down the road. It was being pulled by two magnificent cobs.

When they were getting closer Denny waived them down.

"What can I do for you son?"

"Hi, my name is Denny, and I own the farm up there, pointing to the farm. Where have you come from?"

"My name is Tucker Beany. Head of the gypsies on the east coast of Scotland. The gypsy king. We were in a field just round the bend of the hill along the road, but the police and the estate put pressure on the farmer, and he told us we had to leave. It happens all the way up this valley. We are getting fed up with it. It's soul destroying."

"Tucker, I might have a solution to your problem. How about you come up to the farm tonight for a bite to eat, and we can discuss it. Say about seven thirty?

It was then that Denny got a fright, as a head popped out. Tallulah poked her head out and was hastily pointing at herself.

"Sorry son, this is my daughter Tallulah, and although she is a mute, she is a handful, so I would love to come and speak, but I would have to bring her.

By this time she was standing on the seat looking up to where the men were working. When she saw Tomaz, she started waving furiously until eventually he saw her, and came running down the track. When he got to the caravan, they started to converse in their own made up language.

"What is happening here?" enquired Tucker.

Denny explained about meeting Tallulah at Maggie's place.

"That explains why she was rather animated when she came in the other night. I take her down to the pub, and Maggie gives her a bit of pocket money, for not doing very much. She seems to get on well with the lad."

"Too well pal, and yes bring her with you. Tomaz, get back up that track and get working."

As they took off down the road, she was still waving, as was he, on his way back up the track. Denny knew he had to have a word with him after tonight, but he didn't want to discourage the lad.

Denny had told the men not to cut back the trees on the side of the track facing the estate, but it sat that far back, he doubted anyone could see a vehicle going up or down. They all worked tirelessly for the next few hours, before the track was cleared. Denny went in and made tea for everyone.

"What, no chocolate biscuits Mr. Denny. It's a bit much," said Levi.

"We never bought any at the store son."

"God, do I have to do everything myself."

He walked to the van, and came out with a bundle of chocolate biscuits.

"I told you to get all the stock out of the van. Davie Rae will think he has had a good week when he eventually gets his van back. I sometimes wonder about you Mr. Denny. Let me give you a bit of advice. You can't have a 'brew' without a chocolate biscuit. Get a grip man."

Denny could see that he was serious, and just smiled.

After they had cleaned all the tools, Denny told them that they would have company tonight, so it would be better if they all bathed, as it had been a hard, sticky day and everyone had been sweating a lot.

"Men, I want you to think about accidents, or unusual disappearances over the next few days. We have to reduce their numbers."

They all helped with the dinner, and it was about seven fifteen when they heard a van coming up the drive. Everyone went in to the danger mode, and stood with their guns ready.

Denny looked out and saw it was Tucker, but he was still wary as he had only met the guy for a few minutes. He came to the door and knocked. When Denny opened it he still had the gun pointed at Tucker, just in case there was someone behind him. There was, Tallulah.

When everybody was seated, with the lads plonked on the floor, Tomaz had come through with a tray of soft drinks, and had handed Tallulah hers first.

"Well, son I am not going ask who you or your men are, or what you are doing here. I presume it has something to do with the estate. However, if you want to wipe them out, then fine by me, and if we can help then we would do all we can. Unfortunately, we have to do things within the letter of the law, or we would be persecuted for ever."

Denny sat looking at him. His sixth-sense wasn't telling him very much, and he thought he was a good judge of people, so he asked the men."

"What do you think lads? This might be the break we need."

They all looked at each other, and nodded.

"Tucker, it's a bit of a long story, but these evil bastards tried to kill all of us, and our families a while ago. So, we decided on retribution. Their boss is an MP in Edinburgh, but technically a puppet, as the main man is the guy called Radovan, who is down in the big house. One way or another, we will send all of them sailing in to Hell. I want you to go away and speak to your people. Put it to them that I have a field on the edge of the farm. What I am proposing is, that you can pitch your caravans and vans on it anytime you want, but there will be conditions. Mainly, that hard stands are put in for both the caravans and your vehicles. The access would be from the track that you saw us working on, and it would need constant maintenance. You, being the king of the gypsies, would be in charge of making sure the place would be kept in tip top shape, with no dogs running wild. I am not trying to make demands, but I am not wanting people contacting me about problems from you."

"Denny, that sounds terrific, but I would need to speak to my men to see what they think. Would it be possible for two or three of them to come with me tomorrow to see the field? However, Denny what could we do for you in exchange or can we pay you an annual rent for the field."

"Tucker, there will be no rent, and I am sure you could help us out in some way, but we can discuss that at another time. How about we say ten o'clock tomorrow morning, but before you go please tell me what vehicle you will be in for obvious reasons, and please use the track we have just cleared."

Tucker left about an hour later, after getting something to eat, although it was a struggle to get Tallulah to go with him, until Denny raised his voice at her. When she walked past him, the look on her face just about said it all.

"Tomaz, go and get two of the high powered torches that Andrew gave us. We need to have a last walk around the farm, before we turn in."

The two of them walked to the far side, and when Denny's reflected off the bags of lime, he realised he had made a mistake in not putting bags in the well. He was angry, and turned to Tomaz, and said that would be his job in the morning, along with the young lads.

"Tomaz, did you realise that the lime hadn't been put in the well? If so, why didn't you or any of the others say something?"

Tomaz, just shrugged his shoulders.

While walking along the outer edge of the trees, Tomaz suddenly grabbed Denny by the arm stopping him. He then pointed to where a pair of stunning, amber eyes were caught in the beam of the torch. They stayed as still as they could until the animal moved.

"Bloody hell Tomaz. Look at the size of that male fox. I've never seen the like. It's massive. What a privilege."

Only when the fox moved on, did Tomaz release his grip on Denny's arm. What came to Denny, was the fact that it could have been anyone from the estate, and they had nothing to protect themselves. Another mistake.

Denny told Tomaz to sit down under a large tree where there wasn't any snow.

"Right Tomaz, I'm going to tell you something, so you had better listen or else. I know you like Tallulah, but you have only just met her, so please don't think this is it. Remember, we have a job to do, and there will be plenty of time afterwards for you to get to know her. Please think about this though. If you screw up this mission, because of what you have between your legs, then I will shoot the fucking thing off. Got me?"

Denny was waiting for the thumbs up, which duly came. It was then that Tomaz started his own sign language, which

370

amounted to him asking Denny if it was love at first sight with Helen. Denny thought that the little bugger had out done him.

"Never mind me, its you we're talking about, lets walk."

Tomaz was laughing.

When they got back, Denny's anger had come back.

"Right, please listen everybody. We are making mistakes. Why did no one, including me, think about putting lime in the well? Why did nobody pull Tomaz and I up for going out without a gun. We have to start thinking out of the box, and as from tomorrow we will all have our jobs to do, and we stick to them. Karl, you and Yuri put your heads together, and think of ways to eliminate the people from the estate, and I need to find out what is happening in the cellar of the big house. Remember accidents where possible. Tomaz, I want you to use the scope to record all the comings and goings at the estate."

Everyone seemed in agreement until Levi 'piped' up.

"Seems like you have forgotten us again big man."

"You two will make this place like a fortress. For instance, shutters on the window, more locks etc on the doors. Security lads. Oh, and by the way, after that, you're going home."

"Are you having a laugh Mr. Denny? You can't send us back now. We can be your top snipers. There is nobody better."

Denny just shook his head, while the boys picked up their sleeping bags and headed for the van. In the 'huff'.

The next day arrived with more snow. The men went about their business, which Denny had spoken about the previous night. It was mid morning when Yuri who was looking out the window with the rifle scope shouted.

"There is a black pick up truck coming up the far away track, with three people in it. I recognise Tucker, but I don't know who the other two are.

"Okay men, Let's be cautious. Get the guns."

Yuri ran to the side door and crept round to the front. As Tucker, and the two other guys got out, all the men stepped out the house, with their hand guns cocked and ready.

"It's okay Denny, they are with me."

"Put your hands up lads. Karl search them please. No disrespect lads, but we can't be sure."

After Karl had given a nod, Denny asked them inside.

"No Tallulah today Tucker?"

"No, she is at Maggie's place, although I think it's just company for the both of them."

Tomaz looked disappointed.

The men accepted a coffee, before Denny had said that they should go and look at the field in question. When they got to the top field, it was like the men's eyes had lit up.

"There it is folks. You will see a stream running down the far side, which you can harness for your water. The track entrance can't be seen from the estate, although that might not be a problem soon."

"The field looks perfect son. All the hard stands would be put in by us in no time, and I can assure you we take a pride in where we live. Contrary, to what certain people think. Can I ask you who will be living in the house?"

"At the moment, I don't really know, but something is niggling at me, but I would let you know as soon as I could. You don't have to give me your answer right now, however I feel things are going to escalate here."

The three men walked to the side, and started chatting. When they came back, Tucker said they would gladly accept Denny's offer, and if there was anything they could do to help him, then they just had to ask.

"Tucker, if you get the chance to get rid of any of the men from the estate, without being caught by the law, then please do it."

"Well, Denny we are being plagued by two guys in particular who decide to drive through our camp, playing loud music, shouting obscenities with a rifle hanging out the passenger side. We are no longer going to put up with it anymore. So, at some point soon, there will be two men less on the estate. We'll say goodbye to you."

All the men were getting on with their jobs. Denny was quite impressed with Levi and Bohdi's efforts to put shutters up on all the windows. Not the prettiest, but enough to stop anybody throwing a lighted torch through the windows. Tomaz was busy writing down all the vans and cars going in and out of the estate.

Denny told the men he had to make a couple of calls, so please give him some privacy.

The first was Helen, who was so excited about the call. She had said she had been worried sick, not knowing where he was, or if he was safe. He asked about the boys, and she said they were fine, but missing their dad. She asked when he was coming home.

"Helen, you have to stop worrying me. You will make yourself sick, and you will be of no use to the boys. Unfortunately, it's going take longer than I thought. Too many outside factors aren't helping. I'm confident that we are going to come out of it safe. I love you and the boys, but I need to speak to Willie."

She went and got Willie.

"Hi brother, how many men have you to sent to hell so far? Before you ask, everything is fine here. The men that Gunther picked are all good workers, and very polite to the ladies here. I take it you're going to be over there for a wee while longer?"

"Yeh, it's not going quite to plan. You were right, it's difficult to get rid of thirty odd men. Only two so far, with another two incapacitated. Anyway we have plans. You'll never guess who we have helping us, if that's the right word, Levi and Bohdi."

"Bloody hell Denny, tell me your joking? I bet they still have the same baseball boots, have they?"

"Spot on brother. Now, please put Jinty on as I bet she is 'champing at the bit' to speak to Yuri. Speak soon."

When Jinty came on, he disguised his voice a bit and said that he loved her.

"Oh, I love you too. Wait a minute, is that you Foggerty, you bastard. Get Yuri on the phone this minute."

He shouted on Yuri, gave him the phone, and left him in peace.

He asked the men if the lime had been put in the well. Bohdi had said that that it had, although it still stank, but not as bad as he thought it would be, but it had been done.

"Do you think we can use it again Karl?"

"Not sure Denny. If we need to use it again, then when we have finished here, we will need to really blow it up, and fill in what is left, but it's still an option."

As they sat around the fire after supper, Denny suggested they go for a run up the road tomorrow, carrying on the pretence that they were on a survival course. They all agreed, as they had done it many times before. The lads thought that they were winding them up, until they could see by their faces that they were serious.

"Yuri, can you go with the lads and do once around the perimeter, checking the sheds. Oh, by the way, while Tomaz and I were walking around last night, we saw the biggest dog fox I have ever seen in my life, so beware."

He saw the look on Bohdi's face, before saying that the fox was the size of a pony, had bright glowing eyes and had massive fangs. Everyone was trying not to laugh. That was it for Bohdi though.

"Sorry Mr. Denny, I refuse to go into that forest. It was bad enough seeing that big white stag back in Bavaria, but if anything resembles a devil dog, then I am not taking the chance that I will walk around a tree, and there it is. You can shoot me as a coward, like they used to do."

"How about I boot your arse right around the forest. Instead of shooting you. Either way I am fine with."

"Okay, but I'll need a weapon. Maybe one of these handguns."

"Bohdi. The only weapon you will get is a stick you can find in the forest, so get on with it. If you meet it, then your screams will chase it away."

"Okay for me to get my gun out the van Denny?"

"Yeh, you can get your 'pop' gun, and take it with you Levi."

As Yuri and the boys left the house, Levi ran to the van and came back with his so called 'pop' gun.

"For fuck sake Levi. Let me see that rifle. Do you know what that is?"

Levi looked a bit sheepish, and handed it to Yuri.

"Bloody hell Levi, this is a Winchester Model 70 action. Where did you get this about? This is a highly sought after hunting rifle, and very expensive. I would hate to be you when you show this to Denny."

"Does he have to know Yuri?"

"Yip."

The journey around the perimeter was uneventful, and no devil dog was seen, although Bohdi's head was on a swivel.

When they got back, Yuri said to Denny that Levi had something to show him. Reluctantly, he handed over the rifle.

"Where the bloody hell did you get this? Don't tell me, you got it from Andrew, didn't you.? How much did this cost me?"

"Now Mr. Denny, your getting yourself worked up over nothing. Andrew said he would do us a good deal. We were being thrifty, don't you think?"

"It was Levi's idea Mr. Denny," said Bohdi.

Within seconds, they were wrestling around on the living room floor, with the men poorly with laughter. Denny separated them by straddling Levi, and pinning Bohdi with one hand to the floor. After telling them to calm down, it was Karl who spoke next.

"I've got a great plan Denny. Why don't we take the pair of them down to estate. Open the main doors, and throw them in. What do you think?"

Everyone went to bed laughing and smiling. All except Levi and Bohdi, who were going to the van to start round two.

After they had a very light breakfast next morning, it was left to Tomaz to decide where they were going to run this morning. It didn't take a lot of working out, as after they got their tops off, he pointed down to the field where the gypsies were. It wasn't a problem for Denny.

"Karl, watch over the property, and keep safe. Remember, shoot anybody your not sure about."

"Sound Denny."

They took off at a reasonable pace, but Denny knew that Tomaz would increase it the nearer he got to the camp, hoping that Tallulah would be watching. The blowing snow was making it difficult, as well as really cold. Denny thought that the cold in Scotland was more intense than anywhere else in the world, or maybe it just felt like it. They reached the track before the field, when they heard a shout.

It was Tucker, waving to them from a caravan door for them to come in. They jumped the fence, and went along to his caravan. He ushered them in and asked if they were mad, running bare chested in this weather. Denny explained about the façade, and they weren't doing this for pleasure. Tallulah came through from the back, much to the relief of Tomaz. She gestured that she was going to make tea for everyone and what did they want.

Tomaz moved quickly, and they left for the kitchen area to organise tea.

The tea was most welcome, and they just sat chatting.

"There will be two men less for you to worry about after tonight. They were driving around the field last night, almost hitting one of the children. There will be no more of this intimidation Denny. I will let you know though."

Everyone thanked them for the tea, and said they had to get back, much to the annoyance of Tomaz.

While they were running back, some of the men from the estate started jeering them. They were nearing the first entrance to the farm, when a van came flying past them, with no regard for their safety. Obscenities were shouted out the windows.

"Keep calm everybody, as soon they will all be going to hell. I know I keep saying it, but I am fed up with these arrogant bastards, thinking they can do what they want. Believe in me men. Believe."

When they got back, Denny got on the phone to Stevie.

"Hello my friend. Hope you, and the family are well. Can I ask you a favour, a big favour. Is it possible to keep the lads here until the mission is finished. They are handy as look outs, if we happen to be doing other things."

"Not a problem pal, but as I have said before they have to be kept away from any danger."

Denny thanked him, before telling him about the hi-powered rifle in Davie Rae's van, as well as their camouflage gear.

"Denny, nothing surprises me about these little buggers. I don't know why they latched on to me, and maybe I should have booted them in to touch a long time ago, but they are such likeable characters. Don't worry about the van, as Davie has been known to go on two or three week benders at a time. Keep them safe though."

"I promise Stevie."

He wandered through to the living room.

"Right you pair. You have a stay of execution, as Stevie doesn't want you back for a while, but you must pull your weight. Okay?"

They sat there high fiving each other, and yet last night they were knocking lumps out of each other.

"Denny, can you come here a minute please."

Karl was standing with the scope at the window.

"Have a look at the trees behind the house. Every day about this time, there is a guy walking with a gun. Obviously, just walking the perimeter, just as we do. Take a look at the river he is walking beside. It's on flood. Now, if he happened to slip on the snow, banged his head on a rock, then he would tumble in to the river, and it would be good night for him. He never changes his time or routine. Probably full of alcohol. What do you think?"

"Looks promising pal. Let's see if he changes his routine tomorrow, and if he doesn't, then we go for it the day after. How do you suggest we do it."

"Easy. If you put your eyes on the snow drifts at the back of the trees, then you could bury yourself in one, and lie in wait. You would only need a small peep hole to see him coming, and as he passes, take the boulder you make sure you have, and hit him over the head toppling him in to the water. The boulder, and his gun goes in with him. An unfortunate accident."

"Are you up for it Karl, and would it just be you?"

"Just me pal, and hopefully it will be snowing, but if you can come up with a small diversion at the front of the house, that would be even better.

"Sound pal. Let me think about the diversion, but I already have an idea."

Denny had decided they had to eat a bit better, so he told them they were going to Maggie's place, so go and get ready. Karl said he would give it a miss as he wanted peace to work out his plan for tomorrow.

When they were going up the track at Maggie's, they saw a large four by four sitting at the door. It could only mean one thing, and that was men from the estate were in.

"Listen everyone. We are going in for food, nothing else. If they intimidate us, then we walk away. You pair from Dundee, 'zip' it."

As they entered the bar, Maggie said she was pleased to see them. Denny was under the impression that she had been getting hassle from the estate men.

"Could you do us five meals Maggie please? Whatever you have would be fine by us."

"No worries son. Tallulah and I will rustle something up, so if you want to sit beside the fire, we will be as quick as we can."

They all sat around the fire, drawing looks from the estate men, with the occasional comment, which Denny couldn't quite hear. Ponytail was holding court as usual. There were four of them, all drinking heavily. When the meals came, Denny couldn't decide who was stuffing it in their mouths quickest, Tomaz or the lads.

Ponytail shouted that they wanted more drink, and to get the girl to bring it over. Tallulah walked over with tray full of spirits, and when she had to stand beside ponytail, he put his hand up her skirt a bit and rubbed her leg. Denny wasn't fast enough to stop Tomaz. He bolted over, and sat down in the chair next to the guy. Tomaz just sat wagging his finger, and staring at him.

"What do you want you little, fucking mute. Disappear, before I teach you a lesson."

Denny strolled over.

"I'll tell you what he wants. He wants to stick the knife he has pressing against your ribs into the coward- like heart of yours. Slowly, and I mean very slowly, no sudden movements, lift your right arm, and you will see what I mean."

Ponytail lifted his arm, and sweat suddenly appeared on his forehead.

"If you do that again to the girl, or call either of them a mute, I won't stop his knife being pushed in to your scrawny body. Got me."

The guy nodded.

"Just so that we are clear. At some point, you will wonder if there is a ghost standing at your shoulder. A ghost you can't see, but a cold chill going up your back. A ghost that is waiting to despatch you to the Land of the Dead, when the time is right. Well that ghost is me."

Ponytail went white, and couldn't look Denny in the eye. There was a chill going up Maggie's back, never mind anybody else. She looked at Denny, and wondered who this was.

"Right, let's go lads as there is a stench coming from this lot. The stench of fear. Maggie can I speak to you please. Somewhere private."

Maggie had a small office just inside the main door, so she nodded for him to go in there.

"Maggie, your takings will soon take a big dip when the men from the estate won't be coming in here, so please take this cash, as it will get you through to the Spring, when hopefully the tourists will arrive. Please don't argue. I know it's a lot of money, but to be honest, money doesn't mean a lot to me."

"My God son, this is an unbelievable amount of money, and I really thank you. Why won't the estate men be coming in here?"

Denny went in to his back pocket, and flashed her Shonagh's warrant card.

Maggie stood at the main door watching them leaving. As they drove up the track, She didn't believe for one minute, that Denny was a police officer. She thought he was more the Devil Incarnate.

When they got to the farm, he asked Yuri and Tomaz to have a walk with him to the quarry that Alasdair had told him about. It was about a twenty minute walk, before they came upon what was just a massive hole in the ground. When they looked in, they saw various farm machinery, just lying in various states of disrepair. They didn't spend too much time at the edge.

"Another potential body dumping site Yuri?"

"Yeh possibly Denny, but we all need to have a long talk about this, as I am not sure we are going about this the right way. It's taking too long. It's not that I am that desperate to get home, but the longer we are here, then things can go 'belly up'." We should speak about it tonight."

As they walked back Denny was lost in thought. Was he losing his grip on this venture, or was he just hoping that things would happen, without intervention from him or his men. When they got near the farm he turned to Tomaz and said he needed a word with him about earlier. However, Yuri had said he would do it if Denny would just walk on. Half an hour later, Yuri and Tomaz walked in with Tomaz's face 'tripping' him. He went away to his bedroom.

"What did you say Yuri?"

"I just told him to curb his jealousy, as it might put the mission in danger. I told him that it's not that he couldn't see Tallulah, but not in the same environment that he was in today. I'm not sure I can trust him one hundred percent, so it's a case of keeping an eye on him. We've all been there".

Nothing much was happening. Tomaz was still taking note of vehicles in and out of the estate. The lads were cleaning the guns and knives. All mundane stuff.

It was later on that Yuri called a meeting.

"Okay, men I have spoken to Denny about this, and I want your opinion. I feel the mission has stalled a bit. We were all in agreement, as to how we would proceed with this venture, but we need to hear from all of you, to see if you have any ideas to speed this up. Everyone will have their say. Denny you first"

"I think I have been a bit blinkered, as to how this mission was going to 'pan' out. Obviously, cut and thrust will only work on a short term basis, but even if Tucker gets rid of these two men then I reckon we will still have about twenty men, that we know of, to deal with. I'm sorry, but I think I have underestimated the job we have to do. Karl, what about you?"

"Well Denny I think you are right. Even if I eliminate the guy tomorrow, we don't know if they could get reinforcements from somewhere. Plus, if people keep disappearing, then Police Edinburgh could come down on us, not just that little 'squib' that is in Radovan's pocket. Now, you might think my idea is fanciful, but I think we should blow the fucking lot up.

There was silence before Levi spoke up.

"I said that days ago Mr. Denny. One almighty explosion takes our problem away. You should listen to me more often big guy."

Denny sat looking at looking at Karl, and then Levi, before he spoke.

"But how?"

"Give me a few days, and I will have it worked out, but tomorrow, please remember I need a diversion if I am going to kill the sentry. You worked it out yet Denny?"

"I have Karl, so everyone listen. You know the old shed at the front of the farmhouse. When I give you a signal, you set it on fire. There is petrol in the barn, but don't be seen throwing it on. I then want a lot of shouting and swearing. Enough, that it will attract all the 'wankers' at the house to come to the front. I need them to think we are panicking, so it has to be realistic. Yuri will be standing ready with the water hose ready to douse it, when I

380

see Karl has done his bit. This will be mid afternoon, but Karl will set us straight. He will, however, give us time to get the shed blazing. Any questions?"

Nobody had anything to say except Bohdi.

"You never asked me Mr. Denny, but if you had, then I would have said that we should blow them up."

"How did I know you were going to say that son," said Denny walking away shaking his head, thinking that it would fall off with this pair.

He went through to one of the bedrooms, put his head on the pillow, and went out like a light. It was a few hours later, when he suddenly woke up in a bit of a state. He ran through to the lounge, where everybody was just milling around.

"You must have needed it partner, as Artem would have said."

"Your right Yuri. Things are getting on top of me. Let's get this job done and hopefully within a couple of weeks we will back in the arms of the ones we love. Levi, Bohdi I have another important job for you. Do you know how to 'work' prefabricated sheeting? If so, I need you to make the same type of shutters for the windows, but this time for the outside. There are plenty of sheets in the outhouses, but I don't want them put up just now. Can you do it?"

"Are you having a laugh with us. We come 'frae' Dundee pal. We can do anything you ask us. Oh, and by the way, am I getting my rifle back?"

"Just a simple 'yes' would have been sufficient, and the answer is no. Yuri has it now, and if need be, you will use his. Got it?"

This seemed to placate Levi a little, but Denny knew he would have to keep an eye on them, especially when it was time to leave this place. An inventory of the guns would have to be taken, or maybe an inventory of everything would be taken, or maybe everything would be disposed of.

The boys went to the sheds, and within minutes there was a lot of cutting and hammering going on, so he just left them to it.

After tea, he suggested that they should all go for a wander in the forest. The house was getting a bit claustrophobic for them all, and he knew he had to mix things up a bit. They had never explored further than a few hundred yards from the farm house.

Karl stayed in the house, finalising his plan for tomorrow. Denny hadn't realised the extent of the forest, and wondered about the potential of this farm. Plenty of grazing for any animals, although they would have to be pretty hardy to survive the winter. He thought that wouldn't be his problem though, although he had to have a think about what was going to happen to the place when they returned home. He was more confident than ever that they would all return home.

Suddenly a scream came from Bohdi, and he ran past everyone, at a speed that Tomaz would be proud of. They all got their hand guns out, ready for what was going to be thrown at them. Until Yuri burst out laughing. In front of them were two sets of eyes this time. A male fox and vixen, just standing watching them. Denny wondered why they weren't scared of the men, but he assumed they must have watched Alasdair over the years, so nothing bothered them now.

"Bloody hell Yuri. They are two magnificent beasts. There must be an abundance of rabbits for them to develop like that."

"Mr Denny. That brother of mine is a bloody embarrassment. Maybe we should tie him to one of the trees overnight, and see if he gets over his fears. There might be a better idea though. When we come and stay with you in Bavaria, if I was you I would put him in charge of your dogs. What do you think?"

"Son, that is your brother you are talking about, and there will be no sacrificial rituals on my land. As for you coming to stay in Bavaria, you can forget it, as I love my dogs too much to let you pair loose on them."

Denny had been trying not to smile, but he turned to see Yuri and Tomaz laughing. He couldn't help it, and suddenly burst out laughing, sending the foxes scuttling in to the far reaches of the forest.

Levi was the only one that wasn't laughing.

When they got back, Karl had said that Bohdi had gone to the van, a bit upset. Levi said he would go and see him, as he could do with an early night, plus he would have words with his brother. Denny pointed a finger at him.

"Listen, Levi. We all have our fears, so leave him alone."

"What's your biggest fear big man?"

"Mine? The thought of you pair landing on my doorstep."

Levi went away in the huff.

The wind howled all night, and Karl thought that it would build up a few drifts at the back of the house. As he lay there, he wished this was all over. Killing was becoming too easy for the men. He wanted to be back in Zwiesel, just working in his shop. This would be the last lot of killing for Denny, as it was all getting too much for him.

It was about ten o'clock, when Tucker came up the track with Tallulah sitting in the front. As much as he didn't like doing it, Yuri and Denny walked out with their hand guns ready.

"Sorry Tucker, but you know I have to check the back of your vehicle."

Tucker put his hands up in acknowledgement, and nodded his head.

"C'mon in Tucker, and have a 'brew' as my young lads from bonnie Dundee would say. Tallulah, Tomaz will be through just now."

She motioned that she would make the tea for everyone, and headed to the kitchen.

"Denny, the reason I am here, is to let you know that there are two less men from the estate to worry about. Last night they drove in to the camp, obviously drunk, while wildly firing a rifle in the air.

However, we were ready for them. As soon as they reached a certain point, we boxed them in with a couple on transit vans, and the men went about rendering them unconscious. After tying them up, we stuffed them in the boot of their vehicle, took a chance and drove them to the Fife coast, where we know of a place where the sea is very deep, and despatched them to the fishes, off the cliffs.

We know we will have the police visiting us, but I thought it was courteous to let you know. The police don't bother us, as a visit from them is an ongoing situation."

Tallulah and Tomaz came through with the tea for everyone.

"Tomaz, please ask Tallulah if she has forgotten the chocolate biscuits?" asked Levi.

Nobody could help themselves, and laughed, as Levi had been deadly serious.

"Thanks for coming Tucker, and keeping us up to date. I have no doubt that we will get a visit from the little 'prick' that calls himself a police officer. There one thing though. I know I have no right to ask this, but do you know anyone who can get us dynamite?"

Tuckers mouth dropped open, as he stood and stared at Denny.

"Are you serious son? I thought that when you mentioned that before, you were joking."

"I never joke about something like that Tucker."

"I'll have to have a think about that Denny, as you've caught me off guard. I may have to take one or two of my men in to my confidence, if that would be okay? How much would you be looking for?"

It was then that Karl came in to the conversation.

"It's simple Tucker. Enough to blow the big house to smithereens. Nothing to be left standing. I know it's a tall order, but I feel we could be in danger, unless we do this in one fell swoop."

Tucker sat their looking in to his mug, before he said, "Something has just came in to my head. I will have to make some discreet enquiries, and then I can get back to you. If the person I am thinking about is still alive, then we may have a chance."

"Thanks Tucker. Please get back to Denny as soon as possible.",

Now it was all about Karl. He said he would arrive at the house from the field next to it and then walk through the trees at the back. He told Denny, that as soon as he had disappeared under a drift, then to light the shed up. Karl donned his gear, and only took a hand gun with him.

"Karl, what happens if they catch you?"

"Then shoot me Denny. I mean it."

He took off out the back of the farm keeping out of sight of the house. Even when he was in a crouched walk, you only knew he was there by the movements of his body. Denny had a scope on him all the time.

"Right everyone, get to where you should be. Remember, this has to be believable."

384

At the last minute, Denny saw Karl bury himself in the drift and shouted on the men to light up the shed. With cans of petrol being thrown on from the back, it wasn't long before the shed was ablaze.

"Now everyone, get shouting, and throw buckets of snow on the shed."

Denny thought this was a pure, amateur dramatic farce. They were shouting and swearing, and he saw all the men from the estate were standing at the front of the house laughing and cheering. He then saw one of the men walking down by the river. This was the guy that was sailing in to hell in a few minutes. The guy looked a bit unsteady on his feet.

Even being a few hundred yards away, he got a shock as Karl suddenly sprung out from the drift, and smashed the guy over the head. He toppled in to the swollen river, gun and all. Karl threw the boulder in with him. Just a tragic accident. A text book operation. Denny gave one of his evil grins. He wondered what he might do, when they were all blown to bits.

Karl made his way in to the field he had arrived in, and started running towards the road, jumped the fence, and came up at the back of the farmhouse. He ran in to the lounge, and looked at Denny.

"It would take us forever to get rid of these men at this rate pal. It's done now, but sooner or later they will put two and two together, and then they will come for us."

Yuri was dousing the shed with the hose by this time, and everybody had quietened down. Even the men from the estate must have been getting bored, as they were drifting away. No sooner had Karl changed, when a police vehicle came up the track. This time there were two officers in it. When it stopped the little prick from before, stepped out.

"Oh, for fuck sake, not you again. What is it you want this time, or are you just here to piss me off".

The other guy never moved.

"I'm here investigating the disappearance of two men from the estate last night. There are suspicious circumstances. Do you know anything about it?"

"Why the fuck would we know anything, you little arsehole, and what are the suspicious circumstances. I'll tell you what they are. None, but feel free to look around, but as you don't have a warrant, then not the house, or I might have to shoot you as an intruder."

Denny could see the other officer smiling, while just sitting there. As Denny walked around to the passenger side, and the officer rolled down the window. The 'jumped up' little prick was making a show of looking over by the barn.

"Have you come as back up pal? You've drawn the short straw working with that little 'git' haven't you?"

"Yeh, unfortunately Mr Foggerty, but as you well know, orders are orders. You taking any whisky nowadays?"

Denny stood back from the car, before asking, "How do you know my name?"

"You were a legend back in the force a few years ago Daniel. Although, everybody seems to have forgotten about the whisky, but what the heck."

Denny didn't know how to handle this situation.

"Don't worry Mr Foggerty. I am from a different county, helping that inept officer over there. We have a mutual friend in Shonagh. Don't worry, she hasn't mentioned why you lot are here, but can I give you some advice. When the snow clears, there is a slight possibility that the estate will be raided. However, at this stage, I don't think they have enough evidence. So whatever your going to do, then do it soon. Both you and I know they're scum down there."

"Whatever you do pal, don't be around here when the fireworks go off."

The other officer started to walk back before the guy in the car, winked at Denny, before giving him a stern warning, telling him he would be in trouble if they found anything incriminating."

"Yes, officer?"

"It's Jackson, and you had better remember that."

A slight smile came over his face, although he made sure his fellow officer couldn't see him.

When the officer in charge came back, he got in the car without saying anything, and 'gunned' the car down the road. Denny walked back smiling, and told everyone he needed to speak with them.

"I have just had an interesting conversation with the new police officer. He knows our contact Shonagh in Edinburgh. It appears when the snow has disappeared, there could be a raid on the estate. We could wait for that to happen, but I'm pretty sure the ring leaders will get off with it, due to their boss in Edinburgh. Or we get on with it, and as soon as Tucker gets us the explosives we go for it. What do you think, as there will be no going back from there. This has to be unanimous though. No loose ends."

Everyone said that they should finish what they had started. Denny had detected a rise of anger in their voices, which was what he was looking for. It was Yuri who asked Denny for a word outside.

"Denny, I hate to say this, but I fear that Tomaz will sneak out one night, to try and go down to the camp to see Tallulah. He is really down, and only cheers up when he can get to see here. He is absolutely besotted with her. I can't chain him down, and it must be an awful thing, this love at first sight. Did it happen between you and Helen?"

"No, it didn't Yuri," he lied. What are we going to do about it? Before we came across here, Karl asked me if I thought Tomaz was up for all this. I said I trusted him, but now look what is happening. I'm sorry, but I must have it out with him. What I say to him might sound brutal, but I have five other people to think about. I want you there when I speak to him. Go, and get him please.

When the pair of them came out Denny was sitting on the lid of the old well. Bohdi had wandered out as well for some reason, but Denny bawled at him to get himself back inside.

"Sit down Tomaz. I brought you over here, because I thought I could trust you, but now I'm not so sure. Your brother and I are wondering what your feelings are towards Tallulah. Bloody hell man, you barely know her, and it feels like we are a man down the way you are behaving. Let me say this to you. If her dad brings her here, or we go down to the camp, then you can spend time with her, and after all this is over, then you can fucking stay here for all I care. However, if you screw up this mission then you will be lying at the bottom of this deep dark well. With a bullet in your brain. Got me?"

Tomaz started to lose it. Throwing his arms around, and mouthing what Denny and Yuri could only think were obscenities. Yuri grabbed him by the throat, and pinned him down in the snow. Denny hated to see this. Eventually, Tomaz settled down, and Yuri grabbed him and threw him back on the well lid.

"Listen to me little brother. If, and it's a big if, Denny agrees, I will take you down to the camp for no more than an hour at a time. I will wait for you in the jeep to give you time together, as long as her dad agrees. If she is working over at Maggie's, then I will take you there for the same amount of time, and wait there for you. If you piss me about, then there will be no need for Denny to shoot you, as I will. Okay?"

Yuri looked at Denny, but he didn't say anything for a few minutes, before nodding his head.

"Against my better judgement Yuri. The pair of you get in the jeep, and head down for an hour, and I would appreciate if you could explain to Tucker what is happening, but if he says no, then you are fucked Tomaz. Hear me?"

Tomaz was looking very sheepish, and he couldn't look either of them in the face. Yuri pointed with his head towards the jeep, and they were soon heading down the track. Denny was seething, and went in to speak to Karl.

"When I spoke to you back on the estate I told you I had my reservations about him. This has come at a crucial time Denny. We need everybody to be on top of their game. As I have said before, we need to get the hell out of here. Unfortunately, we need to wait for Tucker getting back to us. I hate it when we are not in control of our own destiny."

Denny shouted through to kitchen for the boys to come through.

"Right boys, we are going for a walk, as I need to talk to you. Levi, you take Karl's rifle just in case. Sorry Bohdi, but one gun happy youngster is enough for me tonight. Don't worry, we have zero chance of seeing the demons with the big red eyes. Remember, if you run away from your shadow, I will use you as target practice"

Denny would never get tired of winding the young lad up.

After walking a while, Denny said to them that Tomaz might not be up for the job in hand. He said that they had better step up to the plate, and they would go back heroes. Although, no one would ever believe their part in all of this.

"Is it that lassie that is turning his head Mr. Denny? Mind you, she is quite a looker, isn't she brother?"

"Just like some of the lassies that are all over me Levi."

"I swear, I will take this gun and shoot your 'balls' off if I hear about your so called sexual exploits again. Stick to 'palm and her five sisters' will you. Just tell us what you want us to do, and it will be done Mr Denny. Remember, I keep telling you, we're proud Dundonians."

"That's imprinted in my brain Levi. When you're big lad I will tell you all about my exploits there."

"Can't wait big man."

They kept walking, before Denny told them to listen carefully.

"Here's what happens if all this goes to pieces. You get out of this farm, and you run east. You run as fast as you can. Eventually, you will come to a village somewhere, and you make your way to Dundee. On no account do you try and save anybody. I promised Stevie that I would not put you in danger, and I will keep my promise to him. Do you realise, that in the near future, there will be a lot of people dead around here, so are you prepared for it?"

"At times we may give the impression that we are just a couple of daft laddies, but let me tell you, we have had a hard struggle through life. We have been in and out of foster homes all our lives. Most of which we have ran away from. We have seen one of our good mates stabbed to death in front of us. Nothing we could do to keep him alive. We have had to steal food at times. There is a lot of bravado about us at times, but it's what we have to do to survive. We owe Stevie a lot, but he has a family of his own now, so we tend to back off a bit. Are we prepared for it? Of course we are."

"Don't worry, I will make sure you are back in Dundee very soon."

"No problem pal. Don't rush, as this is like Butlins up here."

All Denny could do, was his usual, close his eyes and shake his head.

It wasn't long after that Yuri drove up to the farmhouse. Denny could see he wasn't very happy. Tomaz went straight in to the house, but Yuri stayed outside.

"Well Yuri?"

"He was a total pain in the arse when it was time to leave, pleading for more time to be with her. Even Tucker was getting a bit pissed off with the pair of them, although he was fine about them seeing each other. I will keep taking him down on occasion, but there will come a time when we just have to leave him to his own devices. I won't shoot him pal, I couldn't. It would be better if we just left him at the camp at some stage."

"I would ask Tucker if he would let her come and stay here with him, but it would be too much of a distraction for everyone. We will go with your plan of taking him down for an hour every so often, and see how it plays out, but keep a bloody eye on him."

Yuri saw the headlights starting to come up the drive, so he alerted Denny who ran into the house and brought out two handguns.

"Hide it Yuri" he said.

When the vehicle was lighted up with the security light, Denny could see it was officer Jackson.

Denny and Yuri removed the guns from their belts at the back, and pointed them at the police officer.

"Good security Daniel."

"Sorry about this, but can you open the boot while Yuri checks it."

He opened the boot, and after Yuri was satisfied, Denny asked the officer if he would like to come in for a 'cuppa'.

"Best not pal, as I have to get back to village down the road, where I am staying. I phoned in my report earlier, when my so called 'boss' was busy enjoying the hospitality of Radovan. I'm just here to tell you that there is a favourable weather forecast coming within the next ten days, and assuming they can get even a little more evidence, then my bosses will come for them."

Denny walked in to the house, and came out with the notepad Tomaz had been using to jot down all licence plate numbers, along with the times of arrival and departures. He gave it to the officer, explaining what it was.

"This might be all it needs to convince them to move on the estate. Thank you. I need to go now. Hopefully I will see you at some point, but I am taking your advice and going back to my own area. Take care."

Denny hoped he could trust him, otherwise it would be a bullet rather than a lifetime in jail.

When he went in Karl was looking through one of the scopes.

"Do you fancy coming a walk both up and down the main road Denny? I need to try and see the best way to see what is in the cellar. Later, when it's dark I will go down, and look through the slotted windows low down on the building. We know this is a drug factory, but I would like to find out the best possible places to put the explosives, if Tucker comes up with any."

"Yeh, let's go now. Everybody else can look after the farm. "

They wandered down the old track, with only a hand gun concealed at the small of their backs.

"Denny, keep your eyes covered, as if you are sheltering them from the glare off the snow. Let me know if you see anything out of the ordinary."

As they passed the house going North, Denny said, "Karl, are you seeing what I am seeing. Right at ground level, there are small exhausts coming out at the side of the slotted windows."

"Yes I see them, and we probably haven't noticed them due to the amount of snow piled up against the walls. It's the other pipes about a foot high coming out the wall that interests me more. What are your thoughts?"

"Surely, they can only be gas pipes, but we can't be that lucky, can we? Maybe, when we go back, we can check if they have them on the opposite side of the house. On a lighter note Karl, have a look at that waterfall coming down between those hills there. You can hardly see it, because of the trees. There is a small bridge over the water, but for what reason I don't know. It could be that the previous owner wanted to let people go, and view the beauty of the falls. Bit of a hike though."

"Yeh, but let's get our mind back on the job in hand. We will turn around where we can't be seen, and walk back down, as far as the travellers camp. Maybe we should speak to Tucker, and see if he has any news for us."

As they passed the South side of the big house, they glanced across to see the same pipes positioned going in to the wall. Both Denny and Karl just nodded.

Denny's jigsaw was started in Bavaria, and it was going to end in a glen in Scotland.

As they walked in to the camp, they were challenged by two shotgun wielding young lads.

"Who the fuck are you two, and what do you want?"

"My name is Denny, and he is Karl, both from the farm at the top of the hill. We are here to see Tucker."

Just then there was a shout. It was Tucker telling the lads to let them through. Reluctantly they did.

Tucker asked them in, and Tallulah made them all a cup of tea. Afterwards, Tucker told his daughter to go and visit one of the other caravans, as he wanted peace to speak to the men in private.

When she left, Denny explained to Tucker what officer Jackson had said, and now time was of the essence.

"Firstly Denny, can you trust this 'copper'? Before we go any further with obtaining the explosives, then I have to be sure that nothing is going to come back on the camp. Also, the guy that will supply us will want assurances."

"I can guarantee, that you and your folk won't be implicated in any of this. Although, if you are wanting rid of the estate problem, then you have to help us. Okay?"

"Sound Denny. I should have the name of the explosives guy in a couple of days at latest. I know you want to speak about something else, so just go for it."

"I'll speak about Tomaz and Tallulah, but do you have any brave, but fast young guy that would help us when the time comes?"

Karl was looking at Denny, wondering what he was on about.

"Yeh, there is one young lad that fits the bill. He is always telling me that one day he would be King of the Gypsies. You'll have no problem with him. I can guess what you want to say about Tomaz and my daughter. They seem infatuated with each other, and I can't dissuade her in any way. I'm sure Tomas feels the same way."

"When our mission is over Tucker, I think we are going to have a big problem, but I have told him that I am prepared to leave him here in Scotland if need be. I put my faith in him to come over here, and he has let me down, but let's see what happens. Okay, please come up when you know the name of the guy, and where he lives. Karl and I will come with you to see him."

"That will be fine Denny, but I will warn you, that when I knew him he was a bit eccentric. I can't say what he will be like now."

Denny said they would have to go, and to try and make it as quick as possible. As they walked back, Karl had asked him about why they needed to get a young lad to help them. Denny had said it was just an idea he had, but nothing was set in stone.

When he got back, he went back into the house and phoned Helen.

"What is happening Denny, are you any nearer coming home. I'm struggling without you. The boys are missing you. We just need you here."

"No emotional blackmail Helen, I'm dealing with enough 'crap' without this. I trust the three of you are okay? The only thing I can say is that the jigsaw is falling into place."

They talked for another twenty minutes, before he asked to speak to Willie.

"How is Scotland treating you brother? I bet it's colder than it is here. What is all the news?

Denny told him as much as he could, with Willie getting angry about Tomaz.

"Fucking leave him there pal. He's not worth bringing back, or shoot him, and leave him in that old well you have mentioned."

"Not quite as easy as that Willie. I hope to leave this farm as soon as possible. Hopefully, within the next ten days maximum. I trust Gertie is fine, and there is still work being done in the forest?"

"All present and correct pal, but can I say that Helen is not doing well mentally. We are trying to keep her going, but if you are going to be away for any length of time, then you might have a problem when you get back. Anyway, please give Yuri a shout as Jinty is desperate to speak to him. Look after yourself pal."

He shouted on Yuri, passed the phone to him, and left him to it. When he came back he wasn't a happy guy.

"I'm getting grief from her now. As if I haven't enough rubbish here, with that little arsehole," pointing at Tomaz.

Next morning, it seemed like everyone, not just Tomaz, was on a bit of a downer.

"Levi, take Tomaz and bring the corrugated shutters round, and just put them up."

They had just started when there was a commotion from outside the front door of the big house. A truck had drawn up, and two men had gotten out, and were shouting for help. When more men came out, they lifted a body from the back of the truck.

Denny could see it was the guy that Karl had despatched to a watery grave. By this time both Yuri and Karl were standing beside him.

"They have no proof, but they will put two and two together and point the finger at us. So let us be vigilant," said Yuri.

Just then Tucker's vehicle came up the new track. Although they knew it was him, they still went through the drill of keeping their hand guns pointed at him, while Denny checked the boot.

"Come in Tucker. I hope you have some good news for us."

When Tomaz heard Tucker's voice, he came running through from the kitchen, only to be disappointed to see that Tallulah wasn't there.

"Sorry son. She is over at Maggie's."

Denny asked Tucker what he was over for. He said he had located the guy that might be able to help them with the explosives.

"His name is Abe. He used to be in charge of the blasting at the quarry at the top of the valley. It closed about ten years ago, but as he had such a fascination about anything that would go bang, there is a possibility that he can lay his hands on something that would be okay for us. Let me warn you though, he is a bit eccentric, and he continually clicks his left ear, which is bloody annoying, but please don't ask him why, as he can easily kick off. Why, I haven't a clue."

"Right Tucker, are you available tomorrow morning? Karl, and I will pick you up at eight o'clock. We'll take our jeep as it can get through the snow, no problem. Okay with you?"

That was fine with him.

Nothing was happening throughout the day, so Denny got everyone doing odd jobs. He was determined to keep everybody sharp, as he wanted the house blown up within a couple of days.

"Levi, you and Tomaz, go to the barn and bring all the bales of hay nearer the house. Bring all the corrugated sheets to the side of the house."

The day was long, and everyone was glad to eat at night, and head off to bed.

There was an air of anticipation next morning.

"Yuri, we are heading off. I leave you in charge. Keep an eye on Tomaz."

They picked up Tucker, and headed up the valley. After about an hour, they came to a cottage which was set back off the road. As they got out of the jeep, the front door of the cottage opened, and there stood a small insignificant guy, with a large double barrelled shotgun being pointed at them.

"State your business or fuck off."

"Abe, it's me Tucker Beany. We would like your help if possible."

"It's been a long time Tucker. Can you vouch for your two friends?"

"Absolutely Abe. Can we come in?"

Abe nodded, and they followed him inside.

There wasn't any tea being offered, so Karl started to tell Abe what he needed.

"I have the very thing for you. Two boxes of TNT which I procured from the quarry when it closed. There are timers as well. What are you proposing to blow up?"

Karl told him the size of the house, with Abe just nodding, and telling them he had the right gear for them. The continual clicking of his ear was driving Denny crazy, but he managed to contain himself.

Abe went to the bedroom, and brought out two wooden boxes from under the bed. None of them could believe it. He dumped the boxes down in front of the three of them. He saw their concern.

"Don't worry lads, it needs the timers before it will go off," he said laughing.

Denny went in to his money belt, and brought out more cash than Abe had seen in his lifetime, and gave it to him.

"This is for the explosives and your silence Abe. If you ever say anything to anybody about us, then I will come back and 'gut' you. No disrespect."

"None taken son, whoever you are."

As they headed down the road, Denny had said to Karl, that the reason he had been asking about a fit young lad from Tucker's camp, was that they had to be sure that both sides of the building blew at the same time. So it had to be a two man job.

"Tucker, can you bring the guy up to the house later today please."

Tucker said he would, and they drew in to the camp.

When Denny and Karl got up to the farm house, Yuri was waiting outside. Denny thought that this wasn't good. When they got out of the car, Yuri came right out with it.

"Tomaz has done a runner. I'm sorry, but I had just turned my back for a few minutes, and he was gone. I couldn't go looking for him, and leave the boys here."

Denny bent over with his head in his hands, and roared like a wild animal.

"It's not your fault Yuri. Let's wait till he turns up."

He told him about meeting Abe, and what they had in the back of the car. Yuri had said he would take it to the barn, and hide it in a safe place.

"Men, my plan is coming away at the seams, so tomorrow we will end it."

Just then the phone rang, and Bohdi came out saying it was Maggie. Denny ran in and took the call.

"Denny, it's Maggie here. You and Yuri had better get down here quickly, as Tomaz has been badly injured after being attacked by men from the estate. They are still here, but Tomaz is up in one of the rooms, with Tallulah trying to tend to him."

"Yuri, get your hand gun and a knife. Tomaz has been attacked down at Maggie's place."

As they drove down, Denny had told Yuri to follow his lead, but he wasn't prepared to put up with the arrogance of these men any more. When they got down, Tucker was already there.

When they went through the front door, Maggie led them upstairs, and in to the room.

Tomaz was lying with his face all blooded and bruised, but Denny looked at his legs, and knew that at least one of them was broken.

"What happened Maggie?"

She explained that he had been sitting at the bar, when Tallulah had gone over to serve the men, they had done the usual, and touched her legs. Tomaz went for them, but they overpowered him, and gave him a beating, but it was mainly the guy with the pony tail, while the others held him down.

Tomaz was unconscious, and Tucker had suggested that they leave Tallulah to look after him. Denny followed Maggie down stairs, before Denny told Tucker to go back to the camp, as he might not want to see what would happen next. Maggie walked behind the bar, and Yuri and Denny walked over to the inebriated men.

"Here comes the keeper of the mute, men. We will just have the beat them up as well," said pony tail.

He was sitting at the end of a table with his hands on the table, so Denny went and stood at one side of him, with Yuri on the other.

"Do you remember I told you a wee story about a ghost. Well here is another. When I was a child I was scared of ghosts. When I grew up, I realised that people were more scary."

He then plunged his knife up to the hilt through the guys hand, with Yuri doing the same in the other hand. There was no blood to start with, and the guy started to scream, and cry. Denny asked Maggie, who was about to collapse, for the knife she uses to cut up the lemons. Her hand was shaking uncontrollably, when she gave it to him. Denny then went over, and cut off the guy's pony tail, making sure that some skin came with it. He then rammed it in his mouth.

"Ah that's better. I forgot to say pal, that I don't do tears. Sorry about this Maggie, you didn't need to see that."

The other men sat there transfixed.

Yuri was a man possessed, as he started punching them on their faces. He wasn't holding back. Eventually, Denny sat beside the guy.

"Now here is the problem pal. Both my friend and I won't be taking the knives out. So that only leaves you to pull your hands out. Yes, it will be excruciating, but unless you want to sit here all night, while pissing and shitting yourself, then you will have to get on with it."

The guy started to pull his hands along the table. His eyes were bulging, and muted screams were coming from him. Denny just sat with his chin resting on his upturned palm, watching the guy, with his evil grin covering his face. Maggie had disappeared, as she had never witnessed violence like that in her life.

The guy eventually freed his hands, whereby Denny and Yuri removed their knives from the table, then wiped the blood from them on the guy's face. They left the bar, and Maggie was waiting for them.

"I will get Tucker, and a few of his boys to collect Tomaz, so that he can bring him up to the farmhouse. Thanks for your help Maggie."

She didn't say anything. She couldn't.

Chapter 15

Tucker and his men arrived at the farmhouse with Tomaz and Tallulah, about twenty minutes after Denny and Yuri got back. Denny explained to Tucker, that Tallulah might be in a bit of danger being there, but he had said that he couldn't persuade her not to be. Denny had said that he would fix up another bed in Tomaz's room for her. He thanked the men for bringing Tomaz to the farm, and they left.

"Right everybody. Let's get the metal shutters up, as I think there will be a lot of pot shots coming our way. We need to get Tomaz's room fixed up for Tallulah, and we will have a meeting as quickly as possible. Hopefully, Tucker might bring up the young lad tonight."

The shutters were no sooner up, when shots were ringing off them. Everyone knew they were safe, but Denny had told them not to go outside. Yuri and Denny had gone through to assess Tomaz's injuries, and it was obvious that he had a fracture on his right leg, several broken ribs and lots of bruising over his body. Levi had made a temporary splint for his leg and Tallulah had fitted it on. Several times he had woken up, but he was delirious, and just drifted off back to sleep.

Every so often, everyone would flinch when a bullet hit the shutter outside. Denny walked round the front, and saw the guy with his hands all bandaged up, shouting at the men to fire their guns at the farm house, until Radovan came out and ordered them to get back inside.

A couple of hours later, Tucker drove up the track with someone in the passenger seat. Karl and Yuri did their usual, and pointed their guns at the two men getting out. Karl checked the boot. When they were inside, Tucker introduced the new guy as Lash.

Denny explained what he wanted from Lash, and he said it wouldn't be a problem.

"Do you understand son, that you have to be prepared to blow up about twenty plus people, with no regrets."

"I'm doing this for the gypsy clan pal. Not you remember."

"Karl, can you take Lash out to the barn, and show him the gear. I think we have to go for it tomorrow evening early, but Tucker, I want you and Lash to be here from lunch time, so that you can go over and over the plan until it's perfect. Also Tucker, can you get some of your men to roll up in three or four trucks, and park just inside the main gate with their rifles protruding from the windows. On no account do they fire, and at a prearranged signal, they turn and leave the estate to head home. It will only be intimidation.

"Denny, how are Lash and I going to work this if we are on different sides of the building?"

"No worries pal. I will give the signal from the front of the house. It will be me firing my hand gun in the air, and shouting loudly. I expect a few pot shots to be taken at me, but I will be fine. Tucker, I think your camp will be far enough away from the blast, but if you want to position all the vans on this side of the caravans, then that will be up to you, but tell all your people to get on the floor from a certain time. Lash, you will use Yuri's camouflage gear when you head down to the house. There isn't much else we can do at the moment, so I will bid you goodnight, as I have to get an hour or two 'kip,' as I will to be awake all night, watching for reprisals. Although, I need someone to watch my back."

"I'm your man Mr. Denny. I've got the night vision of an owl, partner. What do you say?" said Levi.

Denny was too tired to argue, so he just nodded. You would have thought that all his dreams had come early for Levi.

"Bohdi, tomorrow morning I want you to clear out Mr. Rae's van. Enough for three of us to sit comfortably in the back. Check the engine, and make sure we have enough petrol to get us down the road a bit. Yuri, you understand that we will have to leave Tomaz. He will be in good hands, with Tucker and his folk."

"It's going to be hard Denny, but I fully understand, as will Tomaz. However, if he has Tallulah, then he will be fine."

After a couple of hours Denny shouted on Levi to wrap up warm, get his rifle, and follow him outside. They positioned themselves behind some trees. Levi facing in to the field, and Denny facing the tracks. He thought it was going to be a long night. However, it was only three hours later that Denny

400

whispered to Levi, that he had an intruder creeping up the track. Levi said he had another jumping the fence at the side of the barn, and can he shoot him in the arse.

"Ah, hell just go for it son."

The shot rang out, along with a lot of screaming, with Levi laughing. The guy toppled back over the fence, and hirpled down the field. The other guy took off down the main track, fell on his arse, stupidly keeping his finger on the trigger, and firing off shots indiscriminately. Denny didn't think they would get any more visits, but he left it a couple of more hours before calling it a day.

As they went back inside, Yuri and Karl were standing with their rifles trained on the door.

"Is this what they call being killed by friendly fire lads?" laughed Levi.

"Have you got a joke for everything pal?" said Denny.

Tallulah came through and gestured that Tomaz was awake. Yuri and Denny went in the bedroom.

"Well brother, you have landed yourself in a right mess this time, haven't you? Don't worry, Denny isn't going to shoot you, or so he says."

Tomaz looked at Denny, and mouthed that he was sorry. Denny told him that this would be all over in a couple of days, and get some rest. He said he would leave Yuri to keep him company.

After a while, the sun was starting to rise, and Tallulah made everyone breakfast. It was now just waiting for Tucker and Lash to arrive. He could see that everybody had a look of nervousness about them, so Denny tried to tell everyone to think about what they will be doing in a few weeks time.

Tucker and Lash arrived early. Lash seemed keen to get on with it. Karl took him in to the barn to go over the explosives and timers once again. When they got in the house, Karl wanted everyone's attention.

"Okay, here is how it's going to happen. At four forty five exactly, Lash you will go down the new track, and approach the big house with two lots of explosives. I showed you through the scope when we were out there where they are to be placed. The timers are to be set for two minutes, which will be enough time for your men to get back to the camp, Tucker. Also for us to hightail it away from the house. I am being honest when I say that I know about TNT, although I've never used it, but by my reckoning the blast will be massive, as I reckon there will chemicals in the cellar. Lash, as soon as you've set the last timer, then run like hell, but count as you're going along. If you haven't cleared the trees by one minute fifty seconds, then find the widest tree next to you, and dive behind it. You okay with that?"

"Sounds good to me pal. If I get blown up if the explosives go off early, or I help to blow the house up, I'll be a hero either way. What do you think Tucker?"

"You will that son."

Karl had suggested the he and Lash have a wander through the forest, just to clear their heads.

Tallulah kept everybody supplied with tea and coffee throughout the morning, and Denny had asked Tucker to come through to Tomaz's bedroom. Tallulah was already there.

"Tomaz, please listen carefully. Your brother and I have discussed your situation, and we have come to the same conclusion. We can't take you back with us, for obvious reasons. So if you want to stay here with Tallulah in this farmhouse, assuming Tucker agrees, then within a month, I will have the ownership of the whole farm transferred over to you. Your money in the bank in Munich, would be transferred to The Bank of Scotland in Dundee. Maybe, you and Tallulah would like to try and get this farm up and running. Remember, you are only a three hour flight to come and see us. If it all goes to plan, then we will bring everybody over to see you in a few months. How does that sound to the pair of you?"

They looked at each other, smiled, and then nodded.

The time was nearing, and the darkness seemed to be drawing in quicker than normal. Denny thought to himself, that death and darkness seemed to follow him wherever he went.

Tucker left to get his men ready.

"Remember Tucker, as soon as you see and hear me firing my gun, then get the hell out of there."

He then told Levi and Bohdi to get the mattresses from the bedrooms, and put them up against the windows, with the hay bales from outside, brought in, and stacked against them.

Karl and Lash started to get ready, with Lash going down the new track, while Karl started hiking down the fields on the north side of the farm.

Denny could only watch helplessly. It was out of his hands now.

He walked around to the front of the house, with a scope and his handgun in the small of his back. The men were walking towards the house from either side. He knew that the timing had to be precise. Karl and Lash were hiding behind trees as they were early. Denny's heart was pumping.

"Yuri, when the house goes up, make sure you are with Tomaz, holding him down as the shock will rock this house."

Yuri went back inside as Tucker and his men came up the road, and drove in just through the gate. The men from the estate were in a panic. They came to the front of the house brandishing their rifles.

It was then that Denny started to fire his gun and shout at the estate men. Karl and Lash moved in. When Denny stopped firing, the gypsies reversed out of the gate and headed down the road.

The estate men were all cheering as if they had just scared the gypsies away. Denny then saw Lash taking off through the trees, as well as Karl.

Suddenly, he caught sight of someone running from the back of the house. He had made a mistake. Of course, there had to be a trap door if there was a cellar. Too late.

He ran inside and grabbed Levi and Bohdi and pinned them down behind the bales. He looked through a gap in the shutters, and what he saw frightened him. The explosion was far more than he could ever imagine. As well as the explosion, there was a massive fireball. He kept his head down as the farmhouse shook. After a few minutes there were more explosions, presumably coming from the cellar. It was if they weren't going to stop.

He told the boys to lie still and crawled through to Yuri.

"Yuri, I'm positive that Radovan has made a run for it. When you feel it's safe, check on Karl and Lash through the scope. I'm going after Radovan."

He took off down the field trying to keep an eye on where Radovan was. It was difficult to see him in the trees, but it looked like he had ran to the bridge, crossed over and was now going up

403

an animal track towards the waterfall. Denny didn't know why, but he concentrated on gaining on him.

It was difficult going, and he couldn't see him. He was at the top of the track which overlooked the waterfall. He was going through the trees when suddenly, he was whacked over the cheek with a branch. He had found Radovan. Denny was stunned, and rolled down the banking precariously close to the edge of the falls. He came too, to see Radovan stumbling down the banking, ready to hit him again. Denny slowly got to his feet, and sized him up. Just as he lifted the branch again, Denny landed one of the most important punches of his life

It caught Radovan square on the chin, and put the guy down. He started to roll towards the edge of the falls, before going over, but miraculously held on to the edge while hanging there. He was shouting for help. Unfortunately for him, he was speaking to the wrong person. Denny sat down just above where the guy was hanging, with blood dripping from his wound.

"Welcome to your nightmare you scum. Although I'm not sure you are going to like it much."

Denny then stamped on one of his hands. Radovan gave out a deathly scream, before Denny said, "When you get to Hell, please tell all your men that if I ever get there, then I will kill them over and over again."

He then stamped on his other hand, and watched him fall before blood and brain matter were splattered over the rocks below. Denny started to smile.

The thawing snow would eventually make the river flood, and all trace of him would be gone.

He walked back still feeling a bit dazed, with blood still running down his cheek. When he got a right look at the estate, he couldn't believe it. It was just devastation. There was hardly anything there, except a mangled police car in front of where the house once stood.

When he got to the farmhouse, both Lash and Karl were there. The boys and Yuri were standing out the front of the house, just looking. Not saying a word.

"Yuri, I take it everything was all right in the house. Karl, Lash that was a text book operation. Well done. Okay lads, get the shutters down and put them in the old well. Put the bales back where you got them. All the guns are to go down there also."

He thought the lads were going to cry.

"You heard me. Everything in the well, including the camouflage clothing. Anything that could be traced back to us. Karl take the two grenades we still have, pull the pins and throw them down. If we don't have two, then check these little buggers belongings. Also make sure the gun tally is correct, as I don't trust Butch and Sundance here.

He walked in to the living area and shouted on Tallulah.

"Tallulah, get a needle and thread, and stitch me up please."

She made a gesture that it was going to be sore, until Denny shouted at her to just get it done. While he sat there getting stitched, it reminded him of Moira in Arbroath. The sound of sirens could be heard coming up the road, but there would be a lot more emergency vehicles soon. He thanked Tallulah, and shouted on Karl to get the grenades in the well quickly. As everybody stood outside, Karl dropped them into the well. There was a deep thump, and the lid almost blew off.

"Right, everyone get all the remaining bags of concrete opened and tipped in. Don't worry about the lime. Yuri put some water in later, and cement the lid closed."

As Lash left, Denny shook his hand and thanked him very much, and to tell Tucker he would see him later tonight. Was Denny imagining it, but was there a spring in Lash's step when he was walking down the track.

"Lads, first thing tomorrow, take the jeep to the hole at the far field. Remove the plates, as well as the chassis number, and tip it in. No bloody joy riding though, and no trying to stash it somewhere. Everything has to be spotless now."

Denny was exhausted, and just needed sleep. Maybe, when he got back home.

When he walked in he shouted on everyone.

"Right everybody, please have a think. Have we missed anything? I'm pretty sure we will get a visit from the police early tomorrow, so let's get our story right. We are up here for survival training, with the view to opening a survival school, but the snow has finally beat us, and we are off home. We never saw anything untoward about the big house. My injury was from a tree branch, trying to stop Tomaz sliding down the track in the snow. Anything else?"

They all just shook their heads.

He went in to one of the rooms, and came out with a parcel. He headed of to Tucker's camp.

Tucker welcomed him in, and got the kettle on. As they sat chatting, Denny handed over the parcel. Tucker opened it and exclaimed, "Denny, what the hell is going on, There's a king's ransom in here."

"Appropriate for the King of the Gypsies then pal. Why don't you spread it around your people. I'm sure they will be glad of it."

"Denny, who the hell are you?"

"Tucker, I don't know if you will believe me, but here goes. My real name is Daniel Rey Foggerty, and I own the Albach Trust, which owns a large part of Germany. My estate is in Bavaria, and myself, friends and family all work hard keeping the forests for generations to come. Oh, and just to add, I am a multi, multi billionaire, or so I am told. However, I am still the same guy that spent fifteen years on the Isle of Durma. Maybe, at this point you might want to close your mouth Tucker."

Denny, just started to laugh.

"Bloody hell son. I have actually heard of the Trust, and some of the good it does."

"Can you get all your people organised to take their caravans and vans to your new field at the back of the farm, first thing tomorrow morning. Tomaz needs guidance Tucker, so we will be leaving that up to you. A surrogate father, if you can agree to that. Tomaz, has enough money to make a good go of the farm, so please keep him right. What do you say?"

Tucker leaned over, took Denny's hand in his and said, "Don't you worry son, our community will embrace him with open arms."

Denny got up, and said they would meet again. However, when they did, he wanted to take his two boys on the front seat of Tucker's magnificent caravan, and just drive his beautiful cobbs for a while.

"Any time my friend."

Denny jumped in the jeep and headed back up. After a quick 'brew' from Tallulah, he headed off to bed.

Next morning, the police car came up the track.

"Don't worry everyone. I will do the talking, but I want you two little buggers to disappear, as I don't know what you could be wanted for.

They ran in to the forest, which said it all.

Denny greeted the two officers, and asked them in for a cup of tea and biscuits. It always did the trick. As they sat talking, Denny was very convincing, and in the end they were happy with his story, even to the extent of asking if they could get medical help for Tomaz. Denny thanked them, but said he would be fine with the help he had. After they left, Denny phoned Maggie.

"Hi Maggie. Did you get a fright last night?"

"A fright, you bastard. I thought the world was coming to an end. I take it your phoning to say goodbye Denny."

"Just till the next time, and if you can maybe see it in yourself to pop up and see the youngsters now and again, that would be great. Take care bonnie lass."

Next was Stevie, and he told him he would drop the boys off in the centre in about three hours.

"Right, let's get packed everyone. Levi, get rid of that jeep right now."

The lads jumped in and took off at breakneck speed to dump it.

"Do you think they will remember to jump out before it goes into the hole?" asked Karl.

"God knows Karl."

All their gear was outside, when the lads came running back.

Denny wandered around the front for one last look. Levi and Bohdi sidled up to him, before Levi said, "Nice spot to build a house big man."

Denny could only laugh.

He saw the convoy from the camp heading up to their new site, and said to the lads it was time to go. Levi and his brother ran in to the house, to say goodbye to Tomaz and Tallulah.

Yuri and Denny then went in. Denny gave him a gentle squeeze, and stood aside to let Yuri in next to his bed. He gave Tallulah a hug.

"I love you with all my heart brother."

He turned to walk away, but suddenly stopped in his tracks, when Tomaz said, "I love you too Yuri."

Yuri couldn't believe what he was hearing.

"You can talk you little bastard. You've been pretending all your life?"

Tomaz just shrugged his shoulders, and gave him the thumbs up with a broad grin on his face. Yuri looked at Denny angrily.

"How long have you known? Why didn't you tell me?"

"If the lad didn't want to speak, then it wasn't up to me to say anything."

Yuri was bent over with his head in his hands before he had one last look at his brother, and walked right out the door. As they got in the van, the three men sat on a mattress that Bohdi had placed on the floor.

"Right lads, next stop is Bonnie Dundee, and get rid of these fucking camouflage hats as I told you to do."

The journey was long, and uncomfortable for the men in the back. Yuri wasn't in the best of moods, so any conversation was between Karl and Denny. When they arrived in Dundee town centre, Stevie was waiting for them.

"According to the BBC News this morning, there was fun and games up where you were staying. It wouldn't have anything to do with you lot would it?"

"Not us pal, we were only enjoying ourselves like we were at Butlins, what do you think lads?"

"Spot on big man. Just a bit of fun in the countryside," said Bohdi.

When they were out of earshot, Stevie asked how the pair had behaved.

"They were unbelievable pal. Although still as streetwise as ever. However we would have struggled without them, but please don't tell them that. I hope I see you and your family over in Bavaria some time soon."

"It would be my pleasure pal."

As they hugged, Denny said they would be getting the train to Edinburgh, as they had one more thing to do, before they went home. When they started to walk towards the station, there was a shout. Levi and Bohdi came running over and gave the three of them a hug.

Within eight hours they would be back in Bavaria, even allowing for their little stopover in the centre of Edinburgh.

Denny told Yuri to forget Glasgow, and buy a ticket home from Edinburgh, preferably on the same flight. Denny phoned home, and it was Gertie who picked up. He asked for Willie.

"Hi brother, can you pick us up at the airport in about four hours? There is only one flight from Edinburgh at that time. There will only be three of us. Tomaz isn't coming home. He's fine, but it's a long story. See you then pal, but please don't tell the girls that we are on our way."

After they had been picked up, and nearing Zwiesel, Karl asked to be dropped of at the shop.

"Denny, I feel like I am beginning to bond with you like a brother. However, never, ever ask me to kill for you again, as I won't do it, and we should agree never to speak about this episode again. Okay?"

"Sound Karl. I promise."

When Karl had been dropped off, it was then on to the estate. As they went up the track, it was strange as the dogs started to howl, as if they knew. They parked a bit away from the house, as the workers cars were up near the steps. Both he and Yuri, got out, and just stood looking at the forest, so glad they were home safe.

The dogs howling had given the game away, and Helen ran out of the house with tears tripping her, and jumped on Denny hugging him.

"I'm not apologising for my tears Foggerty. My heart is about bursting."

She then got down, and gave Yuri a massive hug, before looking around.

"Oh no, please no. Please don't tell me. Where is Tomaz? Did he just miss the flight?"

Denny told her to calm down, that Tomaz was safe, as was Karl and he would tell her all about it tonight.

Just then there was screaming coming from the main doors.

"Here comes your fucking screaming banshee Yuri. Good luck with that."

Denny ran into the house and picked his boys up, and hugged and hugged them. They all sat on the veranda, drinking hot coffee with Gertie's biscuits. He thought how he had missed them.

"I meant to say Foggerty, that I find your scar sexy, but evil, so be prepared for a night of passion."

"Helen, I am so tired, I don't think I could raise a gallop, never mind anything else."

"Trust me Foggerty, you will."

Denny didn't do anything for the next four days, except make some phone calls, and a trip to the bank in Munich. He phoned Shonagh, who didn't say much, just that the MP Robertson, had been found dead in his office with a knife wound that had went under his ribs, and into his heart. The police were treating everything as a drug war.

"You don't do things by halves Denny. I will see you in six weeks for my appointment."

"Can't wait Shonagh."

Next was a call to Maria.

"So glad your back safely my lovely boy. What can I do for you?"

He told her to see if the Trust could buy the Ruthven Estate, no matter what state it is in, and to get back to him.

Helen had asked everybody to have supper tonight, as a way of celebrating the return of the two prodigal sons.

Next day, when the men had come in from the forest, Denny had asked them to have a coffee with everyone. As they were sitting around chatting, Denny had given them all a single package. When they opened it, there was stunned silence, until one guy said, "Denny, do you know how much you have given us? We won't have to work for years, if we chose not to."

"Well, here is a story men. I have recently purchased a farm with forestry in the highlands of Scotland. Such a beautiful place. The title deeds will soon be passed to a friend of mine, and due to circumstances, he needs a lot of help. I hope to purchase a large estate just next to it, where there will be firstly construction work, and secondly forestry work. If you're interested, just let me know, but soon though. All expenses paid to get there, and food and lodgings until it is all up and running"

"What fucking farm, and estate Foggerty. When were you going to tell your wife, that's me, about it."

"I keep telling you darling, I just did."

The men looked at Helen, and seeing the look on her face, decided not to laugh.

The young confident lad had immediately said he would like to go, and the sooner the better for him, and could Denny let him know. Two others had shown an interest, so Denny thought it was promising.

It was about seven days till Christmas, but Denny didn't feel in the festive spirit. He knew he had to speak to Willie and Gertie, but it was going to be the hardest talk of his life. He kept putting it off, but although he was sure he knew what was going to happen it wasn't easy. They were all sitting by the fire one night, when he thought it was the right time.

"Willie, Gertie are you going to tell us when you are leaving?"

Nobody moved, never mind said anything. They all just looked at each other.

"How long have you known brother?"

"I've had my suspicions for a wee while Willie, but maybe I was hoping I was wrong."

"Stop, stop. What the hell are you talking about?" said Helen.

"Helen, they are leaving to go their own way darling. Nothing is forever."

"Listen folks. We have been thinking about it for a long time. The world is a big place, and we haven't seen much of it. We are sorry that it is short notice, but we knew that Jean was coming over, and we thought she would be the perfect replacement for Gertie. Yuri would naturally step in to my job, and Ian in to his. There wouldn't be a problem getting anybody to work on the estate. It's not that we wouldn't come back, and see you all."

Helen and Jinty started crying, and went over to hug Gertie, which set her off. Denny just glared at the three of them, with Helen not taking any notice of him.

"Do you know the exact date you will be leaving pal?"

" The twenty sixth or twenty seventh. It depends on flights at this time of year."

411

The snow started to come down heavy, which encapsulated the mood of them all. They were sitting in silence. There was a whiteout all around them.

"Willie, Yuri, do you hear singing? What about you Denny?" said Helen.

Everyone could hear some faint singing coming from down the track. Suddenly, they all looked at each other.

"Surely, this can't be happening. Is everybody thinking what I am thinking."

"It can't be the lads, can it brother?"

"There is only one way to find out. Arno, Udo, go and see."

They all stood watching the dogs disappear into the swirling snow. After a minute, there was a barrage of screaming.

"Yeh, that's Bohdi. Definitely the lads from Dundee. Fuck me. More to the point, why me?"

Denny sat with his head in his hands, with everyone else either laughing, or smiling. The lads were singing Christmas carols, badly. Eventually, this apparition appeared from the whiteout. Two lads, flanked by two dogs, still singing their hearts out. Dressed from head to toe in camouflage gear, except the boots had been replaced by their old baseball boots.

"Alright folks. It's a bit 'parky' out here. Lovely to see you again Gertie. Still think you are looking fit, as are you Mrs. Helen. I think you are wasting your time with Yuri, Jinty, however any chance of a brew bonnie girl?"

It was Willie who started laughing first, followed by the rest. Helen ran down the steps and hugged them, telling them to come on up, and get something to eat and drink. Denny told the dogs to stand down.

"I thought I told you to get rid of all the camouflage clothing, you little buggers?"

"You see Mr. Denny. We thought it would be a waste of your money. The boots? Well we had to sell them for a bit of pocket money. Oh, and seeing as we are here now, is there any chance of a job, at the appropriate rate of course?"

"I see you haven't got over your fear of dogs Bohdi?"

"I just got a fright when I saw them bounding through the snow, honest."

"He's an embarrassment to our name Mr. Denny."

412

"Which is?"

"Levi and Bohdi of course, or as you referred to us back in Scotland, Butch and Sundance. Oh, and can we see the bairns later Mrs. Helen. As long as we don't have to deal with they smelly nappy things."

It was an experience to see the boys sitting down, and getting stuck into any cakes or biscuits put down in front of them. Denny put his head back, closed his eyes, and said to the Big Man above. Please, no more surprises.

The next few days was taken up with everyone getting to grips with the imminent departure of Willie and Gertie, plus the arrival of the lads. During the past few days, Denny had phoned Ian and Neala and asked if they could get over as soon as possible. Willie had already told them about leaving, and Ian was quite philosophical about it, as he and Willie never had that close a relationship.

Denny spent the next few days walking in the forest. Often accompanied by Willie, or the young lads. He wondered about what had happened lately, and did he regret anything.

Not a fucking thing.

Otto had phoned one morning, and asked Denny if he would like to put the dogs to stud to cover a superb couple of bitches he had come across. Denny had immediately said yes, on the provision that he would get three pups. He had an idea.

He asked Levi and Bohdi for a chat.

"I've decided that you can stay here, on the condition you work hard, and look after yourself and carry on your studies, at either night school, or day release. Anything else is not an option. I will convert the lodge for you to stay in, but you will stay in the house until the work has been finished. Yuri will stay down at Jinty's place so that he can oversee the conversion of their house and shop. House rules though. What do you say?"

They started to high five each other, so Denny took that as a yes.

"One other thing lads. Please choose which dog you will be in charge of. No matter what, they will be your top priority after Col and Fin. Everyone else can look after themselves."

"A 'dug' Mr. Denny? You can't be serious. Can you?"

413

"It's either that, or you will be going back to Dundee. Make your mind up."

"Which is the most ferocious one Mr. Denny?" said Levi.

"Probably Arno, but it's difficult to say"

"He'll do for me then. Bohdi you'll be in charge of Udo. We are just here, and we have lodgings, a job, and now a dog each, so get a grip brother."

Denny smiled, and walked away.

Christmas day was upon them. When Denny came down the stairs after a lengthy lovemaking session, he found the fires burning brightly, with the dogs having been walked, and Bohdi making coffee.

"I'll just take a cup up to Mrs. Helen, Mr. Denny will I?"

"Sit on your arse Bohdi as she is in the shower. She will be down with the boys soon. Oh, and a very merry Christmas to the both of you."

Soon, everybody was sitting on the veranda. Gertie had said she wanted to make them breakfast, and surprise, surprise Bohdi had offered to help her. The snow was coming down, and it was a very wintry scene. They decided to exchange presents, although Denny had said to everybody days before that he didn't want any.

First, it was the lads to give presents. Levi went upstairs and brought down two beautifully hand carved cars for the boys. It was then Bohdi's turn. He handed all the girls, a badly wrapped present, in old newspaper. When they opened their presents, there was a lovely scarf. Each one made in Dundee.

"Now, don't get too carried away ladies. He shoplifted them from the Woolworth's store in the Murraygate in Dundee. He actually went in to shoplift his pick and mix, and came out with these."

"Here is me thinking that it's the thought that counts", said Bohdi.

The girls all went over and gave him a 'smacker' on the lips. Much to Levi's annoyance.

"Well Willie, I think you had better stop worrying about flights. You see, I thought this might be your last Christmas here, so a few months ago I ordered a new car for you. My thinking is that if you pass any forestry land that you might think could be purchased, you might stop and make enquiries for me. You can't do that on a plane."

As if on cue, they could all hear the sound of a motor coming up the track. They couldn't see it until it got right up to the house. Here was a brand new, top of the range Opal four by four.

"You'll never get stuck, no matter where you go brother. Not sure you should let Gertie drive it though. Both you and Gertie might like to jump in it, and give the delivery driver a lift back down the road."

When they came back, Willie hugged his brother, as if he might never see him again. They decided it was time to phone Tomaz, with Denny reminding the girls not to be surprised at his voice, which would still be getting stronger. Yuri and Jinty went in to the dining room and called him.

After twenty minutes, they came out, and said everybody had to phone him back, as Jinty's crying had put him off his pronunciation.

Jinty came over to Denny, and sat on his knee, in tears.

"I'm sorry for crying Denny, it was just a shock hearing him for the first time. Please, don't get on to me."

He just gave her a squeeze, before she went over and sat holding Yuri's hand. Willie and Gertie went next, and they could hear a lot of good natured swearing coming from Willie. Plus a lot of laughing.

Again, Denny and Helen had to phone him back.

"How is my little hero Tomaz? We miss you already. Promise me you will come and visit us as often as possible, please. We can't wait to meet Tallulah. Love you wee man."

"Merry Christmas to you and Tallulah. There is a lot of tears flowing pal, due to you not being here. Anyway, before you ask, the dogs are fine. Levi and Bodhi arrived unexpectantly to stay, so I have given them a dog each to look after, if that is okay with you? There is something important I have to ask you. The dogs are going to cover a couple of bitches, that Otto recommended. I was wondering, do you want a pup when they are born? What was that? You want two male dogs, and it doesn't matter how I do it, I just have to get them over there. Leave it with me pal. How is your body feeling?"

415

Tomaz had said he was feeling a bit better, and Tallulah was taking care of him. In a few weeks, he was going to get the men from the community to help him improve, and extend the cottage. He had an idea that he might try breeding horses. Not just cobbs, but different breeds. Tucker had said he would help him, and point him in the right direction.

They said their goodbyes, with Tomaz promising to phone every few weeks. Everyone seemed a bit down.

"Lads, you know where the record player is, so get it set up and look out all the Christmas songs you can, although we can also sing."

"Before we do that Mr. Denny, what did you get Yuri and Jinty for a Christmas present?

"Well son, I have put money into their accounts to have the house in Zwiesel renovated how ever they want it."

Yuri and Jinty looked at each other in surprise.

"What did you get the bairns, and Helen big man"

"I didn't get the boys anything, as I was otherwise occupied, and Helen seems to have got that covered. I don't know if she will like it or not, but I have ordered a pup from one of our dogs, just for herself. Hers and hers alone. If she wants to spoil it then fine. It will belong to her."

"What about you Mrs. Helen, what did you give Denny."

"I gave it to him a few weeks ago. He is going to be a dad again, and this time I know what sex the baby is. Your going to have a wee baby girl husband."

Denny sat there, put his head back, closed his eyes and said to himself. 'I asked for no more surprises Big Man'.

He got up, walked over to Helen, lifted her up in his arms and slowly kissed her. Everyone was either shaking Denny's hand, or giving Helen a hug. Bohdi holding on for that little bit longer hug.

When the boys got the music playing, it was a happy time. They sang, danced and ate until it was almost dark, and everyone knew the celebrations were coming to an end.

"Mr Denny. When we were young, we can remember only one Christmas when our mum was around. Now? Who knows where she is. Anyway, there was one song that has stuck in our heads, and if it's okay with everyone, we would like to sing it for you, without the record player."

Everyone just nodded, and smiled.

The boys stood up, and started to sing a Harry Belafonte song. Mary's Boy Child.

Well, the tears weren't long in coming from the girls, and much as their voices weren't great, they sang it from the heart. When they finished, everybody clapped, and the girls gave them a hug, and Denny thought that might be why they sang it.

The day had come to end.

"Right, you pair sit down. I have something for you. I have each an envelope, in which is a sum of money. It is an advance on your first wage. Each month, I will pay you a good wage, if you work hard. If not then you get 'sod' all. After Christmas, Helen or Jinty will take you to a small bank in Zwiesel, where you will open an account, and at the end of each month, you will deposit an amount into it. The amount will be up to you. Helen will keep a hold of your bank books. How does that sound?"

"Sounds good to us, but it's all in foreign bank notes pal."

"Give me your bloody envelopes, and go and give the dogs a good walk, feed them and make sure they are dry before you put them in the kennels."

Denny put his arm around Helen, and started to walk inside. He couldn't believe he was going to be a dad to a little girl. A precious little girl. Now that was going to be a game changer.

"I suppose you will have thought of a name for the baby, Helen?"

"I sure have, but you will have to wait."

Next morning, Willie and Gertie left without too much fuss. The usual tears, with emotions running high. As everyone watched the vehicle driving down the track, Denny wondered if this was the start of a new era for the estate.

"I'll go and make us a brew Mr. Denny, but one last question. Seeing as we are uncles to the boys, are we uncles to the wee lassie that will be coming along."

"Unfortunately for her, Bohdi."

Epilogue

Shonagh arrived a week later, for her hospital appointment in Munich. Everyone was happy to see her. Denny took her in to the Munich Hospital. She came out from the consultation, and told Denny she was just going to stay in till the morning, as the consultant was keen to do a small operation, there and then.

He arrived back the next day, and picked her up. A few days later she said she was leaving, and said her goodbyes. When Denny took her to the airport, she turned to him, gave him a big kiss, and said to him, "I will never forget you Daniel Rey Foggerty, but I will never see you again. Take care of yourself."

She walked away to the departure gates.

He never saw Shonagh again.

Leon Mayer phoned Denny to tell him that young Wagner had killed himself by continually running into his cell wall.

Ian, and a heavily pregnant Neala arrived soon after. They loved their house, with Ian keen to start his new job. Six weeks later, Lennox Callum McLeod was born.

Jinty went to Edinburgh to escort Jean over, as it was her first ever flight. She was so excited to see everyone, especially Fin and Col. She said that the annex was the nicest house she ever had. Unknown to the lads, she would soon take them under her wing.

Gladys Glover arrived, and was soon sorting out the classroom, telling Denny what she needed for classroom supplies etc. She met Leon and Hans, and they all got on well. She couldn't wait to start her teaching.

When April time came, Denny had asked Helen if she was okay to go and see Tomaz and Tallulah, along with Yuri and Jinty. She had said of course. He had phoned Otto to see if the two pups for Tomaz were waiting at the quarantine centre in Edinburgh.

Otto had said they were fine, and he would bring over the pup for Helen when they got back. The journey wasn't too bad, and when they got to Edinburgh, they hired the biggest car they could, and went and picked up the pups.

He was a bit taken aback how they looked like Udo and Arno. They went and booked in to Maggie's place while Yuri and Jinty went and stayed with Tomaz. Maggie was delighted to see Denny and his family. They drove up to the farmhouse, and Tomaz and Tallulah came out to greet them. Helen immediately hugged Tomaz, and then a big hug for Tallulah. Denny did the same and asked Tomaz how he was. He said he was recovering well, and needed to be doing something now.

"Well bonnie lad, I needed something in my life to get it back on track, and Otto brought me Arno and Udo. So, would you and Tallulah like to come with me."

They walked over to the hatch of the car, and Denny opened it. Tomaz's eyes just lit up. Here were two little pups looking up at them. Tallulah had tears in her eyes.

After they had taken the pups into the house, Tallulah made something to eat for everybody. Especially the pups. They heard a noise outside, and Tucker came to the door. When Denny went out, there stood his beautifully decorated caravan, and two magnificent cobbs harnessed.

"Okay Denny, off you go. I presume you are taking the family with you?"

Denny helped Helen up, and then passed the boys up. As he slowly walked the cobbs down the track to the main road, he pointed out to Helen, that big empty space would be where their Scottish house would be built. Nothing surprised her anymore.

As they went up the road, he looked at the boys, then over at Helen giving her a smile.

Denny had never felt so at peace in all his life.

On returning home, Otto had come over with Helen's pup. He walked up the steps, and handed it to her.

"Thank you Otto, and thank you my husband for such a beautiful gift, and yes he will be mine, and mine alone."

"Everybody, I would like you to meet my beautiful boy Snipe."

In late July, Mali Rey Foggerty, a precious, beautiful little girl was born.